The Autobiography of Jack the Ripper

as revealed to
Clanash Farjeon

Library and Archives Canada Cataloguing in Publication

Farjeon, Clanash
[Handbook for attendants on the insane]
    The autobiography of Jack the Ripper as revealed to
Clanash Farjeon / Clanash Farjeon.

Revised edition of: A handbook for attendants on the insane : the
    autobiography of "Jack the Ripper" as revealed to Clanash
    Farjeon.
Issued in print and electronic formats.
ISBN 978-0-88962-997-4 (pbk.).--ISBN 978-0-88962-998-1 (html).--
ISBN 978-0-88962-999-8 (pdf)

    1. Jack, the Ripper--Fiction. 2. Winslow, Lyttleton Forbes,
1844-1913--Fiction. I. Title. II. Title: Handbook for attendants on
the insane.

PS8561.A695H36 2014   C813'.6   C2014-900408-7
                                              C2014-900409-5

Mosaic Press gratefuly acknowledges the assistance of the Canada Book Fund,
Department of Canadian Heritage, Government of Canada in support of our
publishing program.

Pubished by Mosaic Press, Oakville, Ontario, Canada, 2014.
Distributed in the United States by Bookmasters (www.bookmasters.com).
Distributed in the U.K. by Gazelle Book Services (www.gazellebookservices.co.uk).

MOSAIC PRESS, Publishers

Cover design by Keith Daniel and Eric Normann. Book layout by Eric Normann
Printed and Bound in Canada.

ISBN   Paperback   978-0-88962-997-4
          ePub   978-0-88962-998-1
          ePDF   978-0-88962-999-8

MOSAIC PRESS
1252 Speers Road, Units 1 & 2
Oakville, Ontario L6L 5N9

(905) 825-2130
info@mosaic-press.com

www.mosaic-press.com

The Autobiography of Jack the Ripper

as revealed to
Clanash Farjeon

Handbook for
attendants
on the insane

"If there are ghosts to raise,
What shall I call,
Out of hell's murky haze,
Heaven's blue hall?"

> *Dream Pedlary*
> Thomas Lovell Beddoes
> (1803 - 1849)

Lyttleton Stewart Forbes-Winslow
M.B., D.C.L. Oxon., LL.D. Cantab.
(1844 - 1913)

*Lyttleton Stewart Forbes Winslow was the second son of the famous 'alienist'
and psychologist Benignus Forbes Winslow. He was raised in his father's
private asylums in London and trained as a doctor at both Oxford and
Cambridge. He often served as an expert witness in legal cases relating to the
Plea of Insanity.*

He was also a deeply frustrated and vainglorious man.

*He pushed himself forward at the time of the murders and became very
publicly involved in trying to 'catch' the perpetrator, relentlessly pestering the
authorities with helpful suggestions. The police found his behavior irritating
enough to classify him as mildly suspicious but in the end passed him off as
a pompous oddity. Many years later he wrote in his Recollections, "...night
after night I spent in the Whitechapel slums and at last the poor creatures
came to know me...they welcomed me to their dens and obeyed my commands
eagerly...and found the bits of information I wanted." He claimed that he
had solved the identity of the murderer and by "publishing his clues" had
singlehandedly chased the culprit from England but was careful never to
reveal the name!*

In 1877 Doctor Winslow penned a small volume entitled *A Handbook for Attendants on the Insane*. He thought it droll that the present narrative should reprise the chapter headings of that work.

Also by Clanash Farjeon, a trilogy:

The Vampires of Ciudad Juarez
The Vampires of 9/11
Vampires of the Holy Spirit

Clanash Farjeon is the
nom-de-plume of the well-known
Canadian actor, director and
author, Alan Scarfe.

Contents

for all women
but forever and
most especially
Barbara

On Youthful Eccentricity
as a Precursor to Crime

The strangest thing of all about it is that I was really rather a dull sort of man. Not very imaginative. Not remotely what I had hoped I would be.

I wanted to be like my father. Self-made, successful, to all appearances supremely confident. In the Victorian era it was normal to want to follow in one's father's footsteps. It wasn't thought cowardly or ... what is the phrase your grovellers after my irritating contemporary Herr Freud like to use so much ... 'anal retentive'? How forthright and picturesque. In any case, I earnestly believed in what my father was trying to do.

He was an alienist, like young Sigmund. Yes, I know the word is psychiatrist now, or psychotherapist. Or, to borrow another of your colourful colloquials, 'shrink'. I find the image delightfully apt. Or guru. Spiritual guide. No, no, a hideous phrase. Shall we venture to the middle of the road and agree on psychologist? It was in fairly common usage back in my day as well. My father often spoke the word to describe himself. Indeed, he was the editor of the very first journal in the trade. Fulsomely expressed and scholarly it was. It would put the bulk of your modern, monosyllabic discourse to shame, I promise you!

The choicest epithet our city wits dreamed up for us back then was 'mad-doctors'. We felt that quite unfair, as you can imagine. They also dubbed us hypocrites, frauds ... I wouldn't have thought it so inaccurate if they'd said 'freuds'... sadists, knaves and money-grub-bers. Our sudden arrival on the social scene caused an astonishing amount of animosity. Only to be expected, I suppose. We were new. Forging a new niche. It's very pleasing to see how well it's caught on.

But yes, I wanted to continue my father's work. I'd wanted it all my life. I can't remember a time when I didn't want it. No doubt any modern psychoanalyst would glibly lay the blame for my 'mid-life cri-sis' on that. As well, perhaps, as a childhood spent within the walls of my father's asylums in Hammersmith. Then the pressure to achieve at school. At Oxford. And Cambridge. And what of my intense need to excel in sports? Cricket, rugby, lawn tennis, even golf, for heaven's sake. And, of course, the collapse of the 'super ego' after my father and mother died. A loss of belief in myself and in certain members of my family. A lot of painful litigation to do with my parent's respective estates. Some other rather humiliating court cases too. And then, worst of all, my growing doubts and fears about the validity of my sustaining Christian Faith. Oh yes, all these things together might sufficiently explain the extraordinary outburst of violence that began just before my forty-fourth birthday. But would they really?

To me, its origin remains entirely inexplicable. An unforesee-able visitation. Each time. A summoning. Though I do see now that, despite the horror, the entire issuance was one of healing. For me. I've come quite comfortably to terms with it. Inevitable as a dream.

You may, however, discern some deeper meaning in the strange-ness of my story.

It began, as I said, a month before my forty-fourth birthday, with a kind of botched experiment. Poor woman. I don't even now know her real name. Then the ferocious summer and autumn of 1888. Six more. Then, eight months later, poor Alice McKenzie. A foolish, unnecessary afterthought.

Not surprisingly, in February, 1891, when a woman named Frances Coles was found billowing blood in Swallow Gardens they attributed it to me. But it wasn't. Though I did once have a peculiar scare in New York. I was there some years later giving a series of lectures to the Medico-Legal Congress and a prostitute was found with her throat slashed in a grisly, cold-water hotel on the Lower East Side. I've never been totally certain that I wasn't responsible. As I've told you, they were all like dreams. Mesmeric. Hallucinatory.

In fact, it took a long time to completely accept that I had actually committed any of the murders. Of course, there were clues, oh yes, blood on the cuffs, on the shoes, all over my body on one occasion. And waking up with a woman's uterus under one's bed does give one pause. But, in all honesty, it's only quite recently that I've fully absorbed it.

And how do I feel about it now that I'm sure? Well, this discourse will offer some attempt at explication. I have mentioned, have I not, that I feel quite deliciously and undeservedly at peace? I found my spiritual health again, you see. I could breathe. I could love. I could even enjoy sexual relations with my wife. And I didn't feel the slightest bit guilty. Perhaps I ought to have, but I didn't. There was no remorse. If I should say that all the violence was necessary, a catharsis of the spirit, a primaeval, desperate, flailing search for God, in some odd way, would you think that was selfish? Maybe that's because you haven't tried it.

Blood is ... healing. And I wasn't cruel. Not one of them saw it coming. I'll admit the first was rather clumsy. I regret that. But once I had my method under strict control it was really most humane. There was hardly any noticeable pain. Just release and an almost serene ebbing into the Great Beyond. In many ways I think they were glad of it, poor wretches. You cannot conceive what life was like for them in the East End of London during the late Eighties. An abominable, hopeless cycle of degradation.

The two ambitious hacks who coined my *nom de guerre* did it as a lark. For schoolboy notoriety. I didn't do it for fame. At least, I believe my narrative will prove not so. Though, ironically, it did fall to my benefit in later years. At all events, I disliked the name. I didn't consider 'The Ripper' at all an apt entitlement. I was much more skillful and scientific than that. Remarkably quick ... surely you agree? ... and sacrificial. Respectful, almost. The disemboweling was purest Art. At any rate, so it seemed in my rather over-heated frame of mind at the time. And they were unquestionably acts of love.

You may think that slicing a woman's breasts from her body and putting them on the bedside table is an act of the lowest savagery. Yet I tell you I felt nothing but the most prayerful veneration. Blood is not only healing ... it is ecstasy.

Then why did I stop? Well, you'll have to be patient. I wasn't frightened of being caught. You might say the fever had just run its course.

I was busy again with my career. One odd result of the murders was that I became respectable again. As time went by the general man-in-the-street gave me credit for having singlehandedly chased 'Jack the Ripper' from England. How frighteningly right they were! And it would be disingenuous to say that I wasn't conscious of manipulating, as far as it was possible, this outcome.

There are at least two sides to all of us. Two separable and distinct consciousnesses. Not always simply Jekyll and Hyde. I did know Stevenson slightly, by the way. And was it pure coincidence that the American actor-manager, Richard Mansfield, was performing his own adaptation of Stevenson's novella in a season of plays at the Lyceum at the time of the murders? I met him and we had an evening. I'll tell you about it. Irony of ironies, despite his success and considerable histrionic talent, he turned out to be a boring egomaniac, pathetically vulnerable and vain.

Yes, at least two. Each with knowledge of the other and operating, for the most part, in each other's behalf, yet disengaged and separate. Of course, now that I have the luxury of dispassionate hindsight, I can well see that it is possible to view the whole macabre business as an artful orchestration solely for my own benefit, for the restoration of my career as a mental expert, for fame. But that is barest surface. The heart of it...the blood...goes much, much deeper.

My earliest memory, easy to explain since I was born in Guilford Street, is of the great wrought-iron gates of the London Foundling Hospital. Don't misunderstand me, I am my father's son, but I've always had this nagging, some might say romantic, notion that I was an orphan. I never brought it up before my mother or father. It's just a feeling and, even now that I'm fully healed, I still have it. A hollow sense of spiritual enwaifment.

I can see that you're thinking, "Ah ha! Now we're getting somewhere!" Not at all. It's merely the common ground of our existence, of all our existences, is it not? The reason why God is so vital for our perceptually fragile species. The necessary cushion for all that engulfing nothingness. A mighty fortress and I wholeheartedly agree.

My entire family history was staunch with religious devotion. Going far, far back, generations, to the Puritan exodus to the New World on the Mayflower. Oh yes, I am a direct lineal descendant of the Pilgrim Fathers. My great-great-great-great-great uncle Edward was one of the first governors of Massachusetts. You remember your school lessons, Massasoit, Squanto, all that. He was a great man and I'm very proud of it. A profound faith in the gospel of our Lord Jesus Christ, yes. Four of my father's eight brothers entered the priesthood! Our lay passions have only latterly been inclined toward medicine and the law.

Before I was a year old I was taken by my parents to live in Hammersmith. My father was the proprietor of two private asylums there. The Sussex and the Brandenburgh House. These were the early days when the well-to-do could lodge the members of their families who needed help and rest and the benefit of someone like my father's patience and expertise in smallish private hospitals where things could be kept discreet. The huge charnel houses like Bethlehem Hospital were no place to go if you hoped ever to recover your wits. The whole argument about public *vs.* private management of the mentally ill has gone on ever since and it's really very dull. It's painfully obvious that there is a great and ever-growing need for both.

Our home was a suite of rooms at the Brandenburgh House and I lived there, with the exception of my school and university years, from my first until after my forty-second birthday. I can hear you saying to yourself, "Ah ha!" again. And I admit there is considerable justification for it. Asylum life can be intensely monotonous and, indeed, there is every danger that those who are in constant association with the inmates will themselves become mad. I found my daily contact with the insane quite terrible to contend with. However, I do not believe that those eight murders were acts of madness. No, no, quite the contrary.

In my published Recollections I spoke of the 'past standing out before us in all its hideous nakedness' as old age approaches. I confess I am often guilty of trying to impress my readers with poeticism. My father sprinkled quotes from Shakespeare liberally in all his writings. Well, now that I'm safely beyond old age I can tell you the memories are really very beautiful. I have no need to turn away in horror. I savour them. Indeed, on many occasions afterward, when I had wakeful nights I would call those women individually to my mind and play over every sensuous detail of our *danse macabre* and so find comfort and Lethe's balm.

Please don't misunderstand, there was no sex involved in the normal sense. No contact between tumescent penis and engorged vagina. No trite or vulgar words of fleeting passion. No, our dance of death was infinitely more profound. Something which might have drawn cries of approbation at a *corrida* in Spain or any less sedate realm than this where the relish of blood is still valued. It wasn't at all some trivial adolescent masturbation fantasy. In any case, it wasn't fantasy, was it? You've seen the pictures.

You must grant, at the least, I was well versed in more than one perspective on my subject. I formally graduated as a licentiate of the Society of Apothecaries and was thus enabled to register as a qualified medical practitioner in 1869, even before completing my degree at Cambridge. However, I had earned quite sufficient experience long before that to fully justify calling myself a mental expert. No one truly learns anything of his profession, whether it's legal, medical, clerical, or anything else, until the useless subjects included in the schedule of his examinations are wiped out of memory and room is made for more practical knowledge. But you can see that the groundwork of my credentials was already laid in my father's asylums.

My father was a physician and psychologist. He achieved a position of some eminence though his life, like mine, was unfairly dogged with controversy. He struggled to establish recognition for the plea of insanity in criminal cases in England and eventually he succeeded. He had to work damned hard all his life. Thankfully, he was a man of great vigour and, despite a brief period of relapse like myself, deep, abiding Faith.

He had no wealth given to him. My family were unwavering Royalists and during the American War of Independence they had all their property in Boston confiscated. A great number returned to England where my father and uncle Octavius were born. My father attended university in Aberdeen and New York and London but it took him until his thirty-ninth year to gain a medical degree. He supported himself by reporting on the House of Commons for the Times and, among other things, writing a pocket guide for students on practical midwifery! One of the obituaries, I believe it was the Lancet, after his too early death from Bright's disease in 1874, described him as 'indefatigable with the pen'. It was true. His published work would rival Carlyle's in sheer volume. The Journal of Psychological Medicine and Mental Pathology, which he edited for sixteen years, would regularly run to three hundred pages in its quarterly editions and he wrote the lion's share of it himself. He was an amazing man and I hated him. Of course, I wanted to be him and it terrified me. His love was the tiger that chased me down the rabbit hole and devoured me in my childhood dreams.

He was a great entrepreneur and self-promoter, too. In an obvious, pompous, Victorian sort of way, now I come to think of it. Not supremely sly, not precise and logical and seamless in the plotting, as I have been. In that, at least, I have surpassed him. And in my fame, oh yes, though I have had to bask in it in secret.

He was involved as an expert witness in many of the famous court cases of his day. McNaughton and Townley and the infanticides of Mrs. Vyse and Mrs. Brough. I have followed in his footsteps and surpassed him there as well. It's the main reason I so successfully evaded suspicion at the time of the murders. And the 'Ripper' case opened the door to the crowning successes I subsequently enjoyed. Delicious irony! That's why I say I can hardly believe I was clever enough to have orchestrated the whole thing. But perhaps I was, ha ha, perhaps I was.

My mother was a different matter. From a different kind of people altogether. I'm surprised they ever got married. Well, I'm surprised she ever married him. Though I suppose in his youth his energy was charismatic enough to attract her and he had not yet metamorphosed into the domineering despot that I knew.

Her name was Susannah Holt. She was a dazzling redhead and extremely beautiful, even in old age. Her father was a newspaperman and went by the odd familiar of 'Raggedy' Holt. He took an active part in the popularisation of cheap literature in London and the abolition of the paper duty. He was a bit of an old Bohemian. I'm sure he and my father, who was only fifteen years his junior, must have had a hard time getting along. I can still remember my father's bridling look under the old man's barrage of jocularity and not so gentle teasing.

It was inevitable in the latter years of their marriage that my father and mother would choose to live apart. He had a first bout of serious illness in 1864 and had to give up a great portion of his professional activity, spending much of his time convalescing in Brighton. My mother moved from the Brandenburgh House, which she abhorred and had endured more or less without complaint for nearly twenty years, to a convivial, elegant four-storey Georgian in Cavendish Square. I had my practice there briefly during the early Eighties but they were troubled years for me which I shall enlarge upon fully soon.

Before I leave talking about my family ... and I don't suppose I will ever leave off talking about them entirely in this narrative, how could I? ... I must say a word or two about my grandmother. My father's mother. I never knew 'Raggedy' Holt's wife, nor my father's father. They died before I was born.

My father's mother's name was Mary. She was a well known 'mover' ... 'mover and shaker' you like to say, don't you? What about Shaker and Quaker, ha ha? ... in the religious world of New York, to which she had returned after my father was old enough to attend boarding school. He was the youngest of nine sons! My uncle Octavius, two years my father's senior, wrote a book about grandmother Mary, after she died in 1854 at the age of eighty, entitled A Life in Jesus. It is still revered and widely read in both England and America as a textbook of all that is righteous and good. I can't remember much about her except the softness of the skin on her face and her powerful singing voice. And the smell of her clothing, whether it was perfume, powder or preservative, or all three. I used to sit, small, obedient and slightly squashed, on her left at St. Paul's Cathedral on Sundays when she was visiting.

Oh yes, and I remember my great fascination with her long, braided, white hair. She used to dress it in strict privacy. We were never allowed to see it down. But I did once and I'll never forget it. I think my brother Edward must have put me up to it. In any case, I opened the door to her bedroom without knocking, something which was expressly forbidden. She was seated before her mirror and turned on me with the eyes of a Gorgon. Her underclothes were visible beneath her gown and, as she turned, her flying, waist-length, white hair seemed to completely fill the room. I stood transfixed with terror for a moment then fled with a blood-curdling shriek. It was the single most heart-stopping sight I saw in all my life.

I have mentioned my uncle Octavius and my brother Edward. Octavius was two years older than my father, just as Edward was two years older than me. They were both prolific writers of religious works. My brother became the Vicar of Epping, where our family vault is, from 1873 to 1878, then took up his lifelong position as the Vicar of St. Paul's Church at St. Leonard's-on-Sea. Uncle Octavius wasn't ordained until he was sixty-two. I'm not sure what his profession actually was before that time. I suppose he maintained himself through his writing. An early work of his, The Inner Life, Its Nature, Relapse and Recovery, has always seemed to relate, with an eerie prescience, to the personal history of many members of my family and most particularly my own.

All three, Uncle Octavius, father and myself suffered a period of great inner turmoil in the middle years of our lives. My brother Edward, alone of my close relatives, appears to have escaped unscathed. Though whether his spiritual crisis came earlier, after the business with the dog, I can't venture to say.

Ever since, well, of course, even long before my bloodline's exodus on the Mayflower, my family had been sustained by an abiding, unshakeable faith in the beneficence of an Almighty God and the goodness of his Son and the promise of Eternal Redemption. We have, many of us, had a crisis of faith in middle age in which our basic nature has been overturned in a relapse and then we have been 'born again', the recovery.

Uncle Octavius wrote a small pamphlet in honour of my father after his death and in it he quotes a letter of my father's speaking of his own recovery... "From that time I felt that old things had passed away and that all things had become new. I was conscious that I was born again, had become a child of God, and was cleansed from all my sin by the most precious blood of Jesus Christ. My happiness knew no bounds."... Well, I hope you will forgive my seeming blasphemy when I tell you that my life was born again through the blood of those eight women!

Yes, I did descend into a kind of madness but it was not madness entirely. It had direction. It had foresight. It had almost, dare I say it, a Divine Plan. By which I merely mean that its execution was so skillful, its planning so meticulous, its overall working so unavoidably diabolic as to seem propelled by the urging of a Power much vaster than my own. If I say I believe with all my heart and soul that my actions had the positive approval of a Divine Hand I know you will clap me insane or, worse, in league with the Anti-Christ, and I suppose I cannot deny that as a possibility. But I have not found myself being punished in eternal hellfire for my deeds. I feel quite, quite secure that they were meant to be and that indeed far more good has come of them than harm.

But let me return to some sort of chronology. My intention is only to tell my story in sequential order and as honestly as possible. I hope you will forgive mortal frailty that I did not have the courage to confess during my lifetime but spun an ever more elaborate web of falsehood around myself. It wasn't hard to do. I had such a lot of practice with my father.

Beyond the many memories I have of the asylum and its unfortunate inmates … there were never more than twenty or thirty patients at a time in each. My father's interest was in particular cases for scientific reasons and, of course, in the respective families' ability to pay. I am haunted still by the vision of an elderly woman's slow, arrhythmic dance, endless circles to an unheard tune, in the asylum garden below my window. My father, in passing, would on occasion take a turn with her. I watched her for hours, hypnotised … there are two events from my early years relating to my father that stand out.

The first, when I was eight years old, in 1852, was our attendance, father, Edward and myself, at the funeral of the Duke of Wellington. We had spent the previous night in father's consulting rooms in Albemarle Street and, as he often did, he brought along a patient to act as his valet. In this instance, it was a huge man, one of the terrors of my childhood, with huge hands and huge ears and who did all my father asked of him with slow, thoughtful deliberation, and who I never heard utter a single word in the thirty or more years that I knew him. His name was Casimir Swerdlow, but this is not the place to delve into his story.

On the morning of the funeral we stood among the solemn crowd directly across the Mall from St. James's Palace and watched as the cortège made its way slowly from Buckingham Palace, just newly completed, toward Trafalgar Square and Nelson's Column in the distance. We were standing under some trees, thankfully, because of a constant drizzle. As the nodding black horses and the carriage bearing the duke's body passed my father took off his top hat, I remember being puzzled by an unaccustomed mistiness in his demeanour, and said, without looking at us, "He may have stood aloof but he was a great man. Unflagging industry. Uncompromising honesty. A great soldier and a great gentleman." At that moment, I chanced to look up at Swerdlow's dark, sunken eyes. He, too, had doffed his shabby bowler and was slowly nodding his head in mute agreement and there was a single, glistening tear inching down his freshly-razored cheek. It impressed me deeply at the time but perhaps it was just the rain.

My father was unswervingly conservative. He had been asked on four occasions in his life to run for parliament, once for Cambridge, Norwich, Maidstone and Barnstaple respectively, but had each time declined due to the pressure of his professional commitments. After the funeral we went to the Conservative Club in St. James's Street. Edward and Swerdlow and I sat silent on a stone bench in the foyer for several hours waiting, sipping ginger beer through long straws, while my father talked with the other distinguished gentlemen in a large, smoky room adjacent. I would catch an occasional glimpse of him laughing and telling stories. I remember our furtive amusement at the concentration on Swerdlow's pale face and evident in the deep furrows of his huge, sloping brow as he sucked vacantly on the unfamiliar straw. And I also remember very well that we never moved a muscle from that bench.

The second memory, by far the more vivid and appalling, is from the following year. It was my first appearance before any learned medical body. Father was giving the oration in his capacity as newly elected president of the Medical Society of London. And, for some reason which I cannot recall at this moment, whether I evinced an eagerness at that early age to see what the proceedings of a 'medical society' were, or whether father wished me to go for some secret purpose of his own, I accompanied him to this meeting. Edward was already away at boarding school.

The circumstances of the event, however, are as clear as if it were yesterday. I was dressed in an itchy, hot, black velvet Knickerbocker suit and sat on a straight-backed chair just in front of my father on the speaker's platform facing tier upon tier of eminent gentlemen. How he could possibly have imagined that I would glean anything of value from such an oration at so early an age, even though delivered by my own father, I don't know, and certainly neither of us were prepared for the catastrophe that happened. It was something that he used to relate over many and many a time through the years, much to my bottomless chagrin.

In the midst, I'm sure, of a most eloquent sentence, in which the attention of his audience was most deeply rapt, the proceedings were interrupted by a sudden, fearful scream and I found myself lying on my back on the platform flapping about and squalling in hysterics like a baby.

My obsession with this event often caused me to revisit the text of my father's address, he subsequently published it in its entirety in his Psychological Journal, and I found the precise passage that must have been the trigger of my youthful torment. I can vividly recall the cold sweat creeping down the fine hairs at the nape of my neck as his impassioned rhetoric mounted in intensity.

"...Whatever there is of terrible, whatever there is of beautiful in human events, all that shakes the soul to and fro, and is remembered while thought and flesh cling together, all these have their origin in the passions. As it is only in storms, and when their coming waters are driven up into the air, that we catch a glimpse of the depth of the ocean; so it is only in the season of perturbation that we have a glimpse of the real internal nature of man. It is only then that the might of these eruptions, shaking his frame, dissipate all the feeble coverings of opinion, and rend in pieces that cobweb veil with which fashion hides the feelings of the heart. It is only then that Nature speaks with her genuine..."

It was at that presaging moment I am sure I fell down in this strange paroxysm. Was it guilt of things to come? That would seem to be insupportable. But certainly my piercing protestation interrupted the sanctity of those proceedings and my father was forced to descend from his presidential throne. I think he slapped me in the face to bring me to my senses. Beyond this I can say nothing as to what became of me. Whether I spent the rest of the evening in the cloakroom, or whether the fall wakened me sufficiently to attend to the rest of the oration with fitting seriousness, I am not able to say.

While I am on this subject, I remember that the last time my father came to London previous to his death was to accompany me to Chandos Street to look at his portrait, which he had presented to the Medical Society, and which had just come back from being retouched and cleaned. It hangs now, as it did then, prominently displayed in the entrance hall. He stood for a long time looking up at it, leaning on his cane, then softly spoke a line of Wordsworth's, from The Excursion I think, "...the Mind of Man—my haunt, and the main region of my song..." After that we took a carriage back to Hammersmith as he said he had some papers that he wanted me to see. But let me not stray too far.

My early school days are not remarkable for anything in particular. The first school I went to was kept by a Dame, the house was still in existence when last I looked, in the Hammersmith Road, between Nazareth House and St. Paul's School. From there I went to King Edward the Sixth's School at Berkhampstead and then to a school kept by a Baron Andlau at Clapham Common. This with a view to acquiring a knowledge of modern languages, especially German, which all the boys were supposed to speak during play hours or pay a penny fine.

From Clapham Common I went to Overslade, near Rugby, kept by the Rev. Mr. Congreve...no relation to the great English dramatist of the seventeenth century...and from there to Rugby to the house of the Rev. C. A. Arnold. After my eleventh year I saw Brandenburgh House only on holidays and the odd weekend.

Something happened on my maiden journey to Rugby which is in retrospect amusing. I had gone to Euston Station sporting a new 'topper', as was the wont of any new boy wishing to create a favourable first impression. As we entered the tunnel leaving the station another boy knocked the hat off my head and out the open carriage window. Thus I arrived in Rugby slightly tearful and decidedly bareheaded.

Edward, who, though two years older, had been at the school just a year before me, had earned the nickname 'Bags', due to the fact that on one occasion he had arrived wearing a rather loud pair of inexpressibles. So I was at once called 'Young Bags', in distinction to 'Old Bags', which was then given to my brother. These soubriquets accompanied him to Oxford and me to Cambridge and continued somewhat diminished through the rest of our lives.

I left Rugby in 1861, the year the Prince Consort died. I recall that I heard of his demise while playing in the Old Rugbeian football match. The news had a quite shattering effect on the other members of my side and despite my best efforts to rally them we were thumped eighteen to eight.

The Reverend Arnold was very musical and those pupils of his who possessed any musical talent at all were obliged to take part in the Kinder Symphony. A fine violinist, one Herr Deutschmann, led this curious orchestra. I played a most extraordinary instrument called the cuckoo and two of the other boys... who became learned judges and whose names I dare not mention for fear of being held in contempt of court... played the triangle and the whistle. The performance, which must have been quite dreadful, was, notwithstanding, in every way a great success and we repeated it on many subsequent occasions.

Though it had always been my intention to follow in father's footsteps as a mental specialist, after leaving Rugby School I had not quite decided what course of study I should pursue as the most expedient *modus operandus* for obtaining this qualification. Edward was already at Oxford with the intention of a medical degree as well.

At first I went to read for the matriculation examination at London University, and I commenced to do so with a Dr. Gill, who at that time had a class for the matric. But during the Easter vacation I happened to go to Paris with my father and an old friend of his, Dr. Waller Lewis, the head medical officer of the General Post Office, who, being himself a Cambridge man, persuaded me to abandon London University for Cambridge, which, with father's approval, I immediately did.

I entered at Caius College in the October term of 1862. Father, I remember, took me up there and left me in the charge of Rev. C. Clayton, the excellent, conscientious and good tutor of the college at that time.

I was very anxious to begin my medical studies at once. Unfortunately, before I could register as a medical student at Cambridge, the 'Little Go', or some recognised educational examination, had to be passed. Unless I was prepared to undertake what is called the 'Honours Little Go', which consists of extra mathematics and is intended only for Honours men, a distinction I did not at that time aspire to, I would have to wait until the following October, exactly one year from entering! This I politely declined and struck out on another course.

I wanted to steal a march on the students who had entered at the same term and decided to let the Cambridge 'Little Go' wait and to pass some alternative exam. I had been in communication with the Royal College of Physicians of London, who at that time held a similar examination, and put in my name for this. It was to be held in March, the same as the 'Honours Little Go'. I kept this plan entirely to myself.

At Cambridge it was necessary to 'keep', at a minimum, two-thirds of the actual days that constituted any particular term and my term only expired the very day of my examination in London. I had ordered a cabriolet to fetch me from the college at half past seven. None, however, arrived. Finally, in great impatience, I rushed from my rooms down King's Parade and fortunately found a conveyance of some sort that galloped me down to the railway station. The man at the booking-office told me I was too late but I raced across the line onto the platform and managed to jump on the last carriage just as it was moving beyond reach.

I arrived in London and drove straight to the Royal College of Physicians. I went through the morning examination and then returned to Hammersmith to tell my mother and father what I had been trying to achieve. Their reaction was entirely predictable. I was called a fool and encouraged by being told that I should surely be 'plucked' and "How could I have done such a stupid thing!"

Nothing daunted, I continued with the examination that after-noon and during the whole of the following day. To my immense satisfaction and relief my name appeared on the list and I was able forthwith to register myself as a medical student. I thus gained nine months start on the undergrads who had entered the same term as I had and who were waiting until they had passed the 'Little Go' in October before registering. The time I gained was invaluable since I actually became qualified in London before I had taken my Cambridge medical degree. This was a rather unique occurrence, if not an entirely isolated one.

As a number of my medical friends were migrating from Caius to Downing College, I followed their example. We had more indepen-dence there and Downing was nearer the Medical Schools. At that time it was a small college but soon the numbers began to increase. We put an eight on the river and gained eight places in six nights, rowing to the top of our division. I rowed number six. Lord Justice Collins, Professor Ray Lankester and the Rev. Mr. Macmichael, a sub-sequent 'blue', had oars in the same boat.

In addition to a boat club, the little medical colony who had migrated to Downing from Caius founded an athletic and a cricket club. I was appointed president of these. I have always been of a very athletic turn of mind. I was a great believer in it and though I never actually excelled to any great extent nevertheless in whatever sport I took part I was always well in the front rank. I won in sports at both Rugby and Cambridge.

There is one thing that I am always proud of chronicling. On the twenty-first of July, 1864, I was one of the M.C.C., Marylebone Cricket Club, team to play against South Wales, in which team W. G. Grace, the greatest cricketer who ever lived, played his first match at Lord's. I kept a copy of this match prominently displayed in my study.

In the same year I represented the Next Eighteen as opposed to the First Twelve of the M.C.C. in the jubilee match in honour of the Queen's twenty-five years on the throne. This was also the year that R. A. Fitzgerald, the Secretary of the M.C.C., asked me to captain the first English team that went to America and Canada. This I had to decline because of my studies.

Leaving Cambridge, I was elected at a later period of my life as president of the United Hospitals Cricket Club, of which W. G. Grace was the captain. In this I chose the cup, which is now annually contested for by our hospitals, and I was also president of the United Hospitals Athletic Club. I captained the M.C.C. in many matches and twice again at my old school in Rugby and in, I believe, the only match in which they played against the United Hospitals Cricket Club. This match I arranged myself. These, I know, are not prominent facts in my career as far as my lunacy experiences are concerned but I'm proud to tell you about them and, I hope you will agree, they are worthy of mention.

Even after I was well launched in my professional career I still kept up a regimen of regular exercise. I founded the West Middlesex Lawn-tennis Club, one of the first in England. I also played for Oxford against the All England Club at Wimbledon. As I was a D.C.L. of Oxford I had that privilege. I once even played for the English championship. My last notable appearance was at Bath where I played second for the championship of the West of England. An unfortunate injury to my knee eventually stopped my enthusiasm in the game and prevented further indulgence in such vigorous pursuits.

I remained as keen as I ever was at cricket, however, and when I went up to Lord's it was only with great effort that I could resist putting my name down, as I used to do, to play in the day's match. But discretion is the better part of valour and my loose semi-lunar cartilage, which frequently slipped out when I least expected it, reduced me to a position of playing only mentally from a lawn-chair or a comfortable seat in the pavilion.

Forgive me, I have strayed again.

Despite the fact that my college days were no more than of the usual hum-drum description, like many others I often look back on them with affectionate regret that they are gone forever. Friends made there, never seen since, but, though lost to sight, they still remain to memory dear.

March, 1865, arrived and though I had been at the university for nearly three years and was within three months of the completion of my residence, I had not yet passed any of my examinations. The fact was, having passed the entrance exam in London, I was content to pursue my medical studies, ignoring for the time being the general examinations of the university. I was determined, however, to pass these within my three years and made a supreme effort so to do. Between March and June I had to pass three examinations, the afore-mentioned 'Little Go', the professorial examination in modern history and the Bachelor of Laws degree, or LL.B. I had decided to graduate both in law and medicine in preference to the ordinary B.A. Degree, a fact I never regretted.

This was, may I say, a gigantic task but I accomplished it. I passed the 'Little Go' in March. I had two weeks intervening between this examination and the next. The vacation had just started and I came up to London and joined a class of Professor Stokes, the famed mnemonist, as the professorial modern history examination was crammed full with dates and other facts requiring a prodigious memory to master in two weeks. I also studied like a madman at the reading room of the British Museum. I returned to Cambridge in April and was examined by Professor Kingsley. I had the satisfaction of seeing my name in the Times as having passed first class. Then I commenced my legal studies, having six weeks before undertaking a very complicated and difficult exam in law. I succeeded and took my LL.B. Degree in June, thus passing the three examinations in eight weeks and winning a bet of twenty to one with a titled, conceited undergraduate of the same college, who had scoffed at my achieving this. As I said, I was determined to do it and I did, much to the great surprise of many.

There is one more experience appertaining to my university days which is worth mentioning since it bears on my lifelong aversion to alcohol. It was my first professional encounter with uncontrollable drunkenness, a subject on which I subsequently wrote a great deal. It was a very strange, at least a very unusual, event for any undergraduate to be able to relate.

The tutor of Downing was a man of mark at Cambridge. He was well known for his responsibility in ordering the dinners for which Downing was then celebrated. This specially applied to the catering for the High Table, at which Sunday dinners were a feature of the university so far as the dons of the other colleges were concerned who used to assemble without fail every Sunday and participate enthusiastically in them in our Hall. As I was a fellow commoner, this advantage I also enjoyed. The association with fellows and dons of other colleges raised me rather beyond the pinnacle of the ordinary undergraduate. It had the lasting advantage of putting me at ease with my superiors and being able to create an impression of equality with those in authority.

Our tutor was very hospitable and he was never happy unless surrounded with a number of convivial sparks quite as capable of doing justice to a good repast as he was himself. We had a French chef, also the nominee of the tutor, and I may say that the dinners at Downing in the year 1865 were as good as could be found in any fashionable restaurant in Paris. Except on Sundays, our party at the High Table generally consisted of about six, of which the tutor was quite the ruling spirit.

Downing College possessed a considerable amount of property in Croydon, Cambridgeshire, and its immediate vicinity. The tutor being also bursar, it was his duty to go there and collect the rents. This often necessitated a visit to the countryside and a dinner with the farmers. I remember one wintry night the tutor asked me if I would accompany him on one of these missions. I consented and we drove over in a dog-cart. On our way back the snow was thick on the ground and before long the tutor succeeded in depositing the trap into a snow bank so I offered to take the reins myself, having obvious doubts concerning his sobriety. He consented with a belch. I shall never forget that journey. I had the greatest difficulty preventing him from falling out of the trap and upsetting it. But we arrived safely at the college and I escorted him upstairs to his rooms. On opening his door I saw to my surprise that the Downing Professor of Medicine was there and in an even worse state, so far as sobriety was concerned, than the tutor himself! Having put the tutor safely to bed and tucked him up, I then woke up the professor, who was snoring loudly in an armchair, and half carried him across the quadrangle to his own house.

Poor old man, I can see him sitting there now. He used to give the lectures on *materia medica*. At the first lecture he was quite sober and eloquently impressed upon us all the importance of the subject. But the second lecture was more about tasting his wines, also an important one in his own estimation, as his cellar contained many fine samples. I cannot at this lengthened period recollect in what part of *materia medica* wine-tasting is included. However, this lecture was much appreciated by many of the students who, as you can imagine, turned up in a large body at the next one, only to find, much to their chagrin, that the professor was unwell.

One or two more lectures of much the same description were given during the term and the schedules for attendance at these lectures, as constituting a part of the medical student's curriculum, were duly signed by him and forwarded by each student to the Regius Professor of Medicine.

This same professor was one of the physicians to Addenbroke Hospital and a university examiner for the medical degree. I once attended at a *viva voce* examination out of curiosity. Whether the Downing Professor of Medicine was indulging in a quiet nap it was difficult to say but he had the knack of asking the same question which one of his confrères, assisting at the examination, had just previously asked. Sir Richard Dalby, later the distinguished aural surgeon, who was on that occasion one of the candidates and who had a keen eye for the ridiculous and who knew well the peculiarities of the professor, on several times being asked the same question, replied boldly that he had just answered it! Oh yes, things were very lax in those days.

After leaving Cambridge, I was attached to St. George's Hospital in London where my medical education continued, returning to Cambridge later for two more years of residence in order to complete my required terms there. The time, therefore, between 1868 and 1870, the date of my receiving the medical degree of the university, were spent backwards and forwards between Cambridge and Hyde Park Corner. Though, as I have previously stated, I possessed the degree of licentiate of the Apothecaries Society in 1869, giving me the right to register as a full-blown medical practitioner, which I did.

During the summer of that year my brother Edward was bitten by a mad dog. This quite unpredictable occurrence changed both of our lives forever.

My father originally intended that Edward should take up the medical profession. It was for this reason that I had essentially hedged my bets and graduated with a degree in law as well. When Edward received his M.A. from Oxford he became attached to St. Bartholomew's Hospital as a perpetual pupil. He had completed his first year of study in June of 1869 and we were playing on opposing sides at a cricket match in Surrey. I remember my father and mother and Florence Jessie and the baby were all there.

Oh, good lord, I've neglected to mention the charming lady who was my first wife. Her name was Florence Jessie Winn. We had known each other since we were children. Her father, James Michell Winn, was the resident physician at Sussex House asylum and was, like my own father Benignus, a devoted Christian. So was Florence Jessie and so was I. We had married in the spring of 1866. Our son Percy was born two years later in September, 1868. There was plenty of room for us at Brandenburgh House as my mother had already removed to Cavendish Square and father was now spending the greater part of his time in more relaxed surroundings at our other home on Brunswick Terrace in Brighton.

But to return to the cricket match. I had been having a good run at the bat, up to sixty-nine not out, and the bowler, I can't for the life of me remember his name, allowed me to open up with what I felt sure was a certain stroke to the boundary for another six. Edward was always a tremendous runner, much longer in the leg than I am, and somehow he managed to catch it. There was, of course, great applause at such a feat. Even I clapped him heartily, though he had cut short my innings.

Suddenly, out of nowhere, a large mongrel dog appeared by him on the field and for no apparent reason attacked him savagely. They both went down on the ground and it was some moments before we could get to them. I remember the first players to reach them tried ineffectually to pull the dog off by its tail. Then I ran up and smacked the dog soundly on the rear with the flat of my bat. It wheeled round and lunged with its slavering jaws toward me but luckily the fangs only sank into my shin-guard and I managed to knock the beast out cold with a solid two-handed blow to the top of its head.

Poor Edward was very badly cut up. There were spatterings of blood all down his cricket whites. My father, despite his health being no longer robust, came panting up to us and helped Edward from the field. I remember saying to Edward, "I'm sorry, I'm sorry," and him responding gallantly in his usual bantering tone, "Good heavens, old chap, it was hardly your fault," but somehow I sensed that father thought it was. I looked back as the other lads were bundling up the dog to carry it away and there was a more than sinister trickle of blood and sputum coming from its mouth.

The upshot was that Edward became increasingly obsessed with the unlikely possibilities resulting from this incident and three weeks afterward he suddenly decided to throw up medicine altogether and read for holy orders. This left the field open to me so far as a successor in the same line of practice to my father was concerned. Had it not taken place, I might well have remained in obscurity.

Mad Humanity

Upon receiving my diploma from Cambridge, I at once became associated with my father, who had the enjoyment of the largest practice in lunacy in England, and when I say that at the age of twenty-five I was frequently left in entire charge of this, and, indeed, managed it exclusively for some years before his death in 1874, as he became almost entirely incapacitated due to his failing kidneys, it should be clear that I earned my spurs in this peculiar branch of medicine at a very early period of my existence.

In 1871, I became attached to the staff of both the Sussex and Brandenburgh House asylums in Hammersmith but since, as you know, Brandenburgh House had been my home from the time I was a few months old the experience was by no means a novel one. I felt, however, that I was in full warrant there, subservient only to my father and the medical superintendent. The authority I assumed rapidly developed into one of absolute responsibility and as my father's representative I soon blossomed out into a licensee. Though during the many years I was in residence I was never, on the actual face of it, more than a paid official.

It was during these years that I began to form my rewarding acquaintanceship with that very difficult, acerbic and reclusive man, Henry Maudsley. He was recognised without doubt as the leading authority and foremost intellect in our growing world of mental health practitioners in England. He and I shared some quite entertaining interchanges of opinion during the time of the murders. But in due course.

Now, before I relate the sad circumstances of my father's death, it will be pointful that I finish telling you what he wanted of me after our visit to the Medical Society foyer to view his portrait. As I said, we returned by carriage to the asylum residence in Hammersmith. He didn't say much on the journey except briefly to enquire after mother. I asked him if he would like to stop in Cavendish Square to see for himself, after all it was only a stone's throw from the Society, but he said no.

When we arrived at Brandenburgh House it was already dark. Swerdlow, who was now in his early seventies but still able and willing to serve, though mute as always, came out from the front door with a lamp to greet us. He helped my father down from the carriage and my father hugged him. It was a strange and moving sight. Swerdlow was well over six foot three, though he had become quite stooped, and my father, of less than average height like myself and now frail and shrunk with age and infirmity, seemed almost to disappear in his embrace. How one's perspective changes through life! When I was a boy I thought my father was enormous. When he hugged me I always felt utterly nullified in his arms.

We went in and said hello to Florence, who was still nursing our third son Francis, and then Swerdlow brought a cold supper to the study. Before we ate my father asked me to fetch out some half dozen heavy boxes filled with papers from a storage closet. I had really no conception of what he wanted or what he was about to require of me.

The boxes contained thousands upon thousands of pages of his unpublished writings. The volume of his output was, as I've mentioned, simply staggering just totting up the works that had been published. The sixteen years of his Journal, his work for the newspapers, his pamphlets and broadsides, all that beside what he considered his major works, forgive me if I cannot resist listing them off to you ...

On the Application of the Principles of Phrenology to the Elucidation and Cure of Insanity, 1831.

A Manual of Osteology.

A Manual of Practical Midwifery.

A Student's Pocket Guide to the College of Surgeons.

The Anatomy of Suicide, 1840.

*Physic and Physicians; a Medical Sketch-Book with Memoirs of
Eminent Living Physicians and Surgeons in Two Volumes,* 1842.

On the Preservation of the Health of the Body and the Mind, also 1842.

The Plea of Insanity in Criminal Cases, 1843.

*The Lunacy Act: the Regulation of the Care and Treatment of Lunatics
(with Explanatory Notes),* 1845.

*A Synopsis of the Law of Lunacy, as far as it relates to the Organisation
and Management of Private Asylums for the Care and Treatment of the
Insane. On a Chart.*

*On Softening of the Brain arising from Anxiety and Undue Mental
Exercise and resulting in Impairment of Mind,* 1849.

The Lettsomian Lectures on Insanity, 1854.

It was during the first of these that I fell off my stool in the screeching fit!

*On Obscure Diseases of the Brain and Disorders of the Mind: their
Incipient Symptoms, Pathology, Diagnosis, Treatment and Prophylaxis,*
1860. Eight Volumes!

This last was his *magnum opus* but was merely intended as the
introduction to an even longer work, much of which I assumed was
already written out in his steady longhand on page after page in the
overflowing boxes before me.

"We both know my time is short," he began. "If you would be so
kind to ferret through these trifles and bring them to some order
I would be much obliged. They are the sequel to my Pathology of
Mind. The title I suggest is 'Organic Diseases of the Cerebro-Spinal
System'. There are other things as well. Memoirs, reminiscences,
records of court cases. A long essay in letter form addressed to
Maudsley rebutting his constant irresponsibility ... I would wish that
you give it to him in his hand as well as publishing it. Revive the
Journal if you can. There is much here as well that you will find not
out of date for such a purpose."

He broke off with a sigh and began to nibble at the bread and
cheese in front of him. I don't believe he once looked at me as he
spoke. He just assumed that I would do it. I was feeling that Edward
had been very lucky to have been bitten by that dog and it suddenly
occurred to me that he had slyly used it as an excuse so that he might
finally get out from under father's pressing, insistent control. Alas, at

the time I said nothing, just nodded, serious, obedient, feigning, I'm sure, a humble enthusiasm for the sacred task bestowed upon me. But, oh sweet revenge, in later years, once my health and peace of mind had been restored, I put all those wretched papers to good use!

One incident that had taken place only a few months before will give you some sense of my hidden state of mind that evening as I looked on nodding like a fool.

During 1873, I had written a book of my own entitled Manual of Lunacy: a Hand-Book relating to the Legal Care and Treatment of the Insane. It contained upward of four hundred pages and I was very proud of my accomplishment. The first chapter I had composed, by the by, while enjoying the luxury of a Turkish bath in Jermyn Street. My father had written the preface. It was well received by the public but some members of the press had remarked uncharitably that such a stupendous work could not have been conceived by me alone at the age of twenty-nine, which I then was, and that my father must really be the author. In fact, I had the greatest difficulty in persuading him even to write the preface and he was quite evidently far too unwell to have done more. The egregious spitefulness of these reviews had preyed heavily upon my mind yet my father never made any comment about them. At the time, on that particular evening, oh, how that fact cut across my heart like a knife!

I can hear you clucking, "Ah ha," again. Wait. I've had the last laugh. You will see how.

My father died at Brighton in March, 1874. He was only sixty-three. He had been comparatively well until early February. His visit to London to view the portrait and leave me the charge of his papers had happened quite incidentally to coincide with my thirtieth birthday at the end of January.

But in February he became too ill to leave his bed. On the evening of the seventh oedema of the lungs came on, followed a few days later by dyspnoea and cardiac spasm, resembling, according to his doctor, an acute attack of angina pectoris. His urine was very albuminous and bouts of uncontrollable vomiting now added to his weakness. Both Edward and I were summoned and Uncle Octavius joined us at his bedside a day or two after we arrived. In fact, I spent the two weeks prior to his death dashing back and forth to London on a daily basis. Gradually his kidneys ceased their function and he passed into an uraemic coma at eleven o'clock in the morning on March the third. He died an hour later. The obituary in the British Medical Journal claimed he 'was full of mental vigour to the end', but that is myth-making.

I can't say that Edward and I were much moved though Uncle Octavius was for a time inconsolable. Mother never came, either to Brighton or the funeral.

He was buried in the family vault at Epping, amongst a gathering of 'numerous sorrowful friends and relations'. Sir William Ferguson, Drs. Farquharson, Waller Lewis, Semple, Wane, Seaton, Rudderforth and myself, Mr. A. B. Myers, Mr. J. N. Radcliffe and, of course, my brother Edward and uncle Octavius. Edward was Vicar of Epping at the time and, very generously I thought, in deference to my uncle, who, though now ordained, was vicar of precisely nothing, allowed him to perform the ceremony. It was a dreadful rainy day and I insisted that Florence Jessie stay with the boys in Hammersmith. Her father was kind enough, however, to go out of his way and bring Swerdlow, who stood most dignified and still throughout the proceedings.

As a final postscript let me quote from the Lancet obituary which appeared on March the fourteenth. It will perhaps give you a more precise understanding of the weight of the torch I was being called upon to carry. It is no burden at all now, I wear it lightly, but at the time … well, you'll see. It's probably clear as day to you already.

The Lancet said, and this is merely the concluding paragraph, that my father Benignus "was highly popular in society for his genial philanthropic spirit and his readiness to befriend or advise all who required his aid. He was an active promoter of all medical charities. For years it had been his custom on Christmas Day to give a dinner to three hundred poor people, and on his death-bed he desired the bounty should be continued. His conversational powers drew around him a large circle of notabilities, literary, artistic and scientific. His hospitality was profuse and many will miss the pleasant social evenings, enlivened by interesting and instructive anecdotes, for which his house was noted. The time he found for authorship may be inferred from the fact that, besides his publications, he has left behind a great many manuscripts on his favorite theme, to be edited according to the discretion of his son and associate in practice."

And oh, God yes, I've made good use of them.

The following year, in 1875, I managed to resuscitate the Psychological Journal according to my father's wishes. I edited it conscientiously for a further eight years until my mother's death in 1883, after which the sordid, time-consuming family squabble over my parent's legacy, which I shall soon have cause to describe at length, put a final end to it. I was able to publish many of my father's manuscripts as well as my own and I can say in all modesty that it was a great success. I was actually devastated at the time to see it go but you will appreciate that I had no other recourse.

Those eight years, the bulk of my thirties, were filled with intense activity. We had five children, Percy Forbes, our eldest, whom I have mentioned, then Ashton, born in 1870, Lyttleton Francis in 1873, Darcy in 1875, and last, fully eight years following, our sweet surprise, Dulcie, my dearest daughter. Oh yes, Florence had her hands full too.

After my rounds were finished at Sussex and Brandenburgh House in the morning, I would rush off to town to attend to my private patients there, returning later in the day to the asylum. Cases of every type and description came under my observation, from the comparatively sane individual suffering from slight mental depression to the acutely maniacal raving lunatic. The light and shade...if I may use such an expression in dealing with this subject...were so variable that I never recollect seeing two cases precisely identical.

My father and Conolly and Haslam and most of the other alienists of their generation firmly believed in the use of what they called 'the eye'. This was the supposed power in the medical practitioner to be able to subdue a violent or hysteric patient by the simple 'virtue' of his steady gaze and resolute mind. No, I'm not just blindly jumping about! You will come to realise the significance, I promise you.

I shall cite just one case to which I was called. It was that of a youth, about nineteen, who had nearly killed his brother the same morning and would have succeeded in so doing had he not been overpowered by others in the house. The attack was a sudden one and appeared to come on without any direct cause.

Upon entering the room I found the boy lying on a mattress on the floor, struggling violently, being held down, not without some considerable difficulty, by four men. Much to their surprise, I went straight to the patient, placed my hand on his head and greeted him by name. He turned round on me with glaring eyes and I instructed everyone to leave the room. They did so only hesitantly, uneasy as to what would be my probable fate.

You may find it hard to believe but the boy's paroxysms of violence immediately disappeared the moment we were alone. I remained with him scarce ten minutes during which time his condition became one of absolute tranquility. I requested him to get up and dress, which he did. He then sat on a chair opposite me and we began to discuss matters of interest apparently regardless of what had just happened.

The others were outside, I believe with their ears glued to the key-hole and, not hearing any sounds either of groaning or shouting, they became further apprehensive as to what had become of me. Being unable to restrain either their fear or curiosity, they opened the door with bated breath to see the late raving lunatic and myself engaged in quiet conversation. They were astonished and unable to comprehend such a powerful influence of one mind over another. They were entirely ignorant of the psychic nature of what had taken place.

But you aren't, are you?

You know about Mesmer and Charcot and hypnotism and all that. One couldn't really call it hypnotism, however, though I did become increasingly fascinated with that subject in later life, it was more like what you would call 'faith healing'. A laying on of hands. My father was quite convinced he had the 'power' and in those years I felt I did too. I've learned that it's just a trick you turn on and off. But it does work most exceptionally well if you believe.

You see, those who are called upon to deal with the insane, or those alleged to be so, must not know the meaning of the word fear. Unless the lunatic you are facing understands instantly that you are fearless he will get the better of you. I was always imbued with these qualities. They were as pronounced in me as second nature.

In any case, if you are still a trifle sceptical, you will soon see how I put these powers to the ultimate test with those eight women. For the most part, it worked like a charm. A snake-charm. Though I could do it much, much better now. As I've said, I was in the middle of my crisis of faith then, like father, like Uncle Octavius. Like many people you know, I'm sure. I'm at peace now. I'd be utterly unstoppable now.

Here's another ironic happenstance. I'm trying not to bore you! Have faith, it will all add up in the end.

I was urgently summoned late one summer evening to examine a patient who lived in a lonely part of Clapham Common. I was, I remember, just sitting down to dinner. From the description given to me it seemed a very acute case and, expecting there might be trouble, I sent two attendants in advance to wait outside the house until my arrival. The man in question had been throwing a large amount of money about the common and had so drawn the attention of the police. His family had then come to me with the details.

On arriving at the house and having alighted from my carriage and instructed the coachman to wait at the gates until my return, I looked round in vain for the two attendants. They were nowhere to be seen so I decided to try and force an entrance myself. I passed through the gates and walked up the carriage drive. It was quite dark save for the moonlight, still and unknowable as death. I rang the bell. Suddenly, a man's face appeared at an upstairs window and gruffly asked the nature of my business. I replied that I desired an interview. Without a whisker of hesitation he raised his arm and, presenting a revolver straight at me, fired. Fortunately, he missed.

I ducked under the portico and tried the door, which was locked, but, now more than ever determined to take the house by storm, I forced it. Heedless of what might happen next, I rushed up the stairs and found myself face to face with my previous would-be assassin. He was a raving, dangerous lunatic and I closed with him. Though such madmen are generally gifted with inhuman strength, he found his match in me. He was not the first case of a similar nature with which I had occasion to deal.

There was a desperate struggle during which he nearly got the better of me. But, much to my relief, just as I was becoming exhausted, the two attendants rushed in and between the three of us we were finally able to subdue him. I left them in charge and returned home, thankful to have escaped with my life.

You can begin to see the relevance of these little anecdotes, can't you?

I remember once being seated in my study when, without knocking, a strange man came in and took the seat opposite me. I noticed a thinly disguised agitation in his manner and asked him what his symptoms were. Drawing his chair nearer and suddenly glaring at me, he said, "The fact is, doctor, that I have a great desire to kill everyone I meet." He then took his hat off and I saw that he had a sort of metallic band round his forehead. He pointed to it and continued, "It is only this which prevents me carrying out what I desire to do!" I asked him to give me a more descriptive account of his meaning. He replied, "As I walk along the street, I say to myself as I pass anyone, 'I should like to kill you.' I don't know why, but I have that feeling."

Now, from the moment a patient entered my study, the first thought that always occurred to my mind was, 'Does this man or woman contemplate doing me any harm?' I was always on the *qui vive* for such an emergency. But I was becoming very interested in my man and, keeping my eye upon him, I said, "You haven't answered my question. I still have no idea to what you are really alluding."

Without warning, he jumped up from his chair and attempted to seize what I took to be a weapon from his pocket. I also leapt to my feet and grasped his wrist, while with the other I rang the hand bell. This was the summons for my man-servant, Freddy, who was never far away in the house, to come immediately to the room. Almost at the sound, my good man rushed in. I said calmly, still holding my patient, "Show this gentleman out into the street." At the sight of Freddy the lunatic came somewhat to his senses and allowed himself to be conducted by the arm to the front door. He turned round as he left and said to me, with a silly attempt at a meaningful scowl, "Good morning, doctor, we shall meet again." I replied genially, "Good morning," though I didn't envy the first person he encountered outside!

I followed the description of this event in my Recollections with these words, "This was a curious case of homicidal mania and murderous impulses, the latter evincing themselves whilst in my study. He was, like all other lunatics of this kind, cunning, deceptive and plausible, nothing in his outward appearance indicating insanity but no doubt there was in his innermost nature a dangerous hankering after blood."

You see, after so many years, I'm not at all convinced that particular tale isn't entirely apocryphal. I leave it to you to judge. So often during the composition of those Recollections I came foolishly close to confessing.

Blood … the very heart of life's miracle. And the smell of it is more mysterious and divine than the moist flux from a young woman's vulva after the joyful exertions of *coitus*. Oopsy, I've let the cat out of the bag a snippet there now, haven't I.

"This is intolerable!" Oh, yes, I can hear your impatient brain shouting. "Will you please get on with it! I don't care who you were or where you came from! I want to know how you did it! How you could bring yourself to have done it!"

Well, tell me how am I to show why I was impelled to such appalling barbarity without this preamble? I'm frightfully sorry, there's more! You need to know about the frustrations that began for me after my mother's death in 1883, now surely. And I can't believe you won't find something of interest in the peculiar way my own problems were a kind of mirror for the 'troubles' that were besetting the whole country at the time. And then I'll tell you about the murders. One by one. Every minute detail. Cross my heart.

You needn't worry, I won't let this become some sort of turgid sociological tract. God spare us all, no. It will stay what it is, a High Communion, a fantasia of blood.

To retrace our steps for just a moment, my father believed that most cases of insanity stemmed from 'the excessive indulgence of those passions which God has given us as necessary stimulants for the support and propagation of our animal nature.' Being 'oversexed', to enjoin the shorthand baldness of your modern terminology. 'Moral insanity' was a favourite catch-all phrase much in use during our time. It is a commonplace for you, I know, that in Victorian society any matter of the flesh was treated with risible euphemistic delicacy. However, I'm not sure you fully appreciate why it was so and, in any case, alas, I notice things haven't changed nearly as much as you might wish to think.

Let me cite an amusing example. My uncle Edward, nine years my father's senior, the fourth of Grandmother Mary's nine sons, was once the chairman of a Commission in Lunacy regarding an elderly gentleman named Taylor ... by the by, Uncle Edward became secretary to Lord Lyndhurst, the Chancellor of England, who, incidentally, was a second cousin related through the Copleys ... oh ho ... the sum and total of whose aberrance resided in the fact that he was well into his eighties and yet had recently desired several different women to marry him. I shall never forget this brief snatch of their exchange.

"Don't you think you are rather old to think of marrying?" my uncle asked.

"What has that got to do with it?" Taylor replied, "I suppose you will ask me next how many hairs I have on my eyebrows."

"Do you sleep well at night?"

"No, not very well."

"What do you do when you lay awake?"

"Oh, I can't tell you that. What do you do? Where do you live? What do you do when you lay awake? Come now, let us have fair play."

"Do you sing at night?"

"Sometimes. I believe there is no Act of Parliament against it."

"But you sing at night!"

"So do the nightingales."

There was considerable merriment amongst the gallery at such an absurd line of questioning. Alas, with Uncle Edward, I inherited this sadly humourless streak. It runs through my whole family. Moralistic pomposity. All the way back to Plymouth Rock and beyond, most likely, to the Wynchelouwes of Wynchelouwe Hall in the fourteenth century!

'Moral insanity', if you please! The press had a field day with us. Accusing alienists quite rightly of associating, without the slightest real justification, mad with bad. All so convenient. And we knew perfectly well in the depth of our lying souls that it was purest nonsense. Much the same as so many of your hectoring bible-thumpers do today.

Remember my fainting fit at that lecture? What was it in those words, '…rend in pieces that cobweb veil with which fashion hides the feelings of the heart…'? My father knew! They all knew! Bastard hypocrites!

However, to muddle on. I feel as if you're breathing down my neck! My dear mother died in 1883. Of course, the seeds of my 'eruption of blood' were sown much earlier, that's the point of this long *histoire*, but I only began to sense their stealthy, ineluctable growth at about that time. A black tumour starting as just a pinprick in the pit of the stomach and slowly, slowly engulfing the whole being. At the outset, I thought it was indigestion. How wrong one can be!

After the death of my father, I continued to reside with my growing family at the asylum in Hammersmith though I also maintained consulting rooms, as I've told you, in my mother's home, at 23 Cavendish Square, in the West End. Everything went on well. I had her interests always at the forefront. We were a united, happy family. My mother was a wonderful woman, kind, and beloved by all.

But my eldest sister who lived with her, and who I seem to have thus far neglected to mention, married soon after my father's death and her husband came and hung his hat up in my mother's house. And things quickly changed. The freedom of spirit I had enjoyed in my family's company disappeared. I began to feel like an intruder, even in Hammersmith. As month after month went by, this nauseating circumstance only continued and increased.

One day I went to my mother and told her it was my desire to sever my connection with the asylums entirely. The gist of her reply was, 'Stick to the ship. Your father has left the asylums to you in his will.' I explained more fully my position, the restraint that had come over me since another individual had been taken into the family. She then offered, "In addition to your stipend you shall have one-sixth share in the profits of the asylums." As she seemed so evidently upset at the mention of my dissociation with these asylums, which since my father's decease I had been the sole and only prop in supporting, I reluctantly consented to remain.

But matters did not improve. I felt acutely the shroud of deceit encircling our once convivial home. This feeling was also expressed by others who had previously been our frequent guests. It affected my mother's health. She seemed much worried and harassed and there was no excuse or justification for it. Ultimately I began to hate the very house where I had once spent so many happy days. I did my best to cover my feelings and to give my mother reassurance but the toll upon her health was great and I am certain it was the cause of her premature death. Earlier even than father, she did not reach her sixties.

Before the breath was out of her body, I remember, my odious brother-in-law came brusquely into my study with a paper already drawn which was to give him an equal share in the profit of the asylums. This I indignantly repudiated and, of course, refused to sign. He then replied, "I will make you, or throw the estate into Chancery." By which he meant, of course, to challenge the provisions of my parent's respective wills in court. He proceeded immediately to do this and I was appointed manager of the asylums while the affair should be settled. It took two years.

Two years of constant interference and haggling. There were bitter quarrels and an extremely painful, unnecessary, and to this day unresolved, family feud arose. I felt that, as my father had 'authorised' the trustees to dispose of the asylums to me, I was being shamefully treated. I had no power to do what I liked. I couldn't make a move without the sanction of a court-appointed receiver. This, coupled with the fact that I was called upon to pay the other beneficiaries a certain sum *per annum* before drawing my own salary, made me heartily desire to put a stop to the whole demeaning business. I dug in my heels.

My brother-in-law forced the issue and I was called upon in chambers to vouch all accounts kept by me since my mother's decease until the hearing of this application in court. The amount was close upon eight thousand pounds. I took this into chambers myself, vouching every item and showing clearly a balance on my side. There were at least six solicitors attending these summonses and the months and months it took to complete the matter were utterly depleting.

The time and money spent had months before led to the demise of the Psychological Journal, so dear to my father's wishes. And now to the first ominous soundings of the coming flood in me.

Ultimately the accounts were closed. Then, as I saw that every effort was being made to deprive me of my inheritance and rights, I put in a claim for my sixth share of the profits as agreed to between my mother and myself. During her life it only existed on paper. I never put the agreement into operation. A foolish generosity on my part.

My brother-in-law, always equal to the occasion, of course opposed this. He stated that, as he was living in my mother's house at the time, he was better placed to know her true intentions. I explained that it was only reasonable that, if I received a certain salary during my father's lifetime as an inducement to remain on, I had the additional offer after his decease. But I was very tired of the whole persecution and didn't sufficiently press the matter.

Then, to add insult to injury, the other beneficiaries made formal application to depose me as manager. I, who had been the sole support of these institutions for so many years! I once again rallied my energies and another heavy Chancery suit commenced. To start with I was represented by counsel but I soon lost patience and took the legal matters into my own hands, appeared in person, and argued the case in court. The final hearing came before Mr. Justice Pearson in the Chancery Division of the Law Courts on the twenty-second of April, 1885.

"My lord," I began, "In consequence of your lordship's suggestion on Friday last, to the effect that those interested in the asylums should meet together and discuss the matter, I beg to inform your lordship that a meeting was held on Monday last, the twentieth *inst.*, at which meeting I resigned of my own free will the management, under the court, of the asylums at Hammersmith with which my father and myself have been connected for upwards of forty years. At the same time I refused any remuneration which was then offered me to act as a consulting physician to these establishments. It has always been my earnest endeavour to carry on these asylums satisfactorily, and to protect the good will for the benefit of the estate. In consequence, however, of the furore that has lately taken place in connection with lunacy matters, the value of private asylums is at a very low ebb at the present moment..."

This was indeed true. The tide had been turning for many years in favour of more and more government regulation and intervention, of huge impersonal hospitals that, in my opinion, offered precious little hope of cure. And the public attitude toward the private asylum owner was akin to its feeling for the lowest Hebrew money-lender.

"For the last eighteen months or two years," I went on, "These asylums have been financially managed by Mr. Booker, the receiver appointed by this honourable court, he ordering all provisions, receiving and making all payments, whereas I have not been empowered to interfere in any way in this matter. How, therefore, can I possibly be held responsible for the financial condition of the asylums when I have had absolutely nothing to do with it?

"So far as the treatment of the patients and the medical management are concerned, they are exactly the same as they have been for years. I have it on record, and not long since, that a gentleman came to Hammersmith with a view to placing twenty Chancery patients there. Having inspected the establishment and grounds, he decided that the accommodation offered for the sums paid was inadequate.

"Again, on another occasion an inmate of Sussex House, paying twelve hundred *per annum*, was removed by the Commissioners in Lunacy in consequence of the place not being good enough for such a patient. This is no fault of mine, my lord. My hands have been crippled and tied for many years. I have done my utmost to find a suitable place for the transfer of the asylum, but I have been powerless to act in the matter, and now it appears I am to be held responsible for its financial falling off as well…!"

Justice Pearson interjected, "I do not think there is any occasion to go further into this matter, as I have previously expressed my opinion on your management and I have no reason to alter it."

I nodded gratefully. I remember catching the malignant glance in my brother-in-law's eye, but his counsel, Mr. Robertson, remained silent.

"There is one thing, my lord," I resumed, "On which I should like to make a few observations, especially as much stress has been laid during this summons on the matter. I allude to the receipt of a supposed salary of 1600 pounds *per annum*. My lord, the agreement was as follows, that I was to receive this sum, provided the profits of the asylum admitted of the amount being paid to me. But before I could draw any part of it, the beneficiaries were entitled to receive as a minimum charge, whatever the profits might be, 100 pounds *per annum* each. I had to pay, in addition to this, 400 pounds *per annum* to the medical staff, and was bound by the order of the court to keep up a suitable residence in town.

"Well, my lord, last year the profits, according to the account rendered me by the receiver, amounted to some 1320 pounds, and out of this sum your lordship will see it was impossible for me to receive the 1600 pounds, as agreed between myself and the beneficiaries. Out of the 1320 pounds, therefore, according to the agreement, 300 pounds was paid as first charge to the beneficiaries, rendering my salary just over 1000 pounds. In addition to this, 400 pounds had to be subtracted for the salary of the medical officers, and I may put the expense of the house for consultations, that I was to keep up, at say, at the very lowest, 300 pounds *per annum*. This reduces my salary, which may appear at the first instance a large one on paper, to a mere pittance of 300 pounds *per annum*, out of which sum I have also to pay for the expenditure of certain other actions connected with the asylums. I have nothing further to add beyond hoping that, under new direction and management, things may go amicably with those now interested in the concern."

I then sat down. I had, I suppose, convinced myself at the time that I meant what I said at the last. But you know that I didn't. I wished them all to roast in hell.

After a moment, Mr. Robertson stood up and said, "On behalf of the infants I must press for a sale." My sister's children were as yet no more than toddlers!

The Justice retorted, "Those interests are very remote, Mr. Robertson. As you say, they are still in their infancy. I hope the day is far distant when this question will have to be considered."

I rose again. "There is one thing, my lord, that I have forgotten to say. I resigned my appointment of my own free will and without any restrictions being placed on my actions."

Not only moral pomposity but a fatal yearning after martyrdom! My stigmata were positively oozing with silent, self-righteous accusation. I was so full of it that day I could have been buggered with a rhinoceros horn and turned the other cheek.

Justice Pearson did, in fact, phrase his ensuing judgement in my favour. But I never availed myself of the ruling as to participating in the asylum spoils, though I was now legally entitled to do so. My father left the asylums to me in his will and I had wasted the best years of my life in building up that inheritance only to have it whittled away and undermined by others. It was a severe lesson. The licence itself was transferred to my sister's family and I was never invited to enter the doors at Hammersmith again, not that I had any desire to do so. All I wanted was to wipe my feet on the pack of them and say goodbye once and for all.

During those same years, in addition to the shatteringly unpleasant business I have just described, I had been dealing with a weight of other litigation, all directly in connection with my semi-official capacity at the asylums.

One such notorious case, well, a whole series of cases, in fact, were brought against me by a certain Mrs. Georgiana Weldon. Against me and another consulting physician, several newspaper editors, and, if you can believe it, the great composer Charles Gounod, who was then resident conductor of the Covent Garden Opera House, for once allegedly overcharging her for the rental of the Opera House for a protest meeting! The entire affair was beyond idiocy.

Briefly, Mrs. Weldon was a relatively well-to-do and not unattractive redhead, of fiery temperament, whose husband was some sort of minor official in the royal household. Whether she truly needed confinement or not is, of course, a matter of opinion but her husband certainly thought so and had sought my help in having her certified and committed to the asylum at Hammersmith.

When I arrived to take her thence I found the doors to her apartment barred. But, headstrong as always, I forced an entry. What I had not been told, however, was that the secretary of the Alleged Lunatics' Friend Society…no, this is not some bizarre invention of mine, it really existed…was inside. He was himself a former mental patient and he had, before my arrival, already spirited Mrs. Weldon away, dressed in a nun's habit.

It cost me a small fortune in the end. The judge, a Baron Huddleston, caused me to pay five hundred pounds in damages and my reputation took a terrible beating in the press. It was abominably unfair.

The wretched judge in his closing statement gave birth to what came to be known as the 'crossing-sweeper' summation. Basically, he insinuated that if any common labourer wanted to put someone away in a private asylum he merely had to find, and I quote, "…two medical men who had never had a day's practice in their lives and they would, for a trifling sum, grant the certificates." As you can see, this was a gross and intentional misrepresentation of the facts of what had happened but the damned calumny stuck to me like glue. I was simply made a cat's-paw of the imperfections of the Lunacy Act. I was in no way responsible for any wrongdoing. And far from being unpracticed in matters of lunacy, I was, as you know, reared in its very atmosphere. It was un-Christian persecution, plain and simple, and I bore the brunt of it, at the time, without assistance and without the slightest trace of sympathy. What a galling irony it was to think back to that proudest of days in my life when I received the degree of D.C.L. from the University of Oxford for my thesis on The History of Lunacy Legislation. I obtained this degree at the age of twenty-six, the youngest recipient ever to receive it in the history of the university! And I had, some years later, been made an LL.D. at Cambridge for my researches on the criminal responsibility of the insane. These rare honours had been such a source of satisfaction to me! And now what?! I was forty-one years old and an object of public ridicule. I was in virtual bankruptcy and the cost to my marriage had been dear in the extreme. I ask you, now what?! Some outburst could hardly be entirely unexpected, could it?

Fasting and Feeding

Now, before I tell you about the first murder I want to be sure you understand what life was like in London during the late 1880's. You may think yourself familiar with it but let me fill in a few details. I mean most particularly, of course, for those unfortunate souls who, by the arbitrary circumstance of birth or simple bad luck, were forced, through no necessary fault of their own, to live in the area of the East End known as Whitechapel.

At this period the East End of London was home to nearly one million of the world's most miserable and impoverished people. Whitechapel alone, hardly more than a square mile in area, housed, at a minimum, 80,000 of the very poorest of those. To the average middle-class Londoner the East End might as well have been darkest Africa. It was mythical, sordid…'a shocking place, where I once went with a curate, an evil plexus of slums that hide human creeping things, where filthy men and women live on penn'orths of gin, where collars and clean shirts are decencies unknown, where every citizen wears a black eye and none ever combs his hair.'

It was the home of the Great Unwashed, the Unemployed. An unreasoning Mongol Horde that suddenly, in the late 80's, began making its presence felt, waving banners, demanding attention, eventually, yes, rioting, in Trafalgar Square and Hyde Park and the elegant sanctuaries of the West End.

It is utterly plain why this happened. More than half of the children born in the East End were dying before they were five years old. One in ten of the survivors was pronounced mentally defective, a common result of chronic malnutrition. The 'very poor', those living in squalid tenements with as many as a dozen to a room, or 'doss houses' holding hundreds in fetid communal dormitories, earning less than eighteen shillings a week, numbered well over 100,000, of whom 40,000 were children. There were at least 10,000 more who had no homes at all of any kind.

"They render no useful service. They create no wealth, more often they destroy it. They degrade whatever they touch and as individuals are incapable of improvement," wrote the so-called 'reformer' Charles Booth, a man devoid of charity, whose true vocation was statistical analysis.

Between 1857, when the Lancet estimated that one house in every sixty in London was a brothel and one woman in sixteen a whore, and the turn of the 20th century, when Jack London wrote these words after visiting Christchurch Gardens, Spitalfields, on a January night, let me read the passage to you, "...A chill, raw wind was blowing and these creatures huddled there in their rags, sleeping for the most part, or trying to sleep. Here were a dozen women, ranging in age from twenty years to seventy. Next a babe, possibly of nine months, lying asleep, flat on the hard bench, with neither pillow nor covering, nor anyone looking after it. Next half-a-dozen men, sleeping bolt upright or leaning against one another in their sleep. In one place a family group, a child asleep in its sleeping mother's arms and the husband, or male mate, clumsily mending a delapidated shoe. On another bench a woman trimming the frayed strips of her rags with a knife and another woman, with thread and needle, sewing up rents. Adjoining, a man holding a sleeping woman in his arms. Farther on, a man, his clothing caked with gutter mud, asleep, with head in the lap of a woman, not more than twenty-five years old, and also asleep. My guide told me the women would sell themselves for thruppence, or tuppence, or a loaf of stale bread..." very little of any substance was done by the authorities to alleviate this appalling suffering and misery. The People of the Abyss, indeed.

The winter of 1885-86 was bitterly cold, the coldest for thirty years. There was a large gathering of the unemployed, mostly men, dockers and labourers, held in Trafalgar Square. Afterwards, the crowd marched *en masse* towards Hyde Park where they eventually meant to disperse. There was, however, some uncalled-for jeering and harassment from incensed clubmen as the marchers were proceeding down Pall Mall and it touched off a riot. Thousands of demonstrators streamed through the West End, looting and smashing windows, all the way through Piccadilly and Mayfair north to Oxford Street before the police were finally able to put an end to it.

"How repugnant it is to reason and to instinct that the strong should be overwhelmed by the feeble, ailing and unfit!" stormed a pompous pamphleteer.

Of course, a committee of inquiry was immediately appointed by the Home Secretary to look into the reasons why this had happened and, more importantly, why the police had not been able to control it. And, of course, a scapegoat was quickly found in the person of the Metropolitan Police Commissioner, Colonel Sir Edmund Henderson.

His successor was another military man with no real experience of police work, Sir Charles Warren, of whom I shall have much, much more to say.

At this time the police themselves were a disgruntled lot. They were genuinely afraid for their lives on their beats in the East End. Being urged by 'outside agitators' it was alleged, as is ever the custom of prevailing powers, to strike for better pay and better consideration of their working conditions.

Even my dear wife, Florence Jessie, became deeply troubled by the unrest. I had taken apartments at Rivercourt in Hammersmith and a consulting house in Wimpole Street, just off Cavendish Square, after the court debacle with my family forced our removal from the asylums, and the rioters had come within a few yards of our door. So, it was decided, in the summer of 1886, to move the family to Brighton. My father's house there had been left to my brother Edward and I jointly in his will. Edward was now the Vicar of St. Paul's Church in St. Leonard's-on-Sea, forty miles eastward along the coast. He was busy with his parish and his writing … sorry, Ned, I won't be able to resist telling more about your literary endeavours later on … and kindly agreed to let Florence and little Dulcie take up residence on Brunswick Terrace. I was to stay in London and try to rebuild my practice and somehow make ends meet for us all. The three younger boys were away at school in Repton. Percy was now in his second to last year at Rugby, my old *alma mater*, and not doing well.

In the spring of 1887, feeling myself somewhat lonely and despondent, and exhausted from a winter of constant shifting about back and forth to Brighton, on the spur I took a trip to Paris. I don't know why. I remember finding myself on the boat train and wondering how I got there. But I felt somehow impelled and continued on my journey.

At a social gathering in Paris... I had many professional acquaintances there who turned an understanding ear to my persecutions in England... I was introduced to a Swami. I have always had a deep fascination with spiritualism. In its genuine aspects, not the carnival hokery-pokery which tarnishes its name.

This Swami was a big woman of very singular appearance, a clairvoyant who professed to be able to look into the future and delineate one's character to a fare-thee-well. She was very anxious to discuss with me what she termed the 'righteous life'. I was very impressed by what she said, though at the same time I was suspicious, not to say incredulous. She told me she was a direct disciple of Christ's and that she was destined to play a prominent part in the history of the world and that I was also! I must say she interested me very much.

It is just one more irony that a few years later she was indicted for a series of crimes which sent a wave of horror and disgust throughout France and which earned her seven years of penal servitude!... What is it about my brain that cannot resist the pun of 'penile' servitude?... Alas, the inner life of mankind sometimes seems no more to me than a cavernous echo-chamber of senseless bits and pieces colliding endlessly together like bats in some deep grotto with nowhere to alight and nowhere to escape. Bats in the belfry? Ha! Bats in the grotto! 'Unprofitable strife,' indeed.

Shortly after my return from Paris, I had a dream. I was seated in my study when suddenly a man came in with a hideous mask covering his face.

"Doctor," he said, "I have come to consult you on a most appalling question in connection with myself. I am a well-known man, closely related to the highest in the land, and therefore for certain reasons I think it desirable that my identity should not be known to you. I feel that I am in a position to open my heart out to you, tell you my terrible story and ask your advice concerning it, and I can do this with a much more open mind, conscious of the fact that you are unaware to whom you are speaking."

I reacted with some alarm and moved my chair back so as not to be in close proximity to this strange intruder and his dreadful mask. I replied, putting my hand on a notebook.

"In this notebook are contained the names of persons, which, if I divulged them, would cause an enormous amount of sensation in the world, and would bring misery and ruin to many families. I do not ask your name. I simply ask you to continue your description of your case, when, after careful consideration, I will give you my opinion thereon."

He then unfolded himself and gave an intimate account of the most extraordinary experience that I had ever heard, the precise outlines of which have now, whether fortunately or unfortunately, receded into the mist. I can only recall the immensity of feeling that his relation summoned up in me.

After he had finished, I assured and reassured him that I had heard of similar symptoms, and that I saw no reason why, so far as he was concerned, matters should not right themselves. He seemed grateful, shook me by the hand, and placed in it a thin envelope containing my fee.

"Doctor," he then said, rising from his chair, "Please turn your head while I take off this grotesque disguise from the face of the man who has had to unfold to you such a dreadful history."

I turned my head away. The door opened and the agonised intruder left the house for the outer world again. I did not let him know that beneath the mask I had been able to trace the features of my own face!

It's an obvious truth that we are ourselves every one of the spectral *personae* that inhabit our dreams. This fearful confessional was but a desperate subconscious precognition of everything that was so soon to come.

The summer of 1887 was unusually clement and balmy. It was the year of the Queen's Jubilee and throughout those months the city remained relatively calm, though the homeless and unemployed had taken to invading the West End in greater and greater numbers. More and more were permanently camped out, it seemed, sleeping in Trafalgar Square and St. James's Park, even, as the days wore on, in

Green Park and Hyde Park. I remember much complaint about the daunting experience of taking an innocent stroll on a summer's eve.

Florence Jessie was firmly ensconced in the safety and fresh air of Brighton and I was becoming secretly glad of the separation. The unspoken malaise between us was paralleled by the growing, ominous, palpable tension in London.

One warm evening in August I went through a rather trying experience, again of a horrible nature, and which might have turned out very seriously for me. I was summoned to attend a man suffering from mania incidental to much indulgence in alcohol. Upon my arrival I found the patient sitting on a sofa, his eyes rolling about in a very restless manner. There was a certain amount of subdued excitement about him. His wife, as is often the case where the husband is an uncontrollable drunkard, was herself rather infirm of purpose or she would have taken proper steps to have had him placed in care long before I was called in.

On my entering the room he jumped up from the sofa and, pointing to his wife, exclaimed, "Look at the woman I have brought up! Look at the woman I have nurtured! Look at her now! There she is!"

He then left the room, returning a few moments later, his eyes glaring more fiercely then ever, flourishing a large knife in his hand. After a difficult moment or two, I persuaded him to make me a present of it, which I kept for some time after among my curios. His condition was clearly a dangerous one and, as it was nearly midnight and no possibility of obtaining help, I decided to remain the night on guard.

During the night his craving for spirits seemed only to increase until I determined to stop it at all risks and hazards. I knew that I had the knife safe in my possession. It was only a question of one man's strength against another's. His mania, by this time, had become so violent that, knowing as I did the abnormality of this among lunatics, I determined to assert my authority and power by hypnotic influence. I took the key of the door away from him by force so that he could no longer obtain access to the alcohol. He then fell back on the sofa and I was enabled, by certain psychic influences in which I was by this time most proficient, to produce in him a deep and, what appeared to me, calm sleep.

At seven o'clock in the morning he woke up, the attack having absolutely subsided. I felt sure that I had most narrowly prevented a murder.

A few days later, a woman was brought to me by her husband, a Mrs. Louisa Constance Proud. She was suffering from depression and kept asking her husband why he did not "put her in an asylum and kill the children." She repeated continuously, "Oh, Jack, Jack, you are a fool. Why do you not put me away? Take some poison and kill the children, and then they will be angels, and then we shall have no trouble." At my urging the husband took her forthwith to an asylum but allowed her to come out at the expiration of three days notwithstanding my strong opinion on the matter to the contrary. He then took her to the seaside like an ordinary rational being.

A short time afterwards she killed her infant daughter, aged sixteen months, by setting fire to the bed in which the child was sleeping. She then cut her own throat to the bone with a razor.

In October the weather took a sudden change for the worse. Despite this, the homeless stayed doggedly camped out, mostly in Trafalgar Square. "A foul slurry of vagrants!" screeched one writer. "The scum of London have now seen fit to deposit their sewage at our door!" protested another.

Sir Charles Warren complained to the Home Office that he had to permanently allot two thousand constables just to deal with the worker's demonstrations in the West End. The City Police had had to do the same but with much smaller numbers. I should explain, in case you don't know it, the strange anomaly that the Old City of London, a tiny area in comparison to the whole metropolis, was policed by its own separate force which did not come under the jurisdiction of the Home Office. This will become quite crucial later on since the Old City bordered directly on the teeming poverty of Whitechapel. It worked greatly to my advantage.

The stolid shopkeepers of the West End were fed up and threatened to take the law into their own hands if the police could not bring some end to the intolerable situation. So, Sir Charles proceeded to clear Trafalgar Square of its small army of unemployed and destitute and homeless and then, with the timorous Home Secretary's approval, he banned the use of the Square altogether. But the suppression backfired.

On November 13th, a day which came to be known as 'Bloody Sunday', a terrible battle was fought. A gigantic crowd of the Unwashed, with knives and clubs and bricks and iron bars and staves, swarmed down from the docklands, descended on Trafalgar Square, broke through the police cordon and again briefly took possession. By the end of the day, after four thousand constables, three hundred of them mounted, three hundred Grenadier Guards, three hundred Life Guards and finally seven thousand more constables who had been held in reserve, had struggled for five hours to disperse them, there were counted over two hundred people injured, some very seriously. Three hundred more of the protesters were arrested. It was a black, black day in our history.

Unlike my father, who was almost rabidly Conservative and, had he been alive and his health permitted, would have happily ridden into the Square with his baton flailing, I never had the slightest interest in the shady business of politics. To me it is an entirely hollow world dedicated simply to the propagation of greed and resounding with naught but self-serving pontification. But that day, that day, something almost imperceptibly subtle snapped in me.

I had held such a knot of emotion in check for so long and attempted always to be right and virtuous and compassionate and understanding and civilised for so, so pathetically long that I found myself wishing with all my heart to have been amongst that mob of desperate and reeking and yes, oh, so profoundly unwashed souls and to have been hurling bricks along with them and screaming, too, screaming at the top of my lungs! But, of course, I wasn't. I was in the train on my way back from Brighton after a dreadful weekend with Florence, full of sullen, accusatory silence.

Sir Charles Warren was now universally despised by London's working class. He received death threats. "Beware of your life you dog. Don't venture out if I was you. This is yours!" Followed by a roughly drawn picture of a coffin. But the threat of mob rule had effectively been broken and a month later the Queen personally honoured Sir Charles with a Knight Commandership of the Bath.

My mood was once again deeply aggravated as I boarded the train for Brighton at Victoria Station on Christmas Eve. And I was tired. I was normally, like father, of a happily robust constitution. I never suffered from the common cold and only once during my childhood do I ever remember having been put to bed with a fever. But on this day I felt so tired I could barely mount the steps onto the carriage. I thought glumly at the time that I must be coming down with influenza and how that would add to the trial of an already unpromising holiday season. Frankly, I was not looking forward to it at all. Don't mistake me, I dearly loved my children and, though we were in rather straitened financial circumstances, I had carefully picked out a present for each of them and was carrying them with me, gaily wrapped, in an old Gladstone bag. But the atmosphere between myself and Florence Jessie had become almost inextricably morose.

Yes, I suppose at bottom it was sexual. We had had up to that point a rather typical Victorian marriage. When you look at it objectively it's hard to believe that Victorian women bore children. The hows and wherefores of procreation were subjects never discussed. It was just something that happened, like a dream, in the darkness of the night. A surreptitious matter of wordlessly coaxing up a woman's nightclothes and then almost blinding one's consciousness to the bestial act itself. The proper Victorian woman always kept her eyes closed and her head turned modestly to one side, in a ridiculous pretence that it wasn't actually happening. And Florence Jessie was a good Victorian woman. I don't recall ever seeing her breasts. Her ablutions were always performed in strictest privacy. None of the children ever saw her naked either to my knowledge.

And I was a good Victorian husband. Excessively good. I was not entirely virginal when I married. Given the manner of education of the typical well-bred English public schoolboy this would hardly have been possible. But during the fifteen years of our marriage I had never been unfaithful, though the opportunity presented itself on many occasions, and, most untypically, nor had I ever made recourse to a house of prostitution.

But, yes, yes, yes, I'm sure at its basest level the tension between Florence Jessie and I was sexual. We had not fumbled together in the deep midnight for over three years. It was me. I didn't want it. My unspoken distress and natural reticence in unburdening myself, the old British stiff upper lip, prevented my reaching out to her and deepened over time until my lack of response froze into permanent inaction and though she, being as she was a good and proper Victorian woman, was not supposed to care about such things … the heavens forfend! … and would, of course, never, ever even think of speaking about them, nonetheless it was clear to me that she certainly had taken notice and did indeed care very, very much.

Euphemistic discourse is death. Victorian society perfected it and perpetuated it. How could I have been so unaware that this suffocating politesse was crushing me? How is it that we can so successfully ignore the gaping chasm that exists between reality and the paltry conceptions of our minds? Oh sweet Jesus, don't tell me it's all necessary!

The web of euphemism, how did father put it..."that cobweb veil"...had entirely blinded me, as it had enmeshed a whole society. There was not a breath of fresh air in my life. A vivid sensation of drowning oppressed me in that railway carriage all the way down to Brighton.

No one was there to meet me at the station and a chill wind was blowing off the sea. I was in a sweat, by contrast, shuddering with coming fever. Why did I think of Swerdlow at that moment? The poor man had killed himself eleven months after my mother died. He had surmised something, I imagine, of the uncertainty of my continued connection with the asylums, though that surely cannot have been the entire cause. I had knocked at his small room one night, puzzled at his absence, and found him hanging by a stout cord in his closet. He was eighty-four years old by my best reckoning. In all the years I had known him I had never heard him utter a single word.

I alighted from the brougham at Brunswick Terrace feeling worse than ever. The children were already asleep and Florence Jessie was just helping our new maid-servant to blow out the candles on the Christmas tree as I came in.

"Whatever is the matter, Lyttleton?" she asked, taking the Gladstone bag from my hand, "You're all clammy and white as a sheet."

Her pronunciation of my name bounced madly about in my brain...little tin god, little tin god...I must have been delirious, but I tried my best to put a brave face on it and asked the girl to bring me a pot of lemon tea to my room. After feebly assuring Florence that I would be fine in the morning, I stumbled off upstairs to bed.

As I tossed and turned in misery that night I kept running over obsessively in my mind several prominent cases I had attended in which an attack of influenza had led otherwise quite normal persons to insanity, violence and even suicide.

In particular, a professional gentleman of the highest connections, belonging to many learned societies and a member of one of the leading West End clubs. He had suffered a prolonged period of kleptomania during which he stole without reason many small items from the pockets of other gentlemen's coats in the cloak-room. Among them, two pairs of opera glasses, one box of cigars, seven matchboxes, eleven cigarette cases, fifteen cigar cases, seven card cases, a cigar holder and one tobacco pouch. The man was a non-smoker! He claimed merely to have felt an ... 'intense desire to examine things' ... and to have experienced ... 'a momentary sensation of joy' ... while he held them in his hands. This endless array of small, trivial objects revolved tediously in my brain the entire night.

I felt, inexplicably, much improved the next morning, it can't really have been the flu, and Christmas and Boxing Day passed pleasantly enough. All the normal rituals were observed. After church, the present-giving, the turkey, the stuffing, the plum pudding with a sprig of holly and swimming in ignited brandy, the mistletoe, in the evening the singing of carols as Florence Jessie played the piano. The day following, Christmas boxes for the servants, the postman, the errand boys and a hot meal served personally to the poor of the parish just as father would have done, if not, of force, nearly so lavish.

But despite my feeling better, I had the sensation of walking through it all like an automaton. Edward had wanted us to come to St. Leonard's for the service on Christmas morning but I sent a message declining, laying the blame on my most uncharacteristic bout of fever. Even the children's jolly faces appeared to me as though seen through the wrong end of a telescope. Noises were muffled, distant. The lassitude in my unraveling soul was bottomless. I lay helpless, virginal, spread-eagled. I felt submerged at the bottom of a murky well. But, though my inner state was nothing if not worse than I have tried so ineptly to describe it, except for once or twice catching Florence Jessie looking a trifle quizzically at me out of the corner of her eye, no one really seemed to notice that anything was wrong.

I thought Dulcie strangely subdued, however, on the morning of the twenty-seventh as I set off for the station. She didn't kiss me on the cheek and hug me as she was wont when I bade goodbye and she didn't say anything either. For my part, I couldn't summon the strength to ask her why not, nor could my invention conjure some fatherly jest to elevate her mood.

Yet for reasons unknown to me still, I began to feel a growing lightness of heart as the train sped toward London.

As we passed through Preston Park, where tickets are collected, I thought of Percy Lefroy Mapleton. In 1881, he had brutally shot and murdered a harmless, wealthy, elderly gentleman named Gold while traveling on the Brighton to London line and thrown his body from the train in Balcombe Tunnel. All Lefroy had stolen from him was the old man's watch. Everyone was profoundly startled and dismayed by the act's apparent senselessness.

That night again, back at home in Wimpole Street, I could not sleep. My man-servant, Freddy, did not, as most do, live on the premises, he and his wife and children maintained a modest flat in the Finchley Road, so, at about half past one I prised myself from bed and went downstairs to make a cup of tea. Having done so, I entered my study thinking to read. However, I was drawn unfathomably to the glass-fronted cupboard where I kept odd items of interest from my career. I turned the key and took out the knife I had confiscated from the man suffering from alcoholic mania. I had kept it, as I said, as just another curio. But now, like the respected yet kleptomanic clubman, it gave me a momentary sensation of joy as I held it. I walked to the moonlit window examining it carefully, almost in a trance. As I gazed out into the night, it came upon me with a certainty tingling all my blood what I was about to do. I dressed and went calmly out the front door.

I hailed a cabman on Wigmore Street and instructed him to take me to St. Paul's. On the way, I thought again of Lefroy. One of his friends had told me, after his execution, that he was amiable, kind, even-tempered, of a lovable disposition, and that he had ever displayed this from a child. The thought made me smile. In fact, I found myself laughing out loud, my normal propriety quite vanished. My rapidly unraveling sleeve of care was racing pell-mell toward its so long desired dissolution.

As I alighted from the carriage in St. Paul's Church Yard at twenty minutes to three, it was utterly deserted. I watched the cabman turn and trot his horses back out of sight in the direction of Ludgate Circus. I looked up at the immense dome of St. Paul's, under which all our family had knelt to pray so many times, and whispered fervently..."For You! For You! For You!"...and watched in fascination as the humid exhalation from my lips streamed upward, venomously engulfing Christ and His Infinite Firmament beyond, then turned eastward toward Whitechapel.

I strode briskly through Watling Street to Queen Victoria Street, then on past the Royal Exchange, up Cornhill to Leadenhall Street. Beyond Leadenhall Market the slums of the East End began and I was still less than three-quarters of a mile from that majestic dome! It was not until I reached Aldgate High Street that I saw any sign of life, not even a patrolling constable.

At the corner of the Minories, where the Poor Clares had a convent in Chaucer's day, just across from St. Botolph's, I caught up with a middle-aged woman in soiled ragged clothes, staggering slightly, smelling of drink and urine, clearly a prostitute and much the worse for wear. She turned a bleary eye on me, looked me up and down and cackled.

"Ooee, what are you doing of out so late, your lordship? Ain't it terrible cold though, eh?"

We both stopped moving and stared at each other. Her speech was horribly slurred. I found myself unprepared, tongue-tied as a schoolboy, momentarily quite unable to respond. It was actually a pleasant face beneath the grime. She grunted in amusement and put her hand on my arm.

"You wants to come with me, is that it? Come on then. I don't mind. Cost you a shilling though. You looks like as you can afford it, eh? Bet you can. Come on."

She must have taken my silence for innocence or inexperience or daftness, I don't know. Whatever her thoughts, she led me gently, like a babe, around a corner into a tiny, reeking, pitch-dark alley which I subsequently confirmed was called Golden Fleece Court.

"I knows what you wants, your lordship, I does," she cooed softly. "Ooee, if you 'asn't the look of a unmilked cow."

I remember she had put her gloved hand between my legs, a ratty, rough woolen glove with the finger's ends cut off, and was feeling about for the expected tumescence. There was none. I was a blank. I had not thought to pre-plan any method at all to this madness. The words from a letter of Lefroy's throbbed idiotically in the cavern of my skull... 'Annie, dearest, shall I ever see the silver lining of the clouds again?'

"What's the matter now, eh, your lordship? Lost it in the wars? Come on then, old Fay'll kiss it better..."

She made a motion to drop to her knees and I struck.

Not smoothly though, not with quite sufficient determination of purpose. She was wearing several thick layers of clothing. I don't think the first attempt penetrated her flesh at all. She made a soft squeal of surprise and then opened her mouth again as if to scream. I panicked and in an instant I had smashed her head back into the brick wall, pushing her chin up violently as I did so, at the very least dislocating, if not breaking, her neck. She went limp and began sliding to the ground but I was now possessed of superhuman strength and held her up and forced the knife blade once again, this time cutting deep into her abdomen. I held it there until I felt my hand grow warm and moist with her blood.

I began to master my fear and pulled the blade. With growing excitement I thrust a third time and, as I felt the tissues of her belly being ripped asunder, her eyes popped open wide and looked at me, glinting knowingly in the gloom. I was overcome with a sudden rush of joy and thrust again higher, deeper, piercing the tight knot of her plexus, touching at last with the knife's tip... oh sadly unknown ecstasy!... the pulsing marrow of her heart. She uttered a muffled, gurgling noise, a final, slow exhalation of breath that sounded for all the world like a moan of pleasure.

I heard these words beneath the sound... "I know you."

I pulled the blade again and, holding her still against the wall with clouding marble eyes, pushed it slowly up beneath her chin through the base of her tongue into her brain. I remember a sudden spate of blood shot down the sleeve of my coat and I adroitly stepped aside to avoid further soiling. I suppose I was rather alarmed by the sensation, too, and I let her fall.

Her eyes were still open and not yet quite blank as I backed away. I had an urge to plunge the knife into them, but I didn't. I was torn between further delight and running and took the latter course. I knew she was dead and... I knew I had caught a glimpse of God. And I knew there was more that I had to do!... but in some part of my thrilling, singing blood there was fear and an instinct for self-preservation as deep and ancient as a wolf-howl. I had stepped backward nearly to the Minories before I came fully to my senses and turned to look about me. I crept to the corner of the building to see if I had been observed. A market-cart was clattering down Aldgate but nothing more.

I walked quietly again to the dead woman and looked down at her. What had she said her name was? 'Fay'? Her hair had come unpinned and strands of grey were soaking up her blood. I thought of my grandmother and the stare of a Gorgon that had made me shriek. I knelt down and closed her eyes. The receding life force still had power to tickle mysteriously at my fingertips. I wiped the blood from my hands on her skirt. Rough, rough cloth it was and not easily absorbent. I shook the blood from my sleeve as best I could and cleaned the blade, placing it carefully once again under my arm and down the inside of my waistcoat. It still felt warm as I bid 'Fay' adieu.

I remember whistling softly to myself as I walked calmly away down the Minories, passing beneath the brooding Tower walls like a ghost to Lower Thames Street where I paused in a state of strange euphoria to admire the black silk waters of the river, the blood of the earth, shimmering in the moonlight. I had a momentary thought to toss the knife in but I couldn't bring myself to part with it. Besides, what possible connection could I have to such a murder? And who, alas, would care for the death of poor old 'Fay'?

I continued on, heedless now of apprehension, through the anonymous mackerel bustle outside the new Billingsgate Market and across Pudding Lane where the Great Fire had been unluckily sparked by the King's baker in 1666. But it killed the rats and brought an end to the Plague! As I stood entranced before the enduring elegance of Christopher Wren's Monument to the fire, a hansom came noisily along from London Bridge and I was pleased to hail it home. It was just twenty-five minutes past five when I re-entered the front door of 70, Wimpole Street.

I remember checking my shoes, uppers, soles and inside as well, and returning the knife spotless to its appointed place in the curio cabinet, then going upstairs and washing the remaining blood from my hands and the front and right sleeve of my coat and the cuffs of my jacket and shirt. I left the clothes to dry above the bath. Freddy would send them out for cleaning when he arrived at seven. I told him I had slipped and fallen in a puddle. He enquired if I had sustained any injury and I assured him, no, and that I would have the usual for breakfast, thank you.

As I sat down in my study in a fresh suit of clothes to read the morning papers and wait for hot buttered toast and eggs and tea, I discovered to my surprise that I wasn't in the least bit tired. Quite the contrary... I felt reborn.

Uncontrollable Drunkenness

Now I am aware that other meticulous scholars who have studied the case of 'Jack the Ripper', that irritating *nominis umbra* by which I came to be known to the world, do not believe that there was a murder in Whitechapel during Christmas week in 1887. Or at least, not one that could with likelihood be attributed to me. But you see, I purposely confused the location in my published Recollections on the matter. I dedicated a whole chapter to the 'Ripper' case. Why not? I was rightly taking credit for having put a stop to his butcheries! I wrote that the murder during Christmas week, 1887, had taken place near Osborne and Wentworth Streets. Well, it's only a third of a mile away from the little alley of Fleece Court. And I knew that a woman had been attacked there on Easter Monday in 1888.

Her name was Emma Smith and some clumsy, despicable lout had thrust a piece of wood brutally up her vagina and she died in agony at London Hospital a day later. None of my victims after Fay suffered the slightest pain, nor a second's distress or mental anguish. I do regret that with her there was such a moment. It was due solely to my inexperience.

I have never discovered why Fay's death was not reported, nor why there is no record of it to be found anywhere. And I would hardly have been so foolish to mention it in my Recollections if the Daily Telegraph had not stated in its issue of September 11th, 1888, after I had really got the ball rolling, that the first victim had been murdered during Christmas week the previous year. They got the location wrong and it was clearly sloppy reportage but it served me well. Oddly, a later researcher invented ... or did he? ... the name 'Fairy Fay' for the first victim. He claimed she was killed on Boxing Night, not quite correct, but close, very close, and that she was taking a short cut home from a pub on Mitre Square.

Perhaps she was, perhaps she was. But wait a minute, no, on second thought, I don't recall there being any sort of pub in Mitre Square in those days.

In any case, poor old Fay's fate was left for long unsung. Perhaps the police never found her. Perhaps whoever did disposed of her secretly for their own reasons. Whatever happened, her look, as she was thrust into Eternity remains forever seared into the flanks of my imagination. I have never felt such overwhelming compassion for anyone or anything in my life, nor such a complete Oneness with what you might call 'the existential agony of mankind' ... would you? ... well, then again, maybe you wouldn't ... as I did in that moment when our eyes met and I heard her say, "I know you." We had touched, our two souls, in a way I had never before thought possible.

Freddy brought in my breakfast and I musingly munched away at it, looking out the window at what had become a typical, rainy, London winter morning. I did not have the slightest concern that I could be traced from the murder scene. How could I have been? At all events, as we know, it never came to light. It began to seem in the following weeks and months as if I had imagined or dreamt the whole thing.

I have had patients who are perennially troubled by a recurring nightmare that they have committed some sort of murder in their youth, normally in conjunction with others, friends of their genuine acquaintance. The dream can seem so real that they become convinced that the murder actually occurred. But, questioning their friends, they find that it did not. Your darling Mr. Freud had much to say on this matter, didn't he? The Collective Unconscious. Oh, now silly me, that was his younger colleague, wasn't it? ... I do hope you appreciate my puns! ... Wait a moment though, quite seriously, do you think I was somehow living out a dream from Victorian Society's generalized Unconscious Mind? Is it possible that all the 'Ripper' murders were, in some strange way, just a dream? A necessary dream?

Perhaps part of it was indeed the unconscious result of my conscious awareness of the vital need for social change. Not that I can claim in any rational sense to take credit for the reforms that did slowly begin to occur. I was simply engaged in my own personal search for a more whole identity but the entire collective of British humanity was too.

Bernard Shaw, who was becoming known at the time as a wily and scurrilous proselytiser for the Socialist cause, put it quite succinctly. Noting how the press had vilified the destitute working-class demonstrators on 'Bloody Sunday' as 'animals' and 'scum' and how, just a few weeks after my glorious night of blood on September 30th, 1888, those same mouthpieces of the nobs and over-privileged had made an abrupt about-face and were now screeching that the police were no longer the 'protectors of liberty' but had somehow been transformed, almost overnight it seemed, into 'downtreaders of the suffering poor', he wrote:

"Less than a year ago the West End press was literally clamouring for the blood of the people, hounding Sir Charles Warren to thrash and muzzle the scum who dared to complain they were starving... behaving, in short, as the propertied class always does when the workers throw it into a frenzy of terror by venturing to show their teeth... but whilst we conventional Social Democrats have been wasting our time on education, agitation and organisation, some independent genius has taken the matter in hand..."

By this, of course, he meant me. It was a happy side-product of the general sensation caused by the murders that a bright spotlight was suddenly thrown on the shameful condition of the poor in the East End. It is a sad comment upon us all that nothing else had managed to do this. Maudsley showed me the article with some little malicious delight. I can't remember now if Shaw had used a pseudonym, though I don't believe so. He was quite fond of 'Shendar Brwa', among others.

But do you not find it peculiar that this upheaval in my own inner life should coincide so neatly with the upheaval in the inner awareness, if I may so call it, of Victorian Society in general?

Forgive me, I am getting ahead of myself. And not living up to my promises. Quite out of the blue, immediately upon the christening of the New Year of 1888, my career took a decided turn for the better.

I was summoned, in the first week of January, to examine a man named Taylor, no connection whatever to the comical old gentleman who had embarrassed Uncle Edward in his examination. This Taylor was a much younger man and had committed a double murder at Otley. For no appreciable reason, he shot his own child, remarkably no injury occurred to his wife who was carrying it in her arms, and subsequently a policeman who came to arrest him. I examined the murderer on two occasions whilst he was incarcerated in Wakefield Gaol. He suffered from religious insanity, associated with auricular hallucinations which urged him to commit acts over which he had no control. In his case, the voices were experienced as God-like commands coming from entirely outside his being, in contrast to the gently rippling ocean of my own 'inner voice'.

Early in February I examined a man named Richardson, who had shot several persons at Ramsgate. This was also apparently a motiveless crime. He was arrested and placed in Canterbury Gaol where I saw him. His trial took place on the sixteenth of February. The jury quickly found he was of unsound mind and unable to plead.

As luck would have it, the case of Taylor commenced at Leeds the very same day. I wired to the solicitor, Mr. Gledstone, conducting the defense, as to my position in the matter, and informed him that I would come direct from Maidstone to Leeds, Richardson having been tried at Maidstone, a lengthy journey, but that I hoped to appear in time.

I succeeded in arriving at Leeds that evening and was met at the station by the solicitor and some of the witnesses, who appeared to be in much distress. The case had occupied the whole day and the jury had come to the conclusion that the prisoner was, at the time of his trial, quite contrary to my expressed opinion, of sound mind and able to plead.

The only question remaining was, what was his mental condition at the time of the murder? This was to be decided by the same jury on the following day, with the same witnesses, but with one exception, myself. Everybody had made up their minds that the man would be convicted. The public regarded the case a terrible one, especially as far as the cold-blooded assassination of the policeman was concerned, and one for which no excuse could be given.

The next morning as the witnesses were called the jury were openly yawning during their evidence, having heard it all the day before. Immediately I stepped into the box, however, a change came over the spirit of their dreams. They began to listen attentively and though some junior counsellor tried to trip me up, I held my own. Taylor was found to be, and this was the only possible conclusion, of unsound mind at the time of the murder. The foreman of the jury and several other of his co-members told me afterwards that, had it not been for my carefully reasoned arguments, they would have given the same verdict as they had on the previous day. Sir Clifford Allbutt, who was one of the leading physicians in the North of England, had then testified to the same opinion as I, but even the weight of his great reputation had not proved sufficient to convince them.

I was nearly lynched on my way from the courthouse to the station. I was followed by a large crowd and hooted. You can appreciate it was with a certain amount of satisfaction that I found myself in a sound condition, comfortably seated in a smoking carriage on the London and North-Western Railway, *en route* for home. It is a morbid gratification for me to have to record that a short time afterwards Taylor plucked out both his eyes whilst confined in Broadmoor Asylum and suffering from the same delusions and hallucinations as those so glaringly in evidence when he was placed on trial at Leeds.

I was also retained the same week in a case of murder at Weston-super-Mare. So there was the Ramsgate shooting case in the extreme south-east, the Otley tragedy at Leeds and the Weston-super-Mare case in Somersetshire. Rather a unique experience to be retained in three murder cases in one week! I think the annals of medical jurisprudence do not chronicle an instance similar to this.

Yes, oh yes, I was full of renewed energy and vigour and my life appeared, after the years of drudgery and defeat and turmoil, to be once again on the upswing!

At about five in the afternoon, on the twenty-fifth of February, a prostitute named Annie Millwood was stabbed in White's Row, Spitalfields. I read with interest a report of it in the Eastern Post the following week.

"...The deceased was admitted to the Whitechapel Infirmary suffering from numerous stab wounds in the legs and lower part of the body. She stated that she had been attacked by a man who she did not know and who stabbed her with a clasp-knife which he took from his pocket. No one appears to have seen the attack, and as far as at present ascertained there is only the woman's statement to bear out the allegations, though that she had been stabbed cannot be denied..."

It produced a very strange sensation in me. I re-read the article nervously and again came across the description of the weapon used, a 'clasp-knife', and the time of the attack was... 'five o'clock in the afternoon'. I breathed a sigh of relief. I could surely not have been so foolhardy at such an early hour and I would certainly never, ever have used such a small, inconclusive, and so likely merely disfiguring an object as a clasp-knife. For me, the *coup-de-grâce* had to be singular, instantaneous and fatal. I was appalled as I thought of the poor woman's suffering.

And it became a matter of curiosity to me why the Post's report had used the word 'deceased'. Annie Millwood apparently survived her injuries only to die of 'the sudden effusion into the pericardium from the rupture of the left pulmonary artery through ulceration', in other words 'natural causes', while occupied at the South Grove Workhouse, Mile End Road, some five weeks later, according to the inquest held by Coroner Baxter. She was thirty-eight years old.

At about the same time two other attacks occurred which added to the stir. A woman named Ada Wilson was stabbed twice in the throat by a man who had come to her door in Mile End and demanded money. Her wounds were thought mortal but against the odds she miraculously recovered after a month's stay in London Hospital. I visited her there, out of professional interest, and the wounds inflicted were indeed savage but clumsily executed, panicky, without finesse. Again, I felt relieved. You can understand I did not want to find myself suffering from schizophrenic amnesia... 'O let me not be mad, not mad, sweet heaven...!'

The third attack, on Easter Monday, the most brutish of the three, I have already mentioned. Emma Smith, aged forty-five, was violently penetrated by a large blunt object and succumbed to peritonitis at London Hospital a day later. The poor woman had undoubtedly been robbed and apparently claimed before she died that she had been set upon by several men. It is very likely that she had been raped also. She had been most cruelly beaten about the head and one of her ears had been nearly torn away.

But is it pure coincidence that Emma Smith was a resident of a common lodging-house at No. 18 George Street?

My next victim's last known address turned out to be No. 19 George Street and, strange to say, she sometimes, for whatever reason, used to call herself 'Emma'! But the beginning of my 'autumn of madness' was not to commence until August Bank Holiday and, bear with me, I was engaged in another case well worthy of elucidation before then.

It was that of a civil engineer living at Great Amwell. He was charged with committing a number of criminal assaults. Before his trial took place I had examined him in consultation with some other learned colleagues and it was found advisable to incarcerate him in a private lunatic asylum. A petition was presented to the Court of Chancery to hold an inquiry into his mental condition. It was thought a wise step for the family, as the evidence was so much against him, and it was also considered a humane action in the interests of the prisoner.

The evidence I gave was that I had been instructed by the defendant's family to examine him and that I found he was suffering from incoherent conversation, indicative of insanity. He rambled and was generally irrational and his serious position did not appear to trouble him. I was informed by the son that for three years he had been most strange in his behaviour, at times becoming very much excited, whilst at other times he would lead the life of a hermit. His memory was very defective and he suffered from a great exaltation of ideas and neglected his professional work.

He was in the habit of going about the streets all night and bringing home persons indiscriminately under the delusion that they had been connected to his past history. He once went out of doors with a waste-paper basket on his head instead of a hat. His habits had become most peculiar, burning his clothes, destroying furniture and books for no reason. On other occasions it would be difficult to persuade him to go outside the house and he would sit in a chair in a thick overcoat with a muffler round his neck during hot weather. He would stand for hours in one position in a room having covered the floor with newspapers arranged in a fantastic shape. During his fits of mental excitement he would often rave in a foreign language. I was happy to effect a lunacy commission to be held to help the heirs protect his estate.

I describe these symptoms in an attempt to clarify a change that had come about in me. Instead of viewing such patients objectively, clinically, as I used to do, I found myself feeling curiously at one with them. As though their behaviour were mine and quite understandable, indeed, as though all our collective behaviours emanated from the same source.

I had spent six months now since Fay's death fully engaged once more in my practice, taking my trips as usual back and forth to Brighton and elsewhere, and all the time my delicious secret was as a ripening fruit within me. Fruit born of strange compassion. Fruit that was slowly coaxing me away from the narrow strictures of my solitary Victorian rectitude into a broader consciousness. Into waters rich and rare, and, I hoped, warm and soothing as Fay's blood.

In contrast to the previous year, the summer of 1888 was abominably wet and rainy. I had the pleasure of spending an unaccustomed afternoon with my brother Edward, who had become a prolific writer, like father and Uncle Octavius. He had been persuaded up to London to give an address to the Gospel Temperance Movement in conjunction with the publication of his Children's Illustrated Fairy History of England. He very rarely made such visits, preferring to 'voyage', as he liked to phrase it, *'autour de ma chambre'*.

Since Octavius' death, in 1878, Edward had also rather taken over, in his own mind, the role of 'custodian of the family's spiritual welfare'. At any rate, that was his intended topic for our tea-time conversation in my study. He alone sensed, I think, that some sort of diabolical transformation was going on within me, though, of course, he was unable to put his finger on it. For my part, I found myself increasingly nauseated with his conception of God and His Works. It was so altogether pitiful and puny.

I told you I would not be able to resist making comment on Edward's writings. Perhaps a mere list will suffice, as it did for my father. I want to make it crystal clear to you why I found myself thinking what I was thinking as we chatted. In marked contrast to the grave, messianic zeal of Octavius' God our All, our All for God or The Lights and Shadows of Spiritual Life, Edward's religious passion had become as cloying as tinned milk. Witness the titles and how they grow ever more insipid through the years.

The Power of the Cross, and other Sermons, 1873.

His first publication at age thirty-one, robust sounding, promising enough, but look what follows.

The Way of Pleasantness; or, The Secret of a Happy Life, 1875.
The Higher Rock; or, Readings on the Love of Jesus, 1875.

Within Sight of Home: a Series of Readings for the Aged, 1875, second edition, 1880.

Commonsense Truths for Cottage Homes, 1876, second edition, 1879.

Country Talk for Country Folk, 1876, second edition, 1879.

The Haven where we would be: a Second Series of Readings for the Aged, 1876, second edition, 1879.

Quiet Thoughts on the Sacrament of Love, 1876, second edition, 1879.

The Poor Man's Best Friend; Addresses in Simple Language, 1877.

Thank the Lord this last didn't go to a second edition!

Hurricane Dick: a Tale of a North Country Mission, 1877.

Mission to whom exactly, I ask you?!

Good Tidings of Great Joy, Thoughts for Christmas, 1877.

Little Pattens, Tales for a Cosy Nook, 1877, second edition, 1878, third edition, 1879.

What Came of a Bit of Soap: Tales for a Cosy Nook, No. 2, 1879, second edition, 1880.

Jesus!

The Children's Fairy Geography; or, A Merry Trip round Europe, 1879, second edition, 1880.

Rest in the Lord: Readings on the Higher Christian Life, 1880.

Then a gap of seven years. Edward, as the executor of mother's will and though he tried very hard not to, nonetheless couldn't help becoming embroiled in the demeaning family squabble regarding our inheritance. The incomprehensible fruit of which experience appears to have been...

The Fulness of Redeeming Love, 1887.

And lastly, the book which had occasioned his trip to London and our afternoon together. It's plain to see we had arrived at rather different opinions about Redemption!

Oddly, Edward didn't write much more after his *magnum opus* about the history of England's fairies, which went into umpteen editions, by the way, whereas I went on to become tirelessly verbose, exactly like father. Ha! Oh yes, those endless boxes of papers were finally put to good use. I was lionised after the 'Ripper' murders, on two continents, and my opinions were sought on every subject imaginable. I was ready for them. I had resolved to give them as much nonsense as they could possibly swallow and father's vapid, relentless scribblings were perfect for the purpose. Let the idiots choke to death on it! Damned fine sport!

On Bank Holiday Weekend, August 4-6, 1888, Florence Jessie and the children came up to London for the first time in over two years. It was too rainy and cold for them to enjoy a swim in the sea. We had fun. We went to Alexandra Palace to watch a 'Professor Baldwin' go up a thousand feet into the air in a balloon and parachute back to the ground. We went to the Crystal Palace, braving a colossal crush of holiday-makers, to see a cyclist named Keen race against galloping horses over a course of twenty miles. We saw Captain Dale, the 'Aeronaut', being shot out of a cannon and a Fairy Ballet. Pity Edward wasn't there! The climax to their visit was a tremendously impressive fireworks display over the Serpentine, which wasn't dampened, thankfully, despite the continuous, threatening peals of thunder which rolled on above the crowd throughout.

It was raining hard though as we rode to Victoria Station that Monday evening after seeing the boys off. We were barely in time for the last train back to Brighton. I remember Dulcie wheedled me to come with them and even Florence Jessie seemed to welcome the idea. There was a faint stirring of old passions in our brief farewell embrace but I declined, claiming many pressing appointments the next day.

No, it's not what you might think. I didn't fabricate those appointments because of what I was about to do because I had not the faintest idea that I was about to do it! I had no sense at all of what was to come as I walked in the front door of my once again quiet house on Wimpole Street. In fact, I had, for a moment, the distinctly wan sensation of missing their chatter. I was wet and cold and went upstairs to run a bath.

I remember it was about quarter past eleven when I emerged from the tub and went back downstairs to make myself a cup of tea. As I entered the kitchen I noticed that Freddy had, uncharacteristically, neglected to put one of the carving-knives away in its drawer. He was normally a fastidious and most satisfactory housekeeper. This tiny oversight, I believe, was the sufficient trigger for all that was to follow. Not that I wasn't aware, somewhere down in the secret depths of my searching soul, that my delicious night of blood seven and a half months earlier was calling ever more urgently to be repeated. Oh yes, oh yes, it was necessary! I was like the proverbial fox after having been once among the chickens. The glorious sensations, the ambrosial taste of that night would absolutely have to be experienced again.

I stood staring at the knife for a long moment and, as I did so, the thrill of coming blood cascaded through me without warning, starting in my groin and finally flooding all my being with salivatory expectation. I turned on the instant and went back upstairs to dress.

But I was nervous. Extremely nervous. The kind of wobbly butterflies in the pit of the stomach that I am told actors get on an opening night. It was a very odd sensation to me. Since youth I had always possessed great composure. Almost, dare I express it in cliché, nerves of steel. And now I was shuddering from head to toe with virtually uncontainable excitement. My legs could only with great difficulty carry me down the stairs again to the kitchen.

There I found the cloth sleeve for the carving-knife in its usual drawer. I picked up the knife with wildly trembling hands and inserted it in its protective cover, then, forcing myself to calm lest I draw blood, slid the pampered blade carefully, as I had done with the madman's 'curio', down the left-hand side of my waistcoat. The handle fitted quite snugly against the front of my left shoulder and was nearly undetectable beneath my jacket. The sharp side of the blade was facing frontwards so that I should not risk cutting my own flesh as I withdrew it.

In the vestibule I donned a threadbare overcoat, a pair of old gloves and a ratty-looking deerstalker. Freddy had long been threatening to dispose of these outworn items to the rag-and-bone man, but I had said no, they might yet be of some use. I also had the good sense to put on a pair of galoshes. I hate being unprepared even more than I hate getting wet. I'm sure a wicked smile must have crossed my face as I selected from the stand the stout, cane-handled brolly that had once belonged to my father and went out.

I stopped as I came outside and carefully checked the street. It was now twenty-five minutes to midnight and still raining. All the good and prosperous citizens of Marylebone and Paddington, of Bloomsbury and Holborn, Mayfair and Marble Arch were tucked up safely in their comfortable beds gathering strength for the working day. And here was I, setting out to prowl the night like a ravening beast in search of prey. I felt sure that my eyes were glowing coals. As I walked to Oxford Circus to find a carriage, I struggled to rearrange the liquid grotesquery of my features into an expression of blandest normalcy. Though inside, my mind was now as focused as sunlight through a prism. I fancied I could set buildings alight with my gaze.

This time I asked a waiting carman to deliver me post-haste to Liverpool Street Station. He was a chatty fellow, this one, they are often unaccountably taciturn, and asked me why I was going there so late and on so miserable a night. For some obscure reason I proffered the information that I was a doctor and had been called to an emergency case arriving on the last boat-train from Harwich. This was quite giddy and foolish as I hadn't the faintest idea when such a train might have been scheduled to arrive but it seemed to satisfy his curiosity. And by marvelous coincidence, as we drew up to the station, there was an ambulance standing just outside! I tipped the carman a crown, raised my bumbershoot and walked purposefully towards it, watching until his carriage was safely out of sight before crossing over Bishopsgate into Whitechapel.

It was now twenty minutes to one and the taverns had just shut their doors. As I walked down Hounsditch, a surreal vision presented itself to my eyes. A growling, staggering clutch of lost humanity, rapidly becoming sodden in the rain, raucous or surly by turns, jeering, clasping at me strangely, almost knowingly I felt, though I had been careful to wear such drab attire. I doubled my pace to pass beyond them.

I didn't realise until I found myself outside St. Botolph's where my feet had been leading me. Of course, it was to the very place of my communion with Fay! I crossed Aldgate High Street, then it was just a few steps down the Minories and left into the shadows of Fleece Court. I was startled and disgusted to see a man urinating on the precise spot where I had murdered her. I had difficulty not shouting at him. To me, he was defiling a sacrificial altar. But I turned and waited until he shuffled away without a glance.

I walked slowly into the darkened court and stood for a long time looking at the wall where Fay had faced the Eternal Mystery, reliving every detail of her transport. I made a careful catalogue of my mistakes so that I would not risk repeating them. But as yet my eventual,

perfected *modus operandus* had not presented itself to my imagination
with total clarity.

I remember it was only the ginny stench of the man's piddle, foully
super-imposed upon the lingering residue of a thousand others, that
drove me from my reverie. Was it possible that I had stood there for
more than an hour? It was with alarm and astonishment that I saw
it was now after two o'clock by my pocket-watch as I returned to the
High Street and turned eastward.

The lurching, garrulous crowd had long since dispersed, only a
handful of solitary stragglers remained, and the rain had stopped.
In its place a cold, damp mist was gathering. I crossed Commercial
Street, walking on the south side of Whitechapel Road. Not more
than twenty paces ahead of me, on the north side, a constable with
a swaying lantern turned left, past a now darkened pub, called the
White Hart, I think, into George Yard. The entrance to the yard
was narrow, not more than eight feet wide. I stopped for a moment,
looking up and down the road in both directions, then continued
on to Osborn Street. As I stood in the gloom, watching the steeple
of St. Mary Matfellon being slowly enshrouded by swirling vapour, I
heard a woman's coarse voice behind me. I couldn't make out what
she was saying. I turned and saw her bidding farewell to a tallish
young man, dressed, as far as I could tell under such ill-lit conditions
at fifty yards distance, in the uniform of a Grenadier Guard. I had
not noticed them before and I assumed they must have just emerged
into Whitechapel Road from George Yard and no doubt had passed
the good constable.

The woman was clearly still trying for more with the young man
but after a few seconds he extricated himself, a little over-roughly I
thought, and hurried off toward the City. I checked the road again
in both directions. There was no one. I crossed to the north side and
began walking slowly back toward her.

She was evidently aware of my approach, for she turned to look at
me and squinted, but she said nothing. Yet neither did she make to
move away. As I got nearer I noticed she was rather plump, in middle
age, wearing the typical black bonnet and a longish black jacket over a
long, voluminous dark green skirt. Her boots were very old and worn.

"What's your name, then, my girl?" I offered politely when I had
come within about ten feet of her.

"Emma," she replied in a quiet croak, "'Oo's asking?"

"Soldier not pay you properly, didn't he?"

"What do you take me for?"

There was a surprising firmness of spirit lurking behind her eyes. A dignity maintained despite her fortunes. If I was not careful, I might have come to like her.

"A woman, down on her luck, who could use a few bob."

I paused to let the sum register.

"Where do you live then, Emma, my dear?"

"Just 'ere."

"Lead the way."

She considered for a moment, no doubt sizing up the realistic possibility of worth beneath my costume. I noticed her dark hair and sad, round, motherly face.

"Cost you five shillings," she ventured.

"Very well."

I hadn't hesitated. She, too, was artful, betraying nothing.

"Show it me," she said, something still not quite tallying in her brain about the contradiction that my manner and my dress must have presented to her.

I smiled and took two half crowns from my pocket, letting her see them clearly. We both knew it was a great deal of money for a single assignation. The Grenadier Guard had probably stood her a large gin and paid her sixpence. She thrust out a pudgy, calloused hand.

"Give us it then," she said wearily, with an unsuccessful attempt at feigning continued disinterest.

"For services rendered, my good girl, not in advance."

I put the coins back in my pocket.

"Lead the way."

She gave me an odd, slightly offended look, then, without further comment, turned back into the narrow maw of George Yard. I followed a few paces behind. Even at that remove, the smell suddenly flowing in the woman's wake was vomitous. It put me once more safely beyond danger of softening.

We walked northwards in this processional nearly to Wentworth Street and, just as I was about to speak, I was apprehensive of going so far, 'Emma' turned left into an arched entrance-way. I found out at a later date that these dreadful, dingy, brick tenements were classed as 'model dwellings' and were known collectively as George Yard Buildings.

"This where you live, is it, Emma?" I enquired in a friendly whisper.

"What me? No, never. It's convenient, that's all."

Despite her vestigially proud protestation to the contrary, I knew that even these ghastly lodgings were probably well beyond the means of the poor woman.

"Be quiet, then, there's a good girl."

She gave a half-hearted chuckle, a bone-weary assay at long-obliterated sensuality.

"That's up to you, my love."

She led me up a flight of filthy stairs to the first floor landing. There was a door to some unfortunate's apartment not more than twelve feet to our left. I realised my recent, preparatory admonitions to myself in Fleece Court would not fully suffice to serve the particulars of this occasion. My heart was thumping away in the cavity of my chest like titanic breakers on some barren crag. I knew, whatever the choice, I must be quick and not disturb the occupants.

Before 'Emma' had time to turn to me on the landing, I put my left arm gently round her waist.

"Sssh, now, my girl."

I brought my right hand underneath her chin and, grasping it firmly, with a sudden, violent wrench I pulled upwards and to the side, dislocating the vertebrae in her neck, causing her to lose consciousness instantly. I heard the definitive cracking of bone and cartilage. Other than that there was not the slightest sound. Not wanting any repetition of my error with Fay, I lowered her silently to the floor on her back.

Keeping my left hand on her mouth for safety, with the heel of that palm stopping up her nostrils, I placed the fingers and thumb of the right around her throat and, leaning with my full body weight bearing down onto her neck, I waited, our hearts beating together with gathering insistence, stronger and louder, growing in the grotto of my imagination to a glorious, deafening unison. That hushed and sordid hallway became, to me, a throbbing, echoing cathedral dome, a choir-filled Sistine Chapel!

After perhaps a full two minutes of this ecstasy, during which her body gave a few, odd, involuntary twitches, the pulsations within her reached a desperate, drowning crescendo and then suddenly stopped with reverberating finality as her heart burst. I held her firm for another fifteen seconds or more, joyously drinking in the sacred thrum of that silence. She had never once flickered back to consciousness.

Then I let her go and took the long carving-knife from its hiding-place. It was a beautiful, well-honed, tapering blade. Raising it high above her, slowly, caressingly, I brought it down six times into the slackened muscles of her neck, each penetration enriching our contact. I was at once both 'Emma' and myself. Then, over and over, I plunged the knife into her abdomen, not always deeply, sometimes probingly, gently, like a thoughtful lover seeking to increase his partner's pleasure and make it last. Over and over, I don't know how many times, so infinite was my adoration. Then a final two-handed butcher's thrust, I knew, alas, my time was drawing to a close, a slow, determined pressure breaching the rampart of her breastbone, lodging, at last, in the crimson core, the suffocated membrane of her heart.

I held the knife inside her. When the life force ebbs you can feel its current. Her dying energy crackled up through the lightning-rod of that blade and filled my being as it departed from her, surge after thrilling surge.

Slowly, delicately, I withdrew the blade and sat back for a moment on my haunches, spent. Blood was languidly oozing from her neck. The clothing of her torso too was damp and beginning to be sticky to the touch. I had slashed no artery. There was no uncontrolled gushing forth as there had been with Fay. I had stopped the pump prior to cutting.

I let my breathing recover its normal rhythm. Once calmed, I had an impulse to examine further and lifted her skirts and petticoat. She had on rough stockings held up with garters round the thigh but was bereft of knickers, their absence no doubt serving expeditious in her trade. I raised her garments until I had exposed her pubic region and the flesh of her lower belly. Then, not knowing really what it was I wanted, I took the knife and made a cut into the fatty white roll above her *mons pubis* about three inches long and perhaps an inch deep. It was an indefinite gesture, without purpose, besides, though my eyes were quite acclimated to the darkness, I could not see with any exactitude what I was doing. I began to feel uncertain and as I turned awkwardly on my knee to rise after executing the incision, a sharp pain from my old injury shot through me. It was typical of such a weak-willed moment and served me right.

I got slowly to my feet. My leg was unsteady and I made a few tentative steps to try and firm it, then stopped, holding the wall, flexing the joint. Semi-lunar cartilage, once damaged, remains dodgy ever after. I was usually very mindful to take care. Damn, I thought, damn, I'll be limping now for a week.

The pain brought my attention to bear once more on my surroundings. I took the blade, being cautious to avoid stepping in any blood, and wiped it on her stockings, then replaced it in its sleeve under my arm. Good, my deerstalker had not fallen off. Nor was there noticeable dampness on my hands or cuffs. I looked down at her, much, much happier now, I was sure, peacefully melting away. I checked my galoshes. One had come part way off. I rectified the matter, recovered father's brolly from where I had stood it by the door, and, after what I had hoped would be a final sublime inhalation of the scent of blood and death, though also the admixture of what regrettably came with it ... nothing can ever, alas, be totally perfect ... the stale semen and unwashed excrement indigenous to that scabrous landing, clutching the wall, I made my way gingerly back down the stairs.

I stopped just inside the archway to listen and, hearing footsteps, gently eased back again into the shadows. I saw the swaying, unmistakable pattern of a policeman's bull's-eye lantern approaching on the cobbles. I flattened myself against the wall beneath the stairs but luckily the good constable didn't shine his light toward me and I watched, breathless, as he went on past.

I waited for another five minutes. Knowing, as I did, that most patrolling policemen have a regular round of anywhere between fifteen and thirty minutes duration that they repeat throughout the night, I followed after him, pausing for just a moment to see if I could still discern his light in any direction before crossing Wentworth Street and continuing northwards. My damn knee was playing merry hell but I tried to walk normally ... it's the best thing really, for an injury such as mine was, moderate exercise ... and as I walked I was careful to rearrange my features into that aforementioned bland and innocent and unflappable 'normalcy'. Above all, I reminded myself to walk steadily, purposefully, but without any sense of hurry.

I walked in discomfort all the way back to Liverpool Street Station, taking Flower and Dean to Commercial then Brushfield Street, skirting the Spitalfields Market. It was only now twenty minutes past three! My moment of joy was in earth-time brief but my experience of it had outlived a solar system! The market porters were already busy but I passed unnoticed, just another poor man in a shabby coat.

And yet, as I rode back in a hansom to Cavendish Square I began to feel the pangs of strange dissatisfaction. My groping urges had not found complete fulfillment. Damn me and that quavering indecision that had resulted in the re-ignition of my old meniscus injury! I turned my thoughts to my next excursion. For that, I mused restlessly, I must have a perfectly practised plan that would be flawless under any circumstance. I wasn't happy with improvisation. It was dangerous and, what was even worse, it robbed me of time. Precious, necessary time.

In depressing contrast to the delightful invigoration that followed my encounter with Fay, I felt deeply exhausted as I climbed the stairs for a few hours rest before Freddy came to make breakfast. But, of course, before I did, I had been thorough. Thought you were going to catch me out, did you? I had scoured the few remaining smears of blood from the carving-knife, rinsed and dried the sleeve over a candle before putting it back in the drawer, and left the knife, pristine, re-sharpened, exactly as Freddy had forgotten it, on the counter. I had also checked my galoshes, rinsing and drying them, and replacing them in the vestibule along with the hat and coat. There were a few spots of dried blood on the coat which I had removed with a nail-brush in the kitchen sink. But it was all far, far from perfect. I vowed to be impeccable with my next idolothyte.

The Suggestive Power of Hypnotism

Despite my great fatigue, I couldn't sleep. The manner in which 'Emma' had met her end just wasn't quite right. It nagged on my mind. It wasn't nearly swift nor clean enough. It was still somehow too bestial, too muscular. It required too much effort. And it didn't fully enough contain that electric focused instant I was craving. The moment when time itself would stop and hang suspended and everything would become suddenly blissfully, blindingly clear. I wanted the inside of the Sun, you see. I wanted my confrontation with God Himself to be Absolutely Immaculate.

There was nothing in the morning papers. But, in the Star, later that day I read of it.

"A Whitechapel Horror."

They didn't mention 'Emma's' name, only that she had been stabbed twenty times. I knew it had been far more.

At the inquest, which began on the afternoon of Thursday, August ninth, at the Working Lad's Institute in Whitechapel Road, the true facts of the case began to emerge. 'Emma's' name was Martha Turner, or Tabram, or Staples, or Stapleton, but she had been born Martha White on the tenth of May, 1849, in the London borough of Southwark, not far from the Rotherhithe docklands... once home to Christopher Jones, captain of the Mayflower and, at its western extremity, Shakespeare's Globe! ... She was thus aged just thirty-nine years when I killed her. More than five years younger than I. She looked easily old enough to have been my mother. What shamefully opposite lives we had led.

She was the youngest of five children. Her father had died when she was sixteen. So far so good. But while her father, it was noted, was a decent sober man, Martha quite apparently was not. Four years after her father's death she married a man named Tabram, with whom she had already been living, and they had two children. However, by 1875, the marriage foundered on the rock of Martha's alcoholic temperament. She then took up with a man named Turner. Their relationship continued on and off for some twelve years. He claimed she suffered from hysterical fits when drunk. When I came upon her she seemed quite sober, perhaps merely the result of 'long-engraffed condition'. Both men had given her allowances of money but these had stopped. Turner had been out of regular employment since the beginning of the year and he and Martha had been eking a living as street hawkers. Martha had also taken to prostitution. About three weeks before I crossed paths with her she and Turner had made a final break.

There was considerable suspicion thrown on the Grenadier Guard at the inquest, quite obviously because of the patrol-man's testimony, but it came to nothing. The good constable's name was Barrett, I believe, but in truth I've forgotten. Barrett... Elizabeth Barrett had been immured by her father during the 1840's in the house at No. 50, Wimpole Street! My dear mother's version of her rescue by Robert Browning was a stirring childhood romance.

The coroner did finally give an accurate report of the injuries to the body. According to Dr. Killeen, who had conducted the *post mortem*, there was an inexplicable quantity of blood between the scalp and bone of 'Emma's' head. I knew why. The explosion of the heart. He described all the wounds with scrupulous accuracy, enumerating them as thirty-nine. He incorrectly stated his opinion that death was due to 'haemorrhage and loss of blood'. And there was great consternation and puzzlement about the deep wound to her chest. The thought was that it had been caused by a dagger or a bayonet, *viz.* the Grenadier Guard theory, and that the other wounds had been inflicted with a 'pen-knife'! They could not perceive that the minor cuts were a rhythmical progression, the last a climactic joy!

The murder was variously described as "ferocious butchery", "virulent savagery" and "beyond comprehension". People always say 'beyond comprehension' when they cannot bear to admit that they comprehend only too well.

George Collier, the deputy coroner who had chaired the proceedings, since his superior, Dr. Wynne E. Baxter, the Coroner for the South Eastern District of Middlesex, was on holiday in Scandinavia…Baxter was, incidentally, an acquaintance of mine of long standing…said, as he moved for a two week adjournment due to the uncertainties still present in the case, "It was one of the most dreadful murders anyone could imagine. To perpetrate such a crime, the man must have been a perfect savage…"

An apt description. Not intended as an oxymoron perhaps but poetic nonetheless. It expressed the exact encapsulation of my desire, to be a 'perfect' savage. I was not, like Othello, confused in the distinction between murder and sacrifice. I had no doubts. I knew precisely what I was doing. It was just a question now of the 'perfect' method.

Of course, I didn't attend the inquest of Martha Tabram. There was no serial nature to the murders as yet identified with sufficient plausibility to arouse the public's alarm or, with any justification, my professional interest. In fact…saucy little tin god that I am!…I remember offering barely a grunt in response as Freddy chattered on and on about it on the Friday morning. The papers, too, were filled with lurid exaggeration.

"It's a commonplace," I said, "Merely a sad commonplace," and sipped my tea. But an extraordinary plan was formulating in my mind…I don't know whether you share my fascination with multiple or 'split' personalities? Oh, don't be coy, I'm sure you do!

That morning, out of the blue, it struck me with puckish delight that I could become both the 'perfect savage' and the perfect investigator…both at the same time, and yet remain immaculate!…and I nearly laughed out loud when, at that very moment, my eyes fell upon an advertisement in the Times announcing the arrival on our shores of the "great American tragedian Richard Mansfield" and that, in his forthcoming season at the Lyceum, amongst the traditional selections from the works of Shakespeare, he would be performing his own adaptation of Stevenson's recently published and instantly sensational novella, The Strange Case of Dr. Jekyll and Mr. Hyde!

Later that month, I did make a daring slip. I was seated beside Maudsley at a meeting of the Medico-Psychological Society. We were waiting for Sir John Charles Bucknill to report on his correspondence with Bethlem Hospital regarding the continued, persistent and, in his view, excessive use of restraint, that had been publicly condoned by Sir George Savage, the Chief Medical Officer of the institution, and was in daily practise upon the patients there. Savage, ah yes, I thought, but not 'perfectly' so.

Coincidentally, Maudsley had recently published two very interesting and inevitably controversial papers, The Physical Conditions of Consciousness and The Double Brain. The latter quite *à propos, n'est-ce pas?* However, the subject of our conversation on that particular evening had turned to homicide and homicidal mania. He, being a firm materialist, felt that such behaviour was innate. He was also fond of finding occasion to provoke me, as I had at that time, and have still ... ha ha ... a reputation for being equally firmly in the opposite camp, i.e. devoutly Christian and optimistic.

"How should a human being deprived of his reason, as this man evidently was, become so brutal in character unless he already has the brute nature within him?" Maudsley insisted.

He was an evolutionary pessimist and became more so as the years wore on, and even I must admit that the statistical evidence regarding the steadily increasing number of cases of outright insanity, expressed as a general percentage ranging across the whole human population, can hardly bring one to a very cheery conclusion.

"Perhaps it is only that his brute nature has been so unnaturally suppressed," I countered. "Perhaps our so-called 'animal natures' are not such a peril to society as we have been brought up to believe. Perhaps we should not be so assiduously attempting to transform 'that cobweb veil with which fashion hides the feelings of the heart', as my father so eloquently phrased it, into an unbreachable rampart. Perhaps we should rather make peace with this brute nature and not try so obsessively to stamp it out. It's damaging to the personality and ultimately futile."

Maudsley looked at me strangely. I remembered to check that my bland face was still on.

"You've changed your tune," he said with a smirk, "I thought you considered all bestial acts the work of the Devil. The unavoidable outcome of Original Sin. Surely you of all people haven't taken to the folly of Darwinism?"

Maudsley was a staunch neo-Lamarckian.

"No, no," I replied, backpedalling. "I am only saying that perhaps we should stop trying to euphemise all that we don't approve of into non-existence."

"Hear, hear."

He paused, a wicked twinkle still curling his cleanly shaven lip. He kept his beard trimmed in the manner of a Quaker.

"Are you willing to say, then, that this lunatic was in some 'mysterious way' motivated by the Hand of God?"

My breath stopped. That is what I felt, though I had not put it into words. And here was Maudsley, I'm sure in every sense quite unaware, so glibly trying to catch me out.

"Perhaps the madman himself may believe it. I can't speak for God," I rejoindered. "Religious monomania. We've both seen it many times. Patients who hear their 'voices'. It is a Mystery, indeed."

Rather brilliant and quick off the mark to boot, I thought, congratulating myself.

Maudsley grinned maliciously.

"Ah yes. The Unseen Hand."

"Yes. In any case," I went on with reckless abandon, "I have a troubling suspicion that this murder was not the first, nor will it likely be the last."

Maudsley looked at me hard from under his eyebrows.

"What makes you say that?"

"There were several murders last spring in Whitechapel that bore certain similarities."

"Do you think so?" he said, backing off. He did not follow such matters with the same keen interest as I. "Well, it would hardly surprise me. Not with the conditions there as dreadful they are."

"Indeed."

The gathering began to fall silent. The grand old man was finally mounting the platform to polite applause and we let it rest. What did I think I was doing rambling on like that? It taught me a good lesson. I knew very well that no one, not the press, not the public, not the police, was as yet treating Martha Tabram's murder as anything other than an isolated incident. Why on earth had I blurted that out to Maudsley? Just in order to prove how clever I was later? The 'double brain', precisely so.

Despite not connecting the murders in a series…how could they have really since Fay's corpse had so inexplicably disappeared?…there was such dismay in the East End over the 'brutality' of Martha Tabram's slaying that a Vigilance Committee of ordinary citizens had been formed at St. Jude's. It started out in a small way, only consisting of a dozen or so men who were to patrol certain streets in the Whitechapel area between the hours of eleven at night and one in the morning, but it served to make me the more aware of the necessity of my double-edged plan. And that I would have to be careful, very careful. I had no thoughts of stopping, however. None at all. I was never one to shrink from a challenge.

I found myself gloating over 'the feeling of insecurity' mentioned in the Times. The disturbing fact that "in a great city like London, the streets of which are continually patrolled by police, a woman can be foully and horribly killed a few feet from other citizens peacefully sleeping in their beds, without a trace or clue being left of the villain who did the deed." Good lord, I ruminated smugly, how could any but the most naïve be remotely surprised!

On my weekend visit to Brighton on August 25th and 26th, I found myself staring out the window of the train and pondering what in heaven's name had set me on such a drastic course.

I'm sure you'd like to know too. It goes without saying that's why you're listening to me ramble on, doesn't it?

Who on earth was I? What had I become? What could possibly have induced such a frightfully normal, Victorian, upper-middle-class husband and father and reasonably successful professional man to commit such apparent abominations?

Well, I have mentioned the various familial crises of belief. This, I felt, was mine. But it was not exactly as I summed it up in my Recollections twenty years later.

I wrote that the 'Ripper' was, in my opinion, "…an homicidal monomaniac of religious views, who laboured under the morbid belief that he had a destiny in the world to fulfill and that he had chosen a certain class of society to vent his vengeance on…no doubt the desire to wipe out a social blot from the face of the earth was the cause of his crimes…"

Of course, this was an intentionally disingenuous and veiled interpretation. It's not quite exact to say that I felt motivated by the Hand of God. What I did feel, and this is true, was that I was being compelled, absolutely compelled, to seek for Him. I had become entirely dissatisfied with all the accepted notions of my Christian upbringing. I had to make a fresh search in order to be 'born again'. This personal, knowing, loving, clear and ecstatic relationship with God was what I felt I had lost, or, perhaps, truly never had, and that I thirsted for with all my soul. And that relationship, that affirmation, that contact, was what I sincerely believed I would find only somewhere deep within the flesh and blood of those unfortunate women.

For the women themselves I didn't care tuppence. They were the most wretched of the wretched. I only cared that they should suffer no pain, no mental anguish. And that, at the last, I should fully reveal the God that was within them. I took care of the first concern with all that were to follow. But I did not achieve the second with undeniable finality until November. You'll see the progression. Yet it was only the momentary pressure of circumstance that led to that extraordinary, and, to me, entirely unexpected, climax of my crusade. There was nothing ultimately inevitable about it.

So was it the Hand of God or not? You tell me.

Political machinations within the police force and between the Police Commissioner, Sir Charles Warren, and the timid, shilly-shallying, extremely unpopular Home Secretary, Henry Matthews, also unwittingly assisted a great deal in bringing my plans to fruition.

It so happened that James Monro, the able and fiery veteran who was Assistant Commissioner and chief of the CID, resigned that August in a squabble over a proposed allocation of funds. The resignation took effect on August 31st...you will soon appreciate the significance...and Monro was replaced by Dr., later Sir, Robert Anderson. Anderson had been engaged for twenty years in intelligence work with the Home Office. He was well experienced but overly conceited. He was also in ill-health and suffering from fatigue and despite the excitement that I was causing during the first week of his tenure, he was advised to depart for a month's holiday in Switzerland. This he did, leaving the force in more than its usual disarray.

But the ensuing stages of my quest also brought some able adversaries into the arena. And, of course, I expected and welcomed them.

On Thursday evening, August 30th, I don't know why I chose a Thursday evening, perhaps an instinct for surprise and thus self-preservation was at work. Perhaps, as I suggested with some drollery in my Recollections, it was the influence of the moon or something even more abstruse and deep-seated, I couldn't say, but I had known when I awoke that morning that the coming night would be a night of blood. This time I gave it some thought, however. I was in possession of an old sailor's donkey-jacket with patches on the elbows and an old tug-man's cap, forgotten acquisitions long neglected in a trunk in the attic, and, of course, like any Englishman devoted to his garden, well, perhaps that's overstating it in my case, I had a pair of sturdy Wellington boots. I decided that these might make a suitable disguise. I did not wish to be seen in Whitechapel in my own *persona*. At least, not yet.

As soon as Freddy left for the evening, this was usually about seven o'clock unless I required a late supper, I went up to the attic to fetch the jacket and cap. The 'Wellies' stood neatly on a mat at the bottom of the stairs to the back garden. I tried on my costume and examined myself in the mirror. I found I looked decidedly comical and foolish but then it would not be I doing the looking. I convinced myself that a stranger wouldn't think twice about it. The only difficulty would arise if I encountered one of my neighbours, or someone I happened to know, by chance, on the Metropolitan Line. I had decided on a different method of transportation. Well, I thought, brushing it aside, it's really most unlikely at this hour. I'll muffle myself up well in a big scarf and if any problems present themselves at the outset I simply won't go through with it.

That night, though, I wasn't in the least bit nervous as these niggles ran through my mind. There were no physical symptoms of apprehension or fear. No, the odd thing was, and I remember it was very gratifying to me at the time, that an overwhelming sense of invincibility had begun to accompany my murderous moods. I felt blessed. I felt joyous. I felt the energy of a thousand tigers coursing through me. Nothing whatever could stand in my way.

I settled, too, on a different carving-knife. One with a thicker, stronger blade and a wider back, between a quarter and three-eighths of an inch. The one I had used to dispatch Martha Tabram had been thinnish, the result of good care and many sharpenings, barely of sufficient mettle for its task. It had very nearly snapped in two as I forced my way through her breast-bone. I never normally had cause to sharpen any of these instruments myself. Freddy always kept them honed to perfection and gleaming clean.

I had donned a waistcoat, as before, under the donkey-jacket, and placed the knife in its cloth sleeve with the handle conveniently protruding from beneath the pit of my left arm in the same fashion. I was ready early but I could no longer restrain myself. It was just after ten o'clock as I went out the door. Bugger the consequences!

I had decided not to avail myself of the comfort of a carriage on this occasion and, despite the fact that it had turned cold again and had been raining cats and dogs all day, I didn't bother to take an umbrella. The rainstorm had brought with it ominous, smouldering thunder and crackling sheets of lightning ... 'Rumble thy bellyful!' ... I just turned up my collar. What a summer!

No one was about in the West End. Hardly surprising. I found myself glorying in this misery of a climate as I walked to Oxford Street to catch a bus. Madly out of character.

These buses were horse-drawn, open on the top level, and all the available board space was crammed with advertisements for everything from Sunlight Soap and Nestle's Milk to the latest offerings at the theatre. The drivers had a horrible job in such weather, standing as they did, high above the horses, exposed to the elements. There were only two or three people on the lower level as I boarded. They were solitary travelers, self-absorbed, I could have been God Himself, they didn't afford me so much as a glance. Why should they?

I watched the passing scene with keen interest as we moved slowly east to St. Giles Circus, avoiding the danger of the rookeries by taking the left fork up Bloomsbury Way. I could just make out the looming pillars of the British Museum where, over so many painstaking years, Karl Marx had penned the volumes of his profoundly seminal work, *Das Kapital*. But who was more the revolutionary, he or I? Ha! Then passing Southhampton Row, I was reminded of my birthplace on Guilford Street and the Foundling. The foundling. The Changeling. I thought of Middleton's rapacious character De Flores and smiled. De-flowerer, no. Enflowerer, yes!

Then on, up Theobald's Road and Clerkenwell Road. At the corner of Farringdon I alighted. Just a short, brisk walk and I hoped to catch the last underground train. Why was I doing this? I never traveled this way. But I was enjoying it immensely. It was peaceful. My thoughts were calm and focused. And I was just in time! It was now three stops to my destination, Moorgate, Liverpool Street, then Aldgate.

The Metropolitan Line was a marvel of engineering and human ingenuity. It had taken twenty-one years to complete. The last link, between Aldgate and Mansion House, had been finished only four years previously, in 1884. It was the first of its kind. One of the many motivations for its construction, beyond the obvious one of congested traffic in the streets above, was the efficient, economical transport of low income families out of the slums into the new suburbs that were mushrooming beyond the city in all directions, but particularly west of the West End, in Fulham and Battersea, Kilburn and Kensal Green. In this, the Planners truly did have a Master Plan and it was a good one.

The first thing that drew my attention, as I emerged into the drizzling tail of the storm at Aldgate, were stands of people looking up and pointing. The whole sky to the south was a livid red. Two great fires had broken out on the London Docks, caused, a member of the crowd hastened to inform me with dry-mouthed chagrin, by lightning striking a liquor warehouse. It was an extraordinary sight. Hellish. Appropriate. And it seemed to have created something of a carnival atmosphere, despite the weather. It was only a quarter to midnight and the pubs were still open but I decided the best course was to keep myself to myself and simply observe.

The donkey-jacket was very cosy, more use against the damp, chill night than any of my other overcoats would have been, and I remember wandering for several hours, watching and waiting, as the streets gradually emptied and only the homeless, the mad, the slaughter-men and the prostitutes remained.

Several times I spotted suitable prey but the properly inviting conditions did not materialise. And I was determined to remain a 'perfect brute' and execute my Grand Design!

Then, at exactly twenty minutes past two, I was walking back toward Aldgate Station on the south side of Whitechapel Road, having traversed its length several times as far as Mile End, when a woman came out of Union Street, overtaking me and crossing to the corner of Brick Lane at a brisk pace. On the far side she met another, smaller woman who, after a moment's observance, was evidently reeling drunk. I paused in a doorway to watch and hear what I could of their colloquy. They conversed for nearly ten minutes, I should think. The one who had appeared so suddenly behind me had been, I divined, down to the docks to watch the progress of the fires and she spent much of the time trying to persuade the drunken one, whose name I had gathered by this time was 'Polly', to accompany her. Polly had apparently been turned away from her usual 'doss' for lack of fourpence but she was adamant that she could and would get it.

"I've 'ad my doss money three times today," she boasted, in a high-pitched, warbling, incoherent rasp, "An' I've spent it!" She almost spat the words in violent defiance. "But I'll soon get it back, I will. It won't take me long. Oh, no. Not with such a jolly bonnet as I've got now."

And she laughed. A strange, sad peal of bitterness. I remember distinctly that, as she did, St. Mary's Church clock struck half past two.

The other woman finally gave up her remonstrations and stayed watching for a moment as Polly staggered drunkenly away. She was tottering along the north side of Whitechapel Road in my direction but I came out of the doorway and continued on my path toward Aldgate, passing across Church Lane and the point where the woman of Polly's acquaintance was still standing. I went on to the corner of Commercial Street where I paused and turned to look. The woman was gone. With nonchalant speed, smelling the kill, I hastened back.

Polly was already lost to view in the darkness but I caught up with her again at the corner of Baker's Row. She was talking to a man, I took him to be a porter for he, too, wore rubber boots, but he was clearly in a hurry, on his way to work at one of the markets, I supposed, and paused only momentarily before pushing her away. She had difficulty maintaining her balance and executed a clownish sequence of twirls to do so, all the while shouting obscenities after the man in impotent rage. Then she gathered herself and in a sulk, still grumbling loudly over her ill-treatment, she started across Whitechapel Road toward London Hospital.

Perfect.

"Where're you off to then, my girl?" I called out, affecting a rough accent. I had always fancied that I was quite a good mimic.

She stopped unsteadily.

"Goin' to warm meself at the 'ospital."

"No need for that," I said, aping her slurred Cockney, "I can give you something that'll warm you good and proper."

She was suddenly overcome with a fit of hiccoughs which interspersed her words uncomfortably.

"Oh, can you now?" she said, clutching her chest to stifle the rising dyspepsia, "Where you from?"

She looked me up and down and giggled.

"You ain't from Whitechapel. I knows that."

Another painful belch.

"Off the boats, is you? One o' them Sweezers. Was you the one set the fires, was it?"

She was moving towards me now in a coquettish parody.

I was a bit taken aback by her opinion of my diphthongs and, Lord God of Israel, she was an ugly, wizened little thing. Her eyes were red and swollen with glaucoma and the veins were etched in sharp relief at her temples. I softened my tone somewhat and plunged on.

"Wouldn't you like to know, my dear. Well, then, do you want warming or not?"

"I don't know as I do," she said, ridiculously coy.

I was rapidly getting fed up with her.

"If you do as I say, I'll give you five shillings."

Her eyes popped wide and she grimaced as the acid rose once more into the hiatus of her diaphragm.

"Ooohh."

She paused, swaying. An unwelcome light darkened her mind.

"You wants somethin' partic'lar, then, does ya?"

"I do."

She squinted at me apprehensively.

"You'll 'ave to tell me what. I don't…"

"I'll tell you what. Then you can decide, one way or the other. Show us to a quiet spot first. I don't want to be in a hurry."

"A quiet spot, eh?"

She paused again as her hiccoughs erupted in what I prayed was a final paroxysm. An agonised bubbling of gas and bile mixed that sounded for all the world to me like a drawn-out harrumph of contempt.

"'Scuse me," she said, almost demurely, struggling pathetically for control. An apologetic reflex from better days.

I took out the two half crowns. I'd saved them from my encounter with Martha. Mementos. They did the trick. Polly took one look at them and lurched back across Whitechapel Road, gesturing with her head at me as she did so. I drew beside her as we entered Court Street.

"Wait a moment, my dear," I said.

I pulled her gently into the shadows. Not forty feet ahead of us the familiar beam of a patrolling constable's bull's-eye lantern was washing over the ground and we heard the approach of reinforced metal heels.

"Sssh."

The constable was on his beat down what I later reminded myself was Winthrop Street...I had already developed a clear mental picture of the whole district, as detailed as the street map in my study, albeit the names took longer to stick...As he crossed the end of Court Street he stopped and turned his light for some time in our direction but we were well hidden. We waited. Then he continued on his way out of sight toward Baker's Row.

"What'd you want t'do that for?" she hissed, "'Ere now, you ain't intendin' to do me no 'arm, is you, eh?"

"Of course not, my dear. Now come along, let's earn your doss money," I said.

Under the lone, dim, gas-lamp at the corner of Winthrop Street, I checked my watch. It was eighteen minutes past three. Polly turned into Winthrop Street, shuffling in the opposite direction from the constable. The rough cobbles spread wide for about thirty or forty yards then split into two forks. Further up the right fork I could see light coming from a workshop or slaughterhouse, I didn't know what. Polly took the left, called Buck's Row. It was narrow and extremely dark. We passed a stable yard on our right. I could smell the horses and one was thumping erratically with his hoof against the wood. All else was so quiet I could hear the gusts of the great beasts' breath. On the left, were the looming shapes of soot-blackened warehouses. Beyond, on the right, I could just discern a row of brick cottages.

Outside the stable gate, Polly stopped.

"Quiet enough for you?" she said in a low, mocking tone.

"Mmmm," I murmured thickly in assent, my anticipation mounting.

"What is it you wants then? You only 'ave ten or fifteen minutes 'til the Peeler comes back. You tell me what an' if I will, you give me the 'alf crowns first an' then I'll do it."

"What's your name?"

"Oh, come off it, will you?"

"I want to know," I insisted.

"Polly."

"Well then, Polly," I said, in a gentle, reassuring tone, "What I want you to do is this. I want you to lie down on the ground..."

"Whaa...?" she started to protest.

"I know it's wet, but it's worth five shillings, isn't it? I want you to lie down on the ground and raise your skirts. I want to examine your private parts..."

"Whaaaa...?"

The sound was pure disbelief, but I persisted, steadily, calmly, almost purring. I had jettisoned all trace of the adopted accent. A 'Sweezer', indeed!

"I'm a doctor, Polly," I went on quietly, "And I want you to do as I say. When I've finished examining you with my hand, that's all I need to do, I'll give you the five shillings. It won't hurt, I promise, and it won't take long. It'll be the easiest five shillings you ever earned, you'll see."

Her bloodshot eyes were swimming. The look was childlike, vulnerable, almost embarrassed.

"I wants the money first."

"If you insist, my dear."

I pressed the coins into her chill, chapped palm.

"Now lie down, there's a good girl."

Without further protest, she did so. Close up against the stable gates with her new bonnet pointed towards the row of cottages. I knelt beside her.

"Now lift up your skirts for me. It's too dark to see you. I'm just going to examine you with my hand. I'm a doctor. There's nothing to worry about."

Her bony little fingers obediently raised the skirts, still tightly clutching the half crowns.

"That's it. A little higher. That's right. Now turn your head away from me, that's my good girl."

She did it without demur. It was quite surprising to me that I had so easily and quickly brought her to a state of partial hypnosis. She lay still and calm, breathing softly, with her skirts above her navel. The stays of her corset prevented her lifting further or I think she would have had them over her head.

I placed my left hand gently on her face covering her eyes. Even at that, she made no protest.

"That's very, very good. Now try not to move."

I could hear that my voice had started to tremble with uncontrollable excitement. I drew the knife slowly from its hiding place and placed the tip of the blade just behind her left ear. Her breathing was deep and constant, she might almost have been falling asleep.

My mouth was choked with spittle.

"This may tickle slightly," I whispered indistinctly.

Then, without more ado, I pressed the knife forcefully down into her neck with a graceful, curving stroke, severing her carotid artery and causing instantaneous unconsciousness and death. I quickly turned her face toward me and, positioning the tip slightly lower, repeated the cut, slicing this time all the way across, paring the tissues right down to the spinal column. A shudder of ecstasy rippled through me as Freddy's lovingly sharpened edge struck vertebrae. It was like carving the softest, tenderest pork loin. The sensation of omnipotence was unimaginable. No ordinary, trivial orgasm could possibly compare. I was totally alive! The inside of a tornado!

And my plan had been perfect! The arterial blood was still gushing out irregularly on her left hand side, propelled by the spasmodic rhythm of her dying heart, but there wasn't a spot of it on my hands! For a moment, I waited in the silence, willing it to stop. I had more to do! I stood above her innocently spread, pale legs, so frail, and, unable to wait longer, I pushed up the cuffs of my shirt and jacket and brought the blade straight down into her belly. She was considerably distended in that area despite her skinniness elsewhere. The blood welled up but didn't spurt. The feeling was exquisite. The cutting. The contact. Sublime. I repeated the motion several times, plunging both into and slicing across that womanly whiteness. It was my intent with a few deft strokes to completely disembowel her, but suddenly I heard a man clear his throat somewhere off in the darkness beyond the row of cottages, not more than two hundred yards distant, and the sound of boots approaching at a clip. I stood frozen for a livid fraction of a second with the hairs on my neck in silent stampede, pawing at the night. I had a ferocious impulse to wait and fall upon the intruder and cut him to pieces. But instead I bent down and quickly prised the coins from her hand. In that moment of intense frustration I remember piercing her vagina twice with the point of the blade. Then I fled, without a sound, past the stables and what turned out to be a board school, turning sharply into the fork of Winthrop Street.

There I stood breathless listening. I could hear the man's footsteps slow, then stop. Clearly, he had seen her. Then I heard him cross halfway over the cobbles and stop again, apprehensive. Then a second set of footsteps coming fast. Then men's voices. I was not fifteen yards away.

"'Ere, look," said the first, "There's a woman lying by the gates. Come an' 'ave a butcher's."

The sound of the second man's hobnails drew closer.

"I think she's dead."

The first man then evidently knelt down beside her.

"I can 'ear 'er breathing."

That wasn't possible! I had felt the galactic swirl of her soul rushing out with all that blood!

"No, she's all limp," said the first again, "She must be dead."

"Perhaps she's just dead drunk," said the second.

It was obviously too dark for them to see her wounds and the growing pool of her blood was all on the gate side.

"No. She's proper dead. Looks to 'ave been raped as well."

"Pull 'er skirts down, poor thing."

Then I heard the men walking toward me. They passed the board school, not seeming to hurry, and I watched them off into the dim lamp-light at the corner of Court Street and beyond. I waited until I was certain they were out of sight, then dashed tiptoe to Polly's corpse again, but, alas, before I had come ten paces round into Buck's Row I saw the beat constable's bull's-eye appear at the far end. My precious minutes were gone! I backed slowly away, hugging the wall.

This time I didn't wait to listen. I began walking at a calm and steady pace up Winthrop Street. I wiped the blade on the inside of the donkey-jacket, put it away and checked for my cap. As I passed opposite from where I had noticed the light before, I could see it was a slaughterhouse. Not Jewish though. Barber's was the name and three men were inside busily dispatching a sow. They didn't look up.

At the end of Winthrop Street is Brady Street. Under the gas-lamp there I paused to check my hands and clothes. Some slight smearing on the hands which I dispersed, a few tiny flecks of blood on my boots and right sleeve, nothing to notice. I congratulated myself in sullen consolation. The time was ten minutes to four. I decided to walk north in order to be clear away from the Whitechapel district as quickly as possible.

I was so full of solar discharge I could have walked with ease to John o' Groats! Carefully, I traversed the east end of Buck's Row. The constable's light was still moving. It was not until I was passing the Hebrew's Burial Ground that I heard his shrill whistle, indicating he had found her. I hastened on, continuing north on Brady Street, crossing the Weaver's Fields to Bethnal Green Road, then successfully traversing a circuitous maze of depressing, dingy by-ways to Hackney Road and Old Street, past St. Agnes' Well and all the way back to the corner of Clerkenwell and Farringdon Roads where I had alighted from the bus. I had covered some five miles in just over an hour. It was no little concern that it would soon be starting to get light, and the main thoroughfares were already becoming busy, so I hailed a passing carriage at Hatton Gardens, asking the carman to drop me at Park Square on the north side of Regent's Park Circle. Wimpole Street was just being kissed with sunshine as I entered the solemn quiet of home at twenty to six.

I rushed to clean all trace of the murder away and ran a bath but my mood was understandably morose. There was so much more that I had wanted to do! How to find the time. And a secure location. Those were the burning questions. I also knew that the police would now be certain to suspect the possibility of a past and coming series of murders. Well, I reflected, that being so, I would have the better chance of bringing to fruition the double-brained exquisitude of my plan. The thought cheered me considerably. I would somehow make sure that the odds were more fully in my favour before making my next move.

I was right. On August 31st, the headline in the Star read:

"Revolting Murder. Another Woman found Horribly Mutilated in Whitechapel. Ghastly Crimes by a Maniac."

They went on, linking the loose character of the women, the late hour of the crimes, the close proximity of the locations and the seemingly pointless violence of the mutilation, concluding:

"…all three tragedies…are the work of some cool, cunning man with a mania for murder."

The only error that they made, and would continue to make, was linking the brutal beating and violation and subsequent death of Emma Smith on Easter Monday to the series. Dear 'Fay' was the first victim of the three, as we know.

And I was right, too, in thinking that now my opposition would become more formidable. Scotland Yard reacted swiftly to the murder and appointed F. G. Abberline as Chief Inspector in the case. He was arguably the most able investigator in all England at that time and had a particularly extensive knowledge of the Whitechapel area. He, like Wynne Baxter, was a respected acquaintance. It's an odd and amusing coincidence that Abberline and I were almost as alike as twins, many people had remarked on it, though in justified vanity I can say that he was very much the more overweight. Besides that, and the fact that my hair, alas, was graying while his remained dark brown, we were strikingly similar in appearance. From our height and complexion to the bushiness of our moustaches and mutton-chops and the sadly balding condition of our pates, we could easily have been mistaken for brothers. I rejoiced in his arrival as a worthy adversary.

I was also, even at this early stage, though I did not discover it until much, much later, beginning to stir the waters of panic in the highest circles of the government and the following little exchange will show you how far the Home Office unwittingly assisted me through the paralysis of imagination endemic to the bureaucratic mind.

Apparently, on August 31st, the very day I had sacrificed Polly on the altar of my obsession, a clothing firm, named L. & P. Walter and Son, of Church Street in Spitalfields, sent a letter to the justifiedly despised Home Secretary urging him bluntly to tackle the matter of the killer's capture with the obvious expedient of offering a substantial reward for information leading to it. A few days later they received a reply…oh yes, British Government Offices always reply…signed by one Edward Leigh-Pemberton, Legal Assistant Under-Secretary to Henry Matthews, stating that:

"...the practice of offering rewards for the discovery of criminals has for some time been discontinued; and that so far as the circumstances of the present case have at present been investigated, they do not in the Home Secretary's opinion disclose any special ground for departure from the usual custom ..."

Ah yes, the wheels at Whitehall grind slowly, if they grind at all. You'd need an impeccably sharp wit to sever those endless miles of red tape and cut away the stultifying flesh of so much unexamined tradition. The usual custom!

During the first week of September, I, too, put pen to paper. I was impatient to begin my double role, my perfect duplicity! I wrote to Sir Charles Warren, the Metropolitan Police Commissioner, offering him any assistance, in my professional capacity as an expert in mental pathology, that he wished to call upon in the case. Saucy Jacky! He replied politely, of course, but in the negative.

During the whole of the autumn of 1888, I communicated by letter with Sir Charles many times. I gave him all sorts of clues, some intentionally misleading, some cheekily exact, but he never did anything more than to courteously confirm having received them. I knew very well from past experience that it is no easy thing persuading the police to accept suggestions from outside sources!

As a specific, particularly ironic, instance of this, during that September it so fell out that a man, dressed in a brown pea-jacket and cap, dropped quite unpredictably to his knees before my daughter and another friend of hers in Brighton. Producing a large Bowie-knife, he commenced to sharpen the same. Fortunately, the young ladies were able to find refuge. You can imagine my distress on finding that their description of the man was similar to some that I had made to them of suspects in London. Of course, I at once communicated with the Brighton police and attempted to convince them that the event was likely only childish imagining but, alas, as I knew in advance, they didn't listen and there resulted an unnecessary "scare at Brighton". In mirrored perversity, on every single occasion that I gave important information to the police in London they treated it with disdain.

I think I could have told them straight out that I was 'Jack the Ripper' and shown them bloody hands and a bag full of guts and they would still have turned me away with a patronising smile!

One idea I gave to Sir Charles Warren, and a good one too, though partly tongue-in-cheek, was that the police constables on their beat should be supplemented with off-duty asylum attendants in plain clothes, 'shadows' experienced in dealing with lunatics. These attendants would have been quickly aware of suspicious behaviour in a way that the untrained constables would not. But Sir Charles only responded with the usual printed acknowledgement and that was all I ever heard of it.

However, the real reason I communicated with Sir Charles immediately after Polly's death was to firmly establish my interest. It would certainly have been no surprise to him since criminal insanity was my long-established area of expertise but I wanted it to be official. Indeed, on the afternoon of September 6th, I specifically arranged an interview with the Criminal Investigation Department at Scotland Yard in order to give them my opinion of the case!

As you will see, it was a master-stroke to play out my bold pilgrimage in this double guise. It provided me so much more freedom of movement.

Let me quote once more from my Recollections, my shambling, autobiographical reminiscence that I published over twenty years after the murders.

"... Day after day and night after night I spent in the Whitechapel slums. The detectives knew me, the lodging-house keepers knew me, and at last the poor creatures of the streets came to know me. In terror they rushed to me with every scrap of information which might to my mind be of value. To me the frightened women looked for hope. In my presence they felt reassured, and welcomed me to their dens and obeyed my commands eagerly, and found the bits of information I wanted..."

Ha! Euphemism! A veritable triumph of euphemism!

'Came to know me', indeed! 'Bits of information', indeed! If you can appreciate the broadness of my definition. Ha! What a phenomenally brilliant, diabolical scheme! Forgive me, but I felt absolutely on top of the world as I attended Polly's inquest, dressed in the sober costume of the perfect Victorian gentleman. And I was, oh yes, I was, I was! Oh yes! Perfect. I was investigating myself investigating myself investigating myself. And at the core of that blood-onion was God. I knew it.

At the inquest, which began on the first of September, the good doctors were unable to come to any satisfactory view of the manner of Polly's death. Whether it had taken place on the spot where the corpse was discovered or whether the body was dumped there after the fact. Whether the murderer was left-handed or right. And, once again, everyone was entirely baffled to discover any motivation for the crime.

I did learn, with great interest, that little Polly's name was really Mary Ann Nichols. She had been born on the 26th of August, 1845, off Fetter Lane, near the Law Courts and Lincoln's Inn Fields...a stone's throw from the scene of my Chancery humiliations!...She was the daughter of a respectable locksmith, Edward Walker, and his wife Caroline. The place of her birth was no more than a third of a mile from Farringdon Station on the Metropolitan Line...where I had been within moments of missing the last train on the second leg of my journey to our brief encounter!...Do we all travel so little distance in a lifetime? And are all our fates so meaninglessly the whim of blind, blind chance? Not mine, I prayed, not mine. And if not mine, I realised in ecstatic epiphany, then not Polly's, nor your's, nor anyone's, nor any living thing's down to the humblest protozoan, nor any motion of any material or immaterial particle in this whole infinite, wheeling Universe! My fumbling search for God was the Hand of God Itself! What other possible interpretation could there be?

Of course I was fully aware, even as I sat there listening to the proceedings of the inquest, that this philosophical position is a commonplace, the stuff of childhood sermons and Sunday singing. It is the very definition of Faith. It is, in its dilute, mundane form, the skimpy stuff of all my brother's, of all my uncle's, writings. But I was impelled to rediscover it in this visceral way. I needed the Ultimate Proof and that proof I knew was in Polly's blood. I might have held it that night living in my hands had I not been so cruelly interrupted!

On the 16th of January, 1864...about the time my father first fell ill with Bright's disease...Polly married William Nichols, a printer's machinist. They had five children between 1866 and 1879...those tired, white, swollen loins had borne five children! I remembered their softness and unappreciated beauty with reverence and bowed my head...but, in 1880, the marriage had foundered. There were conflicting interpretations of the cause, his infidelity or her desertion, but it had propelled her ineluctably down the slippery slope at the bottom of which I had saved her.

She had made a last, futile attempt to bring herself back to respectability in the previous May. She had left the confines of Lambeth

Workhouse to take a position as a domestic servant with the Cowdry family in Wandsworth and had written a letter to her father, saying, as best I can recall, that she was "settled in her new place", that it was "grand, with trees and gardens, back and front" and "newly done up", and that the Cowdry's were "teetotallers and religious, so I ought to get on." But by July she had clearly once more weakened in her resolve. She absconded with some clothing valued at three pounds, ten shillings, and was back in Whitechapel.

On the third day of the inquest the woman appeared whom I had seen her speaking with that night. Her name was Ellen Holland and she shared a room with Polly on Thrawl Street. She clearly liked her and I remember the foreman of the inquest jury, a Mr. Horey, I think, asking her:

"What name did you know her by?"

"Only as Polly," Mrs. Holland replied.

"You were the first one to identify her?"

"Yes, sir."

She was weeping.

"Were you crying when you identified her?"

"Yes, and it was enough to make anybody shed a tear."

Indeed, I found my own eyes watering as I listened.

I was gratified at the testimony of PC Neil, who had discovered the body and questioned some of the local people soon thereafter. He stated that no one in the area of the murder, not the keeper of the board school, not the watchmen at the wool warehouse or the cap factory across the road, not even the residents of the cottage immediately next door to the stable yard, had heard anything suspicious that night. Neither could the three slaughterhouse workers, nor a watchman for the sewage works on Winthrop Street, nor the two men who had found the body first and whose conversation I had overheard, offer any clue. They had seen nobody. There was not an "atom of evidence". The inquest was adjourned and reconvened again and dragged on nearly to the end of September but still they could not find "the slightest shadow of a trace".

Ha!

I remember an interesting discussion with a colleague, during a break in the inquest proceedings that first week, on the subject of masked epilepsy and the possibility that the killer might be suffering from it in some form. I had consulted in many such cases.

"During such a seizure," posited my friend, "He might perform the most extraordinary and diabolical actions, and upon returning to consciousness would be in perfect ignorance of what had transpired when the attack was on him, and would conduct himself in an ordinary manner."

"Quite likely," I agreed. "I can recall a very proper lady who, while in the midst of conversation, would grow deathly pale and, to the horror of her visitors, pour forth a volley of profane oaths. A few minutes later she would resume the conversation as though nothing at all had happened."

My friend nodded seriously. Not in all the days of eternity would he have suspected that he was discussing these issues with the perpetrator himself!

Heavens, I can remember telling Sir Charles Warren in a letter, even writing to the newspaper that the murderer was "in all probability a man of good position and perhaps living in the West End of London," and further that "when the paroxysm which prompted him to his fearful deeds had passed off, he most likely returned to the bosom of his family." What ferocious audacity! But did any of them have ears to listen or eyes to see? No, of course not. It's been well over a century since I wrote those words and still no one has seen it. It's surely high time to claim my due.

I have said that my actions remained in my memory like a dream does, part real, part unreal. But I was not at all in "ignorance of what had transpired", as my colleague phrased it. Not at all. It was, however, as though the murders, the bloodlettings, my adventurous excursions into God's own delicious Reality, were somehow separate from my ordinary, earthly self. I could keep them entirely apart, in an emotional compartment all their own. That was the reason that I was able to act with utter calm and equanimity in talking with others about the 'Whitechapel horrors'. I was able to investigate myself investigating myself with perfect clinical objectivity.

And no matter how often I tried to tell the police or my colleagues or anyone else that the killer was most likely not of the 'lower classes', none of them really wanted to believe me. Such a beast could not possibly have money or position! No, no! Humankind never wants to stare reality in the face. Good golly gosh, no, that would be bad taste.

We must at any cost maintain our pretence to civility, to the airy-fairy smugness of spirituality, to that will-o'-the-wisp irrationalisation 'godliness', for Heaven's sake, that we all know in our wicked hearts is a pack of lies. Why do we have Saints and Devils? Why does our true nature insist on being so out of touch with itself? We are not condemned to Plato's cave, we commit ourselves there all too willingly! It's surely the very summit of irony, is it not, that people of sophisticated intellectual gifts and education would call 'Jack the Ripper' a madman? I was the sane one! I was putting myself back together! I was becoming One again with my true nature and with God! I was aware!

During the first week of September there was a great hue and cry in the newspapers about a Jewish slipper-maker named Pizer. 'Jack' Pizer as it turned out. He was nicknamed 'Leather Apron' because of his trade and was rumoured always to carry a long, sharp knife. He was considered mad by most who knew him because of his "sinister expression" and "repellent grin" and the fact that his "eyes were small and glittering" and "always darting about"! He never looked at anyone levelly. Poor chap, I should have given him lessons.

He came under suspicion of being the killer because he had been known to beat up prostitutes in the East End and bully them for money. It took the police over a week to find him. He was being sheltered by relatives and was in terror, with good reason, of being torn to pieces by the mob.

I don't think Abberline or anyone else involved in the investigation really believed in his guilt but they were forced to try and hunt him down because of the intense public clamour against him which had been stirred up by the press. And, from the same quarter, the police force was coming under attack as "shamefully inadequate", even being unfairly vilified in the New York Times, of all places, as "the stupidest in the world".

By the seventh of September they still had not found him. I knew that Henry Matthews was enjoying a parliamentary recess, that Sir Charles Warren had gone on holiday to the south of France and that Robert Anderson was to leave that day for his much needed 'rest-cure' in Switzerland. Taking it all rather lightly, gentlemen, weren't we, leaving it to the subordinates?

I decided to strike again.

The Tragedy of the Passions

I mentioned my great frustration at being unable to fully satisfy my desires with Polly. I was absolutely determined not to let that happen this time.

Though I had been to Whitechapel on several occasions during the first week of September to attend Polly's inquest, and had let my interest in the case be known in the highest circles, I was still not quite ready to venture to the East End in the small hours entirely as 'myself'. There was a strange sense of uncertainty, of not completely trusting in my own identity. A vestige of concern that without some form of mask I would not remain sufficiently able to control the situation. A quibble that threw itself most savagely to the winds that night.

"A strange turn of phrase," I hear you thinking. But that's what it was like, you'll see. Perfect freedom. Perfect abandon. Invincibility unbounded. Pure omniscience. The final, total obliteration of 'I'!

The seventh of September was a Friday. A chilly evening, though not raining, and very dark, the new moon rising. I was half sincere in my Recollections regarding the influence of the moon on the timing of the murders. How they either fell on the change into the last quarter or the new moon's rise. There was one exception, but even then it was only a day outside the parameters of the calculation and there was good reason. I'll tell you about it in good time.

Maudsley had invited me to join him at the performance of Mansfield's Dr. Jekyll and Mr. Hyde on Saturday evening. In preparation, though the impulse to kill again was at a fever pitch within me, as soon as Freddy had departed... I had excused him from his duties until Sunday after church as he was to give the bride away at a niece's wedding on the Saturday afternoon... I took my copy of Stevenson's novella down from the shelf and sat quietly in my study to re-read it. I wanted to remind myself of every subtle detail.

I had met Stevenson once or twice. He had signed the leather-bound copy in my hands with a respectful dedication. He had signed one for Maudsley also, the duality of Man's Nature being our mutual absorption. Robert Louis was perhaps a half dozen years my junior but there were certain interesting parallels in our lives. We had each rebelled in our own way against stern, puritanical fathers and the general hypocrisy prevalent in Victorian society.

His lifelong struggle against lung disease has a more than anecdotal resonance here. He used to call the horrid, mucoid mouthfuls of blood that he was forced more and more frequently to expectorate or drown, "Bluidy Jack"! And were we not both engaged in our own obsessive search for good health? Of course, I was physically very robust, I don't mean that, but spiritually. Stevenson, too, wrestled with the problem of evil all his life. I don't suppose he managed to burst so successfully through its 'cobweb veil' as I did. Though, out there in Samoa, who can say?

He told me that the story of this 'strange case' had come to him in a most vivid dream, a nightmare, and that Fanny, his wife, had shaken him awake in the middle of it. He laughed, I remember, as he related how irritated he had been with her for interrupting this 'fine, bogy tale'!

And indeed it is! As I read it through again that evening slowly, thoughtfully, I was thrilled time and time again by the accuracy of its insight. How well Stevenson managed to give expression to the secrets of my own heart! Even in the dedication to Katharine de Mattos there is an enigmatic line that for some inexplicable, feral reason always sends shivers cascading through me.

"Still will we be the children of the heather and the wind."

Oh yes, I know that Stevenson may merely have been speaking of the unbreakable connection between true friends, true lovers, but to me, to me, the sentence is profoundly magical, the pure poetic voice of our eternal mystery.

My excitement and recognition grew with every page. Yes, I was that "Juggernaut"! Yes, I was the "man in the middle with the black, sneering coolness"! Yes, I, too, was going "my own dark way"! Yes, I had "concealed my pleasures" and "stood already committed to a profound duplicity of life" and "with an even deeper trench than in the majority of men" were "severed in me those provinces of good and ill which divide and compound man's dual nature"! Indeed, indeed, I felt "I was the first that could thus plod in the public eye with a load of genial respectability, and in a moment, like a schoolboy"...like Shakespeare's wretched Lear in the storm!... "strip off these lendings and spring headlong into the sea of liberty!"

But was "this familiar that I called out of my own soul", was this "being inherently malign and villainous"? Was "his every act and thought centred on self"? "Drinking pleasure from any degree of torture to another"? "Relentless like a man of stone"?! Yes, Robert Louis, yes, and that was good! I had no queasy pangs of conscience. I was no longer a tortured duality. I was the One, the Godhead, "tasting delight with every blow", gloriously filled with "boldness, a contempt of danger, a solution of the bonds of obligation"! That tedious, witless, suffocating 'obligation'! I was through the looking-glass, the cobweb veil. I was "sharpened to a point", "tensely elastic". It was no "ugly idol" that I beheld in the glass. Indeed, "I was conscious of no repugnance, rather a leap of welcome". Oh, such a joyous leap! It was myself, whole, simple, robust, uncomplicated! Natural, human, lively, express and admirable, single, One! At last! Oh yes, Robert Louis, oh yes, I hope Samoa was good to you! I hope so! Though, you died of your 'Bluidy Jack' at the age of my liberation. Perhaps you too saw God's face before the end. Perhaps. I hope you did.

It was well past one o'clock before I stirred abruptly from my reverie, from my glorious bath in the warm ocean of those words. I dressed and went out, still enthralled, into the deserted, fog-enshrouded streets. A Juggernaut.

I had put on the same threadbare overcoat that had served for my encounter with 'Emma' Tabram, the same old gloves and galoshes and shabby deerstalker, and the same stout blade that sent 'Polly' to her reward was nestled snugly, as before, under my left arm. As always, it was razor sharp. Thank you, Freddy. I had also brought a smallish burlap bag which I found in the cellar and had prepared for its task the previous evening by carefully lining it with some old shammy rags. They were saturated with years of shoe polish and, now firmly stitched in, I felt they would serve to make the bag satisfactorily leak-proof. I had folded the whole very neatly and placed it beneath my waistcoat on the right hand side.

Again I brought no brolly. High above the swirling, smoke-saturated fog I occasionally glimpsed a peeping star as I floated airily through Cavendish Square to Oxford Street.

Cavendish Square. Ah, Doctor Lanyon's address, and my dear mother's once, and mine, now and forever the usurped property of my loathsome brother-in-law. The 'citadel of medicine', so deeply intertwined with my family's history. But I no longer cared. Why should I? It was a new moon. I was a new man... 'Cal, Cal, Cal, Caliban!' ... Ha! I leapt and clicked my heels. Oh yes, "you who have so long been bound to the most narrow and material views", oh yes, I echoed Stevenson with the certainty of coming triumph, "you who have denied the virtue of transcendental medicine, you who have derided your superiors—behold!"

Behold me if you dare! The perfect brute!

I hailed a hansom and instructed the po-faced driver in a roughish, foreign accent... a 'Sweezer', why not?... to take me with all the haste his horses could muster to the London Docks at Wapping. I alighted just before we got there at the corner of Cable and Ensign Streets. It was seventeen minutes past three.

I heard the carriage off into the distance, making a brief deceptive jaunt down Dock Street, and then made my way into Whitechapel through the impenetrable gloom of Backchurch Lane.

I avoided the strong temptation to revisit Fleece Court or Buck's Row, taking Commercial Road west and north, through Church Lane, crossing Whitechapel High Street, moving quickly past the White Hart at the bottom of George Yard, then further northward up Commercial Street past Thrawl, and Flower and Dean, and Fashion, and the Queen's Head, and the lolling, shivering, snoring homeless under Christ Church, then the Britannia on the far side, stopping finally to watch the porters at Spitalfields Market, already busy at quarter to four, the first real sign of life.

Of course, I had heard the furtive scurrying of footsteps along the way and the sighs and grunts of complainant *coitus*, even once a raucous call for my attention through the all-embracing fog, but nothing to spark my interest. And I was following an overpowering inner impetus, a 'voice' that swept me along. I don't know why I stopped to watch the porters but no sooner had I done so than I noticed the form of a small woman standing slouched in the darkness against a wall at the corner of Brushfield Street, away from the lights of the market. I knew on the instant it was my bride to be, but I waited silent and observing for the better part of ten minutes. She was quite motionless, undoubtedly asleep on her feet. Finally, I walked toward her.

As I came close, she stirred and opened her eyes and looked at me, not speaking. I leaned casually on the wall beside her. She was truly a tiny woman, less than five feet tall, though buxom and thickly waisted.

"Tired, my girl?" I began sympathetically.

It was my own voice. No attempt at disguise. I noted the occurrence at the time with surprise and satisfaction. I had neither thought nor planned it.

She yawned and nodded, coming round to an assumed routine. I forestalled her assumption.

"No, it's not what you think," I said, "I'm not here for that. I'm here for information. I'll pay you for it."

She frowned and her sleep-starved eyes began to focus on me more sharply. I noticed the mark of a recent contusion on her right temple.

"I'm a doctor. A psychologist. Do you know what that is?"

She shook her head vaguely, without commitment.

"I want to try and catch this vicious murderer. To do that I need to understand his mind. You can help me. Will you?"

"You don't look like no doctor."

Her voice was low and husky.

"No, that's on purpose. Do I sound like one?"

She didn't respond.

"The police are at a loss. They've been helpless to find this fellow Pizer for nearly a week now."

She grunted in amused disgust.

"What, Jack? Go on with yer barrow. 'E never did it."

"Why do you say that?"

"'E's nothing but a poor 'alf-wit."

"Do you know where he is?"

No reply.

"Well, alright, I don't think he has anything to do with it either. From what I gather he's just a petty thief and probably a bit mad but certainly not a killer."

"'E just wants 'is mama."

She cackled.

"Quite so. What I need to understand is how it can happen. How could these poor women let themselves be so easily caught off guard? Why would they go with a man they suspected was going to treat them badly? Surely one must be able to tell."

"You can't never tell."

We were silent for a moment, then she looked at me probingly.

"It's a chance you 'as to take, don't you?"

"Yes. I can appreciate that there may not be much choice sometimes. What's your name?"

"Annie. 'Dark Annie', they calls me. What's yours?"

"Holt. Doctor Thomas Holt."

A lie, yes, I do apologise. But it was my grandfather's surname and his middle name became my own. Not that these basically irrelevant facts can be offered as mitigation in any rational sense.

"Well, Annie, what do you say, will you help me?" I went on, open, friendly, myself. "I'll pay you five shillings."

I took the two half crowns from my fob pocket. She eyed them hungrily. Poor woman. I could divine a buried dark intelligence somewhere deep beneath those threadbare rags and years of neglect. 'Dark' Annie and 'Raggedy' Holt. A fine pair.

"I don't know what kind of 'elp I can give ya."

"I'd like to see some of the places you might go, you know, if I were a man who wanted something from you."

She looked suddenly vulnerable, as though she had a brief suspicion but her mind was too tired to entertain it and it vanished. I went on.

"Show me the kind of place you think it would be foolish for a woman to go with a man. The kind of place you've been and perhaps thought you were lucky not to have been murdered yourself."

"Whatever good will that do?"

"I told you I'm a doctor of the mind. I'm trying to think myself into this terrible man's heart and soul. That's how we'll catch him. And I'm not familiar here. I need to see the kind of secret place you go."

She looked at me and held out her hand and I gave her the coins.

We crossed back over Commercial Street, taking the narrow lane of Wilkes Street north to Hanbury. On the north side of Hanbury Street she stopped outside number twenty-nine. A dismal, three-storey brick row-house that had once been filled with the clicking hand-worked looms of the weaving trade but, since the ruinous advent of steam power, had been converted into lodgings for the working poor. A sign above the door proclaimed, in scrawled, white-painted letters, 'Mrs. A. Richardson, rough packing-case maker'.

"There's a 'allway straight through 'ere into the back."

"What's there? A garden."

She cackled again.

"More like a yard, I'd say."

"Yes, of course. Have you been yourself?"

"Many's the time."

"Don't they keep the door locked?"

"No. Too many lodgers going in and out. Too many keys to remember."

"How many people live here, would you say?"

"Twenty at least. P'raps more."

"Will you show me?" I said.

I was giddy at this reckless plunge and suddenly I became aware of footsteps approaching from along the street behind me but I was careful not to betray to 'Annie' the slightest apprehension. A clock somewhere was striking half past four.

"Will you?" I repeated.

She nodded unenthusiastically, "Yes, alright."

And the footsteps passed. It was a woman. On her way to work at the market, I supposed. She didn't turn back to look at me as we entered the house. My plan could proceed. In any case, I was now at such a pitch within I doubt I could have stopped had I tried.

Annie led the way through the front door and down a long, musty darkened hall smelling of unseen cats, past a flight of stairs, and out into a small yard not more than twelve feet by eighteen. Three stone steps led down to bare earth. In a few places a rough attempt had been made at paving with flat, odd-shaped stones. There appeared to be a woodshed at the rear and, by the waft of its unmistakable redolence, a privy. The yard was fenced off on both sides by wooden palings, tight together, just over five feet in height. There was a cellar entrance to the right of the back door.

I walked down the steps into the yard. To one side there was a water tap. I stooped to examine something underneath it. It was a water-soaked leather apron! A ridiculous coincidence or a message from on High? You choose.

"Here, Annie," I whispered, "Come and look at this."

She had been hesitating by the door but now let it close softly and came waddling down to the bottom of the steps. Though malnourished she was still quite plump. It's not uncommon.

"What do you think? It's a leather apron." I pretended innocence. "Go on. Are you playing games with me? Is this where Jack Pizer lives?"

"No. Mrs. Richardson's boy comes in sometimes an 'elps 'er with the packing cases."

"I see. Funny though, isn't it."

She evidently didn't follow my point.

"All right, then," I went on, "Let's say you've brought a man here. Now show me what you'd do. Would you stay by the steps or go to the woodshed?"

"Doesn't matter. Whatever 'e'd want."

"But you'd have to be careful not to be overheard, wouldn't you? Otherwise someone might get up and turn you out."

"Not likely."

"Well, at all events, this seems a safe enough place. For you, I mean. A man would have to be a fool to try any funny business here. It's a certain trap."

At that precise moment we heard the front door bang. Someone was coming down the hall! I grasped Annie gently by the elbow.

"Come on. Let's not be seen. I've more to ask you."

It was just starting to get light and I hurried to hide us behind the woodshed as the back door opened. I think Annie, too, was beginning to quite enjoy herself.

A young man came out and looked down at the cellar door, then sat on the steps and removed one of his boots. He took out a small knife and carefully carved a piece of leather off the boot's toe. Clearly, it had been pinching him. All this took several minutes during which Annie and I stood breathless, close together. The stench of the privy was overpowering. I prayed that the young man would not decide to come and use it! Compared to that fetid midden of untreated excrement Annie's body smelled almost fragrant.

Mercifully, after putting his boot on again and sitting for a moment or two picking his nose, he got up and went back inside. A woman's voice called out sleepily, "Good morning, John." I didn't catch a reply but I fancied I heard the front door close a second later.

Even though I now knew that people were waking up in the house and dawn was streaking the sky, I was determined to execute my plan. I was quite beside myself with excitement yet my outward show remained a preternatural calm.

"Come on, we'd better go," I said disingenuously as we emerged from our hiding place. Annie was almost smiling.

"I thought you 'ad more to ask me."

Bless thee, oh, bless thee, sweet foolish lady.

"Well, yes," I said, and stopped as we approached the steps again. "How is it possible, I mean, what sort of position would you have to be in, you know, for a man to actually take you by surprise like that? So you wouldn't have time to cry out or defend yourself. I really can't see how it could happen."

"They was drunk, I s'pose."

"Yes, I imagine so." I tried my best to feign embarrassment. "I'm sorry, Annie, to seem rude but do you always make love to a man while facing him? Or do you sometimes turn your back?"

"Well, mostly, if it's wet like, we satisfy 'em standing, y'know. Frontways or backways, doesn't matter."

"Forgive my innocence," I said, my focus absolute, "How might it work 'backways'? Could you demonstrate?"

The sad little woman turned her back and leaned forward putting both her outstretched hands on the wall between the steps and the wooden fence, then stuck out her bottom toward me. It was singularly unprovocative. I think she was almost giggling.

"Yes, I see. Then he'd come up behind you like this..." My knife was out. "...and lift your skirts?..."

There was no possible reply. In one blessed, glorious, God-drenched instant, I had taken her by the hair, pulled back her head, and sliced the life from her before she had time to make a sound. Her pudgy little hands still held the wall as the blood gushed from her jugular straight downwards on the ground. Much like the pig I had seen dispatched by the men in the slaughterhouse on Winthrop Street. The sound was reminiscent of someone tossing out the slops. Only a few drops spattered the wall itself and not a drop touched me. Perfect.

At this precise moment of my joy someone opened a door into the yard of the adjoining house beyond the fence. I ducked down my head and listened. I heard shuffling footsteps and a yawning sigh and a loud fart and a voiding of heavy catarrh and whoever it was crossed the yard, presumably to the equivalent privy because a rusty swing-door slammed.

I held Annie firmly by the collar until her hands dropped from the wall and then lowered her gently to the ground. At any other time she would have been a ton weight. We bumped the fence very slightly as I raised her again to turn her on her back. Her eyes were still open and yet not fully clouded but I could tell she was already in the Hands of the Almighty, not looking at worldly things like me.

The footsteps in the next-door yard returned from the privy and, after another horrid snortling and another guttural venting of rheum, stumbled back inside. I went speedily to work.

"Bless you, Annie," I said, as I took the blade and made a second deep, deep cut through the tissues of her neck. A thrill went through me as her heart made a last, unexpected convulsion, sending a final eruption of blood toward the palings and then stopped. I paused to savour the unfathomable silence, my blade still singing inside her, then, quite unpredictably, I set to prising at her vertebrae. I was evidently desirous of cutting her head clean from her body but, when after a few strenuous moments it would not more easily come away and wanting the knife still sharp, I turned to more important pleasures.

I stood upright to sniff the air. She was lying now with her head lolling loosely not six inches from the wall and her feet pointing to the shed and the privy. I stooped and lifted her black skirts with the point of the knife. She had on two layers of filthy petticoat and a large pocket or bag for her belongings was tied underneath around the waist. I casually slit this open and noted the contents. An envelope, a pair of combs, a piece of cloth for patching, two farthings. Precious little. I scattered them about. Noticing two brass rings on the ring-finger of her left hand, I tugged them off and kept them, I don't know why. I flopped the arm back down across her breast and, repossessing the two half crowns, set to my delicious task.

She wore stockings but no knickers. This was quite obviously the custom. A noisome, otherworldly odour rose damply from her loins as I pushed her knees sideways and cut her belly open from the pubes straight upwards at a single stroke to the sternum. The woman had on two bodices, at least. No need for warmth now.

Having opened the intestinal cavity I quickly cut away two large hindering flaps of flesh and tossed them over her left shoulder, then pulled out lengths of small intestine, casting the whole haphazardly on her right side to expose my intended prize. The uterus. That ghastly infinitude, the well-spring of our Being! I wanted it. I wanted all of them! I sliced around the now shriveled organ with great dexterity, carving through the top of the vaginal passage to preserve the cervix. I intended to miss the bladder but failed, excising part of it as well, though I avoided spilling forth the contents of her rectum, thank the Lord.

Having successfully severed the object of my desire from her rapidly cooling, clammy flesh, I paused again to wipe the gore from my hands on her petticoats. As I did my gaze fell upon the dark mystery of her navel and, cheekily, I could not resist trimming it away with a circle of stomach flesh around it. The bottomless placental maelstrom, the fundament of the Ouroboros! This unpremeditated prize I placed with the rest of the purloined sweetmeats and wiped my hands again. Then I took the oily, polish-cloth-lined burlap from beneath my waistcoat and carefully wrapped the still tintinnabulant, shimmering organs. Ecstatic, heavenly music to my eyes!

I stood again. It was nearly sunrise. I went to the water pump. Below it was a bowl of clean water ready. Had He set it there for my coming? Leisurely, I washed my hands, and Freddy's wonderful blade, rinsing a small splotch of red from my right cuff as I did so. I put the knife safely away. For some devil-may-care reason I took the basin to the privy and, holding my breath, poured its cherry contents down the awful hole. I had a strong need to urinate but decided to delay it. I then returned to the pump. One motion was sufficient to refill the vessel with clean water.

I heard someone coughing in the house as I gathered up my burlap bag. Noises of the coming workday from the streets beyond were filling the yard. I looked at my watch. Twenty-five minutes past five. I didn't give Annie so much as a farewell glance as I mounted the steps and crept in the back door.

I stood in the hallway a moment listening. A host of morning sounds. Throat-clearing, humming, the clatter of crockery, tired footsteps, a baby crying. I went along to the front door and peered out. A dray-cart was passing. Three market-men were hurrying heedless to work. I waited, then joining in the rhythm, walked out into the awakening world of Hanbury Street and no one noticed me! I knew it. Not a soul. I had stuck my head in the lion's mouth again, this time daring it, positively daring it, to snap shut and prove my quest a falsehood. But it didn't, it didn't, you see! I got away with it. I got away with it all.

I walked toward Spitalfields and Commercial Street. Most of the traffic was going in that direction. I crossed over to the flower market and stole a rose. I turned north, swinging my grisly package nonchalantly, smelling the fragrant petals like Romeo come love-shocked from a tryst. It was just as though no one could see me! No one! I was invisible!

I started whistling, walking more briskly now, enjoying the chill of the morning, crossing Shoreditch High Street and on to Old Street and the familiar environs of St. Agnes' Well. Here I hailed a carriage for Wimpole Street. Why be more careful? I was invisible. I had the driver drop me directly outside No. 70!

Now, what the devil was I going to do with parts of a woman's belly, her navel, uterus, a piece of cervix and a raggedy chunk of bladder? Why do you ask? I wasn't a cannibal! I just wanted to look at them. To look, do you see, at my leisure. To plumb them with my eyes. And to own them.

I had prepared two plain glass jars with a clear solution of spirits of wine and left them ready in the kitchen. Once I had made sure Freddy's blade was properly spotless and in its place and washed all remaining traces of Annie from my clothing, I slithered those lonely relics from their greasy bag into the jars and lovingly sealed them tight. Then I cremated the bag with its remaining smear of innards in the stove. It whuffed up the flue in a votive rush. I checked after a moment to ensure there wasn't a trace.

I went upstairs, cradling the jars under my arms, and ran myself a steaming tub. Leaving the jars by the bath for a moment, I went into the bedroom, undressed, put on a silk robe, taking my costume, my investigator's disguise, my priestly vestment, and stowing it all safely away in the attic under the dust-covers.

I lay in the soothing heat, staring at the jars. Annie's two brass rings adorned my pinky. What secret, intense and inexpressible joy! But more. I wanted more and more and more. I was the Juggernaut! I thought of Robert Louis and Maudsley and Mansfield and my theatrical evening to come and I was filled to bursting with a cosmic swell of satisfaction. Finally, after two musing, mesmerised hours, the hot water trickling, keeping my Pierian Spring at a constant, comforting temperature, bugger the expense, I yawned and toddled off to bed. But not before locking my hard-won trophies in a small trunk and sliding it far back beneath the box-spring.

It was afternoon when I was roused from a deep, rejuvenating slumber. The telephone was ringing downstairs. Where the devil was Freddy? And then I remembered, of course, that I had given him the day to attend his niece's wedding. I was gloriously alone. Exactly as I had planned. Of course. I wondered briefly who was calling. Probably Maudsley to remind me of our visit to the theatre. So what? I lay back again luxuriant. I could still feel ripples of vibration rising from Annie's pickled organs underneath the bed. A fascinating and magical thing, the life force. As palpable as sunshine. Finally, I bestirred myself and went downstairs. The telephone rang again. It was Maudsley.

"Ah, there you are, Lyttleton," he snapped, "I've called several times."

"Sorry, I was about an urgent case. I've only just got in."

"You've seen the papers?"

"Of course," I lied.

"The Hand of God was at work again last evening, eh?" he chortled.

"Very funny. You know I wrote to Warren offering my help. I told him we had a religious monomaniac on our hands and offered some thoughts on how to catch him but, as expected, he has declined."

"Thinking of taking matters into your own hands?"

Maudsley was impossibly prescient.

"Perhaps. How did you guess?"

"You've always been utterly predictable."

I couldn't help but smile.

"Have I now."

"Oh, yes, yes. In any case, look here, I'm afraid I can't join you for supper as planned. I'll just meet you at seven o'clock sharp outside the theatre."

"Very well."

"I'm told Mansfield's been having difficulties with this one. Half houses at best."

"Yes, I'd heard."

"The murders no doubt. This last will finish it. He'll have to make a substitution. We're just in the nick."

"I shouldn't be surprised. Though one would have thought this gruesome business might have had the opposite effect. People love nothing if not a drop of blood."

"Mmmm," he said, "It'll be interesting. I'm looking forward to it. See you there then. Seven o'clock."

And he rang off.

Mansfield was so confident in the piece that he had actually opened his run of plays at the Lyceum on August 4th with a performance of Jekyll and Hyde. And two nights later I had made away with Martha Tabram. It was much, much more than coincidence, surely you must see that by now!

There was a positive 'Jekyll and Hyde' fever that summer in London. Mansfield had not originally intended to open his season until the first week of September but a German actor named Bandmann was scheduled to begin performing a pirated version of the same work on August 6th. As well, Howard Poole had already appeared in his own compilation at Croydon on July 26th. Apparently, Stevenson and his publishers, Longmans, had strenuously enjoined him not to do so and proclaimed in the press that Mansfield's was the only authorised adaptation. It had no effect.

But, I ask you, why was it that this little novella was creating such a sensation with the public at the same time I was having my own bloody conference with God? Oh, yes, I think it was far beyond mere coincidence!

However, Poole's performance attracted little attention and Bandmann's was universally panned. I had read Clement Scott's scathing review several weeks earlier.

"Mr. Bandmann's Dr. Jekyll is a canting, sanctimonious humbug of Pecksniffian appearance; his Mr. Hyde a malevolent dwarf-like creature with large teeth. Its monkey-like tricks only provoked laughter and derision where they should have inspired terror."

Bandmann withdrew the piece after its second night.

Mansfield, in marked contrast, had created an undeniable sensation. The critics concurred that, "on the plane of all that is weird, sombre, saturnine and mystical", there had been nothing in the experience of living theatre-goers comparable, excepting perhaps Henry Irving's performance as Mathias in The Bells. This was the role, twenty years earlier, that had brought Sir Henry lasting fame. And now Mansfield seemed poised for a similar triumph. And he was here in London at Henry Irving's invitation and in Sir Henry's very own theatre, the Lyceum!

Nevertheless, despite these glowing critiques and doubtless excellent word-of-mouth, the prudish British public were staying away in droves. The main reason being that some few articles in the press had pilloried Mansfield, claiming the horrific nature of his transformation into the character of Hyde was somehow encouraging the murderer! Good lord, how perfectly daft. Besides, I hadn't yet seen it! But I was looking forward to it immensely and perhaps to a meeting with Mansfield himself afterwards. I felt a brief pang of remorse that I was causing him financial difficulties.

The evening papers were full of Annie's murder. The Star was particularly florid.

"London lies today under the spell of a great terror. A nameless reprobate—half half man—is at large, who is daily gratifying his murderous instincts on the most miserable and defenceless classes of the community. There can be no shadow of a doubt now that our original theory was correct, and that the Whitechapel murderer, who has now four victims to his knife, is one man, and that man a murderous maniac. Hideous malice, deadly cunning, insatiable thirst for blood, all these are the marks of the mad homicide. The ghoul-like creature who stalks through the streets of London, stalking down his victim like a Pawnee Indian, is simply drunk with blood, and he will have more ..."

Amazing, don't you find, the public's appetite for such fulsome tripe? Gosh, perhaps it was all because Edward and I never played 'Cowboys and Indians' when we were children! Though, come to think of it, perhaps it was indeed. We were always far, far too serious. Deathly so.

I arrived at the Lyceum at about a quarter to seven, having supped pleasantly and alone at a favourite restaurant in Garrick Yard. A middle-aged busker was at work outside the theatre, accompanied by two small urchins banging drums. First he sang a song, to the tune of "My Village Home", I think. A frightful thing.

"Come listen to the dreadful tale, I'm telling, In Whitechapel four murders have been done..."

And on and on *ad infinitum*, you know the sort.

Then, to my amusement and surprise, he launched into a rather clever mime involving a leather apron and various masks, of a vampire, of comedy and tragedy, and Jekyll and Hyde, with the street-urchins running around in circles and screeching blue murder. The act culminated with the mimed death of one of the children, complete with up-raised, gore-stained rubber knife, and the shrill-whistling arrest of the other by the busker, now wearing a bobby's helmet. The little boy loudly and eloquently protested his innocence, whereupon the busker scratched his head, took the leather apron and began trying to fit it on several of the waiting theatre patrons, amidst the usual banter and repartee. Some of the patrons took it good-humouredly, some decidedly did not. And then he came to me.

I do not know what it was about me that made the busker stop abruptly, but after giving me a very odd, quite chilling look, he silently backed away.

At that moment, Maudsley appeared at my shoulder.

"What's the matter, constable?" he called to the busker with a chuckle, "You've recognised your man. Arrest him!"

The busker ignored the comment and, on the instant, resumed the forced jollity of his banter with the crowd, holding out the bobby's helmet for donations. I had ferreted out a sixpence but he passed me by without a glance.

"Seems like there's blood on your money, old chap," said Maudsley, "Tut, tut."

I actually glanced down at the sixpence to check! My two talisman half-crowns, my good luck charms, were safe in the fob-pocket of my waistcoat. What had the busker seen?

"Funny fellow," I said, and smiled, flipping the sixpence casually in the air, "A lot of them are quite, quite mad."

"The mad have second sight."

"I sincerely hope not," I replied with a mock shudder. "You've got the tickets?"

"Good lord, no," he said, "I thought you had them."

I laughed and we followed the line into the theatre as the house manager opened the doors.

The performance was as the critics had described it, quite startlingly magnificent. The only departure from Stevenson's plot, other than the necessary elaboration of already suggested detail, was the addition of a love story between Jekyll and Agnes Carew, the daughter of Sir Danvers Carew, the member of parliament murdered by Hyde. The adaptation was by Thomas Russell Sullivan from a scenario imagined by Mansfield. But, sadly, the house was scattered though it was a Saturday night. Sorry, Richard.

Mansfield's Jekyll was brilliantly conceived, a haunted man, a man set apart, filled with a ceaseless terror of the devilish, uncontrollable change which might come upon him at any time without the slightest premonitory warning, at any place, in the street, in the house of friends, even in the hoped-for haven of his sweetheart's arms.

His transformations into Hyde had been the talk of London for a month and now I saw why. No one could believe there wasn't some trickery to it. He was accused of using acids, phosphorus, all manner of chemicals. Some ready wit had declared it was "all perfectly simple. He uses a rubber suit which he inflates and exhausts at pleasure!" But it was quite evident to both Maudsley and myself that he affected the change merely with the muscles of his face, the tones of his yielding voice and the posture of his body.

He could poise in a crouching position balanced on his toes, swaying, then suddenly bound forward or scale a vertical surface with astonishing agility. And he knew to perfection the intricacies of theatrical timing! The dread expectant horror he managed to convey to the audience when Hyde was coming! An empty stage. Gloom. Oppressive silence. They had seen Hyde before. But the anticipation, the prolonged anticipation, every nerve whetted, all eyes searching the black corners of the stage for the next expected onrush of the demon! The hushed and breathless spectators held fast in hypnotic fetters. And then at last, with a wolfish howl, a panther's leap and the leer of a fiend, Hyde was suddenly, miraculously in view! Women fainted regularly at such moments and had to be carried from the theatre.

But the last act was the best. During twenty minutes Mansfield held the stage alone with but one interruption. The scene represented Dr. Jekyll's cabinet in broad daylight. Here was a man overwhelmed. He now knew that the drugs, with which he had with some success controlled the changes, were accidental and not to be duplicated. Hyde now possessed Jekyll. The Juggernaut's mission was very nearly complete! Mansfield's soul-sadness, his tender despair, his haunted anticipation as the convulsions seized him, his pitiful, agonised attitude as he stood before the mirror dreading to remove his hands for fear of the demon's face they would reveal, his cry of joy as he discovered that the change had not yet come and he was still Henry Jekyll!! Oh yes, these produced an effect in me quite as thrilling and more profound than any vulpine flamboyance preceding.

Strange, is it not, that an actor can represent liberation, understand it, taste it, revel in it with utter abandon on the stage, and yet abhor it? Can they truly be believed? The Stevensons, the Mansfields. Surely they are teasing, I thought, playing with us, these artists. Surely they know that the release they experience when representing the unfettered animalism of a Hyde is identical, in small, to the ecstasy of that freedom itself!

How can they then, when donning their oh so sober, righteous public masks, pay lip service to such outdated concepts as 'evil', 'demonic possession', 'the Devil'? How can they pretend to be shocked by violence and murder when they are thrilled by its enactment in their imaginations? They must be quite insane. Certainly living a damaging and duplicitous self-deceit. The cobweb veil enshrouds them all. You also, yes, you also, forgive me for saying so. Come now, step outside your stuffed up, double brain for once. Admit you know what I'm talking about. God is Blood, you pious fraud, Christ's Blood streaming in the firmament, and you know it! We are One.

During the applause at the curtain, which would have been thunderous had the house been full, Maudsley said:

"I think we should go and offer our congratulations. I believe he's had a difficult day."

I nodded enthusiastically.

At the end of the calls, after several grand though gracious bows alone upon the stage, Mansfield quieted the applause and came forward. The curtains fell together behind him.

"Ladies and gentlemen, I thank you for your kind appreciation of our efforts," he began, "However, as you are aware, alas, not everyone thinks as you do.

"The gentlemen who have said in the journals that there is no necessity to make the play so strong, that there is no use in displaying so horrible a character upon the stage or of lingering over the agony of Jekyll, seem to forget that as long as the actor acts, he will consider the highest form of his art the display of the most powerful passions of men. I do not delight to hear that just so many women have fainted of an evening in the theatre…"

There was a flutter of feminine laughter.

"…but I, my art, and my nature, receive a fresh stimulus and inspiration from the breathless silence and the rapt attention of my auditors.

"In reply to the criticism that the moral contained in this story of Jekyll and Hyde could be taught equally persuasively by gentler and prettier means, I have only to point to the great masters, and ask why Shakespeare…"

Ah, father would have been in his element!

"…piled horror upon horror in Richard the Third and Macbeth, why Othello smothers the beautiful Desdemona and then cuts his throat or stabs himself, why everybody is killed in Hamlet, and why even Romeo and Juliet carries us to the tomb? Oh, you may say, 'But the sublime thoughts, the language of Shakespeare!' 'Oh yes,' I will reply, 'Find me a Shakespeare today and I will surely engage him.' In the meantime I am highly satisfied with the thoughts of Robert Stevenson and the dramatisation of my young friend and scholar, Thomas Sullivan. For myself, I give all I have.

"To those who have loudly proclaimed that my impersonation of Hyde encourages evil, I can only reply that I do not believe art, true art, can ever give impetus to anything but the high perfection of man and his society…"

"Stuff and nonsense!" muttered Maudsley.

I assumed he was now impatient to get on and beard this actor in his lair.

"…However," continued Mansfield, "We are sensitive always to the effect we have and wish in no way to offend. So, to that end, I would like to announce a special benefit performance for the

Suffragan Bishop of London's Fund to take place next month on Friday, October 10th..."

"To open a laundry for the employment of reformed prostitutes, I don't doubt!" hissed Maudsley.

"...The play chosen for that occasion will be a surprise for one night only..."

It turned out to be a soppy, weightless comedy entitled Prince Karl.

"...Sadly, also, I must announce that there will be only two further performances of Dr. Jekyll and Mr. Hyde after this evening. On Thursday next, September 13th and Thursday, September 20th. It will be replaced on October 1st with A Parisian Romance, in which I have happily had some modest success in America depicting an aging, comi-tragical roué, one Baron Chevrial..."

Here he skillfully gave just the slightest hint of the characterisation to come. It was greeted with silly, sycophantic giggling.

"...Please tell your friends. I thank you and bid you all a fond goodnight."

He bowed again to light applause and disappeared through the curtains. The life of an actor-manager must be quite awful. So endlessly selling oneself and one's wares. Not much above begging. Pure hell. Besides, I thought smugly to myself, why act such stuff when one can do it!

"Christ Almighty," moaned Maudsley, "What a let down! A hawker! An arse-licker! The smarmy coward's all yours, Lyttleton, if you want him. I've heard quite enough!"

Ever unpredictable and irascible, once outside Maudsley lost no time in hailing a cabriolet, bidding me a brusque farewell, and dashing off home to the comforting silence of his books. Why had he bothered to come? But I was intrigued and feeling giddy and, after giving Mansfield a few minutes grace, went round to the stage door and announced myself to the doorman.

Gruff and unwelcoming, as they all seem inevitably to be, the hunchbacked little man told me to wait. He would find out if 'Sir' was receiving. 'Sir', indeed. Mansfield was barely in his middle thirties and had only just begun his rise to success. He had struggled for years in obscurity in both England and America and was merely fortunate that Henry Irving had seen him in New York the previous year. And here he was at the Lyceum, following the great Sarah

Bernhardt's sold-out run as Sardou's *La Tosca*, acting for all the world like Irving himself! By the time I had sat on that perishingly hard bench by the door for twenty-five minutes, I was ready to slit the little popinjay's throat! All the other members of the cast and stage-crew and their guests had long since departed. All paying obeisance to the ghastly doorman. He grudging them all a terse goodnight.

Finally, after a lull of at least five minutes in which no one came or went, the malformed gnome got up and made a great show of locking the doors, then turned to me and said, with a sordid, malevolent smirk, "I'm sure Sir will be most 'appy to receive you now."

He clambered up two flights of dingy stairs and hobbled down a moth-eaten hallway. I followed, though I had pretty much lost interest. What was the man after all? Just another ambitious American shamelessly grovelling before the public whim. Maudsley was right. At the end of the hallway, the pop-eyed dwarf stopped at a door and knocked.

I heard Mansfield's tired voice quietly saying, "Come."

The little horror grinned, grasped me painfully by the elbow with his bony fingers and fairly shoved me through the door.

The atmosphere in Mansfield's private dressing-room was a pleasant contrast to the hallway without. Not that it was all that spacious or lavish, no, but it was tastefully furnished, well-lit and orderly. I approved. I felt that Maudsley had perhaps been a trifle harsh in his judgement. Economic survival is ever, I knew, of pressing ubiquity.

Mansfield himself was a surprisingly small, unprepossessing-looking man. Balding like myself, seeming for all the world like a bank clerk, not the wildly charismatic demon of less than an hour ago. He wore *pince-nez* and had apparently been poring over some account books before I entered.

As I was thrust into the chamber he stood and removed the *pince-nez*, putting them down on his dressing-table.

"Hello there," he said genially.

"Thank you, Roger," he added, nodding to the ghoul who bowed and closed the door.

I introduced myself and we shook hands.

"Ah yes, of course, the famous psychologist. What a pleasure. Come in. Come in."

He opened the hall door again for a moment and looked out, then, satisfied I suppose that the shrivelled ostiary was not listening at the keyhole, closed it once more behind me.

"Please sit, doctor." He gestured me to a stuffed armchair. "May I offer you some refreshment? A glass of cognac?"

I saw he had an empty snifter placed by the account books and a half eaten plate of food. Uncharacteristically, I said yes I would. He poured out a far too generous portion for me from a large decanter, then replenished his own glass and sat.

We looked at each other for a moment.

"I must congratulate you on a marvelous rendition of a great work," I said.

"Thank you. But it's all for nothing. I'll have to take the play off, as you heard. The Philistines are always with us. The police were here to question me this afternoon."

"Really? Whatever for?"

"Some joker made them think that I must be this Whitechapel murderer because of the way I play Hyde."

"You were certainly very convincing," I said. "I assume the police were satisfied with your answers?"

"I should damn well hope so. Last spring, when they claim the first of these murders occurred, I was in America! The night of August 6th I was dead asleep in my hotel. I'd just arrived to an exhausting opening weekend. The night of August 30th and last night too. I can't think how they imagine I'd have the energy for murder, doing what I do!"

"It's comical," I agreed. "Well, I shouldn't worry. The police are only clutching at straws. They've spent days trying to put their hands on this 'Leather Apron' character without success. He's just some poor simpleton with a bad temper who doubtless has nothing whatever to do with it. It's both funny and sad. Alas, I'm afraid we shall be an international laughing-stock."

The cognac was already having its effect. I realised I would have to be careful. I had very poor and unhappy brains for drinking, as I've mentioned. Nonetheless, I couldn't resist developing a fresh subject.

"Tell me something," I ventured, "I'm fascinated by what Stevenson has to say. I've met him, you know. We have had parallel lives in many ways. We were both strongly affected by our father's beliefs and have had to combat our own feeling of being hemmed in and strait-jacketed by convention. Quite in common with our whole society. And in my observation of the insane over many, many years I have come to understand what really sends these poor souls toppling into the abyss. It is their inability, in the majority of cases, to contain their passions sufficiently to play this social game. They pine for liberation from it and either explode, like Hyde, or, more frequently, turn inward and destroy themselves."

I could see Mansfield was quite taken up with this line of thought.

"Oh god yes, I understand completely," he replied, looking serious in the way that only Americans can and nodding his chin energetically. "I've often thought that what I do must be good for my health. And I hope, in a lesser degree, for my audience too. I get a chance to let these passions out every night. To let off some steam. Oh yes, I'm lucky."

"But only in play," I said.

"Well sure, but it's still a 'liberation' for me. It's a serious kind of play."

I couldn't resist.

"Have you ever found it dangerous? I mean by that, has it ever made you desire to experience the real thing? Has the temptation come into your mind, even ever so slightly?"

Mansfield looked at me strangely.

"What, actually to commit murder?"

I nodded, smiling innocently.

"Hell no. Acting the murderer is damn well exhausting enough for me." He was laughing now. "But here's a thought, maybe you should tell all the asylum owners in England to start putting on plays!"

"And a good thought too," I said, and joined his laughter.

We paused. I was beginning to feel quite light-headed.

"I'm just on my way to Whitechapel," I suddenly confided, surprising myself. Up to that moment I had no thought to do so! "Purely out of professional interest. The streets will be charged with excitement there tonight. Would you care to join me? Who knows, we might snare ourselves a murderer. It's well known they return obsessively to the scene of their crimes. But perhaps you're too tired."

"No, no," he said, his eyes crinkling with amusement, "You fascinate me. Lead on."

"It could prove dangerous for you."

"Be damned."

He downed the remainder of his cognac and pulled out a fresh bottle from a drawer. I quickly began to wonder what kind of unhappy pickle I might be inflicting on myself.

"Let's make a night of it!" he said with a flourish, gathering up a long cape and rakishly donning a slouch fedora, and we went out into the musty hallway. Mansfield carefully double-locked his dressing-room door as we did so.

"Goodnight, Roger," he said pleasantly in passing to the bunch-backed toad at the stage door.

"G'night, Sir," came the reptile's reply, with a lop-sided, fawning smirk, beneath which ground the decaying teeth of purest malice.

"Some years ago I had a man-servant named Roger," I said, once we were on the street.

"Better looking though, I'll wager. A more handsome personality, too!"

We chuckled.

"They're all like that," he said, "It's a lousy job. They rule their little fiefdoms with an artful despotism."

"Ever the result of thwarted liberation," I rejoindered.

A hansom cab was there by the kerbstone waiting for him. The driver doffed his cap.

"Evenin', m'lud," he said.

'Sir', now 'my lord' for heaven's sake! 'How do these blasted actors merit it?' I thought, a mite sniffy. No more drink for me.

"We want to take a little spin through Whitechapel, there's a good chap."

"Whitechapel?" the man said in surprise. "No, it wouldn't be safe for you, sir. Not tonight of all nights. Was near to riot in the streets today. The police caught a suspect. Some Jew. The mob would of tore 'im to bits if…"

Mansfield cut him off with a good-natured smile.

"Oh, come on. What's life without a little real danger?" and he winked at me as he stressed the word 'real', "My friend here will protect us. He's a doctor. Well versed in these matters. You're not afraid, are you? We'll pay you well. Now come on, come on, let's have no more delay."

Mansfield leapt aboard before the driver could demur further. He muttered glumly, "Have it your own way then," hoping, I'm sure, that we might change our minds as we got nearer, and we were off.

I learned some interesting things about Mansfield as we clopped slowly down the Strand, past the Law Courts and Ludgate Circus and St. Paul's, to Cannon Street. He needed little prompting to talk about himself and less and less so as the level in his bottle went down.

He had been born in Berlin while his mother, one Erminia Rudersdorff, a renowned *prima donna* of Dutch descent, was on tour. She was the daughter of a musical prodigy, a violinist and con-cert-*meister*, Joseph Rudersdorff. She had spent her youth in Dublin and was fluent in at least five languages. Maurice Mansfield, Richard's father, was her second husband. He was a wine merchant with his business in Lime Street near the Leadenhall Market. On our way, at Mansfield's insistence, we detoured directly past the building. It was now a cloth manufacturers or some such thing. Mansfield was getting quite tipsy and there were tears in his eyes at the sight of it. His father had died when he was only four. But, how delicious, we were not two hundred yards from Fleece Court! And Mitre Square! You'll become very familiar with that locale soon.

In his early years Mansfield himself had lived in Upper Berkeley Street off Portman Square. Just the other end of Wigmore Street from All Soul's Church where I married Florence Jessie and our children were christened. Oh, this may be mere coincidence to you but it wasn't to me!

Mansfield also regaled me with another amusing anecdote and its serendipity positively resounded within me. It had to do with his first appearance on the stage as a young boy. Now, can you guess at the reason for my interest? His mother was dressing for a concert in which she was to sing at the Crystal Palace. He insisted on going along and neither refusal nor threats dried his tearful determination. Finally, his mother relented and he was hurriedly dressed in his best black velvet skirt and coat.

At the theatre he remembered being much awed by the vastness of things, the lights, the strange noises, the apparent confusion, and he clung close to his mother. She took him into her dressing-room and admonished him there to remain.

When an assistant knocked on the door to say that Madame's turn had arrived and that the orchestra was waiting, she strode majestically forth, as was her custom, from her own room straight to the centre of the stage. Her appearance was greeted by a roar of applause which she acknowledged with queenly bows. She did not notice a subdued tittering beneath the ovation, however, and signaled the conductor to begin. The music quieted the applause but did nothing to stifle the increasing hilarity of which she soon became painfully conscious. Glancing about to see what could be the occasion, she discovered Richard beside and somewhat behind her, frightened to death, but firmly clutching the hem of her long train in his little hands!

Resonance, resonance. A mother, a father, what's the difference? Children must break through the cobweb veil. Cut the umbilicus and spray the world with blood! Or don't you see that?

We were traveling now on Aldgate, St. Botolph's on our left, the Minories and Fleece Court to our right. How I ached to tell him about Fay! But I had been careful only to seem to sip more brandy all the while and was able to resist.

I instructed the driver to turn north on Commercial Street. Our passage had until then been quite unobstructed, only a few scattered knots of frightened people and frequent pairs of patrolling constables, but suddenly here there were throngs of jostling rowdies in our way. It was just before midnight, nearly closing time.

"Last call!" Mansfield cried out, fully swelled now with the effect of the liquor, "Let's get ourselves a taste of the local vintage!" and at the corner of White's Row he bounded from the carriage. I followed suit.

"Don't desert us, my good man!" he shouted to the driver, who was managing the horses with difficulty and looking singularly distressed, and plunged theatrically into the crowd. They made way for him but I could tell from their faces how easily things might get out of hand. I did my best throughout the evening to provide a counterfoil.

"Look," he said, pointing in two directions, "I spy public houses there and there! Say which tickles your fancy."

On the other side in front of us was the Queen's Head and farther along, at the corner of Dorset Street, the Britannia.

"Either. Whichever tickles yours."

"Both at once then!" he declaimed merrily, already on his way. We crossed over to the corner of Fashion Street and entered the Queen's Head.

Now a pub in Whitechapel in those days had no gilded mirrors, mahogany carvings or windows glittering with cut glass, but it was not quite the sordid, spittle-strewn, Hogarthian gin-palace that you might expect either. There was a tavern for every three hundred and forty-five Londoners, every two hundred in Whitechapel. They were usually places where class distinction might be relaxed a little, but, nonetheless, a pair of 'toffs', one in evening dress, occasioned quite a stare as we came in and made our way through a distorted sea of sweating, rosaceate faces to the bar.

"Two large brandies. The very best you have, good sir," Mansfield said jovially to a great bulldog of a man behind the counter.

It still gives me a tremor when I recall that at that moment I had my first glance of Mary Kelly though I did not speak with her that night. She was sitting with a man who I came to know was Joseph Barnett and two other older women at a back corner table. I noticed her, I remember, because she wore no hat and the light was catching her ginger hair. She looked quite surprisingly respectable too in her clean, white apron. Elizabeth Stride, I learned afterward, was also a frequenter of the Queen's Head though I don't believe she was present on this occasion. She had more than once been taken into police custody for drunk and disorderly behaviour in this very pub but I never met with her there.

"Slummin', eh, guv'nors, is you?" piped up a sweet-faced little man perched on a rough stool beside us.

"Mmm," I nodded, "You've had some excitement here today."

"Not 'alf. Streets'll be deserted ten minutes from now, see if I'm not right."

"Thought they'd caught the murderer, did they?"

A few other inquisitive faces had gathered around us. I motioned to the bulldog to replenish their glasses.

"Yes, indeed, didn't they an' all," said a plump woman with a wall-eye, "But Mrs. Fiddymont saw the real culprit early this morning. Oh, much obliged, guv'nor, decent of you, I'm sure."

She had received the benefits of my gesture from the barman.

"She told them. 'E came into the Prince Albert bold as you please and ordered an 'alf from 'er."

"'Is shirt was all torn an' there was blood on 'is face an' 'ands," chimed in another.

"What time was this?" I asked.

"Just on seven o'clock this morning," said the plump woman. "She was 'aving a chat with Mary Chappell. 'E 'ad 'is 'at drawn down over 'is eyes an' looked quite terrifying, she said. 'E caught Mary staring at 'im an' bolted."

"Didn't anyone think to follow him?" Mansfield queried.

"Oh yes," said the little man, "Joe Taylor followed 'im to Bishopsgate. Walking awful fast though 'e was. Strange and springy-like. Joe caught up to 'im an' said 'is eyes was all wild an' staring."

"Did he say anything else? Did he say how old the man was?" I asked.

I was understandably curious.

"'Bout your age, guv, I'd say," twinkled the little man.

"Really."

"Oh, yes. More or less exactly, I'd say."

The others laughed.

"But, not to worry, guv, 'e 'ad short, villainous, sandy sort of 'air an' a ginger, twirly moustache an' 'orrible 'ollows in 'is cheeks. Don't worry yourself, guv, we'll vouch it weren't you."

I laughed with them. I thought I caught Mansfield's strange look again out of the corner of my eye. But, in retrospect, there was probably nothing in it.

"What is it about you, doc?" he said, grinning. His voice had suddenly taken on an unwelcome slur.

At that moment two constables came in and gave us all a quick once over. They eyed Mansfield and I suspiciously but decided to leave well enough alone as to our presence there.

"Near as nothing to 'alf twelve, Tom," one said to the barman, "Time to close up and go 'ome."

The barman nodded.

"Good night, gentlemen," the second constable said to us pointedly as they went out. Many of the other denizens were already obediently slipping away into the night.

"We'd better scarper, too," I said, looking at Mansfield, using the colloquial. He was downing my untouched brandy.

"I suppose you all knew the poor woman that was murdered," he said.

I took note, with mounting apprehension, that his eyes had become decidedly bloodshot. If I envisioned him in different attire he would have looked a regular.

"Little Annie Sievey? I should say," offered the plump woman, "You knew 'er, didn't you, Mary?"

The red-haired young woman from the back table was just passing by with her companions on her way to the door.

"Dark Annie, is it? No, rest her soul, hardly at all. Not any more now, that's a sure thing."

And she was gone. It was a pleasant voice, with more than a hint of Irish brogue.

"She kept 'erself to 'erself but we all knew 'er. She 'ad 'er share of airs and graces but she didn't deserve this," said the second woman with a sentimental sniff.

"No, indeed not," I concurred solemnly.

I had to get them all to trust me, you see. This was how I might eventually gain time! I took advantage of this golden opportunity to introduce myself and explain my opinion of the killer's nature and the methods which I thought could lead to his capture. I enlisted their help and assured them I was not one to rest while such a fiend was in their midst. I was quick about it though as I could see Mansfield was getting bored and impatient.

"Will you show us where it happened?" I asked them in conclusion.

Of course they would. Our strange little entourage bustled out of the Queen's Head and, with the grumbling coachman following, made its way past Christ Church and the homeless shivering in the yard under its protecting steeple, turning right on Church Street at the Ten Bells, then down the narrow, tenebrous alleyway of Wilkes Street to Hanbury. My very passage with 'Dark Annie' herself! Mansfield kept pace, though a few steps behind, silent and morose, in a brandied world of his own. All the while my new companions told me a great deal about the little woman whose womb lay silent, jarred and preserved, beneath my bed.

She had recently had a fight with one Eliza Cooper in the street outside the Britannia over a piece of soap, they said. Ah, that explained the bruising. She had once been well-to-do, they said. Her husband was a veterinary surgeon but he had died, leaving her with no allowance. She had a sister in Brompton. She used to go to Stratford to sell crochet work. She was very clever with her fingers. She had intended to go hop-picking this day. She had a regular man named Stanley or someone called 'the pensioner', maybe they were one and the same, they weren't quite sure. Tim Donavan, the lodging-house deputy at Crossingham's, had done wrong to turn her out because she couldn't pay. She had drunk her doss-money but he shouldn't have turned her away at that time of night. He knew her, she'd been there four months. He was to blame, they said. They were sure of that.

Wilkes Street emerges into Hanbury on the south side. To our right and on the north was No. 29. Lights were still on in the building and in the houses adjoining. Two constables were stationed by the door, allowing no admittance to the crime scene. We discovered that the immediate neighbours had been making a killing all day letting gawpers view the back yard of No. 29 from their rear windows. The traffic had been steady in and out and there were still a few customers even at this time of night.

I introduced myself to the two bobbies on duty. One of them turned out to be the same PC Neil who had discovered Polly only the week before! We chatted amiably but they were firm in not letting Mansfield nor I through into the back yard and Mansfield, alas, decided, in his eerie, drunken state, to get pointlessly shirty with them for their refusal.

"Do you know who I am?!" he shouted, quite out of the blue, rearing up and waving his right arm in a grand manner.

Ah, here we go, I thought, the true man at last. I had been steeling myself for the moment. And, sure enough, without being asked, he told them. At length.

"Some of your comrades dared to accuse me of being the murderer this morning! What do you think about that?!" he went on, after enlarging roundly upon his accomplishments, without so much as a pause for breath.

I was trying unsuccessfully to calm him.

"You probably think I'm just some hack American!"

What on earth had provoked this?

"I'm not Irving, you think, not the sanctified Duse, oh no, Miss Irving pissing Terry or your *belle dame* Madame Sarah, no, no, no! But let me show you something! Pharisees!"

He had completely lost control. And now the silly fool was doing it, yes, he was transforming himself into Hyde before their astonished eyes. His face had turned quite black, his eyes were fiery coals under fisted, threatening brows. He was truly unrecognisable. To this day I haven't a clue how he achieved it. Is it possible, I thought, that my visage changed in such a manner when I performed the deed itself?

"What do you say now? Do I look like a murderer now?! What do you say to your precious Sir Henry now!!" he rasped out viciously.

The madman was dashing about the street in a frenzy of rage. A hideous, spine-chilling gargoyle. The women were gasping, mesmerised, too afraid to speak. Then, in what seemed an impossibly short instant, he was back again confronting the two hapless, dumbstruck policemen.

"Why don't you arrest me if it's so, you mental midgets?! Can't you see? It's obvious, for god's sake, isn't it? I'm the slasher! I'm your man! Arrest me! Put me in irons!"

He was beside himself, screaming at the top of his well-practised lungs directly into the poor men's faces. A livid, ghoulish, animal snarl. They, for their part, I don't know how, responded to the whole absurd situation with quite admirable British patience and unflappability.

"You'd better take your friend 'ome, I think, sir," said PC Neil to me levelly as I finally managed to come between them.

Mercifully, Mansfield seemed somewhat to regain his senses and looked about blinking for a moment, realising, I suppose, where he was. Then, with a stunningly overdone, mock-tragical peal of laughter, he dashed to the waiting carriage and leapt in, his long cape flapping behind him like some parodist's premonition of Count Dracula. Significant in any way, is it, that Stoker was for twenty-seven years Sir Henry Irving's manager? Well, anagogical, at best.

Mansfield's long-suffering driver cast his eyes heavenward. What a spectacle!

"He's drunk, but a danger only to himself, I fear. My apologies," I said to the ever-placid constables, calling out to my guides as I hastened to follow him, "Thank you all for your good company. I'd better see him home. We'll meet soon again, I'm sure."

Mansfield slept all the way back to his hotel, thank heavens, snoring like a grampus. I mused smugly, as I listened to his wheezing, droning rattle, what a huge success the evening had been. By this quite unexpected means, I had been able subtly to introduce myself to the intimate world of the murders as an innocent, much-interested party. I had begun to get the confidence of the common people of Whitechapel and the police would surely tolerate me now with a blind eye, stalwart and patronising as ever…Thank you, Richard, thank you! You were the answer to my prayers. The perfect ruse and my unwitting smoke-screen ... But, good Lord preserve us, I thought, as I watched his slack, exhausted face, what impossibly strange paranoia lurking hidden within the hearts of men can be released by overindulgence! And I found myself enjoying a solitary smile.

After a ridiculous hiatus at the hotel, in which two night-porters actually had to carry Mansfield from his carriage like a casualty of war, the grateful driver kindly dropped me directly to my door at Wimpole Street.

I never spoke with Mansfield again. I received a cordial note from him the following day thanking me for getting him home and offering two complimentary seats at any other of his offerings of my choice. As you can appreciate, I had neither the time nor inclination to take him up on it. I telephoned Maudsley on Sunday morning and told him the gist of what had transpired expecting to share a good laugh but his response was characteristically ill-humoured and terse.

"The stage is a puerile ambition," he barked.

And that was that. Yes, I know, I know, it's time to get on with it, all this side-tracking, you're interested in the murders! Forgive me, though, there's a great deal to this narrative besides the gore. I must relate in some detail what happened during the month of September. It's still three weeks yet to the 'double event' and another five after that to the crowning glory. And I must begin to weave the oddity of the Maybrick family into my story, it cannot be fully complete unless I do. They became much involved in its strange *dénouement*. You'll just have to be patient.

A Manual of Lunacy

That Sunday afternoon, the ninth of September, I lay down on Florence Jessie's favourite stuffed-brocade ottoman in the parlour for an unaccustomed nap. You'll indulge me, it had been a busy weekend.

Freddy arrived punctually after church and pottered about as usual. He was careful not to disturb me though I know he must have been curious. When I awoke, at half past three, I told him all about my evening with Mansfield, and the beginnings of my efforts to effect the Whitechapel murderer's capture, over a delicious cup of tea with scones and jam and clotted cream. 'What if he'd looked under the bed upstairs?' I hear you thinking. Well, that's why I had been careful to place little Annie's preserved organs in a locked trunk. It was padded, specially made for the purpose, there was no chance of the jars rattling about though one might have heard a bit of sloshing. But what of it? And, oh yes, during my nap I had been dreaming of further embellishment to my store of dainties!

I was anxious, too, in a quite genuine way, though this may seem bizarre to you, to continue my investigations. Ah yes, the double brain. I knew that the inquest into Annie's murder would begin before the week was out, as it happened it was convened on Wednesday the 12th, and I wanted to be in conspicuous attendance. But before that, on the Monday and Tuesday, I was required to give evidence before Mr.

Justice Field at the Bristol Assizes. I had also, of course, to keep up with my professional work. After all, I still had a family to support.

I was called in for the prosecution in what became known as the 'Clifton lunacy case'... Thomas Lovell Beddoes, one of my favourite poets, was born at Clifton... 'So out of Life's fresh crown fall like a rose-leaf down. Thus are the ghosts to woo; thus are all dreams made true, ever to last!'... Ha! Magnificent!... The case concerned an action brought by a young lady against two doctors and the mother superior of the Roman Catholic convent that they had illegally incarcerated her in a lunatic asylum. I had made it a clear condition in giving evidence that I considered the doctors were justified in every way, but so far as the authorities of the convent were concerned, in their behaviour previous to the certification of the lady, I thought that the plaintiff had good grounds for her suit.

She was the daughter of a clergyman but was found somewhat unruly and difficult to govern and had been sent to various Catholic schools. In 1883, she went of her own accord as lady boarder to the convent at Clifton and remained there for ten months. But she felt there was an unpleasantness in the demeanour of the mother superior and some of the other nuns and, after a time, she decided it would be better to leave the convent and take rooms outside. They, however, persuaded her against this and she consented to remain.

Once, having been requested by the nuns to take her meals in her room, being of a quick and proud temper, she promptly retired there, locked the door and refused to come out. She claimed that her food then became of distinctly inferior quality to that previously supplied. She declined to eat it and put it outside. On one occasion she was so disgusted with the fare on her plate that she threw it all down the stairs. Shortly after this the mother superior, accompanied by the convent nurse and several of the nuns, arrived in her room, seized her by the wrists, and took the key forcibly from her. She grew indignant and struck the nurse in the face. Two nuns were placed in charge of her and she was ultimately locked up in the room. Not long after this the mother superior summoned a doctor to examine her. Upon completion the door was locked again and five days later a second doctor came. The result of this was that she was sent to Brislington House Asylum, where she remained a few months and was then liberated. She considered her treatment to have been in every way unjustifiable.

Mr. Justice Field, who at that time was nearly stone deaf, became, for reasons best known to himself, very angry with me during my testimony. I assumed it was because, being more or less an unwilling witness, though not opposed to the doctors, I had to fence with the questions put to me by our counsel, Sir W. Phillimore. One question was:

"Do you consider that 'rambling, incoherent conversations, refusal to answer questions, and vague statements of ill-usage' are sufficient to justify the certificate?"

My honest reply, though unfortunately unsought, perforce had to be, "Yes, rambling and incoherent conversations may in some cases be regarded as signs of insanity."

Justice Field then demanded that I answer the whole question as to whether the certificates justified inferences of insanity. I replied that I could not do so without being given the opportunity of analysing them. As I had already faced a considerable amount of argument with the learned counsel on the matter Justice Field got very indignant at what he thought my audacity and I felt for a moment that this irate, deaf old judge was about to commit me for contempt of court! I had previously met him at a dinner and he seemed a kind old gentleman but the defects of his aural apparatus were so blatant it seemed insupportable that he should still preside in a judicial capacity on the Bench. I had been called in to advise on purely *ex parte* statements and not on any other evidence. At all events, the opinion I had originally given to her solicitors was finally upheld.

I returned to London on the evening of the eleventh and wrote a letter to the Times in which I made public my lunacy theory and posited that the murderer of Martha Tabram, Polly Nichols and Annie Chapman was one and the same. Oh very well, I confess I had already penned a brief anonymous missive in the same vein three days before, signed 'A Country Doctor'. I was warming to my task!

I have a copy of the paper here.

"To the Editor of the Times.

"Sir, - My theory having been circulated far and wide with reference to an opinion given to the authorities of the Criminal Investigation Department, I would like to qualify such statements in your columns.

"That the murderer of the three victims in Whitechapel is one and the same person I have no doubt."

Of course, I couldn't mention Fay.

"The whole affair is that of a lunatic, and as there is 'method in madness', so there was method shown in the crime and in the gradual dissection of the body of the latest victim. It is not the work of a responsible person. It is a well-known and accepted fact that homicidal mania is incurable, but difficult of detection, as it frequently lies latent. It is incurable, and those who have been the subject of it should never be let loose on society.

"I think that the murderer is not of the class to which 'Leather Apron' belongs, but is of the upper class of society, and I still think my opinion given to the authorities is the correct one—*viz.*, that the murders have been committed by a lunatic lately discharged from some asylum, or by one who has escaped. If the former, doubtless one who, though suffering from the effects of homicidal mania, is apparently sane on the surface, and consequently has been liberated, and is following out the inclinations of his morbid imaginations by wholesale homicide. I think the advice given by me a sound one—to apply for an immediate return from all asylums who have discharged such individuals with a view of ascertaining their whereabouts. I am your obedient servant, *etc*."

'Oh, rare Ben Jonson!'

Every time I re-read that letter I am both awed by its cunning and puzzled by one thing. The use of the word 'gradual'. My evisceration of Annie had sadly been anything but gradual. That was a slip, an error in the perfection of my duplicity. It was the secret voice of my deepest longing, unnoticed by me at the time, a subterranean exudation, the anticipation of future bliss, of luxury yet to come!

You see, some had been arguing in the press against the murders having been all the work of one man. The fact was raised that the force of imitation is very strong in the insane and that a murder committed in a terrible way often has its imitators. Well, obviously, there are plenty of examples of precisely that. I visited a prison once and in the course of a conversation with the chaplain he informed me that a youth had been executed the previous week in whom he took much interest, so far as his spiritual welfare was concerned. He had been convinced the boy was truly sorry and the following Sunday he alluded to the case in the pulpit as an example of repentance at the eleventh hour and how gratifying the result was to him. The boy was guilty of a very revolting murder. The chaplain's sermon was grave and sincere but before the week was out one of his congregation performed a murder in a similarly horrible way. Some years ago a lunatic jumped from the Duke of York's column and a few days afterward several others followed his example! One insane person is seen flourishing a knife in the street, the power of imitation is so great, of course others will be found doing so too. Of course, of course, of course!

There had been a number of regrettable instances just the previous week. A labourer in Hoxton had come home drunk and slashed a table-knife across his wife's throat shouting he was going to make a 'Buck's Row murder'. Mercifully, the attack was not fatal and the man, one Henry Hummerston, was rightly sentenced to six months hard labour.

A woman had been leaving the Forester's Music Hall on Cambridge Heath Road when she was accosted by a well-dressed man who asked her to accompany him. Near to the spot where I had dispatched Polly...intentional, not coincidental, there's a difference!...the man seized her by the throat and dragged her down a court where a whole gang of women and men stripped the unfortunate woman of her necklace, ear-rings, brooch and purse and brutally assaulted her. When she tried to shout for help one of the gang laid a large knife across her throat, saying "We'll serve you as we did the others." A departure from the 'High-rip gangs', these were pimps merely keeping a prostitute in line, but the woman was eventually released, and recovered, thank heavens.

Of course, I had thousands of imitators! Puerile ambition! What could I have done? At least I tried to set the record straight. Sly, yes. Veiled, yes. But within the skeins of my deception lay the truth.

All the idle theorising in the press was a positive help to me. In the editorial column next to my letter the opinion was put forward that the murderer had leapt over the wall between the garden at No. 29 Hanbury Street and No. 27 and then into the garden of No. 25 to make his escape. No doubt the writer had been impressed with the almost superhuman agility of Mansfield's Hyde. The papers were always chock-a-block with such nonsense. Did you know that some larky lad had thought it amusing to scribble on the wall of the yard near to where Annie's body was found, "Five. 15 more and then I give myself up"? Oh yes, I had help from all quarters!

More erudite publications like the Lancet occasionally managed a drop of sense. On September 15th they wrote, admitting to their bafflement, "...It is most unusual for a lunatic to plan any complicated crime of this kind. Neither, as a rule, does a lunatic take precautions to escape from the consequences of his act; which data are most conspicuous in these now too celebrated cases. The truth is, that under the circumstances nobody can do more than hazard a guess as to the probable condition of mind of the perpetrator of these terrible tragedies..." But you can, can't you.

In delightfully macabre resonance with my letter of September 12th was also the following, printed directly beneath!

"A Thames Mystery.

"Yesterday afternoon, shortly before one o'clock, a human arm was discovered on the foreshore of the Thames, near the Grosvenor-road railway bridge, on the Pimlico side of the river. A constable took it to the Gerald Street police station, and Inspector Adams, by the instruction of Superintendent Shepherd, called in Dr. Neville of 123, Sloane Street, who, as a medical officer in the Turkish War, has had great experience in such examinations. Dr. Neville gave it as his opinion that the arm was the right arm of a woman and that it had been in the water some two or three days. He thought that it had been cut off after death, for if it had been cut off in life the muscles would have been more contracted. The limb had been cleanly severed from the body with a sharp weapon. It had string tied tightly round it and Dr. Neville suggests that this was in order that it should be carried. The age of the person to whom the limb belonged cannot be said offhand. Superintendent Shepherd at once sent information all over the metropolis and the Thames police have set on foot an examination of all the waters above and below. The fact that the limb was found off Pimlico gives no clue to the place where it was thrown into the river. The police records of missing persons have been carefully searched but they yielded nothing that could be described as a clue. Within the last week there have been reported to the police an average number of mysterious disappearances of women but as far as can be ascertained not one of them can be connected with the present case. It is impossible to form an opinion as to whether another revolting murder has been committed in London or whether the arm has been placed in the water as a grim joke by some medical student."

Delicious! Was Someone helping me? And there was more to it. It became known as 'The Whitehall Mystery'. The left arm was found a fortnight afterward and finally the torso. I'll tell you about them in due course. And what was that 'average number'? Would you care to hazard a guess?

The inquest into Annie's death began, as I had presumed it would, on the morning of September 12th at the Working Lad's Institute and went on, in tandem with the continuing enquiry about Polly, with various delays and adjournments nearly to the end of the month.

I was quick to learn that another Vigilance Committee had been appointed on Monday the 10th while I had been away in Bristol. It was composed of sixteen local tradesmen, the majority of them were Jewish, under the presidency of one George Akin Lusk, a respected builder and contractor. Other leading members were Mr. John Cohen, Mr. Joseph Aarons, the proprietor of the Crown Tavern, and a Mr. Harris, the secretary. Amongst the remainder were a cigar maker, a picture-frame maker, a tailor and an actor!

It was called the Mile End Vigilance Committee and one of the main reasons for its formation was the ever-present frisson of anti-Semitism. Joseph Pizer, 'Leather Apron', who had at last been apprehended, amidst yet another hostile demonstration, at the house of his relatives on Mulberry Street that very morning by PC Thicke, was known to be a Polish Jew and there was rising anti-Jewish sentiment, not only in Whitechapel but throughout the city. There had been several violent incidents in the streets already and Samuel Montagu, the Jewish MP for the Whitechapel Division of Tower Hamlets... who, incidentally, maintained a second home in Brighton just as I did... was very anxious that prominent Jewish citizens should be seen to be in the forefront of the effort to apprehend the killer.

Xenophobia. Never surprising. The population of London had swelled by twenty-five percent, adding a million souls in the twenty years preceding. Primarily due to the exodus of hopefuls from the British farm... 'Too late, dear children of the sun, for London's Feast is past and gone!'... and the immigration of Jews fleeing the pogroms in Poland and Russia. A great sadness for the ill-advised former since their life expectancy in the fresh air of the countryside had been fifty-one years, in the foul slums it was a mere twenty-eight. For the latter, I'm sure anything would have seemed an improvement to the persecutions of their homeland. However, the general economic depression, the grinding poverty, the fierce competition for jobs, well, you don't have to stretch your mind too far to understand the commonly held opinion that "no Englishman could have perpetrated such a horrible crime as that of Hanbury Street, it must have been done by a Jew." Old folk myths emerged with renewed force from the blood-boltered 'collective unconscious'. 'Passover was a festival of human sacrifice and the ritual slaughter of Christians.' Why not?

No wonder Montagu was the first to offer a reward for the murderer's capture. One hundred pounds. He nearly had the police engaged to print and distribute the posters but the Home Office got wind of it and the plan was scotched.

Bless you, Leigh-Pemberton, you pudding-headed twit!

Nonetheless, the Vigilance Committee, being a private body, did announce its intention to offer a substantial reward and had already posted handbills to that effect in shop windows throughout the East End. Amazingly, however, they had great difficulty in raising the money because people felt it was the duty of the Home Office and by the end of the month they were still only able to offer fifty pounds. Finally, in desperation, on September 27th, Lusk sent a petition to Queen Victoria herself but it too was obfuscated into nullity by the starched minions of Sir Henry Matthews.

Poor Sir Henry, he had a terrible time of it. I believe it was pure sadism on Salisbury's part that he refused to let him resign. By the by, I have been utterly shocked and dismayed to discover that there was indeed some truth to the rumours circulating the previous year that the Prime Minister had actually condoned a Fenian plot to assassinate the Queen on the occasion of her Jubilee with a bomb in Westminster Abbey! My own misdemeanours pale in the comparison!

But let me return to the Jewish question.

I agree, and it's scandalous, that here have certainly been a disproportionate number of Jewish names among the suspects. Isenschmid, Klosowski, alias George Chapman, Kaminsky, Pizer, Kosminski, Cohen, Jacobs, Lipski, even though this last had been hanged the year before! More about him shortly. I'm sorry, but you'll see I couldn't resist stirring the pot just a little.

Pizer appeared as a surprise witness on the first day of 'Dark Annie's' inquest, after two days of hard questioning at Leman Street

Station. He was given this opportunity to clear his name. I was astonished by his age. From all that I had heard said of him I had assumed a man of not more than twenty. He looked to my eyes forty at a minimum. Abberline, who had motioned me to sit beside him, whispered in my ear that the case against Pizer had proved groundless, despite the fact that he had been picked out of a police line-up and accused of threatening a woman in Hanbury Street with a knife on the morning of the murder by one Emanuel Delbast Violenia. Abberline told me he had become reluctantly convinced that this Spanish-Bulgarian vagrant was lying and probably half demented.

Pizer was described in the East London Observer as "a man of about five feet four inches, with a dark-hued face, which was not altogether pleasant to look upon by reason of the grizzly black strips of hair, nearly an inch in length, which almost covered the face. The thin lips, too, had a cruel, sardonic kind of look, which was increased, if anything, by the drooping, dark moustache and side-whiskers. His hair was short, smooth and dark, intermingled with grey, and his head was slightly bald on the top. The head was large and was fixed to the body by a thick, heavy-looking neck. Pizer wore a dark overcoat, brown trousers, and a brown and very much battered hat, and appeared somewhat splay-footed. At all events, he stood with his feet meeting at the heels and then diverging almost at right angles. His evidence was given quietly and distinctly were it not for the thick, guttural foreign accent."

Now, do you find that ever so slightly biased in the syntax, or is it just me?

Wynne Baxter questioned him about his attempt to elude arrest.

"Why were you remaining indoors?"

"Because my brother advised me."

"You were the subject of suspicion, were you not?"

"I was the subject of a false suspicion."

"It was not the best advice that could be given you."

"I will tell you why. I should have been torn to pieces!"

To think that a man should object to being hurled into eternity for something he didn't do! What audacity! What is it about these occasions that inevitably turns to farce? When I reflected on the number of poor wretches who had met with grossly unfair treatment at the Old Bailey I could not refrain from a sardonical grin every time I passed by and observed the grandly solemn figure of Justice with the sword and scales, the emblem of the supposed purity of English Law. I myself had received much discourtesy there, great want of respect, and had very often been handled in a way that I considered most blatantly unwarrantable. Utterly one-sided. A dark blot upon our constitution.

What else did I discover during those interminable days? Oh yes. Quite a lot of facts, quite a lot of data, statistics, you know, places, names, all that. And that among a dozen men there will at best be only one or two with even a fragmentary quotidian of intelligence.

Little Annie. She was forty-seven when she died. She was born Eliza Anne Smith in Paddington. Her father, George Smith, was a Lifeguardsman and had married her mother, Ruth Chapman, in 1842. They had moved to Windsor. On the first of May in 1869, Annie married John Chapman at All Saint's Church in Knightsbridge. Was he a cousin of some sort? ... my brother Edward married our first cousin, Octavia Ellenor, my uncle Thomas's daughter, at St. John the Evangelist's in Notting Hill on the 5th of November, 1866 ... They recorded their place of residence as 29, Montpelier Place, in Brompton, her mother's house. Then they had lived at No. 1, Brook Mews, in Bayswater, then at 17, South Bruton Mews, just off Berkeley Square. Doesn't sound half bad, does it? Except that those were the homes of their employers.

In 1881 they moved back to Windsor where John took a job as head domestic coachman for Josiah Weeks, a farm bailiff, at St. Leonard's Mill Farm Cottage. Not too bad at all. And they had children. Emily Ruth, born 1870, Annie Georgina, 1873, and little John in 1881. But John was born a cripple and the following year Emily Ruth died of meningitis, Annie turned more and more to drink and the marriage collapsed. The little boy was sent to a charity school and the middle child ran away with a traveling circus from France. Annie received an allowance from her husband for a few years but he died of cirrhosis of the liver, ascites and dropsy on Christmas Day, 1886, at the age of forty-four. Then she took up with a man who made wire sieves. That's why the woman had called her 'Sievey'. And then she met me.

Abberline also divulged that early that morning, the first day of the inquest, Jacob Isenschmid had been arrested and taken to Holloway Police Station. He and another man named Piggott had replaced

Pizer as the leading suspects. This Isenschmid was a pork butcher and known to be insane. He had been taken to the Islington Workhouse and then, on the advice of Dr. John Gray, to the Grove Hall Lunatic Asylum in Bow. I offered to examine him but Abberline declined.

Apparently, the reason for his arrest was his habit of continuously sharpening a long knife. Good lord, I thought, I'd better warn Freddy! Isenschmid also styled himself as the 'King of Elthorne Road'. He told Dr. Gray he could build a church by himself and that he would soon be a Member of Parliament and would blow up the Queen with dynamite. He clearly must have known more than I did of the Fenian plot. Perhaps there was a darker, more political reason for having him out of the way! Most interesting to me, however, was Abberline's description of the man's persistent delusion that 'everything in the world was his'. Delusion? I found myself entirely in sympathy. Such yearning, though perhaps muddled in the mind of a madman, is, for the sane, a Grail. Grail. 'Gradual'. Ha! Sing Alleluia! Ha, ha!

Ultimately, of course, I was the one who cleared Isenschmid and so many others of suspicion but many of them remained in unfortunate confinement as my pilgrimage wore on. Oh yes, I reached the Delectable Mountains! But you'll have to wait.

Well, actually, I'm rather bored with all these 'interesting and instructive anecdotes', too. Not very 'enlivening' in truth, are they? No. I really will try hard now to be brief.

John Richardson, the landlady's son, the one who Annie and I had watched from behind the privy sitting on the steps attending to his shoe, was the first witness. He said he'd been there at about a quarter to five, which was very likely quite correct. But then there was a discrepancy.

A Mrs. Elizabeth Long was the second witness. She was the one who had seen Annie and I in the street outside before we ventured through the hallway to the yard. She claimed that the time was half past five because she remembered hearing the clock at the Black Eagle Brewery in Brick Lane strike the half hour as she entered Hanbury Street. Well, I'm sorry, she was wrong. It was striking half past four.

The woman was looking directly at me, I fancied, as Wynne Baxter questioned her further.

"Did you see the man's face?"

"I did not and could not recognise him again. He was, however, dark complexioned..."

I certainly was not!

"...and was wearing a brown deerstalker hat."

That I was.

"I think he was wearing a dark coat but cannot be sure."

Yes, I was.

"Was he a man or a boy?"

"Oh, he was a man over forty, as far as I could tell."

Well done.

"He seemed to be a little taller than the deceased."

A good eight inches, I should say, I was stooping!

"He looked to me like a foreigner, as well as I could make out."

Well, I can't keep right on apologising for every mindless reflex of my fellow citizens, now can I.

"Was he a labourer or what?" Baxter went on.

"He looked what I should call shabby genteel," the good woman proffered.

An excellent description! A perfect oxymoron.

She had also heard us speak and reported it more or less correctly. Abberline uttered a deep sigh. His frustration was palpable. The poor man had nothing to go on and the mounting pressure on him to secure a conviction, any conviction, must have been well nigh unbearable.

Albert Cadosch, the farter from next door, was the last witness. He had heard more than I thought considering the voluble nature of his expectorations, but nothing that might provide any clue. He, at least, reported the time more or less correctly. He said that as he left for work and passed Spitalfields Church it had just gone half past five.

There was nothing more of interest in all the painstaking depositions and cross-examinations that followed for the remainder of the month. Save, of course, the brow-scratching that went on over the medical expertise of the perpetrator. But that didn't really catch fire until Wynne Baxter had coaxed Dr. George Bagster Phillips, the divisional police surgeon, to reveal the full extent of Annie's abdominal mutilations. He was hesitant about doing so at first, within earshot of the press, because of their horrible nature. He was very old-fashioned both in his dress and decorum.

In the meantime, on the 19ᵗʰ, I wrote a letter of rebuttal to the Lancet, spinning, spinning my cobweb of debate. 'The net that shall enmesh them all!'

"To the Editors of the Lancet.

"Sirs,—Being more or less responsible for the original opinion that the individual who committed the wholesale slaughter in Whitechapel was a lunatic, I beg to trouble you with this communication.

"In the interview I had with the officials at Whitehall Place I gathered that this was also their theory. In your issue of the 15ᵗʰ *inst.* you say, 'The theory that the succession of murders which have lately been committed in Whitechapel are the work of a lunatic appears to us to be by no means at present well established.' Of course, it is impossible to give a positiveness to the theory unless some more evidence can be established; nevertheless, to my mind the case appears tolerably conclusive. The horrible and revolting details, as stated in the public press, are themselves evidence, not of crimes committed by a responsible individual, but by a fiendish madman. You go on to add that 'homicidal mania is generally characterised by one single and fatal act.' Having had extensive experience in cases of homicidal insanity, and having been retained in the chief cases during the past twenty years, I speak as an authority on this part of the subject. I cannot agree with your statement."

Do you know, I actually found myself indignant as I wrote!

"I will give just one case which impresses itself upon my recollection."

It will recall itself to yours, too.

"A gentleman entered my consulting room. He took his seat, and, on my asking what it was he complained of, replied, 'I have a desire to kill everyone I meet.' I then asked him for further illustration of his meaning. He then said: 'As I walk along the street, I say to myself as I pass anyone, "I should like to kill you"; I don't know why at all.' Upon my further questioning him on the matter, he jumped up and attempted to seize a weapon from his pocket, and to give me a further, more practicable, and more realistic illustration. I was enabled, however, to frustrate him in this desire. Another case in which I was retained as expert was that of Mr. Richardson, who committed murder at Ramsgate (his homicidal tendency was not confined to one individual) and was tried at Maidstone this year; and there are many others that I could mention. Homicidal lunatics are cunning, deceptive, plausible, and on the surface, to all outward appearance, sane; but there is contained within their innermost nature a dangerous lurking after blood, which, though at times latent, will develop when the opportunity arises. That the murderer of the victims in Whitechapel will prove to be such an individual is the belief of—Your obedient servant, *etc.*"

Now, you can't say I wasn't trying to help, can you?

In that same edition, which wasn't actually published until the 22nd, there was an utterly witless bit of theoretical posturing from Henry Sutherland placed in the column just above mine. He went on about the Hunt case. The two were totally chalk and cheese! The only snippet of sense in his epistle was the "opinion that should the Whitechapel murderer or murderers be apprehended, it will be proved that he or they are of perfectly sound mind." Surely, by now, you will concur, or have I yet more convincing to do?

In the British Medical Journal, which came out the same day, there was a wondrously pompous editorial. Maudsley was mentioned and his description of 'impulsive insanity in which murder was the insane correlative of love.' Dear Henry, for all your brilliance, you never got past your double brain. Neither, alas, did you, Robert Louis. You had neither the courage to venture so far. Into the Truth beyond!

The editorial also quoted Rev. S. A. Barnett, the vicar of Whitechapel. To wit, "…within the area of a quarter of a mile most of the evil may be found concentrated…" And his suggested remedies? Police efficiency. Adequate lighting and street cleaning. Removal of public slaughterhouses. Reform of tenement ownership. The editorial's conclusion? "…All civilising influences tend to improve the brain, especially in young people; and in this way the establishment of evening classes, well-conducted clubs, and athletics tend to lessen ruffianism; while throwing open the school playgrounds at all times, and maintaining discipline in school, may train the child to civilised life."

Ah, the Great Illusion of Progress! Pour on the Repression! When will you all start listening to me?!

It was the British Medical Journal that let the cat out of the bag in that same volume. A small news item stated:

"Dr. George Bagster Phillips gave some remarkable evidence at the adjourned inquiry respecting the mutilations found on the body of Mary Anne Chapman. He expressed the opinion that the length of the weapon, which must have been very sharp, was at least five or six inches, probably more."

Correct.

"The mode in which the knife had been used, he said, seemed to indicate some anatomical knowledge. The reports published in the daily press are incomplete; it is therefore desirable to state that the parts removed were a centre portion of the abdominal wall, including the navel; two thirds of the bladder (posterior and upper portions); the upper third of the vagina and its connection with the uterus; and the whole of the uterus."

This started the ball rolling on the 'Burke and Hare' or 'American doctor' theory. Nothing was too far-fetched or sensational. Why, at one point, serious consideration was given to the possibility that the outrages were the work of an escaped gorilla!

Wynne Baxter unwisely included this in his summation, on September 26th, the last day of the inquest:

"...Within a few hours of the issue of the morning papers containing a report of the medical evidence given at the last sitting of the Court, I received a communication from an officer of one of our great medical schools..."

The same wag who bunged that arm in the Thames?

"...that they had information which might or might not have a distinct bearing on our inquiry. I attended at the first opportunity and was told by the sub-curator of the Pathological Museum that some months ago an American had called on him and asked him to procure a number of specimens of the organ that was missing in the deceased. He stated his willingness to give twenty pounds for each and explained that his object was to issue an actual specimen with each copy of a publication on which he was then engaged. Although he was told that his wish was impossible to be complied with he still urged his request. He desired them preserved not in spirits of wine, the usual medium, but in glycerine in order to preserve them in a flaccid condition and he wished them sent to America direct. It is known that the request was repeated to another institution of a similar character. Now, is it not possible that the knowledge of this demand may have incited some abandoned wretch to possess himself of a specimen?..." Oh, ho!

Baxter had at once communicated this information to Scotland Yard. Of course! Why not? A trade in illicit utera. How absolutely ghastly! How typically American!

Needless to say, a huffy refutation to this damaging theory, this "grave error in judgement", appeared in the Lancet on the 29th, on behalf of the whole medical fraternity.

Ah, the medical fraternity. Dr. Phillips, despite his thoroughgoing expertise, thought that Annie had been partly strangulated before her throat was cut, an opinion echoed in the Lancet, because of the livid swelling of her face and tongue. There are more things in heaven and earth, dear colleagues! Though, of course, he was dead right about the syncope.

At all events, Baxter continued:

"... the injuries have been made by someone who had considerable anatomical skill and knowledge. There are no meaningless cuts. It was done by one who knew where to find what he wanted, what difficulties he would have to contend against, and how he should use his knife so as to abstract the organ without injury to it. No unskilled person could have known where to find it, or have recognised it when it was found. For instance, no mere slaughterer of animals could have carried out these operations. It must have been someone accustomed to the *post mortem* room ..."

"... enabled," as the Lancet editorial put it, "to secure the pelvic organs with one sweep of a knife."

Oh, Glory! One sweep! No meaningless cuts! How sweet the savour of recognition!

The upshot of all this diligent examination of minutiae, of all the expert testimony and intense synaptic circumlocution, was the banal verdict, the same in both cases, Polly's and Annie's, on the 22nd and 26th respectively, of "wilful murder against some person or persons unknown."

Ha! Ha! Ha! What a resounding conclusion! What a pathetic waste of time and energy!

And that very day the second arm was discovered on the grounds of the Blind Asylum in the Lambeth Road!

Rumour, too, was rife that I had fled to the North Countree since a young woman had been found murdered and disemboweled at the bottom of a railway embankment at Birtley Fell, near Gateshead, on September 22nd. It was even erroneously reported that her name was Savage. I liked that. Two weeks later it became apparent that it wasn't a copycat killing after all. The perpetrator was a man with the unlikely appellation William Waddle, a simpleton who said he thought the victim was his wife. Besides, by then I had made it pellucidly clear that I was still in London.

As well as my attendance at the tedium of those inquests and keeping up my practice on the intervening days, and trips back and forth to Brighton, and the family crisis of what to do with Percy who was already turning twenty during this last week of September and whose examination results at Rugby had proved insufficiently promising to gain him entrance to either Cambridge or Oxford, to the former of which his cousin Gilbert, fully two years his junior, was to be admitted at Clare on October 8th, I had often been to Whitechapel in the evenings. I had developed more than a passing acquaintance with two of the ladies who will figure largely in the ensuing pages of this narrative and the good constables were now, to a man, benignly anaesthetized to my amateur sleuthing.

Can you appreciate that, by the 30th, I was positively slavering for blood?! I'm sure you can! You are too! Confess!

Alright, I'll describe exactly how it happened. It's no accident that I sent two more sad souls scurrying within an hour of each other.

It was a night, in retrospect, that smacked more of puckish pranksterism than the Olympian reverie that followed a month later. But my relations with Mary Kelly needed careful and patient nurture to bear their full fruit. Then yes, oh yes, I was in love. A Hercules, climbing trees in the Hesperides! You'll see, you'll see. But first…

On the evening of the 29th, I told Freddy that I was going once again to Whitechapel. He encouraged my crusade and was always very interested in the details. He left Wimpole Street at about half past six, after preparing me a light supper.

"Be careful, won't you now, sir. And wrap up warm. It looks fair to be a nasty night," he said.

I chuckled at the quaint contradiction in his phrase and said not to worry, I would see him in the morning after church as usual.

"I'll be careful not to rouse you, doctor."

Freddy was by now accustomed to my nocturnal perambulations and knew, though normally I too attended church on Sunday mornings, on this occasion I would be likely to sleep late.

The moment he was out the door I began my preparations. It was no longer a question of disguise. Though, of course, in my frequent night-time visits during the last few weeks I had not dressed in my best clothes. The easy familiarity that was achieved with the 'poor creatures of the streets' by this careful lack of ostentation proved to be invaluable. The beat-constables were amused by it and would often give me a sly, mocking wink as I passed by.

I put on an old, dark overcoat and a rather battered, broad-brimmed felt hat, as protection against the rain, and a pair of soft-soled boots. I took two items from Freddy's surgery this time, the same keen carver that had won Annie's treasured curios beneath my bed and a shorter, brilliantly-honed paring knife. I had prepared another, larger burlap bag and lined it with more oilcloth. In the cellar, too, I came across an old piece of builder's chalk and thought, yes, yes, I'll take that. And, stranger still, since I have never much enjoyed tobacco, though I occasionally indulge in the odd cigar, a very old, and very dirty, clay pipe. I took it up to the kitchen and washed it. Why I took the pipe I haven't the faintest idea. Perhaps I fancied myself as an embryonic Sherlock Holmes. Yes, yes, that was it! A Study in Scarlet. Had its appearance in Beeton's Christmas Annual been a kind of punctuation to my destiny? In coterminous resonance with Fay? ... 'The Stagge and Sheepe may be co-terminate, In Nature's finall strife!' ... Conan Doyle was a doctor, was he not? My apologies. I can hear you thinking, "Hell's bells, he's taking this a bit far, isn't he?" Am I? In any case, thus armoured, I went out.

Freddy's meteorological prognostications were coming true, it was raining, a wind was picking up and it was cold. But, as my good angels would have it, a carriage was passing directly outside and I was happy to ride in comfort all the way to Whitechapel. What a relief no longer to be forced to scuttle through fretful tunnels to my destination like the mad scopophobe Duke of Portland on his journeys from Welbeck Abbey to his city home in Cavendish Square! It was twenty minutes past nine as I calmly entered the Queen's Head.

I gathered, though I did not enquire directly, that Elizabeth Stride had been there earlier in the evening with Mrs. Tanner, the deputy of her lodging house at 32, Flower and Dean Street. On several previous occasions over the past fortnight I had gained her consent to follow on her nightly rounds in the hope of turning up some clue and I had more than once stepped in to defend her from the crude advances of some inebriate ruffian. She would be grudgingly grateful, though out of pocket, and had come to view me, I think, as a protector and benefactor, since, of course, I also made more than adequate compensation to her for any financial loss.

She was a strange woman, originally Swedish, and had her life been kinder might even have been considered attractive. She had a penchant for invention. She told me she had borne nine children. That her husband and two of her sons had been drowned when the Princess Alice sank off Woolwich and that her front teeth had been inadvertently kicked out in the disaster. That she was the daughter of the gentry in Sweden and had attended the university of Stockholm. All of which was quite untrue. But she was not without charm, there were flickers of genuine intellectual life and she was able to converse in rudimentary Yiddish. She earned a meagre subsistence charring, "among the Jews," she said, as well as by prostitution. She, among so many others, was obstinately convinced that the Whitechapel murderer would be found to be 'of the Hebrew persuasion'.

I had become more or less a regular now at the Queen's Head and it was frequently difficult to extricate myself, my presence always drawing quite a crowd anxious to share with me their views or plumb my own concerning the hour's latest rumour as to the identity of the fiend. Even Mary Kelly popped her head in the door that night.

"Nice to see you again, doctor. I'm sure we're all thankful to you for looking after us. Has anyone seen my Joe?"

They hadn't and she was gone. But no Elizabeth.

Finally, it was after eleven, I took advantage of a heated altercation between some new acquaintances over the efficacy of the police using bloodhounds in the case and, having offered my opinion that it would avail nothing, merely serve to make the police appear even more foolish than they were, I made my departure.

Now I know you will term this pure coincidence but not ten minutes later I came upon Elizabeth Stride on the arm of a pock-faced young man, whom I took to be some sort of junior clerk, at the corner of Settles and Commercial Street. At my appearance she immediately shooed him away. I can't say at all that I blamed her. I perceived a froth of unwholesome dribble on the young man's chin as he passed me by with a hollow, jaundiced glare.

"Good evening, my dear," I said as I came toward her.

"Can you lend us a bob, then, doctor?"

In truth, there was barely a trace of Swedish in her peculiar drawl, only the cast of her eyes revealed that she was continental.

"I can do better than that."

I produced the two half crowns. My talismans!

She smiled. Her mouth was crooked. Her fleshy lips drew up oddly on the left hand side.

"Is there some occasion? I'm obliged."

She took them.

"It's a rainy night," I said, affecting a casual shrug.

I don't know what she did with all the money I had paid her. I learned at the inquest that she had been to the Swedish church for charity on both the 15th and the 20th. Perhaps she had to give it to her lover, a dock-man she had been living with on and off for the past three years. He was considerably younger than she, a testament to her fading charms.

"What say we take a stroll down by the Radical's Club. We've never been there," I suggested, as I pinned a small red rose I had just purchased from a flower-girl on her jacket.

"You're a smart one, doctor," she said with a wry grin.

She set off and I followed, as was our customary practice, some twenty or thirty yards behind. She crossed Commercial Road, passing Christian and Batty Streets, to the corner of Berner where she paused and waited. I loitered in a doorway. It was just gone half eleven.

During the next ten minutes two different constables stopped and spoke to her. I didn't hear what they said. But the streets were still busy with people and each in turn continued on their respective beats. A few moments after the second constable departed I saw her catch the eye of a shortish, middle-aged man on the other side of the road. She looked quickly towards me and began walking south on Berner Street in the direction of the aforementioned club. Her instinct had, of course, been right and the man hastened to go after her. I followed.

Now, the International Working Mens' Educational Club was about a hundred yards down Berner Street, in Dutfield's Yard, on the right hand side. It was a Socialist Club and its primary membership was eastern-European and Jewish. This was the meaning behind Elizabeth's dubbing me a 'smart one' as I pinned the rose. It was, in her opinion, and, she assumed, my own, likely a good location for fishing. The club had a side kitchen-entrance beyond the wooden gates into the cobbled yard. These gates were usually left open, though, in walking past them the week previously, I had noticed there was also a wicket door cut into the more northerly of the two. At the far end of the narrow court inside there had once been a stable.

The portly little man caught up to Liz, I'll call her that from now on, it was what they all called her, 'Long Liz', coined not because of her height, she was quite short, but for her surname Stride...remember Elizabeth Long?...and they continued on past the entrance to Dutfield's Yard, stopping in at a small green-grocer's shop just two doors further on, then crossing Fairclough Street. I was able to see that, indeed, the gates to the yard were wide open.

They would pause from time to time and the little man must have told her a bawdy joke or two because I heard her laugh. This aimless, wandering dance went on for twenty minutes or more as the man's attentions heated up and he began pawing and kissing her in earnest. Then one of the constables I had seen before came round on his beat again and after that, for some reason, the little man got cold feet or Liz simply tired of his clumsy advances and he hurried off on his way down Ellen Street. Liz came back toward me.

"Cheeky little bugger bought me this," she said indignantly, holding out a small bag of cachous, "And he had the breath of a corpse himself, rude blighter!"

"Let's keep trolling," I said, amused.

Immediately she passed me by and ambled off again toward the club. We continued this cat and mouse for another forty minutes with little result. The pubs closed and the streets became more deserted. I watched an elderly man nervously boarding up the green-grocer's shop. The constable made one more round just after half past twelve. I was careful on each circuit not to let him see me. I had a good sense of his rhythm now, his beat was a long one, almost half an hour.

Liz was getting quite fed up as we came together again outside the School Board building opposite the yard. A man hurried past us and I leaned one arm casually up against the wall to obscure my face.

"No luck. Maybe some other night," she said hopefully.

Her teeth were chattering.

"Just a few minutes more," I said, firm but gentle, after the man had gone, trying my best to look encouraging.

"I'm horrible wet and …"

"Wait now, here's a likely customer if ever I saw one."

A young man had turned the corner and was proceeding down Berner Street from Commercial Road, evidently drunk and angry about something, muttering obscenities.

"Go," I whispered, "I'll watch him. I won't be far."

"Oh, alright," she grumbled, "But, look here, this is the last one tonight."

"The last. I promise."

I waited as Liz crossed over the road and met the man just outside the front entrance to the club. He was round-faced and broad-shouldered, wearing a dark jacket and a black cap with a peak. In no time he had accosted Liz rather roughly and pulled her into the street and then … damnation! … another man suddenly entered Berner Street from the same direction.

The first man took no notice of his approach. Liz began casting apprehensive looks toward me as she tried to fend off the young man's increasingly aggressive mauling. As the second man approached, something in his carriage told me he might be Jewish, the ruffian threw Liz down on the footway and she let out a muffled scream. The beast was actually attempting to mount her then and there in the midst of the puddled street and the Jew stopped, fearful, not knowing what to do. In the silence at the cessation of his footsteps the young rapist turned from his predations to look up.

"Piss off if you know what's good for you, 'Lipski'!" he snarled.

I discovered that the Jew's real name was Israel Schwartz. Poor Lipski's fate was to be reborn as an insulting taunt.

'Lipski' looked over the street at me, for some reason I had taken the clay pipe out of my pocket at that moment and was fiddling with it in my mouth, and assuming me, I suppose, to be an accomplice, thought better of interfering and hurried on his way, breaking, after a few steps, into a run. Why he claimed to the police that I had chased him, I really can't say. In fairness, it was only the Star report the next day that added the knife in my hand. Because, of course, I hadn't followed him at all, I had gone directly to Liz's aid.

"Get up, you young brute!" I said sternly, pulling her attacker roughly to his feet. "Let's see if you've got a knife about you then." I began to pat him down. "It's going to go very hard for you if you do, I promise you."

Something in the force of my demeanour and the certainty in my 'eye' convinced the young fool that I must be a detective, or, at the very least, not with impunity to be challenged, and he broke from my grasp and dashed off after the Jew.

"He wasn't our man," I said to Liz, as I helped her unsteadily regain her feet, "He hadn't a weapon of any sort. Look, here's another."

Another man was hurrying down from Commercial Street.

"In here," I said, pulling her gently backwards by the arm past the gates into the yard, "You don't need any more trouble."

The instant we were in the darkest part of the entryway, perhaps ten feet beyond the gates, I twisted her to the ground in a rapid motion pretending I had caught my foot in a rut, she hadn't time to cry out, and, grasping her neckerchief in a choke-hold with my left hand, with one swift slash I cut the life from her, severing her left carotid artery and windpipe at a stroke. We were motionless for a moment and the man we had seen a bare ten seconds before passed down the sodden street beyond the gates, oblivious. Some people simply cannot sense when they are in the presence of the Miraculous! I registered, with the omniscient, circumpolar, perceptual clarity that was the familiar of such moments, that the man was carrying a small black bag.

The candent glacier of my love looked down at Liz. Her eyes were staring wide. The only sound was the blood rushing from her neck, a Castalian head-water…into which, no doubt, you think I should have thrown myself…a rippling rill down the carriage-rut which fanned rapidly out into the yard beyond. And yet, oh yes…though you will say it is impossible…though I had rendered her incapable of vocal utterance, I heard her voice echoing to the walls…

"…I know you…!"

In perfect simultaneity, a tremulous tenor voice, from somewhere upstairs in the club, chimed mournfully in with a snatch of a Russian ballad to honour her passage…'*Recondita armonia*!'…The *Missa Solemnis*, at Heaven's rendering, could not have resounded in antiphony more exquisite!

Think you've caught me out, you opera *buffone* you, with my little reference to Cavaradossi's aria? Don't be so smug. I didn't die until 1913 and even then, so what!? I'll have you know I attended the premiere of Tosca at Covent Garden and found it to be mellifluous trash!

This passion play of mine was no soppy Sardoodledom though, I promise you. Look that one up, you Clever Dick! Hockery, dockery, dick, if you think it's all 'coincidence'!

The divine and infinite harmony into which I was impaled scintillate for that infinitely tiny slice of time, and yet I had circumnavigated the Universe, was cruelly interrupted with a sudden clash of carriage-wheels and hooves. I had to dart backwards and slide behind the opposite open gate as a two-wheeled barrow, drawn by a pony, clattered noisily into the yard, shattering the peace of our farewell and barely missing the curled foetus of Liz's body. The pony shied towards me as they clanked by.

The driver, too, had evidently noticed something for, after stopping the barrow by the side door, he came cautiously over to the body and poked it with his stick. Then, after exhaling a rather panicky grunt, if I may so term it, he ran hell for leather into the club.

Taking that as my cue, I moved swiftly to Liz's corpse and wiped my blade on her jacket. The ebbing pulse of her Divine Constituence throbbed through me as I did so. Ah, mutability! I had observed her stowing my talismans in an inside pocket of her long, bare-rubbed, black jacket, it was trimmed with greasy black fur, and I retrieved them. Then, after pausing a moment to observe the street, the good constable was not likely to return for another five minutes, I walked casually a few doors north and turned into a narrow winding passage that I knew would bring me out to the relative safety of Backchurch Lane.

I've hinted, have I not, that Liz was merely a decoy duck? I was very well aware that in Dutfield's Yard I would never be allowed sufficiency of time to enlarge upon my desires. A complete, over-arching vision of this night had had its cloven incubation during those tedious hours of inquest and the first fruit of its engendering had just fallen out much better than I could have devised.

I was bursting with self-congratulatory elation as I paused at the corner of Backchurch Lane and heard the hue and cry begin. Now! Now, I prayed, I might finally speed full sail into the Uncharted Waters, my Azores behind me!

Of course, you'll want to know by what circuitous, ineluctable magnetism I was then drawn to Mitre Square, won't you? It wasn't just some idle meander! But you won't be satisfied until you've heard the actual names of the thoroughfares, the alleyways, the bypaths. Jesus wept, can't you put that sphincter-scratching pedestrianism aside?! For the sake of all the Saints in Heaven, you fool, I flew!

Alright, alright, I'll take pity on you. After waiting until I sensed that the ensuing panic and brouhaha had fully settled its blinkers on the locus of the body in Dutfield's Yard, I passed calmly down Backchurch Lane to the corner of Gower's Walk, traversed the railway tracks from the Goods Depot, entering Great Prescot Street. I paused briefly at the corner of Leman Street. I observed a momentary hubbub at the Police Station there as three constables dashed out and raced the other way. I continued on Great Prescot to Mansell and turned left again on Swan Street to the Minories. There I turned right but, resisting the impulse to homage at Fay's urinous shrine in Fleece Court, turned left again before I reached it into the oasis of the City and Crutched Friars. There I turned right into Jewry Street, then left on Aldgate, crossing over immediately into Mitre Street and the welcoming gloom of Mitre Square.

There now, does that make you feel better? It doesn't change the truth. I flew! Perhaps it took twelve minutes from the viewpoint of your shriveled little mind but I know. I know, do you see! I was there! It took no time at all!

And nobody saw me. Not even the City constable I followed from Aldgate on. Since you're so obsessed with the time, it was now exactly, precisely, perfectly, half past one.

The constable entered Mitre Square and shone his bull's-eye about for a few seconds, then re-emerged and went on his way, turning the corner out of sight at King Street. I floated effortlessly through the square to Church Passage on the opposite side. It was utterly deserted, dingy warehouses and disused tenements, and dark. Perfect. Now all that I required was perfect timing and a perfect victim.

And it happened just like that, perfectly. I stopped a few paces before reaching Duke Street as I could see a man's back leaning against the wall at the passage end. And I heard voices. I learned later that they belonged to three Jewish gentlemen who were just leaving the Imperial Club. I caught a glimpse of them on the opposite side making their way down to Aldgate. At the same time, the man whose back was toward me, I took him to be a sailor, extricated himself from the woman I shall soon describe and made off toward Bevis Marks. The woman fairly fell into my arms.

"Steady on, dear," I said quietly, catching her. "Is something the matter?"

"Oo, la," she gasped, "I've come over all queasy like."

I recognized her, though I could not remember her name. She was clearly weak from lack of nourishment and smelled strongly of stale spirits. She had, I discovered, been newly released from Bishopsgate Police Station where she had been taken but a few hours before, hopelessly drunk. She was in a fever sweat, despite the chill and rain, and near to fainting.

"Come along, then, my dear," I said gently, picking her up into my arms like any bridegroom at the threshold, "I'll see you to your lodgings. I've a carriage waiting."

She was light as a feather and I bore her swiftly back down through Church Passage to my practiced rendezvous. She was both mentally and physically incapable of resistance, my only real concern was vomit.

"I shall get a damn fine 'iding when I get 'ome," she slurred weakly as we crossed to the very darkest corner of the square.

"Just wait here," I whispered.

I laid her down softly beside a grating. No trembling newlywed at the nuptial couch could have deposited his bride with greater delicacy. She looked up at me with watering eyes, a partner in Romance, a novitiate at Communion, humbled by the Mystery.

"'Oo are you?" she whispered, smiling beatifically.

"A friend."

She never took her eyes from mine as I slowly drew the longer blade, I had used the short paring-knife in Dutfield's Yard, and, tenderly turning her compliant head away, I carved her neck through like poached salmon.

Oh, Glory, Glory!

You will say this was impossible. Too perfect. Too easy. But I tell you that is exactly how it happened and I knew it was a Gift! I fell to my knees. "For You, for You, for You!" *Gloria in Excelsis!*

As the life pulsed rhythmically, languidly, from her left carotid artery, a peaceful bubbling, not a spate as it had been with Liz, I set quickly to my work. Thus far there was not a spot of blood upon me.

I had been most careful in Dutfield's Yard to avoid stepping in any and I took the same caution here.

I raised the layers of clothing from her loins. Lord God, she was a scrawny little creature. More than half her weight must have resided in these endless skirts and petticoats, the pockets of which were stuffed with all manner of items. I heard them given this careful accounting at her inquest:

"...a large white handkerchief, a blue striped bed-ticking pocket, two calico pockets, a cotton pocket handkerchief, a dozen pieces of rag, a piece of coarse linen, a piece of shirting, two small bed-ticking bags, two short clay pipes"...mine was long and tapering..."a tin box with tea, a tin box with sugar, a piece of flannel, six pieces of soap, a comb, a white-handled table-knife"...blunt no doubt..."a teaspoon, a red leather cigarette case, an empty match box, a piece of flannel with pins and needles stuck in it, a ball of hemp..."

Survival. Vain fetishes we all shore up against our ruin.

Like the others, she wore no undergarments, no drawers to slow the passage of my singing blade...'my sword of Spain, the ice-brook's temper'...as I opened her wide from the groin to the breast-bone. Yet her hide and the underlying musculature was surprisingly tough and, though I held the weapon firmly in both hands, in the speed and insistence of my slicing I found myself bouncing her lightly on the ground.

But you will agree from the *post mortem* evidence that, for the greater part, my attack upon this little woman's body was inspired! I whittled her like an art-work, throwing aside the obstruction of intestines, spleen, stomach, fat and deftly removing her left kidney...Michael Kidney was Liz Stride's dockman lover!...my father died of kidney failure, slipping away into uraemic coma!...and most of the desolation of her womb. These, as you know, I took with me.

I was carefully wrapping them in my oil-cloth specimen case, when a second constable's bull's-eye appeared from the north end of the square. An unexpected and damnable interruption! I lay down with my back to him and froze, breathless, curling around my beloved on the ground to obscure her. His light washed over us briefly. We cannot have been as much as eighty feet from him but, seeing no movement, I assume, he luckily turned and retraced his steps. Perhaps we seemed no more than a bundle of refuse, I can't say.

Had the sound of his footsteps made toward us I should have been forced to make a premature dash for it.

I rose again, holding my breath against the stench, the point of my blade must unfortunately have pierced her cloaca, and placed the steaming viscera, now neatly wrapped, into the pocket of my coat. I knew the other constable whom I had followed to the Square would return within moments from his beat on the south side. But my sculpting was incomplete! Her blanched white features faced the wall in virginal modesty, eyes demurely closed, a Madonna. Waxen incongruity, I thought and made it match. With the taint of her excrement still dripping from my stiletto, I slit through her cheek, severing the tip of her nose and right earlobe, a few minor finishing touches, dancing the tip of the blade on her lips and eyelids, and she was done, a Beauty! No Rodin marble amidst the perfect green of a Parisian garden could have radiated a more eloquent aura. Mute testament to God's Love.

There was blood on my hands. Rather than tarry longer I cut away a piece of apron, wiped the speckled gore from Freddy's cherished carver, stowed it, and flew like a phantom from the square past Kearley and Tonge's, through the narrow passage to St. James's Place, as a massed choir of seraphim, cherubim and thrones sang out in joy, Hosanna in the Highest! A deafening crescendo, a coruscating tidal wave of sound across the wide circumference of Heaven's Vault!

I stopped to wipe my hands. They were vibrating like steeple bells on a Sunday morning as her life force dried upon them. The glorious voices were sadly fading away and I carefully folded the piece of her apron inwards to preserve the lining before placing it in my pocket. I noticed that my fingers still smelled faintly of faecal matter. I would have to find somewhere to wash.

After several deep breaths, to make sure I had sufficiently recovered Jekyll's bedside face and subsumed Hyde's again within it, I sauntered off in the direction of Hounsditch. There was one more phase to my plan. I had an urge to jump up and click my heels, I felt frolicsome, a jaunty Puck.

I passed out of the City into Whitechapel again quite undetected, skipped down the pitch dark alley of Gravel Lane, through Ellison and Middlesex to Goulston Street where I knew on the east side near the corner of Wentworth Street were the Wentworth Model Dwellings, a mostly Jewish tenement. There, on the brick facing of Nos. 108-19, I chalked the following, much debated, *graffito*.

'The Juwes are not The men That Will be Blamed for nothing.'

Saucy Jacky! Ah, the power of the Word!

Only the City Police, in the person of Detective Constable Daniel Halse, reported my subversive fragment of Horatian ode correctly. In wildly obscure resonance...'to summon as in dreams the voices and the forms of long since buried men!'...Or is it? Ha! Sir Charles Warren and the Home Office inanely attempted to soften the enigma of my slur by changing the position of the word 'not' and placing it in front of the word 'be'. It was Sir Charles, too, who rashly ordered the little poem erased, fearful that my japery would cause a riot. Of course, it had been part of my plan from the outset to rub up the already considerable friction between the Metropolitan and the City forces, in the same way that I had intentionally queered my spoor by slipping back and forth between one jurisdiction and the other. Which was mightier, the chalk or the dagger? You choose.

To this day, I promise, I haven't the faintest notion why I wrote the word as 'Juwes'. Perhaps in some unconscious part of my mind it was connected to the medieval spelling of my own name and the Wynchelouwes of Wynchelouwe Hall. But no doubt you'll think that's pure poppycock.

I dropped the bloody, shite-smeared scrap of apron directly beneath my handiwork and sped on. Why Constables Halse and Long claimed that the rag was not there on their passage down Goulston Street a few minutes later is anyone's guess. It's possible the wind had shifted it to a more conspicuous position when they did finally discover it at nearly three o'clock. All I can tell you is that I had made my escape back into the City by ten minutes past two...even taking into account my somewhat reckless sidestep through a close in Dorset Street to wash my hands...perhaps I was just snatching a sweet, predestinate whiff of Mary Kelly...cheekily stopping to stand for a moment and admire the facade of Bishopsgate Police Station as I did so. I was so enraptured with the wild success of my escapade that I walked all the way home.

As I passed the Stock Exchange and the Bank of England in Threadneedle Street I beheld this comical sight. A hansom carriage, normally licensed to convey two passengers, came pelting out of St. Swithin's Lane with three beefy constables clinging to the rear and I can't say how many more inside. The carriage careened on one precarious wheel, heedless of collision with any passing innocent, around the corner and up Cornhill. I imagined rightly that they had been summoned from Cloak Lane Station to Mitre Square. My amusement was equally great when I read, many years later, in the memoirs of Lieutenant Colonel Sir Henry Smith, then Major Henry Smith, the Acting Commissioner of the City Police, that he was one of the passengers inside. His description of the event was most charmingly colourful!

I went on, whistling a jolly tune, an indefatigable spring in my step. I savoured the prayer and beauty of St. Paul's, guffawed as usual at the sombre hypocrisy of the Law Courts, even stopped to toast myself, sharing an unaccustomed pint with three porters by Covent Garden Market. I was frightfully thirsty. Then, after traversing the early morning hush of Soho, I arrived in Wimpole Street at five minutes past five. There I cleaned up, put the uterus and kidney in separate jars, filled the jars with wine-spirit and lay in a hot bath, as before, regarding them with wonder.

I don't suppose you will appreciate at all the wide-eyed shudder that thrilled through me as it slowly penetrated my steeping consciousness … the little woman had been suffering from Bright's disease!

After carefully placing my new treasures beside their companions and sharing a lengthy votive pause, I locked the case again, restored it to its hiding place and finally flopped contentedly into bed. It was exactly six o'clock. Clear morning light made a kaleidoscope of the gently wafting curtains. The solar wind of the life force streamed up through me from the jars in its passage to the Firmament and I was rocked by those loving, maternal arms into a deep sleep.

The Tragedy of Mental Obscurity

I awoke refreshed, feeling for all the world like Thomas Jefferson, like Garibaldi … a red shirt! … another William Morris. Lord, how it would have made father seethe to know that the Socialist League met regularly now at Kelmscott House in his beloved Hammersmith!

I'm sorry if it seems my mystic *hejira* was becoming a trifle … as you would say … 'politicised', but I simply couldn't resist putting my finger up the hypocritical bum of the Home Office. 'Concerned to protect the Jews', indeed! The British ruling class has always been gaggingly phony about its so evidently smouldering anti-Semitism. And I like Jews. Really I do. But I promise, after this momentary baiting of those Lilliputian gods, and, I admit, it was probably puerile on my part, I returned to my pilgrimage … '*puro e disposto a salire alle stelle*' … purified and ready to mount to the stars!

Now, I defy you to continue your pose of rational scepticism when I relate the following.

On the 27th of September, the Central News Agency at No. 5, New Bridge Street, near Ludgate Circus … I had passed there walking home! … had received, but for some reason had not immediately published, this infamous letter. It was written in a flowing educated hand which the syntax and punctuation belied.

25 Sept: 1888.

Dear Boss

I keep on hearing the police have caught me but they wont fix me just yet. I have laughed when they look so clever and talk about being on the right track. That joke about Leather Apron gave me real fits. I am down on whores and I shant quit ripping them till I do get buckled. Grand work the last job was. I gave the lady no time to squeal. How can they catch me now. I love my work and want to start again. You will soon hear of me with my funny little games. I saved some of the proper red stuff in a ginger beer bottle over the last job to write with but it went thick like glue and I cant use it. Red ink is fit enough I hope ha.ha. The next job I do I shall clip the lady's ears off and send to the police officers just for jolly wouldnt you. Keep this letter back till I do a bit more work then give it out straight. My knife's so nice and sharp I want to get to work right away if I get a chance. Good luck.

Yours truly

Jack the Ripper

Dont mind me giving the trade name

A postscript was written sideways, as you see.

wasnt good enough to post this before I got all the red ink off my hands curse it. No luck yet. They say I'm a doctor now ha ha

Now, what about it? Wouldn't you swear I wrote that? But I didn't! "No time", "love my work", "soon hear", "funny little games", "ha ha", "clip the lady's ears off", "doctor", "ha ha", and, by the by, I also relish nothing more than a good, cold mug of British ginger beer.

And what do you say to the fact that the editor did hold the letter back, only telling Scotland Yard of it on the 29th? Chief Constable Williamson and the others had quite a jolt, I'll wager, that Sunday morning after!

A second missive, a blood-stained postcard, written in a similar hand though much less interesting from my point of view, clearly taking advantage of known information, was received by the Central News in the first post on Monday.

> *I wasn't codding dear old Boss when I gave you the tip. You'll hear about*
> *saucy Jack's work tomorrow double event this time number one squealed a bit*
> *couldn't finish straight off. had not time to get ears for police thanks for keeping*
> *last letter back till I got to work again.*

> *Jack the Ripper*

The two souses at the Central News, whose infantile invention these letters were, must have thought themselves thrice blessed by the inconceivable synchronicities apparent in the first! I sincerely hope, too, that it frightened them a little. It certainly thrilled and frightened me.

In another way, I was angry about it. I am not, nor ever have been, "down on whores". I loved those women! And the name, the name was so excruciatingly trite. My grandfather was partly to blame, I suppose, championing the penny-dreadfuls. And, of course, I could see from whence their witless inspiration came. W. H. Ainsworth's soppy romances about Jack Sheppard, who was really nothing more than a common thief, the success of Nellie Farren's recent burlesque at the Gaiety, Spring Heeled Jack, Sixteen String Jack, oh yes, the list of bugbears, forebears and bogy men goes on and on. And, indeed, 'rip' was, from a literalist's point of view, an apt description. Though surely you can vouchsafe by now that my eviscerations were not the work of some pea-brained Ourang-outang! It was utterly infuriating to me to have this perfect attestation of the Divine, this exemplar, this sunset and evening Star, trivialised by a pair of pub-crawling hacks! You can understand why I refrained from using such a juvenile anonym in my own letter to George Lusk later in the month. And I confess I did write quite a number of others. I'll tell you about them in due course.

Charles Moore, the senior of the two gay hoaxers mentioned above, actually telephoned me on the Sunday afternoon, wanting to quiz me about the murders! It had not gone a quarter to three and yet he was already more than tipsy. He had somehow got wind that I had been in Whitechapel on the previous evening and asked if there was anything about the present murders that might occasion me to change my opinion of the killer. He was artful not to drop any hint at the time about the letters and it was only later that week that I first began to twig that he and Tom Bulling might have been the perpetrators. I was equally devious in my response.

I told him that I certainly had not changed my mind and was gratified to see that some of my esteemed colleagues were beginning to come round to my point of view. To wit, Doctor Edgar Sheppard and Sir James Risdon Bennett. I reiterated that, in my humble opinion, our man was a homicidal lunatic goaded on to his dreadful work by a sense of duty. That religious monomania was evidently closely allied with his homicidal instincts, because his efforts were solely directed against fallen women, whose extermination he probably considered his mission, and that he possibly imagined that he received his commands from God. That the diabolical cunning of such a man renders his capture red-handed extremely problematical. That a man of this nature would be sure to read the newspapers carefully and gloat over the result of his crimes. The savage hacking and cutting of some of his victims showed without doubt that he was under the influence of a religious frenzy, and every horrible detail he probably considered redounded to his credit and proved that he was performing his mission faithfully.

Helpful to a fault, self-deprecating and scrupulously honest, the inescapable harvest of my upbringing!

I also mentioned to Moore that I had told Scotland Yard that I could very probably run down the murderer if they would follow my lead. Lunatics can frequently be caught in their own trap by humouring their ideas. I had proposed the simple expedient of placing an advertisement in a prominent position in all the newspapers, reading:

"A gentleman who is strongly opposed to the presence of fallen women in the streets of London would like to co-operate with someone with a view to their suppression."

I suggested that there be half a dozen detectives at the place of appointment to seize and rigidly examine everyone who replied. I expressed my dismay that Scotland Yard had refused to entertain the idea and lamented that, since it was quite impossible for me, as a private citizen, to seize and detain possibly innocent persons, it had to be abandoned. I sensed that Moore was now quickly tiring of this

interview...many and subtle are the uses of being thought a harmless crackpot!...for he hastily brought it to a conclusion and rang
off. The only thing that we had been able to agree on was that the
police must be completely dazed since, despite all their precautions
and carefully laid traps, the murderer had quite apparently escaped
them with ease. The gist of our little chat appeared in the papers the
next day. Ha!

Now, what about this, you Unbeliever?

I shall read in full the Weekly Herald report on the matter. I think
you'll find it's worth it.

"Another Ghastly Discovery in London. A Mutilated Body at
Westminster. About twenty minutes past three o'clock on Tuesday
afternoon..."

Yes, Tuesday, October 2nd.

"...Frederick Wildborn..."

Ha! Wild born but civil bred, no doubt.

"...a carpenter employed by Messrs J. Grover and Sons, builders
of Pimlico, who are the contractors for the new Metropolitan Police
headquarters..."

No less.

"...on the Thames Embankment, was working on the foundation,
when he came across a neatly done up parcel in one of the cellars. It
was opened, and the body of a woman, very much decomposed, was
found carefully wrapped in a piece of what is supposed to be a black
petticoat. The trunk was without head, arms or legs and presented
a horrible spectacle. Dr. Bond, the divisional surgeon, and several
other medical gentlemen were communicated with, and from what
can be ascertained the conclusion has been arrived at by them that
these remains are those of a woman whose arms have recently been
discovered in different parts of the metropolis. Dr. Nevill, who examined the arm of a woman found a few weeks ago in the Thames, off
Ebury Bridge, said on that occasion that he did not think that it had
been skillfully taken from the body. This fact would appear to favour
the theory that that arm together with the one found in the grounds
of the Blind Asylum in the Lambeth Road last week belong to the
trunk discovered on Tuesday, for it is stated that the limbs appear to
have been taken from it in anything but a skillful manner."

God pardon us our disciples.

"The building which is in course of erection is the new police depot for London. The builders have been working on the site for some time now but have only just completed the foundation. It was originally the site for the National Opera House and extends from the Thames Embankment through Cannon Row, Parliament Street at the back of St. Stephen's Club and the Westminster Bridge Station on the District Railway. The prevailing opinion is that to place the body where it was found the person conveying it must have scaled the 8 ft. boarding which encloses the works..."

A simple matter. I had done much the same two nights previous, sailing over the fence by the Goods Depot railway in a single bound.

"...and, carefully avoiding the watchmen who do duty by night, must have dropped it where it was found. The body could not have been where it was found above two or three days, because men are frequently passing the spot..."

Yes, but no one really looks, do they.

"...One of the workmen says that it was not there last Friday because they had occasion to do something at that very spot..."

Absolutely certain, hmm? No doubts whatever?

"...It is thought that the person who put the bundle there could not very well have got into the enclosure from the Embankment side, as not only would the risk of detection be very great, but he would stand a good chance of breaking his neck. The parcel must have been got in from the Cannon Row side, a very dark and lonely spot, although within twenty yards of the main thoroughfare. The body is pronounced by medical men to have been that of a remarkably fine young woman..."

Ah, euphemism. Clearly she had firm, plump breasts.

"...The lower portion from the ribs has been removed. The *post mortem* examination was held this morning and the result will be made known at the inquest."

Despite its amateurish aspects, I found myself in admiration of the perpetrator's daring. I even had a very peculiar sensation that I might somehow have been involved, that the deed had been committed by some other parallel facet of myself, in some unknowable side-show hall of mirrors. The same absurdly irrational feeling that came upon me some years later after the murder of that failed actress in New York, poor Carrie Brown. Her nickname was 'Old

Shakespeare', since, like father ... yes, I own to it, like myself ... she was over-fond of quoting the Immortal Bard.

Further, there were many titillating, inescapable resonances in the warp and woof of the little soul's biography who so submissively embraced her death in Mitre Square. It's only right and proper, after all, that I tell you something about her. I relate it as I learned it during my obligatory appearance, and very diligent attention, at the two days of her inquest. Wynne Baxter conducted one inquest, Elizabeth Stride's, with his usual rigour, at the Vestry Hall in Cable Street, on October 1st, 2nd, 3rd, 5th and 23rd. The other was held, with equal care to detail but mercifully much greater dispatch, before S. F. Langham, the City Coroner, at the City Mortuary in Golden Lane on October 4th and 11th.

The little votary's name was Catherine Eddowes. She was born in 1842 ... the same year as Edward ... in Wolverhampton, in the midst of a brood of eleven children. Her father George was a tinplate varnisher. They moved to London when 'Kate' was two. The census of 1851 recorded the family living in Bermondsey. Their life was no frolic. Kate's oldest brother was born a half-wit. In 1854, the youngest child died of convulsions at five months and the following year Kate's mother died of phthisis. Dispersal followed. Her older sisters were in domestic service but the younger children were sent to the grim environs of the Bermondsey Workhouse and Industrial School. Kate was fortunate to be rescued and returned, for a time, to Wolverhampton to live with her aunt Elizabeth. But she robbed an employer and ran away to Birmingham, taking up with a man named Thomas Conway.

The letters 'TC' were apparently tattooed on her left forearm but I hadn't noticed.

She lived with Conway for some twenty years but they were never married. They had three children, a girl and two boys. Finally, in 1881, they had separated. Her sisters gave the inquest conflicting reports as to the reason. Elizabeth claimed Conway used to beat her, Emma blamed the failure on Kate's excessive drinking. She then formed a relationship with a man named John Kelly and they had lived together, on and off, in a common lodging house at No. 55 Flower and Dean Street for the last seven years ... Liz Stride was living at No. 32! ... there was no doubt that I had recognised Kate, and she me, from my rambles of discovery amongst those rotting slums...but Kate had become estranged from her siblings, and her daughter Annie, due to her indigence and scrounging. That autumn, she and Kelly had been down to the Kentish countryside near Maidstone hop-picking...they had only come back to London on Thursday, September 27th!...and for all their exertions they were without money.

Kate put her name down as 'Jane Kelly', with the fictitious address of No. 6 Dorset Street...another Mary Jane Kelly lived at the rear of No. 26 where I had washed my hands!...on a pawn ticket for a pair of boots that was found in one of the tin boxes in her possession. She and Kelly had 'popped' the boots for half a crown at Jones' Pawnshop in Church Street on the morning of the 29th and shared what turned out to be a last breakfast together at Cooney's. They had parted company in Hounsditch at about two in the afternoon. Kelly had warned her to be careful of the fiend and to be home early. Kate had replied:

"Don't you fear. I shan't fall into his hands."

But somehow, in the interim, she had managed to inundate her system with drink and 'fall' is, as you know, precisely what she did. When James Byfield, the station sergeant on duty at Bishopsgate, enquired her name as the constables brought her in, she had mouthed the single word, "Nothing."

I believe that, far more than any of the others, little Kate was aware. She 'knew' me. I think it is very much within the bounds of likelihood that she had divined I was the murderer even before our paths crossed that night. Why else would she have accepted death so placidly, almost, dare I say it, with welcoming arms, unless she knew, by some strange instinct, that it was preordained? It was exactly as though the little drama we played out together had been rehearsed in every detail. On the other hand, I suppose, like Liz, she might simply have been told that I was a doctor and so trusted me to be her good Samaritan and, true to my promise, help her home. Perhaps she thought my knife a magic wand. I cannot submit which may be the truth now with any surety.

Which do you think? Will you be daring and give credence to the former possibility?

In any case, in the humdrum workaday world, I had certainly stirred up a storm of outrage.

"We hear startling news of abounding sin in this great city. Oh God, put an end to this and grant that we may hear no more of such deeds. Let thy gospel permeate the city and let not monsters in human shape escape Thee!"

Amen!

So implored Mr. Spurgeon in his homily at the Metropolitan Tabernacle on Sunday, September 30th, and I'm sure his prayer was echoed from pulpits throughout the land.

Suddenly everyone was outvying the other to offer a reward. Sir Alfred Kirby, Colonel of the Royal Engineers, Tower Hamlets Battalion, offered one hundred pounds and the services of fifty militia men. The Financial News editor, Harry Marks, sent the Home Office three hundred pounds on behalf of his reader-ship. Both were refused. But the Lord Mayor of London, at the suggestion of Sir James Fraser, the Commissioner of the City Police...not to be confused with James Frazer, the mytholo-gist...mythologiser?...who was then only thirty-four and whose rise to prominence had just begun the previous year with the publication of his essay on 'Totemism'. The first volumes of his *magnum opus*, The Golden Bough, were two years away. How his theory of our progress from savagery to civilisation, through magic to religion to science, fascinated me. How it paralleled my own evolution, from innocence to experience and my triumphant rise to higher innocence...Ha!...how young I felt and feel!...Ha, ha, ha, ha!...offered five hundred pounds and private donors followed suit. By Tuesday, October 2nd, the total possible reward to anyone who could provide information that might lead to the killer's arrest was well over fifteen hundred pounds! And it was also suggested that a full pardon should be offered to any accom-plice, not involved in the actual killing, if they now came forward. But still the Home Secretary remained obdurate. Even a shocked telephone call from Queen Victoria herself could not soften the resolve of Sir Henry Matthews, nor his chinless amanuensis, Sir Evelyn Ruggles-Brise. How the two of them must have sweated over this issue! 'How, how can we now give in to popular feeling and yet not be covered in ridicule and contempt?' Silly, silly, silly little men. The public would have covered them under a mile-high cordillera of stallage had they been given the opportunity!

The newspapers and magazines, from the scholarly to the scurrilous, all shrieked in horror and every callous leg-man in Fleet Street was suddenly scribbling a jeremiad. It became a deafening caterwaul, ululating, disharmonious, a strident clarion demand for social change.

Thus, the Pall Mall Gazette:

> *The sights and sounds of Whitechapel are an apocalypse of evil. The main thoroughfares are connected by a network of narrow, dark and crooked lanes, every one containing some headquarters of infamy. Underneath the prosperous stratum of Jew dealers the district seems to swarm with a nomadic mob of dehumanised men and women and unchildish children.*

The Weekly Herald:

> *The East End of London with its slums, its rookeries, its gin-palaces, its crowded population living in poverty, and not knowing where its tomorrow's dinner will come from, has claims of the most pressing kind on the West End, where idleness and luxury are the temptations that assail virtue and charity, where in the gilded saloons, at the gaudy parties, in the ball room and the theatre are wasted in empty show or worse that wealth which is entrusted to those who have it for the dispensation of mercy, for feeding the hungry, clothing the naked and spreading truth where error holds sway.*

The British Medical Journal:

> *It would be most lamentable if this anxious period of mental disturbances, horror and grief should pass away, leaving behind it only the records of an unprecedented series of crimes .... There is a much deeper lesson in the story. We do not echo the vague outcry of blame against highly-placed officials which usually arises under such circumstances. The true lesson of this catastrophe has*

*been written by the Rev. S. A. Barnett, the vicar of
Whitechapel, whose life has been spent combatting the
terrible conditions of social degradation and public
indifference of which these murders are the outcome and
the evidence.*

The Lancet, in summation:

*It does not reflect creditably on our boasted civilisation to
find that modern society is more promptly awakened to a
sense of duty by the knife of a murderer than by the pens of
many earnest and ready writers.*

Hear, hear! But really, as you might say, 'What else is new?' And
what about this? The Star published a leader: "Is Christianity a
Failure?" and for several days thereafter they were deluged with a
voluminous correspondence earnestly discussing the issue! My goodness, how my modest little murders did get people in a tizzy.

Of course, doubt and questioning were much in the air. Mrs.
Humphry Ward's novel Robert Elsmere had just been published and
had rapidly become a best-seller. The story of a young clergyman who
resigns his orders to take up social work in the East End of London!

But let me ask you to reflect on something. The carnage and utter
immorality of colonialism was in full swing at the time. I'll leave aside
the bottomless misery caused by my fellow countrymen. Let's just
examine the Belgians for a moment. Did you know that the mad
King Leopold II was once under suspicion of being 'Jack the Ripper'?
In truth, there can be no comparison between us. Just think of the
horrors of slavery! This rapacious, evil king callously closed his eyes
to the deaths of ten million Africans in his country's frantic scramble
for the profits from ivory and rubber. Your precious Henry Morton
Stanley was part of this. Well, to be just, he wasn't American, he was
really a Welsh bastard named John Rowlands, reared in a workhouse.
Progress? Coagulated sap from the jungles of central Africa was
shipped to 'civilised' Europe in vast quantities and transmuted into
pipes, gaskets, wire insulation and tyres, tyres, tyres! Did you know
that in the process of collecting this pallid, sticky gold, the practice
grew up of delivering baskets of hands and other body parts to the

white overseers, along with the sap, just to show that sufficiently rigorous methods had been used in meeting the all important quota?

Ten million people! And that was just in the Congo. An unfathomably vicious crime against humanity like so many others preceding and following without cessation to the present day! What humanity, that tut-tuts and exults in masturbatory hand-wringing about the mis-termed 'violence' of my little religious observances and yet cannot bear to look at itself?! No one in England at the time could dare to face the fact that these insignificant murders were being committed by a man exactly like themselves. I doubt you can credit it now, can you, in all truthfulness? A man who was merely struggling to find a way out of the morass of his internal conflict, to burst through the crippling neuroses imposed by his Victorian *Weltanschauung*, and become once again a Whole Being, pure and unafraid, basking in the Glory of God's Eternal Goodness! As my old friend and colleague, Batty Tuke, summed it up, in a letter to the British Medical Journal, after my desperate night in Miller's Court, "...there are incentives to crime that are unappreciable by the great mass of humanity...", if I may take him far out of context and far, far beyond his meaning. Sorry, Batty.

What is it about our species and its 'cobweb veil', the smothering cocoon of illusion that we seem incapable of doing without? Why are we so unwilling to see the wood for the trees? Why can't we cleanse the Doors of Perception and be at home in the Infinite? Why? It was my opinion at the time that the only way to do God's Will was to break through these shackles of everyday conscious life and come face to face with His Blessed Mercy and Protecting Love in that Beauty beyond worldly understanding. That He would provide the safety net against Perfect Dissolution. That Wholeness and Peace lay there and were attainable by Right Action. Why else would I have been doing this? I was attempting, in all straightforward honesty and good faith, to follow the teaching of Our Lord and Saviour, Jesus Christ.

That is why I was less than amused when Moore showed me a copy of a letter that had been received by the Star, but not published as it was thought decidedly unhelpful to the ongoing public debate regarding the 'failure of the Christian ethic'. The letter had been forwarded to Moore by the editor of the Star because he wanted someone to share privately in what he considered a good joke. I made a dry pretense of mirth when Moore put it under my nose but really, at the time, I found it infantile. A 'cheap shot', in your vernacular. Here it is.

"Sir. Why do you try to put the Whitechapel murders on me? Sir Charles Warren is quite right not to catch the unfortunate murderer, whose conviction and punishment would be conducted on my father's old lines of an eye for an eye which I have always consistently repudiated. As to the eighteen centuries of what you call Christianity, I have nothing to do with it. It was invented by an aristocrat of the Roman set, a university man whose epistles are the silliest middle class stuff on record. When I see my name mixed up with it in your excellent paper I feel as if nails were going into me—and I know what the sensation is like better than you do. Trusting that you will excuse this intrusion on your valuable space. I am, Sir &c., J.C."

Moore told me that the Star had received a second letter in the same hand, signed 'Shendar Brwa'.

Though I did agree with Shaw about disciples and some of the prissier groanings of St. Paul, I was totally unwilling to mock the agony of the Crucifixion. But, yes, of course, throughout history religious observance has too often been little more than a cobweb veil of lies, a mendacious cloak of zealotry in the service of domination and cold avarice. However, I was trying my best to fashion a fresh path.

The violence inherent in the nature of the human animal is not itself a danger to society, it is the two-faced attempt to smother that primal energy in the name of 'civilisation' that has in the end provoked the greatest bloodshed!

Let me briefly list some of the ludicrous alternatives put forward to combat the clearly excruciating and unswallowable notion that the perpetrator of these hideous murders might be a normal, English, family man.

I have twice made oblique reference to the woman from the Isle of Wight and her obsession with Edgar Allan Poe's hirsute culprit in The Murders in the Rue Morgue. Well, I had 'soundlessly disappeared', I grant her that. But, truly, the Song the Sirens sang is not beyond all conjecture!

Further to that absurdity, I was, at various suggestion:
'Badly disfigured by disease.'
'Missing my privy member.'

'Suffering from syphilis and using the part cut off from the woman as a kind of poultice to suck off the virus from my ulcers.'

How singularly revolting!

'Chinese.'

'Malay.'

'Suffering from sunstroke.'

'An East Indian hill tribesman, preserving the female generative organ as an amulet.'

Not quite, but close.

'A follower of Buddha.'

'A Thuggee offering human sacrifice.'

'Possessed by the phases of the moon.'

Yes, we've discussed this.

'A woman, in disguise as a slaughterman. Or a midwife.'

Why not?

'A foreigner of any description.' Pole, Russian, Frenchman, Belgian, German, it didn't matter. 'Germans were fond of skinning people and pasting these second skins on as disguises, using American glue.' Americans always do seem to be singled out with an especially snotty brand of puckered indignation, don't they? And on and on *ad infinitum*. They should all be 'kicked out of the country into the sea!'

Hear, hear! Don't forget to include the Royal Family!

'A Jew.' 'Well, of course, he hides himself away in an old vault in the Jews' Cemetery, don't he?'

Of course.

'A madman.'

Alright, I'll stop.

My personal favourite was the letter from a widow who granted that I might be an Englishman but was piously convinced that 'respectable females' had nothing to fear from me. She was quite plainly a neighbour of mine though, alas, she didn't vouchsafe her name.

"... I feel certain it was him whom I saw one night in the Devonshire Street end of Cavendish Court on or about the 30th of August. Although conducting himself in a disgusting manner he allowed one to pass without a murmur ... I fervently hope that, when in the agony of his own death he takes the last look for mercy, the sigh of his soul may be Jesus, sweet Jesus ..."

Well, thank you very much, my dear, I hoped so too.

But is it possible that it was me that night? Doing what, exposing myself? I hardly think it likely. The weather was vile. She was not certain of the date and did not specify the time of night, though I had been impatient and left early, but, in any case, I recall walking directly from Wimpole Street to Oxford Circus, not passing by Devonshire. Yet, as in all similar instances, I could never be perfectly sure.

Meddling monkey or busy ape? Both the aforementioned ladies may have been correct, in their way.

All this feverish avoidance, what is it really, the fear of Death? The Grim Reaper? Is that what causes us all to split asunder after birth into a double-brained monstrosity? The conscious half struggling pointlessly to maintain a fantasy of control, the unconscious knowing the truth all the while. Nineteenth Century European Man was perfect in his Mind and crowed the superiority of his rationalism over all other races, the 'White Man's Burden', setting himself apart with chilling finality from the natural world. To the ultimate ruin of both. What is so problematical in accepting that we are One? The fact of our common mortality proves it so! Ah yes, the Conqueror Worm. No, the ruffian on the stair.

'Rule Britannia, Britannia rules the waves, Britons never, never, never shall be slaves!'

This schizophrenia, this hubris, has never, I think, been more pronounced, in all the sorry, deluded history of our species, than among my Victorian contemporaries. What can you say to the fact that William Gladstone, whose party, by the by, I helped bring back to power in the election of 1892, took relish in inviting prostitutes to his home and then harangueing them about the sinful error of their ways while feeding them cakes and hot chocolate? And you think I'm crazy?! He, too, was quite unshakeable in his belief that his work and God's Work were one and the same. Or William Morris, that great artist and poet and champion of the lower classes, enjoying the freedom of his comfortable inheritance? Or Shaw and the Fabians with their dilettantish credo of 'gradualism'? *Cunctator*, indeed! Wits, theorists, coffee-house procrastinators! 'Cork-headed, barmy-brained gowks!' Or the other side of the coin, horror of horrors, my father. And myself. Oh yes.

Delay, delay, delay, or fight, fight, fight, or work, work, work, anything but face the apparently unbearable fact that we are not 'going' anywhere! All our high-minded thrusting forward is nothing more than pretence, side-step, window-dressing and busy-work at best. At worst, in those in whom it is truly unconscious, a lethal combination of blind egomania and unacknowledged terror!

But what is humanity to do on this earth for Eternity, they wail in strident unison, if not to 'progress'? What dismal paucity of imagination!

Sorry. Oh dear, I promised I wouldn't, didn't I. '*Si peccavi, insciens feci.*' And I'm getting ahead of myself.

It inevitably descended into farce. The police were barraged with an endless fusillade of quaint suggestions as to how they should proceed. You are already familiar with some of my own slyly disingenuous advice. Consider these gems:

"Dress up policemen as women. Don't forget they must be clean-shaven. They should wear chain-mail corsets and a thin, steel collar for protection, flexible, of course, with a broad tapering piece bent up under the jaw, attached to the terminals of a storage battery so as to deliver, by the deft flick of a switch, a powerful electric shock to the assassin and thus discomfit and disable him and render him capable of arrest."

No mention was made of the inevitable shock to the transvestite constable!

"'Daughters of Eve' should carry papers pasted with birdlime to slap on the back of the assailant unawares so that he might be later clearly identified."

When, during an attack, the unfortunate woman should be able to retrieve this from her handbag seems to have escaped the writer's notice.

"Female dummies might be placed in all the particularly dark and lonely spots, attached with arms and legs on springs that would be suddenly released when touched, entrapping any attacker like an Octopus and emitting a shrill, whistling sound."

"Let the police beware! The killer uses a chloroform-soaked handkerchief. Be sure to arrest anyone who comes too close and blows his nose!"

"Clear Whitechapel of policemen, except a hundred pairs of detectives and an equal number of prostitutes, sufficiently paid, perhaps two shillings per night, as decoys. Too many will only frighten our man away."

This one was not bad: "Hold a public meeting to discuss fresh ways of trapping the assassin and, since he would be bound to attend out of self-interest, lock all the doors."

Another similar to my own: "Place an advertisement in the papers thus: Medical Man or Assistant Wanted in London, aged between 25 and 40. Must not object to assist in occasional *post mortem*. Liberal terms. Address stating antecedents."

Pity I was too old!

And lastly, this delightfully bloodthirsty epistle, Abberline himself showed it to me:

"Dear Inspector. The officers, once arrayed as pitiable women of the street, should wear soft velvet-covered collars underlaid with fine, sharp-pointed stings that the infernal beast may be thus wounded. Then may the officer turn quickly round and take hold of the murderer above the hand, forcing it with all his power into the breast of the scoundrel. Thus the monster must bear his own knife into his own breast or let fall it. Don't give this idea to anyone except the Chief of Police, as your lordship may warn unconscious that way the bloodhound. For who can say this criminal don't belong to a rich family. The officer or officers should look at every suspicious woman or all women in general. The Devil may know what is often in such a petticoat!!!!"

Good heavens, burning, scalding, stench, consumption, pah, pah, pah! An ounce of civet, please!

I was particularly amused by my characterisation as a 'bloodhound'... Do the names Barnaby and Burgho spring readily to your mind perchance? If not, they soon will... To me the breed has always epitomised the empty-headed baying of lop-bollocked bureaucrats, though I'm acutely aware how very, very unfair that is to the dogs.

And who, indeed, 'can say this criminal don't belong to a rich family'? Well, not rich, but comfortable. At least we were before all the undignified scrabbling that ensued upon my father's death, and continued on for those many wretched years, had so separated and reduced us.

On the third of October the Metropolitan Police placed posters with facsimiles of the two concocted missives from 'Jack the Ripper' outside all their stations and asked the public's help in trying to identify the handwriting. They also sent copies to the press which were published in several newspapers the following day. From that moment on, of course, the silly appellation was on every tongue, as it remains to this day.

My sole concern attending the inquests was that the Jew, 'Lipski', would be called and perhaps have some memory of my face. He was the only person, beside the abusive young man who pinioned Liz in the roadway, who had had a good look at me. I felt sure the young blackguard would not show himself for fear of incrimination. But the Jew, that was a worrying possibility. I discovered that he had gone to the Leman Street Station on Sunday evening with an interpreter to inform the police what he had seen. Despite their best efforts to keep his evidence secret, the Star also ran him to ground and published an error-strewn version of his story on Monday, October 1st. I was relieved to read in their account that the man, whom they described only as Hungarian, did not have any very clear recollection of me. Later on though I was told that he had given a fairly accurate description to Chief Inspector Swanson. But, thanks to the mealy-mouthed desire of the authorities to suppress any evidence that might stir up animosity toward the Jews, this man was never called to testify at the inquest! I found out that his name was Israel Schwartz, though I don't think even the investigators were quite sure. I never set eyes on him again.

'For thou hast striven with God and with men, and hast prevailed. Bless you, son of Jacob.'

The discussion concerning my degree of anatomical expertise was renewed. Dr. Frederick Gordon Brown, the City Police Surgeon, and Dr. Philips, who had also been called to Kate's autopsy, were unable to agree. The latter felt that the murderer of Dark Annie had been a different person because of the greater skill shown in her evisceration. 'There were no meaningless cuts'! But he didn't think to imagine the different situations. In Hanbury Street it was dawn and I had plenty of light, the reverse was true in Mitre Square. What the devil did he expect?

I learned a good deal more about little Kate that week but not from the professional men. I heard it in the pubs of Whitechapel, particularly from her common-law husband, John Kelly, whom I was at a loss to console. He was drowning his sorrows in the Princess Alice when I came across him. It was Wednesday evening, October 3rd, the day after he had been to Bishopsgate Station and then to the City

Mortuary to identify her corpse. Surprisingly, he was a pleasant-look-ing man with an honest face, sporting a small moustache and a few unshaven hairs beneath his lower lip. He was seated amongst a mot-ley rag-tag of condolence as I came in.

"Oo, look now, John," said an old man sitting beside him comfort-ingly as I approached, "'Ere's the good doctor."

"Good evenin', your lordship," said a woman I knew on his other side. "It's been somethin' terrible this 'as for poor John. 'E still can't 'ardly believe it's 'appened."

"I'm sure," I nodded in genuine sympathy. "Do you mind if I sit down with you?" I said to Kelly, "I'd like to ask you a few questions if you're up to it."

"No, no, do," he said.

He was a bit unsteady on his stool and the look in his tired eyes was vague and otherworldly, a distance born of pain. I could tell from his face that he wasn't an habitual drinker. The older man made room next to Kelly and I sat down. The crowd pulled close to listen.

"I'm very sorry for your loss."

It was true, I was.

Kelly nodded ruefully and tears welled up in his eyes.

"My poor ol' gal," he spluttered.

"'E didn't 'ave no clue it was 'er till yesterday," said one of the gag-gle, a broad, capacious woman with a purple, cross-veined face.

"How did you find out?"

I directed my question to Kelly.

"It were the pawn-ticket," chimed in the older man, now standing at my elbow.

"'E read about it in the papers. In Cooney's. An' then 'e saw she 'ad the letters 'TC' tattooed on 'er arm an' that was it. 'E knew," said the flush-faced woman.

"You could 'ave blown me over with a feather," Kelly sobbed.

"I don't know 'ow 'e 'ad the strength to go to the police at all, after that. Really I don't," said the woman, dabbing her eyes too.

I know you may deem this special pleading but I had a constant struggle with my own emotions throughout the interview.

"I knew before they took me down to see 'er." Kelly was more con-tained now. "I knew it was 'er for all the way she was cut up. She never went to 'er daughter's at all."

"Was she intending to?" I asked.

"Yes. An' I wish to God she 'ad."

His lower lip was still trembling.

"Maybe she did, John," suggested the woman, "She'd got 'erself some lolly someplace."

"No, she never. 'Er Annie moved away from King Street more than a year ago. 'Er sister Liza told me after I'd fetched the police to 'er this morning."

"They should never 'ave let 'er loose from the station, that's what I say. She'd be alive now. It's a sin what they done, doctor, 'pon my soul it is," the woman added vehemently.

"Now, now," said Kelly, "She likely gave 'em such a time of it they 'adn't a choice."

He was grinning softly now into his beer in private remembrance.

"Does no one at all in the whole district have any clue as to who this dastard might be?" I asked with my best Jekyll face. "Alas, it goes without saying that the police still haven't anything to offer."

They chuckled ruefully, then shook their heads.

"No one," they concurred, in patchwork unison.

"Do you think it's possible she might have known the man?"

"No," said Kelly, dismissive. "Why? She was 'armless. Jolly. Always singing. 'Oo that knew 'er could have brung themselves to cut 'er up like that? My poor sweet ol' gal. We'd lived together seven year an' never 'ad a quarrel."

"I don't know, John," said the woman, "The super down at Mile End says she told 'im as 'ow she did. She'd come back to claim the reward money, she said, for she knew the man."

"She said a lot of things," Kelly rejoindered. "She never said nothing like that to me. Never."

"You can't be too sure, though," I said, "She might have. Didn't she ever say a name?"

"Not as I know of," replied the woman.

I'm sure that every hair was stiff upright beneath my clothes! My intuition had been correct! She did know me! She had gone to her death willingly, the bride of Christ!

Mile End casual ward was where Kate had spent the night before her death. As you can imagine, I went there bright and early the next morning and was audacious enough to interview the superintendent but he could confirm nothing more than what I had been told already. And no, she had never mentioned a name, so that was that. I felt great compassion for poor John Kelly. He was a decent, simple man. However, I did not consider he had anything to gain from the truth.

Did you know that at Bishopsgate that night, as she was being discharged into my care, little Kate had finally given her name as Mary Ann Kelly? But I forgot, you don't have any truck with resonances, do you.

You won't find this entertaining then, either.

After having heard nothing but 'Jack the Ripper', 'Jack the Ripper' for two full weeks and having listened to a stream of mind-numbing theories on the etymology of the word 'Juwes', I decided on another little jape.

On Sunday evening, October 14th, I was very tired and stayed at home reading and catching up on some correspondence. A letter of congratulation was overdue to my younger cousin Reginald. He had graduated in Law from Caius in 1881 and had been called to the bar at Lincoln's Inn the following year at the age of twenty-four. I reflected with sadness about Percy who was still so badly floundering. Reginald had wasted no time in bolstering the proud tradition of the family, as an author his work was already voluminous. In 1885, he had published The Law of Private Arrangements between Debtors and Creditors in eight volumes. Then, in 1887, The Law relating to Protestant Nonconformists and their Places of Worship, equally vast in scope and detail. And now, this year, an enormous analysis and critique of The Deeds of Arrangement Act, which had passed the Commons just the previous autumn. It, too, was in eight turgid volumes! Dear sweet Jesus Christ in Heaven, I thought, yet another 'eminent Victorian' in the bud. I made my note to him succinct and cobwebbed, I could not bear to do more.

Then I sat back to look over the new edition of the Lancet. As I've predicted, you won't find this of any consequence, but what should greet my eyes, a report on a lecture delivered at London Hospital by my dear young friend Freddy Treves, he was then surgeon and lecturer on anatomy there, recounting his attendance the previous spring on a case of hernia into the foramen of Winslow!

The significance of this, to me, was monumental! Besides the fact that such cases are extraordinarily rare, this obscure orifice, situated between the greater and lesser sacs of the peritoneum, was named for the great Danish anatomist Jacob Winslow whose renown had flourished in Paris during the first half of the last century. But what was deeply poignant, he had suffered a spiritual crisis and converted to Roman Catholicism after reading the treatises of Jacques-Benigne Bossuet. Further, he had taken Jacques-Benigne as his baptismal name and that, in consequence, was the inspiration for my own father's name, Benignus!

What is more, but of absolutely no moment or meaning, you mugwump, this Jacob Winslow became an anatomist because he could not bear the sight of blood! He never once himself performed an operation!

Also of paramount interest to me was Freddy Treves' theory that this particular hernia, which had ultimately caused the death of a young twenty-six-year old laundry keeper, was the result of the foramen being abnormal, a reversion to a lower anatomical type.

"...Even in animals with large great omenta, as in some of the *carnivora*, the foramen of Winslow is much larger than in man. In the present case it is reasonable to assume that with the abnormal position of the intestinal canal was associated an abnormally large foramen of Winslow..."

I sat transfixed for a long while, looking at those words, letting them swim in my mind.

Foraminose means 'full of holes'! Abnormally large *carnivora*! For Amen of Winslow!

A decision had been made. I stood abruptly and went upstairs, retrieving the jar containing Kate's kidney from beneath my bed and carrying it back down to the scullery. After carefully rescuing my prize from the preserving spirits with a pair of tongs I placed it on a cutting board and began, with the help of the razor-sharp paring-knife which had so gently caressed the neck of 'Long Liz', to trim it up. I removed the rag-end portion of the suprarenal gland, cut away a length of ureter and a few vestigial scraps of vein, finally dividing the organ longitudinally, leaving the small remaining segment of renal artery intact on one side.

As I went methodically about my dissection, humming contentedly, a host of seemingly unrelated details swirled up from somewhere deep within.

Richard Bright, though more than twenty years my father's senior, had been a respected professional colleague. He was appointed physician extraordinary to Queen Victoria on her accession. His Reports of Medical Cases, Selected with a View of Illustrating the Symptoms and Cure of Diseases by a Reference to Morbid Anatomy is one of the classics of medical literature and, collectively, the non-suppurative inflammatory diseases of the kidney honour his name. In addition, in 1818, he had published a volume entitled Travels from Vienna through Lower Hungary...the birthplace of Israel Schwartz!

I noted with satisfaction, once the two halves of the kidney lay innocently spread upon the cutting board, that my original suspicion had been correct. The bases of the renal pyramids were considerably congested and the tissues were pale and bloodless. Little Kate was certainly suffering in an advanced stage of nephritis.

Now, what to do for packaging. I went down to the cellar to see what I could find. Amongst the odds and ends of tools in a musty drawer on the workbench I found a small, green, cardboard box with a neatly-fitting lid, which contained a circular, leather-bound, tape measure, about four inches in diameter. It had belonged to my father. There were no markings on the box of any kind. Perfect. Leaving the measure in the drawer, I remounted the steps to the scullery.

I was sorely tempted to wrap the half kidney in the pages of Freddy Treves' dissertation concerning the eponymous hole but discretion prevailed and I instead filled out the package with shreddings from the wood-box. After patting away the surface moisture from the purloined organ as best I could, I placed the portion with the artery attached into the bed of shavings. I then returned its sister hemisphere to the jar, screwing the lid back on securely.

Now, a message. I left the kitchen and returned to my study. Selecting an old nib pen that I would not miss, I went to the hearth and scuffed up the point to a roughness. Then, taking out some small sheets of plain notepaper, I sat down to practice a disguised hand. The resultant scrawl is something with which you may be familiar. It was written rapidly, on perhaps the fourth or fifth attempt, with my left hand. I wanted it to appear jagged and suggest a violence of temperament. I think I succeeded pretty well.

"From hell"

A suitable return address.

"Mr Lusk"

I thought it only right to forward this sweetmeat to the men of the Mile End Vigilance Committee. Surely they were more likely to affect my capture than anyone else.

"Sir"

The word became interpreted as 'Sor', and, indeed, it looks like that as you can see, but really it was only the effect of haste and my discomfiture at the novelty of left-handed penmanship.

"I send you half the Kidne"

The capitalisation was a resonance of Michael. The mis-spelling either error or inspiration, I can't remember which, but I've grown fond of it.

"I took from one women prasarved it for you tother piece I fried and ate it was very nise I may send you the bloody knif that took it out if you only wate a whil longer"

Lord, in retrospect my latter efforts at displaying an untutored orthography were pretty unimaginative, weren't they?!

"signed Catch me when you can Mishter Lusk"

I had covered the whole page.

Satisfied at last with my handiwork, I returned to the kitchen. There I disposed of the trial pages in the stove. Then I folded the note twice and placed it, with more shavings as a dampness buffer, on top of the bisected kidney in the box. After once more examining the contents for any possible speck of incrimination, I popped the lid back on and returned to my study, placing the box on my desk on a folded copy of the Times in case of any soil or unexpected leakage.

I wrapped the box with artful clumsiness in brown paper, I am not, in any case, gifted in such matters at the best of times, and tied it up with string. I then sat down and scratched on the address, slantingly, with the damaged pen, again, of course, with my left hand. I smudged it a little afterward but left it readable.

"George Lusk Alderney Rd Globe Rd Mile End"

Finally, I affixed two penny stamps, carelessly asymmetric, above and to the right of the address. I lifted the box, there was no leakage nor staining, and returned with it once more to the kitchen, placing it on the counter while I scoured clean the knife and cutting board. I buried the damaged pen deep in the rubbish bin.

Then, after turning out the lights, I went back upstairs to my bedroom, carrying my gift box, and the jar sloshing with its mirror image. I returned the jar to its locked sanctuary and put the box on the broad sill outside my window in the cool of the night air, although I was confident the kidney's saturation with wine-spirit would keep it from stinking for a day or two. Then I went to bed.

The following morning after breakfast I put the box, still no suppurations or offending odours were noticeable, in a briefcase with my other correspondence. I told Freddy I had several trivial errands in the City and would return about eleven o'clock.

"Anything I might be of help with, sir? It's perishing cold."

So much the better for my meaty oblation.

"I can't think what," I said. "Thanks all the same."

The air was raw with damp as I went out but I was quickly able to find a carriage and asked the driver to take me to St. Paul's. I was well aware that my little packet was an inch or more too deep to be deposited without crushing through the slot of a pillar-box. But more, I wanted the franking to register its origin as close to Whitechapel as possible.

It was a frightful day. As we neared the river at Ludgate Hill, the carriage became enveloped in thick, choking fog. Nonetheless, I stayed fast to my plan and alighted at the cathedral steps. I saw the driver off and walked the remaining half-mile to Lombard Street through a swirling, smoke-filled smother.

Another unnecessary consequence of poverty and greed!

I entered the post office. The custom was slight but, true to the habitual manner of all postal workers, not one raised an eye to look at me. In the muffled distance of an adjacent room I heard a persistent, racking cough. Against the wall there was a receptacle with an opening of sufficient size. With my back to the counter, I dropped my waggish offering in. There followed a very slight, hollow, only to my ears sinister, thud, and that was all. My other correspondence I pushed into a regular slot. I glanced round in parting to make sure that my presence had still sparked no attention. It hadn't. Then, pulling my collar up against the cold, I ventured out once more into the tubercular cloud.

I hailed another carriage home at the corner of Cheapside and Bow Lane. It was precisely two minutes past eleven as I walked briskly in the door at Wimpole Street.

"Good as your word, sir. Punctual as always," Freddy said cheerily as he helped me with my coat. "The fire's cosy in the study. Go on and warm yourself, doctor. There've been several calls. I've just made a nice pot of tea."

One of the calls was from Maudsley regarding a case in which we had a mutual involvement. It concerned a man named Thomas Babcock, a chemist by trade, who stood accused of poisoning his wife and two infant children but whom I considered to be innocent. It was apparent to me that, after a quarrel between Babcock and his wife which resulted in him leaving the house, his wife had quite idiotically administered an overdose of chloroform and morphia to the children in order to quiet them and, finding that they subsequently could not be roused, had taken her own life in the same manner. Babcock discovered the bodies on returning home and, terrified that the blame would fall upon him, he had carried them from the house in a trunk and deposited it in a warehouse.

He was arrested three months later. During the five weeks of his incarceration before the trial he began to behave in an extraordinary manner. He wrote a number of strange and incoherent letters to the press. He began mumbling to himself and making erratic statements, claiming to be Jesus Christ, demanding that his fellow prisoners treat him with respect, that he was the 'hero of the trunk tragedy'. He became absolutely indifferent to the issue of his guilt, laughed without reason, failing utterly to realise the seriousness of his position, any mention of the deaths producing hilarity in him. I had asked that Maudsley examine Babcock and make an independent report. A gamble and, alas, a fatal error.

"The man is not insane," asserted Maudsley, almost before I had time to say 'hello'.

My heart sank.

"He refused to answer a single question rationally," he went on without a pause. "He giggled and grimaced and hummed even though he knew exactly what I was talking about. If he were insane he would have taken no notice at all or made an attempt at some disjointed response. He was simply determined to turn the interview into nonsensical gabble."

"You don't find it to be the incoherence of true mania?"

"Certainly not! All that religious drivel he spouts, that he'd been alive before the universe began, that he'd helped God to create it, that he'd written all the books in the world, he doesn't believe a word of it."

"No?" I questioned. "But you can't deny there has been a long history of mental disorder in his family. It has had a profoundly adverse effect on his mental constitution."

"I knew you'd say that," Maudsley snapped. "If I were you I'd look more closely at his personal history. The man has always known what he's doing. He still does."

There was no point arguing with him in such a mood. I agreed to differ and that was that. More was the pity for poor Babcock.

Another call was from a friend of mine, a surgeon at Charing Cross Hospital. He told me of a patient who had been admitted two nights previously suffering from appendicitis. He was a young man from Vienna who claimed to have been robbed of a large sum of money, three months past, by prostitutes in Leicester Square. He was still determined to revenge himself, he said, and wished that this 'class of individuals' should be killed. My friend told me that the young man had asked permission to attend at several operations and that he was evidently of unsound mind. I told him that he ought to inform the police himself, that I had rather worn out my welcome in that regard, but that I would follow it up with an independent investigation of my own.

I discovered that the young man in question had been confined to an asylum in Vienna and later on in Paris. I wrote to the hospitals asking for particulars about his admission and discharge and other facts relating to his case. I never received any answer whatever to my communications. Clearly, the same reticence is found in Paris and Vienna as in London, where those professionally engaged are bound by the sanctity of their oath not to reveal to the outside world what goes on in the precincts of their office or comes within their knowledge whilst in the performance of their functions.

My friend at Charing Cross Hospital never received anything more for his pains than the usual printed acknowledgement from the CID. The police authorities, from Sir Charles Warren downwards, were very much at sea. They were engaged in looking for a murderer who might be anything, from a well-dressed man in his brougham to a coster in his donkey-cart. The rich were now equally suspected as the poor, the educated and refined man as well as the opposite. They worked night and day, originating theories, acting upon every conceivable sort of official suggestion, but all without avail because they ignored privately offered clues. It's almost beyond belief that they did not recognise their own incompetence. Important information, that was placed *gratis* in their hands, was ignored on the grounds of nothing more nor less than their obstinate assurance that they alone were the persons who should detect the crime and bring the murderer to book. Thank you, mutton-heads!

The unfortunate man who had been carrying the small brown doctor's bag, and whose image had been so brilliantly etched in my memory as he hurried past the entrance to Dutfield's yard, was an exception. They gave him a very bad time. He had apparently also been seen by a Mrs. Fanny Mortimer who lived at No. 36 Berner Street and was standing at her door, she said, between about half past twelve and one. She must have gone back inside at that moment because she did not see me leaving the yard not more than a minute later. Perhaps I truly was invisible! However, neither did she mention the passage of the pony and barrow, driven, I discovered, by a Russian Jew named Louis Diemschutz.

The owner of the bag, which became so absurdly famous solely because it was such obvious ground-bait for the police and press to snap at, voluntarily turned up at Leman Street Station a few days later. Thankfully, he was at last able to prove his innocence. He had just left a coffee house in Spectacle Alley and the bag was full of empty cigarette boxes. He was a member of the International Working Mens' Club and only lived a few paces away in Christian Street. His name was Leon Goldstein. But what Unseen Hand had urged him onwards home instead of entering the yard? The mournful tenor must surely have seemed a beckoning Lorelei, a Siren song of invitation, yet he had scurried by without a glance!

There were now scores of private citizens, besides myself, who had decided to take matters into their own hands. The loud complaints against the inefficiency of the police had grown into a howl of protest. Amongst my fellow prowlers, now nightly patrolling the streets of Whitechapel hoping to catch the murderer, was no less a personage than a director of the Bank of England. He was so obsessed by a special theory of his own, that the killer was a cattle butcher off a ship...our own dear Queen also became rather shrilly convinced of this typically xenophobic notion...that he disguised himself as an ordinary day-labourer and would explore the common lodging-houses clad in heavy boots, a fustian jacket, with a red handkerchief around his head and a pick-axe in his hand. This incongruous apparition would wink stagily at me whenever we passed by each other on our respective searches!

After dropping my little present for the Mile End Vigilance Committee at the post office in Lombard Street I decided I would give my very public attention to the case a few days pause and wait for the reaction.

I wrote no further letters during that autumn. Nor did I receive any.

"Ah ha!" I hear you thinking, you oh so careful student of the case…what do you call yourself, a 'Ripperologist'?…"What about those two letters you yourself mention in your Recollections?!" And, do you know, as I look back now over that chapter, I certainly find it confusing. Or is it that even I can no longer unravel its diabolical cunning?! But let me try. My apologies that it may require quoting myself at length.

First of all, the facts. The data. I both wrote and received those letters, but a year later than I claimed. There is clear evidence of this falsehood in the pertinent chapter of my book. I'm truly not sure whether I was being careless or artful, but on page 264 I had printed a facsimile of the front of an envelope or postcard, and then, below it, part of the contents or obverse side. I'll describe them in a moment though I'm sure you've already had a look. Beginning directly beneath the facsimile, continuing on the page following, I state, quite out of the blue:

"…During the month of August 1888 a man was seen whose description, as then given me, corresponded with the man who was found writing on a wall under an archway. The inscription read: 'Jack the Ripper will never commit another murder.'"

Who? What the devil am I talking about? Is this just some age-befuddled reference to my little poem about the 'Juwes' on the brick facing of Wentworth Model Dwellings?

Then I followed straight on with:

"On 4th October I received a letter purporting to come from 'Jack the Ripper', and expressing an insane glee over the hideous work he was carrying out. This letter was in the same handwriting as the writing found under the archway. Another letter was received by me on

19th October, also in the same handwriting, which informed me that the next murder would be committed on 9th November ..."

There can be no doubt that I am referring to the year 1888. However, consider the aforementioned facsimile.

The front of the postcard or envelope is addressed simply to 'Dr Forbes Winslow, London' ... my goodness, so easily found amongst four million, I must have had no small opinion of my fame, I hear you thinking. Clearly there were more deceptive reasons for my brevity. But I was famous, oh yes, I was! The postcard got to me, didn't it? ... but now here's the rub. The franking clearly shows "London W.C., OC 7, 89"! The seventh not the fourth and a full year later! There is also a tuppence ink-stamp with the letters W.D.O., Western District Office. On the postcard below I had penned the terse message, "This week you will hear of me—Jack the Ripper." Not what you would call a particularly effusive expression of 'insane glee'!

Now wait, there's more. On page 273, I wrote:

"... The peculiarity of my correspondence with 'Jack the Ripper' was that his letters were never stamped."

What am I trying to imply? There was the tuppence ink-stamp on the facsimile. That the perpetrator was working for the Royal Mail? Had I forgotten that I purposely refrained from stamping them and the post office sent them on anyway because of their possible importance?! Am I just crowing once more about my own or, is it, perchance, a veiled admission?

I go on:

"One was written on half a sheet of cheap notepaper."

I can only assume I am referring to the brief message I claim to have received on October 4th yet was franked October 7th.

"It was in a round, upright hand, and evidently written by someone who was not accustomed to using the pen. The writing is distinct, with an absence of flourish, but written with deliberation and care. The scrawl is not a hurried one; the address on the envelope is even more hurriedly written, with less care, than the letter."

What a load of waffle-headed gobbledegook!

"It bears the postmark of the Western district, whereas the previous letter I received was from the Eastern."

There was no previous letter mentioned, only the one following on the 19th!

"There was a smudge upon it which I was always under the impression was blood, and which, by the use of a magnifying glass, proved to be the case."

By the by, and *à propos* of absolutely nothing, it was impossible, in those days, to differentiate with any certainty whether blood was of human or animal origin, even under the strongest of available microscopes.

"The other letter I received was signed P.S.R. Lunigi…"

The blood-smudged card was signed 'Jack the Ripper'.

"… giving his address as '*Poste Restante*, Charing Cross'; this is the one in which my correspondent informed me that a murder would take place on the 8th or 9th of November."

In fact, I had not even begun to formulate my plan to murder Mary Kelly and disrupt the Lord Mayor's Show by mid-October.

"He requested the reply to be sent to the Charing Cross post office, giving his address as 22, Hammersmith Road, Chelsea. On making enquiries, however, I found that no such road existed."

What a surprise.

Then, on page 274, I included a full page facsimile of this 'other letter'. In places nearly illegible, it read:

"22 Hammersmith Rd Chelsea. Oct 19th 88"

It's obvious the 88 has been written over! Indeed, I recall first writing 89 in error, having got into the habit over the course of the year, and had to amend it. I clearly didn't care a fig it was all so sloppy!

The letter begins:

"Sir I defy you to find out who has done the Whitechapel murder in the Summer nor the last one You had better look out for yourself or else Jack the R may do you something in your house to before the end of Dec mind now the 5th of Nov there may be another murder so look out old sir…"

Old sir, bah!

There followed some quite illegible crossings out. I think it may be "M Devil frank frankly" but I have no recollection now what thought, if any, was then in my mind.

"… Tell all London another J ripper open will take place some one told me about the 8th or 9 of Proximo not in Whitechapel but in London perhaps in Clapham or the West End. Write to the *Poste Restante* Charing X address to P S R Lunigi &c Oct 19th."

Well, I confess that I concocted the letters as supporting evidence to prop up a much later position. I'll tell you about that in due course. But I am astonished now at my cavalier negligence in the manner of its elucidation in my book of reminiscences. I can't see much art in it at all. If I had actually written the letters during October, 1888, as a kind of *raison d'être* or excuse, should I have needed one, for my presence in Whitechapel on the night of Mary Kelly's murder, then it might have been clever, but no. And really, what odd schoolboy invention conjured the name 'Lunigi'? Half way between *lungi* and lunific, a loincloth and a silver alchemical? Luigi, the Italian lunatic? Ha!

One final punctuation to all this slipshod, earlier in the chapter, on pages 255-6, I had stated, "…in the letter I received in October 1888 the writer told me that the murder would be committed either on the 7th or the 9th…" I didn't even bother to make the dates properly coincide!

I was tired, I suppose, and just dashing it off. I'd published volume after volume of glib twaddle by 1910, using all those boxes of notes father left me to collate. Yes, I was tired. But no one has divined the reason for my messy little cobweb of errors over the last ninety years, now have they?! No one has noticed the confession between the lines!

It was nearly four days before anything was heard from George Lusk. He had received my jocose xenium on the evening of the 16th but kept it in his desk for thirty-six hours before showing it to some fellow members of the Vigilance Committee on the morning of the 18th. I imagine it must have nosed sweet and ripely! They had then taken it for examination, first to a doctor's surgery in Mile End, then to London Hospital, then to Leman Street Station where Abberline had the singular delight of adding it to his list of evidence and sharing this 'latest horror' with the City Police.

Poor old F.G., when I saw him on the twenty-third, the last day of Wynne Baxter's inquest into the demise of 'Long Liz' Gustafsdotter, he looked frightful. He told me that in the three weeks preceding some eighty suspects had been detained and questioned and over three hundred more had been diligently traced down and followed. He, too, used to spend late nights in Whitechapel, like the banker, like the eager young reporter who had been arrested dressed as a woman, like myself. I often saw him there and we would compare notes. I sensed that even he was growing rather impatient with my suggestions and advice though he was always gentlemanly enough not to show it. During the days he had had to carefully examine more than a thousand dockets and many more thousands of pages of police reports and the now impossible deluge of vague clues and pet theories and most often mindless suggestions from an ever-helpful public, none of which the poor man could unfortunately afford to ignore. He had lost his appetite, he told me, and indeed his normally taut waistcoat seemed to hang in limp folds beneath his jacket. No more fried lamb's kidneys for breakfast, I'll wager! I noticed that his hair was starting to turn gray. Apart from the colossal bags under his eyes, we were becoming ever more like twins.

"Theories! We're drowning in bloody theories!" he said, in a hoarse, tired voice.

"Nothing turned up in the search?" I asked.

Between the 13th and the 18th, the police detectives had conducted a massive and exhaustive house-to-house search through a wide area of Whitechapel and Spitalfields, prying into every cupboard and attic and cellar and outhouse, mostly with the occupant's willing assistance.

"Not a blasted thing of any use," Abberline grunted balefully and shook his head.

"What about the dogs?"

Tracker dogs. Bloodhounds. Remember Barnaby and Burgho? The use of dogs had been suggested soon after I had wooed and wedded 'Dark Annie'. A dozen or more years previously, after the brutal slaying of a girl in Blackburn, Lancashire, they had tracked down her murderer, William Fish, and uncovered evidence that led to his subsequent execution. Following my sublime duplexity of September 30th the idea was taken up in earnest. Despite misgivings at the Home Office, and some pathetic quibbling over finances, Sir Charles Warren had conducted several successful trials with the abovementioned champions on October 8th and 9th in Hyde Park, even acting as their quarry himself on two runs, and had given orders that no further victim should be touched until the dogs could be brought upon the scene. It was one of the many reasons for my caution during the ensuing weeks.

"Brough's frightened they'll get hurt. Or poisoned. He hasn't been paid properly for them either …"

Edwin Brough of Scarborough was the bloodhound's owner. I can't believe that anagrams don't intrigue you!

"...He's taken Burgho off down to Brighton now for some dog show..."

Abberline was aware, I think, that I had, some years previous, been an avid breeder of champion mastiffs. Crown Prince was my pride and joy. But that happy diversion too I had relinquished due to the competitive malice and witless controversy that had come to reign endemic amongst the very members of the club I had founded.

"...The other's still with a friend of Brough's on Doughty Street..."

Doughty Street! A stone's throw from the Foundling!

"...Speaking of Brighton, how's the family?"

"Oh, fine, fine. Oldest son's turned out to be a bit of a pip. But the others are doing splendidly."

"That business at Tooting about the dogs getting lost was, as usual, blown out of all proportion by the press, by the way. Never mind that the whole idea is daft. It's all well and good to sniff out Sir Charles bloody Warren in the green of Hyde Park. It's quite another thing for them to track a man here in the slums of Whitechapel."

"Quite," I agreed.

The upshot was that, due to the government's shilly-shallying and the lack of a few pounds worth of insurance money for the dogs, Brough took them back to Scarborough in a huff. They were gone by the end of the month.

"What do you make of the letters?" I asked.

"Hoaxes. Pranks. All of them," he snorted, "The stinking kidney too. Just some medical student farting about."

"Yes. I suppose so. But the kind of farting about that might bring down the government when all's said and done."

Abberline looked at me narrowly. I was feeling dangerously besotted with my hidden power.

"It might, Lyttleton. You know it just might. There was an old devil named Simeon Oliphant came into King Street Station last week saying he'd misplaced a black bag..."

I raised my eyebrows.

"...He blathered on about being able to cut off the desk sergeant's head and then replace it on his shoulders in such a way that he would never know it had been removed. He said he could prove by arithmetic that every man and woman in the world was the same as bloody God! Bring down the government, you say? Oh, ho, ho, ho, it might indeed."

It was a strange, mirthless little chuckle. The dear chap was very near to breaking, I could see. And, at that moment, Wynne Baxter regretfully announced the verdict of the inquest jury. It was, for Liz, as it had been pronounced for Kate by the City Coroner twelve days before, 'Willful murder against some person or persons unknown.' Well, to be accurate, in the City case, Langham, following his summation of the medical evidence, convinced the jury to state it in the singular, 'Willful murder against some person unknown.'

Ha, ha, ha!

Spiritualistic Madness

That evening, it was a Tuesday, I gained my first intimate knowledge of Mary Kelly.

I had seen her on several previous occasions and she knew me by sight. She was just leaving the Queen's Head with another woman as I came in. It was only eight o'clock but she was already extremely drunk.

"Not live with me, is it?!"

She had her back to me and was screaming at the top of her lungs toward a man I recognised sitting at the rear of the tavern. It was evident that her Irish brogue waxed far less charming and decidedly thicker when in her cups.

"Not live with me if I get the money! Well, don't then, you stumbler! Just tell me what am I to do if you can't bring in a farthing, just tell me that?!"

Her female companion had noticed my presence and was tugging at her sleeve to little avail, gesturing rather inconclusively with her head in my direction.

"Stop your pulling at me, Julia! I'll come when I'm ready!"

She pushed the other woman away and advanced again on the man. He was trying to ignore her, burying his face in his glass. The swaying denizens looked on, cheering or booing by turns, like fanatics at a football match.

'The mistress of the world! The football of ruffians!'

"What did you say to me, you stammering looby?! Don't you dare turn your cowardly face! Are you going to feed us then? Are you? Are you the one's going to give McCarthy his guinea? Jesus, Mary and Joseph, I'm the one's just stood you all the liquor, you po-faced gobshite! You were happy enough to be swilling it down! Not live with me, is it?! Hah! It's I'm the one's not living with you!!"

With that, she hoisted high her skirts and kicked the poor fellow off his stool, sending him sprawling on the filthy, sodden floor against the wall. Then she turned on her heels and marched fiercely back toward me. She was sweating, her eyes ablaze, her face a furnace, her auburn hair burning in the gaslight. A banshee. A Gorgon. A Juggernaut. Big. Tall. Worthy. Almost beautiful. And young.

"What about you?!" she shouted imperiously, pointing at me, still too lathered for it to dawn who I was, "Fancy a dingle with a young, strong woman who'll root up your sorrows and leave you drowning! This milky white Catholic boy here will mew that he don't like it, but... oh, it's you again, is it, doctor...?"

She paused ever so briefly but I could see I was not to be spared in this overflux of Milesian temperament.

"... Lord save us, if you haven't got the pallor of a true blue rabbinical as well. What is it you want with us, doctor, tell us now, forever lurking in doorways? Does it give you a tickle downstairs, watching our trouble, does it? Why don't you put away those funeral eyes for once and let Mary give you an honest spanking? Only cost you two guineas. Cheap at the price..."

She was rubbing up close around me, a malevolent, fire-breathing witch. I kept firm eye contact with her and made no attempt at escape. I am grateful to say that only a few of those present were laughing. Tom, the bulldog barman, chimed in gruffly.

"Give over, Mary. The doctor..."

"... Can make up his own mind, now can't he?! What is it, your lordship, afraid I'll be catching? It's so easy, eh, isn't it, looking down at us from your pedestal, like the great man of science that you are. Examining us from on high like so many specimen bugs. Poking and prodding with gloved hands on your scalpel. Like the Romans at Christ's crucifixion. But all the time itching inside, why don't you confess it! Itching in holy terror at the hot, raw flesh of a woman! Why is it you can't just... aaaaccchh! ..."

She let out a tremendous yell of frustration and disgust.

My unflinching gaze had had its effect. My funereal 'eye'.

It was believed by some that if you photographed the eyes of a victim soon enough after death they would reveal a reflected image of the murderer.

"...Aaacch, to hell, Julia, let's get out of it!"

Her voice was suddenly quiet. The pressure-cock had released its steam. She cast her eyes with hatred over all the men in the now hushed bar, over all the men, I imagined, in this grasping, sordid world, and muttered, "The cheek of the dirty buggers. Damn the whole pack of them to hell."

With that, she caught her companion by the arm and they slammed out the door. The room was silent. It took me a long moment to remember to breathe. My soul was singing in an afterglow as though I had been kissed. In that minuscule lacuna in the inexorable flow of time, before the gabble resumed and twittered gently back through the filter of my astonished consciousness, my whole being became suffused with a crystalline vision of all that was to come.

What had I been doing playing politics? Fretting over the trivia of foible and bias and prejudice and injustice. In that schoolboy rigmarole I had lost my way! What did I care if the whole human race disappeared in a maelstrom of its own devising? That was not what mattered! What mattered was coming face to face with God my Maker! That must be the sole and perfect purpose of my restless seeking, my quest, my crusade, my pilgrimage, to venture beyond the Delectable Mountains, beyond the Garden of the Hesperides and the Isles of the Blessed...even, yes, even beyond the proliferating multidimensionality of the Rev. Abbott's Flatland!...to a Great Free Nowhere beyond which all Dimension is obliterated in the cathedral infinity of Christ's Passion! The Solar Wind scathing cataracts of adoration from my temples! My very flesh torn away by that Eternal Light! My bones and gristle and fibrous substance vaporised in the howling cauldron of Love Everlasting! *Jubilate Deo!*

No more dallying with golden apples or graven images. Mary Kelly was my Juggernaut, beneath whose wheels I was panting to be crushed. In her loins I knew I would meet God.

I turned slowly from the door and ambled toward the back of the tavern. Not more than a second had passed since her departure. The miserable object of the banshee's wrath had regained his stool and was now sitting glum and isolated, nursing flat beer and staler pride. I have already once mentioned his name, Joseph Barnett. He was a stolid, stocky, four-square looking man, about thirty years of age, no taller, I judged, than Mary, with fair hair and moustaches and pale blue eyes set disconcertingly close together.

"May I sit with you a moment, Joe?"

He peered up at me, then nodded civilly enough, considering he, too, was quite drunk and, perhaps, rather like myself, in a state of shock.

"May I ask Tom to replenish your glass?"

He nodded again. I waved to the bulldog barman, he nodded in turn. For some reason we were spared a gathering consort, deference to the bruise of domestic strife, I supposed. It could also have been that, without Mary beside him, he wasn't particularly popular, I can't say. For my part, I found him pleasant enough, if rather taciturn, but that may have merely been the consequence of his tongue-lashing. In any case, it suited me perfectly. Our private *tête-à-tête* provided many helpful morsels of information. And an invaluable object which I will reveal momentarily.

"The fair sex can be difficult to fathom," I offered.

"Difficult to fathom. Too true. Too true," he agreed ruefully, jutting up his chin in the accustomed gesture of resignation. "Impossible's more like."

We shared the age-old, secret, long-suffering smile of the not so loyal order of men. Tom placed two dripping pint mugs before us. I put a shilling in his palm.

"Have one for yourself, Tom, and bring Joe another in due time."

"Much obliged, doctor," Tom said, wobbling his jowls, then, on painful knees, rocked back to his station behind the bar.

"Cheers." I raised my glass.

"Cheers. Cheers, doctor. Ta very much."

He took a long draught. I sipped.

"It's hard when you can't find work."

I knew he had been a porter at Billingsgate fish market but had recently lost his license over an accusation of petty theft.

"Can't find work. Yes, very 'ard," he said.

His weak eyes were unable to sustain my gaze for more than a moment at a time. Not so much shyness as an inchoate selfhood.

"She has a fiery temperament."

"Fiery temp'rament? No, not really. Just in 'er cups."

In the compulsive pattern of his speech, the repetitive echo of my phrasing, I recognised the familiar, diffident residue of childhood abandonment. I had seen many such cases but I will spare you the tedium of their elucidation in this reconstruction of our colloquy.

"A common trait of the Irish."

I did not wish to listen to him demur at my commonplace and say she was really a sweet young thing. I wanted to hold fast to my untamed image of her and pressed on.

"How long has she lived in London?"

"Four or five year. She 'ad a 'usband what got blown up in the mines. In Wales."

"Dear, dear. But she was born in Ireland?"

"Yes, I think so. Limerick."

There was a young lady named Kelly, who was found with a hole in her belly ... for Amen of Winslow ... sorry!

"She 'ad a job in service with a French woman when she first came. In Knightsbridge, she said. Used to take 'er to Paris but she didn't like it. Still fancies 'erself as 'Jeannette' though, if you please. Moans on about 'aving 'ad a lot of nice frocks. Huh! I never seen 'em."

"And how long have you known her?"

"Since Easter last year. She was dossing at Cooley's. 'Orrible place. She's been a tidy sight better off with me, I'll tell you straight."

"I dare say. Where do you live now then?"

"'Ad a room to ourselves in Dorset Street for near the past year. Mostly to ourselves. She brings 'ome stray cats."

"What do you mean?"

"Cats. 'Ooers. Like that one she was with. Laundresses, my bloody arse. Bloody krauts an' bloody 'ooers."

It was a peculiar usage, from which, of course, I gathered that Mary's companion was of German extraction but I saw no purpose in questioning it.

"I see. Yes. That would make it difficult. I see."

He had already drained his glass and, as I had instructed, Tom, the bulldog, came tottering over on his in-bowed legs with another pint. All torso and wasted extremities, the sad result of nutritional deficiency in youth, I mused.

"Not much of a drinker, are you, doctor?"

I had barely touched the first one.

"Not much, I'm afraid. No."

"Go easy now, Joe. You've 'ad a skinful already," Tom admonished.

Joe snatched up the fresh mug and downed it at a gulp in response, staring at the barman insolently, then proceeded to lick off his wet moustache with child-like gravity. The burly keeper was roundly unimpressed. He picked up the empty glass.

"I'd pack 'im off 'ome soon, doctor, an' I was you. 'e'll only start talking daft."

I nodded. Joe's blurring eyes followed Tom's return passage to the counter unsteadily. His rickety tick-tock gait brought to mind a steward I had once observed during a stormy Channel crossing, tea-tray balanced precariously at the end of a graceful, upstretched arm, wending his way on tip-toe through a slithering maze of sea-washed lounge-chairs and helpless passengers staggering to retch over the rail of the nauseous, pitching deck.

"Is there a danger of being turfed out of your digs?"

Joe looked at me blankly for a moment, then down at my still full pint. I could see he was thinking of snatching it up but, even in his state, could not quite bring himself to such effrontery. I was wise enough not to offer.

"What digs? I'll not be living with 'er if she's ... I've got to piss ..."

He rose to his feet, swaying, fumbling in his jacket.

"... I've told 'er. And that's flat."

I have no idea if he was actually searching for it, but something metallic made its way through a hole in the inner lining of his left-hand pocket and tinkled to the floor under the table. I bent to look but he was gone, lurching towards the lavatory door. It was a single latch-key. I had an instant reflex to call out and tell him but the honesty was fleeting. I waited for a moment, covering the key with the sole of my boot, then casually leaned over and picked it up, slipping it unseen into my own breast pocket. When he returned from the urinal he seemed to have forgotten and Tom, the barman, stopped him before he could sit down and told him to go home, which, after a few seconds surly looming and a vague gesture of protest toward my unconsumed pint, I assume he did, for he stumbled grudgingly out the tavern doors without a word of parting.

Yes, I know what you think about coincidence! But, to me, that latch-key was more than a leprechaun's gift, much more than a pot of gold at a rainbow's end! It was a sign, an omen, a beckoning light-house beacon! It was Acceptance!

Since we're discussing the subject, let me bring to your attention the spiritualist, Robert James Lees. He was a self-styled clairvoy-ant and…is this totally unconnected?…a friend of Keir Hardie, the young Scottish socialist, founder and editor of The Miner, who had just been defeated as a Labour candidate in a by-election in Lanarkshire. I was unaware at the time that Lees had offered his assistance to Scotland Yard on three occasions in early October only to be dismissed as mad and sent away with the usual polite rebuff and this despite the rumour of his close ties to the Queen. Apparently he had once, at a palace séance, spoken in the clear, unmistakably Teutonic tones of her beloved Albert.

Lees claimed to have had a psychic vision of the murder of Martha Tabram and to have come face to face with the murderer boarding an omnibus in Shepherd's Bush. I normally, as you know, avoided public transport but if he had said Oxford Street on the night of August 30th I might have, had I known of it, been a trifle concerned! He also made some rather accurate predictions regarding the play-ful dance of my knife about little Kate's ears. And a few weeks later, I believe he did almost sniff me out, guiding the police to the house of a prominent West End physician in Harley Place, a mere hundred yards from my door. The doctor, I'll call him 'Mason' for the nonce, was an acquaintance, an unstable man with a strong sadistic streak. His wife told me she had once come upon him in the cellar savagely torturing a cat. So, you never can tell…'stones have been known to move and trees to speak, augurs and understood relations have by Maggot Pies and Choughs and Rooks brought forth the secret'st man of Blood'…!

Yes, yes, alright, I can hear you! Yes! I grow more like my father with each unnecessary oblique referent!

Now I already knew perfectly well where Mary Kelly and Joseph Barnett had been living despite my questions to him on the subject. I had known since the third week of September that their room was in Miller's Court. Don't you remember? I had stopped there to wash my hands after laying little Kate to rest and chalking up my enigma about the 'Juwes'. I knew the exact location of the doorway. I had merely to discover if the latch-key would fit. And … you may actually be amused by this … I decided to leave it to chance!

In the two and a half weeks following my chat with Joe and the wee hours of November 9th, I visited Whitechapel during darkness only once. On the 5th of November, Guy Fawke's Night. Do you honestly not find it in any way meaningful that the poor dupe was executed on my birthday in 1606?

But perhaps you don't know much about this peculiarly English little celebration. It commemorates the Gunpowder Plot, a failed attempt by a group of justifiably disgruntled Catholics to destroy the reign of King James I. It was to begin by blowing up the Houses of Parliament on their opening day, November 5th, 1605. Fawkes was apprehended at midnight on November 4th breaking into the cellar of the parliament buildings where piles of fuel and faggots had clandestinely been stowed. The task of setting them alight had fallen to him and he has had the dubious honour ever since of being the patron of many a glorious fireworks display and inspiring little children throughout the land to be creative. They make effigies of him out of whatever comes to hand, the more hideous the better, thick blood oozing from the gaping mouth, a hangman's noose tightly cinched around a straw-filled neck, and, showing off their artistry in the streets, are encouraged to beg of any passing pedestrian, "A penny for the Guy!" After their pockets have been lined with sufficient coin, they burn the effigy with Bacchanalian delight, dancing and whooping around the pyre, and chanting …

"Please to remember the Fifth of November, Gunpowder Treason and Plot! We know no reason why gunpowder treason should ever be forgot!"

I think I can say with confidence that I have managed to make the ninth of November equally memorable. In any case, I took a quantity of coppers with me to Whitechapel that evening.

What I found out was of vital importance to the execution of the plan that was now positively bursting within me. I discovered from his brother that Joseph Barnett was indeed no longer living with Mary at No. 13 Miller's Court. He had finally summoned up enough courage to make good his word and, at the beginning of the month, he had decamped to Buller's boarding-house in Bishopsgate. It was possible, I was told, that another friend I had more often seen her with, Maria Harvey, another "stray cat" and "'ooer" as Joe would have it, might be lodging with Mary instead. I could have spent the night watching just to make sure, but that too I decided to peril on the cast of Urim and Thummim!

What was happening to me? I was overcome with such a powerful surge of expectation that nothing could subdue it. I was borne on the Wings of the Divine! You know that I was normally most fastidious in my preparation, I had never believed in leaving things to Chance though I was well aware of the seeming enormity of its role in my affairs, but now I had lost all qualms and inhibition, I was eager, more than eager, I was rabid, to engage the Juggernaut! I was St. George before the Dragon's Lair! I could hear His stamping feet. I could smell the cordite exhalations of His breath! I was as rampant within as a woman in the birth throes! I was beside myself to meet Him!

Now, for just a moment, before I attempt to satisfy you with a full account of my glorious night of transubstantiation, I might even be so shameless as to say carnification … 'that miraculous image, the carnified or bleeding host' … I must digress and introduce the Maybricks to my story.

James Maybrick was a Liverpool cotton merchant addicted, among other things, to the peculiar habit of eating arsenic. It was, alas, not all that uncommon. I had seen several similar cases. Dr. Fowler's Medicine, a much-used tonic at the time, contained a small amount. The takers, mostly men, claimed that it 'strengthened' them. In other words, enhanced their virility. *Arsenikon* translates as 'potent' from the Greek. But I suspected the fatigue so often complained of by such patients might sometimes be the result of hypothyroidism.

I met him only once. It's most chillingly ironic in the light of all that subsequently transpired but it was on the afternoon of November 8th, a Thursday, at a musical gathering held in the home of his younger brother Michael, by then a very popular song-writer, using the *nom de plume* or *nom de théâtre*, Stephen Adams. It was a sort of preview for one of his forthcoming ballad concerts … does it not at all stir you that a later frothy concoction of his was entitled 'We All Love Jack'?! … I had been asked along by my new young acquaintance Arthur Wing Pinero, who had worked as an actor with Irving and been given a leg-up by him. He was now well known as the author of several clever farces and was making a packet at the time with a sentimental piece, Sweet Lavender, but, surprisingly, he became the progenitor of 'realism' in the British theatre in the nineties with his play The Second Mrs. Tanqueray, which was very fortunately headlined by Shaw's favourite, Mrs. Patrick Campbell. Michael Maybrick and Pinero were neighbours and dwelt at Wellington Mansions on Regents Park. I'm sure I was only invited because of my association with the sensation of the moment, to wit, the murders and, though I was not really looking forward to a lot of inane questions, I felt my attendance might stand in purposeful counterpoise to the deed I was now bound and determined to enact in Whitechapel that very evening.

There was quite a large crowd and the performance by Michael and his librettist, Frederick Weatherly, who I believe were both homosexual though I am not always a good judge, I found to be unbearably silly stuff. There was a piece to celebrate James Maybrick's fiftieth birthday sung sweetly enough, but to my ears painfully off key, by his young American wife, 'Florie', *née* Florence Elizabeth Chandler... Florence Jessie and Long Liz!... She had been born during the Civil War in Mobile, Alabama. Her father was a wealthy member of that so-soon-to-be-shattered Southern White Society, but when he suddenly died before Florence was a year old her mother was suspected of poisoning him and they were effectively banished from the state. A quickly married second husband died shortly thereafter, also in suspicious circumstances, on a steamer bound for Scotland. However, more of that later.

James and 'Florie' had just arrived by train from Liverpool that morning. The trip had been at her urging in order that she might attend the Lord Mayor's Show the following day. I remember he and I exchanged some pleasantries about horse-racing and cricket, it was just possible that we had played on opposing sides in a match at Lord's some twenty years before, and, mercifully, nothing about the 'Whitechapel horror'. I discovered that his former Liverpool business-partner, Gustavus Witt... Liz Stride's maiden name was Gustafsdotter!... maintained an office in Cullum Street... not three brisk minutes walk from Mitre Square!... and I also recall receiving the distinct impression as we spoke together that things were far from right between he and his pretty, vivacious young wife, but nothing more. Except that he had a pallid, sweaty countenance and that I took an almost instant dislike to him. I never saw him again alive.

November the ninth has been, since the 13th century, the traditional day of the 'Lord Mayor's Show' in London, an annual festival and celebration. A magnificent parade from Mansion House to the Royal Courts of Justice in the Strand for the investiture, where normally the Prime Minister himself will speak though the Lord Mayor is second in rank only to the Queen within the City, followed by a return to Guildhall and a sumptuous banquet attended by the twenty-six aldermen of the wards, the two-hundred-and-six common councillors and representatives of the livery companies, of which the Lord Mayor must at least be a member of one...the Apothecaries, Armourers and Brasiers, Bakers, Barbers, Brewers, Butchers, Carpenters, Clothworkers, Coach and Coach-harness Makers, Coopers, Cordwainers, Cutlers, Drapers, Dyers, Fishmongers...'rippers', ha!...Girdlers, Goldsmiths, Grocers, Haberdashers, Innholders...the chronically repressed?...Ironmongers, Leathersellers, Mercers, Merchant Taylors, Painter-stainers, Parish Clerks, Saddlers, Salters, Skinners, Stationers, Tallowchandlers, Vintners and Waxchandlers. No 'mad-doctors'. Butchers and skinners though, why wasn't I invited?

The new Lord Mayor, the Right Honourable James Whitehead...no descendant, I think, of the author of Richard Savage...had been duly elected from the ranks of the court of aldermen on September the 29th. I had only the most vestigial intention of ruining his day, I promise, though my timing turned out to be perfect. The news of Mary Kelly's murder interrupted his procession just as it was passing St. Paul's at Ludgate Hill and nearly set off a riot. However, I'm getting far ahead of myself. By that time I was not even in London.

I made a polite exit from the Maybrick festivities at about a quarter to five and returned to Wimpole Street. Freddy had laid out a cold supper, not being sure at what time I might extricate myself from the party, and I told him I would be grateful of it later on but, for the moment, I had to attend to some correspondence. We discussed the forthcoming Lord Mayor's Pageant and agreed that he should be free from any duties concerning my welfare as it was customary for him to treat it as a holiday. He and the family would rise early, hoping for a fine day, and stand for hours in the crush waiting for the pompous circus to pass, then, flushed with empty-headed civic pride, cheer at the top of their lungs for they knew not what. Lord, I mused…in retrospect I see it was quite uncharacteristic, a foreshadowing…what cynical devils have the cunning to organise these pharisaic master-pieces of social deflection. Despite my huge excitement I was oddly grumpy. Perhaps, I told myself, it was the banality of the music which I had so recently been forced to suffer. However, as soon as Freddy had bade his farewells, I shook it off and sat down to gather my thoughts.

I had the key and I would not waver, I would put my fervent trust in the Lord…'the breastplate of judgement, *doctrina et veritas*'…I had received my message from on High. I did not touch Freddy's meal but went upstairs, lay down on my bed and fell almost instanta-neously into a heavy but expectant sleep.

It was after midnight when I awoke still fully dressed in the suit of clothes in which I had attended the Maybrick's tedious matinée. I had sweat right through them and got up to change. To say that my mood was alarming is not to begin to describe it. I felt myself to be an invisi-ble, ethereal spirit wafting in the outer rings of Heaven but within the circle of that sensation was a white-hot fire. A focus so intense that it might have cut through the lead-plate doors in the vault of the Bank of England. I was the supernatural elixir within Jekyll's alembic or a Paracelsian athanor, my quicksilver perfectly fixed.

I stripped to the skin and took out two sets of long winter under-wear. One I put on, then folded the other neatly on the bed. Then I pulled on a thick pair of woolen socks. After this my customary linen shirt and collar and bow and the inexpensive woolen suit and waistcoat I had worn on all my recent peregrinations in Whitechapel. Freddy had wanted to dispatch it to the launderers but I had told him no. I had found it easy enough to scrub the material clean of the flecks of little Kate's and Gustafsdotter blood. I took the extra set of undergarments and two small hand-towels from the airing cupboard on the landing and went downstairs.

Leaving these items on a table in the hall, I descended to the cellar for the yard of brown, American cloth and coil of stout twine which I had secreted there late on Guy Fawke's Night. I also fetched out another of my queerly fashioned, oil-cloth sacks from its hiding place behind some other oddments on an upper shelf and ascended again to the kitchen. This time, instead of sliding my two beloved blades from Freddy's carvery down the sides of my waistcoat, I wrapped them, the longer one, as before, still in its protective scabbard, between the other necessaries in several generous folds of the dark cloth, carefully mind, so there could be no danger of any suspicious protrusion, finally cinching the whole bundle firmly round with hempen fibre and tying it with a slip-knot.

I took the package with me to the vestibule and donned once more the same felt hat and overcoat, lacing up a different pair of black, felt-lined, soft-soled shoes ... 'a delicate stratagem' ... 'kill, kill, kill, kill, kill!' ... and, making assurance doubly sure that I still had the key to Paradise warming my left-hand waistcoat pocket, I stepped out into the freezing night. It was already more than half past one.

Madness, perfect madness. If any constable had enquired what my little packet contained what should I have blurted out? What could I have done if they had insisted on looking? I hadn't given it a second's thought. I didn't care. I was Invincible!

This time I was not lucky in finding a carriage and walked in my trance through the wind and rain ... 'a little tiny wit' ... all the way to Charing Cross Road, nearly into the menace of St. Giles, before I was able to hail one. What was I thinking?! A few more steps and I might have found my own throat cut! But perhaps it was the working of good fortune after all, the driver did not find it in the least surprising when I asked to be deposited at Spitalfields Market.

Our voyage was slow and somnambulatory. As we passed along the glistening, deserted streets I turned over in my mind all the preceding nights that had led me here. My fumblings with Fay in Fleece Court, my tantalising foretaste of divinity to come in George Yard, my slipped semi-lunar cartilage, my experiment in Mesmerism with Polly, her tear-filled child's eyes, the snorting horses, the squealing pig, the idyll of Annie, the backhouse, my first treasures, the uterus in the wine-spirits, the fun I had with Long Liz Gustafsdotter, 'Lipski', her rescue from the lecherous ruffian, the black bag etched in sharp relief, the shattering cart, my flight over the railyards to Mitre Square, Kate's pliant fall, her look of ecstasy, the sweating kidney, and, arching over all, the music, the music, oh, the swelling, beckoning music, not that simpering rubbish at the Maybrick's but the Sublime Song that I was longing with all my simple heart and soul to hear again ... '*L'amor che muove il sole*' ... longing to bring to its glorious, blessed, deafening Finale!

It was five minutes to three when I alighted from the carriage outside the market at the corner of Commercial and Brushfield Streets.
The Ten Bells public house lay darkened across the way. I looked up
at Christ Church and smiled. The rain was turning heavy and only a
single cart was in evidence, its contents covered by thick canvas. Lights
shone within but I saw no porters. I stood for a moment, drinking in
the sound of the downpour, getting my bearings and checking in all
directions to see if I had been observed. Looking along Commercial
Street toward Whitechapel, I saw a small woman covered in a shawl
scurrying from Fashion Street past the Queen's Head and over the
road to enter Dorset Street. I decided to wait a minute or two before
making my way there. During this time no constables appeared, but
it was now or never and I knew it.

As I turned into the shimmering avenue of my dreams I could just
make out a man's back disappearing south into Bell Lane. No one
else at all was visible. I flew like a phantom the few steps to Miller's
Court and glided down the narrow stone passageway to her door.
The dim gas-lamp on the wall opposite had not yet been extinguished
and illuminated me for all to see ... Ha! ... as I took the key from my
pocket and slowly, silently slithered into Valhalla ... 'enough of tears,
ye Gods, enough of wail!' ... closing the door behind me. The noise
of the rain muffled a slight creaking of the hinge and the mouse-like
creep of the lock-spring.

I stood stock still and dripping in the pitch dark room. I could
hear the stuporous, rhythmic exhalation of her breath and listened
for a full minute to be sure that she was alone.

The air was laden with the unmistakable smell of metabolising ale.
Perhaps, I thought, it was as well that the gas-lamp outside still shone
for I slowly began to distinguish the positions of the room's pathetic
furnishings. There were two windows to my left covered with some
ill-hung curtaining or clothing, I couldn't make out which, and a
faint glow trimmed the edges. She lay asleep to my right and I could
feel with my hand a small, bare, table between us, its top a feverish,
ghostly glimmer. There seemed to be a second table and possibly a
chair in front of me and across the tiny room I could just delineate
the shapes of the fireplace and a standing closet to its right.

With Ophidian stealth I moved to the table by the window. Her
clothes were carelessly strewn about on the floor around the chair

beside. Without a sound I set my burden down, then picked up the discarded garments one by one and folded them neatly on the chair, finally placing her boots together beneath it. Then I slipped loose the knot, unfolded the linen cloth and laid out the contents of my packet with delicate care. The knife blades caught the sullen, red reflection of the window's rim as I turned to look at her.

I could now discern the outline of her recumbent form. She was sleeping on her right side close against the wall. Above her head ecto-plastic rectangles of moulding stood out on the partition. I knew that this room had been separated off from the rest of the house and that the walls would be paper thin. The utmost silence was essential. Her bare left arm lay peacefully on the coverlet and at her shoulder I could just make out the pale flounce of her smock.

'But while I say one prayer...'

'It is too late!'

I took off my coat and hung it on the back of the chair, then placed my sopping hat over it secured by the left-hand ear of the toprail. It had been my plan to doff my other outer garments to keep them clean and I did so, methodically folding them and piling them beside my surgeon's tools that nestled on the hand-towels on the table. The winter underwear was to protect me from the chill but my excitement was of such intensity that I could have been submerged beneath the polar ice and still felt warm. Besides I suddenly felt ridiculous, obscenely insufficient to the grandeur of the moment standing there thus clad, and on an impulse I stripped them off as well. To accomplish this I also had to remove my shoes and socks and finally there I stood before my Maker, stark naked as He made me... 'a poor, bare, forked animal'... As a last gesture of obeisance I took off my wedding ring.

In my mind I was perched on the western-most crags of Skellig Michael, high above the crashing waves, facing the full force of the Atlantic blast, all comforts of my beehive cell behind me, raw, nascent and precious in the eyes of God.

At that exact moment she murmured something in her sleep and turned on her back. I imagined quite clearly that her eyes opened and she looked at me and smiled, offering languid arms wide in welcome, but in truth she didn't wake. Without averting my gaze I picked up the longer blade and advanced, prehensile toes grasping the filthy floorboards, a white-skinned ghoul, a Juggernaut. I reached the bed and, light as a cloud, knelt upon it straddling her. Still, still she did not rouse. The perfection of her face throbbed in the gloom. She was just Florence Maybrick's age. I raised my eyes to Heaven for some sign. None came but I could wait no longer. I grasped her gently by the hair with my left hand, then, with a silent, bestial exhalation of release, I slashed the blade deep into the innocent, ivory luminescence of her neck with calamitous violence. Her body convulsed and her arms flew up in a willowy, wind-blown parody of defense. I bore down savagely with all my weight, riving vein, artery, gland and ganglia, until the implacable metal rocked on bone.

'Oh, blood, blood, blood!'

Blood was everywhere, spurting in my face and on my chest, signing the wall in staggered rivulets. And now, I'm sure, her eyes were open and aghast and though there was no sound I heard it nonetheless, an echoing, boundless accusation streaming far out beyond the Firmament, her voice calling, calling… 'Help, help, ho, murder, murder, murder!'

After a breath-stopped eternity the hallucination of her pleas subsided and the panicked pulsations of her blood slowed and ceased. It was welling up like hot mud in a gentle gurgle on the bedclothes and I could hear it dripping beneath us onto the floor. I could hear no music. Gradually it seeped through the puzzled agony of my consciousness that I had ejaculated in slimy, mucoid gouts upon the coverlet.

The humiliation was beyond all bearing. Why, why was this?! Never before had I betrayed the slightest sexual arousal. My execution of His Will had been vestal pure. And now this. Out of all cognizance, this demeaning, disgusting emission!

"What do you want of me, oh Lord?!" my mind screamed, "Where are You? What are You?!"

In a paroxysm of rage and confusion I threw the coverlet and sheet aside, cut through the front of her chemise at a stroke and plunged the knife into her belly, slicing beneath her rib-cage in a blind frenzy of seeking, rending away wide strips of flesh and mounding them up on the table.

"Where is the Music, Lord?! Where is my Heavenly Choir?!"

Nothing.

Like a gibbering lunatic, with the encumbrance of her skin and muscle now torn away, I gouged out all her inner organs, the stomach, spleen, the pancreatic gland, the liver, kidneys and the rest, ripping them savagely from their interstitial moorings and casting them heedless about me on the bed.

"Where? Where are You?!"

No reply was vouchsafed in that hysterical, brain-bashed silence.

I hacked into her chest, chiseling a wide circle of tissue around each fat-engorged young breast, undercutting them beneath as you would fillet a fish and wrenched both bobbling slabs away clean from her ribs. I poked the knife up and down between the intercostal muscles on each side and forced my fingers into the opening, yanking down on each individual bone, separating them slightly, exposing her heart and lungs.

"Speak to me, my God! Give me a Sign, some Sign, some Gesture of Approval!"

Nothing at all broke through the sickening vacuum of my isolation.

Unable sufficiently to prise the ribs from the ligaments and reach her soul, with growing desperation I plunged my gore-stuck hands up into the gaping cavity of her abdomen and, almost without further cutting it seemed, excavated her heart from the vessels of her thorax and held it upwards to the uncaring ceiling with tear-filled eyes and palms imploringly outstretched, an Aztec High-priest before the sacrificial Altar of the Sun in Tenochtitlan.

"Is this it, oh Lord?! Is this the prize? Isn't this what You wanted after all?"

My mind was melting. The still twitching, fibrillating organ dropped from my hands to the grimy, splintered floor. I slid from the bed, pulling my sad, eviscerated rag-doll close to the table side, then with a silent howl of renewed horror I attacked her loins... 'on horrors head horrors accumulate!' ... carving away again great swaths of skin and fat and muscle and tendon from her lower belly, pulling out her organs of increase, everything, ovaries, uterus, intestines, bladder, buttocks, bowel, scraping away her vagina and rectum raw down to the pelvic arch... 'Is this nothing? Then the world and all that's in it is nothing! Nor nothing have these nothings if this be nothing!' ... I ran deep slits down both her thighs and cut away huge, livid chunks of the frontal musculature, exposing each femur. My blade was losing sharpness and I strength as the automaton poignard continued on, in seeming independence of my will, making long and irrelevant gashes in the helpless flesh of her flaccid, hanging calves.

'Cold, cold, my girl…?'

I retrieved the shorter blade deftly from the table and, gaining a brief second wind, set to work with it on her face in a malicious fury of revenge, slicing off her nose and ears, slitting her lips, peeling away the skin off her cheeks and forehead upward from the eyebrows as though preparing a chicken for the soup-kettle. Finally, as the crucifixion of my woe abated, I tattooed jagged, meaningless striations down her arms. I left her eyes alone. I don't know why.

I stood back gasping and began to sob…'*Eli, Eli, lama sabach-thani?*'…Father, why hast thou forsaken me? Outside I heard only the cruel drumming of the rain.

'Thou'lt come no more…'

I was blank. Lost. Solitary. Wretched. Naked. Bathed in gore to the very lips. All the sacred underpinnings of my life were gone. Vanished. He was not there. He was Not There! Either He never was or else, like Nietzsche's madman, I had killed Him. But from that moment it is certain, dead He was to me. To those of you who cling to Faith and believe I was merely making God a scapegoat, laying the blame on Him for my trivial, sexual inadvertency, I say no. To those of you for whom the absence of God is an easy commonplace and to whom the minotaur's cavern of my despair may seem a paltry, perhaps even a comical thing, I can only say that at the time I felt utterly dumbfounded and betrayed and hollowed out and gutted to the roots.

My tears eventually subsided and, like a reprimanded child, with both knives in my hands, leaving the door ajar, I went outside into the rain to wash, no more the Juggernaut, an empty wraith. Had anyone been looking into Miller's Court at half past four that morning what a revelation would have greeted their astonished eyes! The gas-lamp had been extinguished but whoever had done so had apparently been, soul and brain, dead to the *tragos* of our pageant within, nor had I noticed it, though I at least had some excuse.

I must have stood on the worn flagstones of that tiny, desolate court, beside the pump where I had washed my hands after the ecstatic delirium of my double venture, for at least ten minutes, numb to the icy deluge, hoping it would flush my agony away. It did not. As

I ran the blades mechanically between my fingers to rinse them I had a sudden, vainglorious impulse to cut away my privy member and the offending appendages beneath. I went so far as to spread my legs and place one knife in my groin at either side. I turned my eyes upward to the black, indifferent sky, forcing them open, bolding the pitiless drops to scourge away the salty exhibition of my grief.

"Is this what you really want, oh Lord?" I murmured without conviction.

My exhaustion was complete and I had to raise my hands to relieve my stinging eyes but only the strange, hypnotic lassitude of my state of mind, I believe, prevented me from actually carrying through with the emasculation and so ending my life.

I went back in. It smelled like an abattoir. My bare, wet foot bumped into her heart on the floor. I picked it up. It was hard to hold on so intense was the energy marooned within it, like an electric football, and, in a suicidal gesture of contempt, I took it outside, still naked, strode down the narrow passage and flung it far into the street. I can only surmise some lucky stray found breakfast for there was never a mention of it at her inquest.

I suddenly felt cold and hurried back into the room to dry myself on the cloth and hand-towels. The instinct for self-preservation reigned profound somewhere beneath my abnegatory daze. I pulled on both sets of underwear and my socks and shoes and felt my way to the mantel. On it I found a clay pipe and some other items and a candle. This I took back to the table and lit, after some difficulty, with a match from my jacket pocket. Being careful not to look at the bed, I gathered up the cloth and towels and the twine and my oil-cloth sack, I had no further wish nor use for it, and took them to the grate. The cloth and towels were understandably quite damp and I went to the closet to search for kindling. There I found a number of cotton shirts, one oddly small, a brace of overskirts, a waterproof cape, a crepe bonnet and what I took to be a petticoat and one by one I lit them in the fire, coaxing the cloth and towels to burn along with them. At the last, the oil and polish-soaked burlap and the twine provided quite a blaze. For some unfathomable reason, whether sentiment or superstition, I left Mary's clothes where I had folded them on the chair and placed her boots to warm by the hearth.

'Mary, Mary, quite contrary'...my gorgon grandmother's name was Mary.

Once certain that everything of mine had been consumed, I finished dressing, restored Florence Jessie's nuptial gift to its wonted place upon my ring-finger, and continuing to avert my guilty, coward eyes from the carnal, bleeding torment before me, I fancied I could hear the gristly snap and pop and squelch of cooling flesh, I snuffed the candle and went out the door, the key again in my waistcoat pocket, the knives secure under my arms... 'so petty, so foolish'... It was not quite five o'clock, still dark and raining.

It mattered not a fig to me whether anyone was in the streets to observe my escape and I couldn't tell you if they were. I'm sure I made a sorry sight indeed for anyone who might have taken notice, my face a histrionic mask of bereavement and self-obsession, as I staggered blindly I knew not where. I have not the slightest memory of what path my feet took but at length I found myself at Fenchurch Station purchasing a first-class ticket for the early local train to Southend. Why I was doing this or what, if anything, was leading me I hadn't a clue. I knew not a soul at this seaside town, in fact I had been there only once in my life, with my mother and grandmother and Edward, I think, as a boy of four or five. I seem to remember that it was then I learned to swim. As you know, I retained a strong athleticism ever afterward.

I was alone in the compartment, save for a severe and overflowing matron dressed in black who eyed me with suspicion not because she could in all the days of the world possibly have imagined the truth but because I could see that she assumed I was that most typical of men, a drunkard creeping sheepishly home to his wife and family after a night of debauchery and womanising. I recognised all too well the hidden prurience behind her saintly sniff... 'in filthy sloughs they graze and wallow'... But I was grateful that she would never deign to converse with such a reprobate as I and as we rumbled through the tunnel out of the station my shattered inner world began a slow and painful reassemblage.

'A childish toy.' 'No sin but ignorance.'

Marlowe's phrases from The Jew of Malta ran tedious circles in my brain... 'her lips suck forth my soul!'... Was I Faustus? Had my pact been with the Devil? I thought not. Why had I been so gullible and stupid all these years?

'I count religion but a childish toy and hold there is no sin but ignorance.'

I had always fervently repudiated anything resembling the so-called 'Higher Criticism', that braying, insidious rationalism that triumphed logic over faith, all those super-intellectual Germans and their English toadies. It wasn't Darwin, no no, his theories by themselves were not an argument against God nor had he intended them to be so, indeed they had come to seem eminently sensible. Yet now I felt quite certain that I was possessed of unimpeachable inner proof that there was not, nor ever had been, nor ever would or could be, any cogent, organising Power or Principle, any Absolute at all beyond or beneath the superficial, momentary, changeable workings of the world. Everything was fleeting and arbitrary and, worst of all, unknowable. I began to agree with Robert Elsmere's wife. What was the use of a rampart of euphemism and metaphor? If the Gospels were not true in fact they were of no value whatsoever. A Sunday playschool for weaklings and lick-spittles. Instead of a Juggernaut, I mused, I would become an *Übermensch*! Why not?

My *volte-face* to this radically opposing view of life was slow, however, as tortoise-like as our sedate procession on that early morning train. We emerged from the tunnel with the gasworks on the right and Tower Hamlets cemetery on the left. I wondered idly if Samuel Montagu had reserved a burial plot within it, but of course not, how silly, he was a Jew, orthodox and very wealthy besides. Then, for some unknown reason, my mind strayed from Montagu to my father and his loathing for the reformer, Charles Bradlaugh. How smugly delighted he had been when Bradlaugh was defeated in his run for election in Northampton riding, once while I was still at Cambridge and then again a few weeks before his death. How it would have galled him to know that Bradlaugh had at last been successful though. Because of his staunch refusal to take the customary oath of office because it mentioned God, he was denied his seat in the House of Commons for six more years until, after repeated re-election by his constituents, the government was finally forced to capitulate. Bradlaugh was a liberal, you see, a supporter of the workers' protests in Trafalgar Square, a champion of women's rights. In 1877, he and Annie Besant were prosecuted for publishing a book, The Fruits of Philosophy, that advocated birth control, though they later fell out due to her espousal of socialism. And this very year he had triumphantly seen the Affirmation Act passed through parliament, allowing unbelievers to merely affirm, not take, the oath in the courts of law as well as in the House. But more than all the other reasons, my father hated Bradlaugh because he was an atheist.

We passed the blackened row-houses of Bromley-by-Bow, the Hackney Marshes, the larger gasworks at West Ham and East London cemetery where Long Liz lay buried at the expense of the parish in an unmarked pauper's grave.

In Bradlaugh's Plea for Atheism, he wrote:

"...The atheist does not say 'there is no God', but he says 'I know not what you mean by God; I am without idea of God; the word God is to me a sound conveying no clear or distinct affirmation...The Bible God I deny; the Christian God I disbelieve in; but I am not rash enough to say there is no God as long as you tell me you are unprepared to define God to me.'..."

How father would have huffed and puffed...'Desolater! Who shall say of what thy rashness may have reft mankind? Take the sweet poetry of life away and what remains behind?'

True, I was desolate, but I could also find no vestige of the Hand of God, no 'sweet poetry', in the endless tenements and ill-kept warehouses I saw before me sweeping by without the carriage window. Nor could my frenetic cogitation sustain any satisfactory concept, any convincing definition of what I might have meant by God. The only image that constantly thrust itself into my weary mind was my own father's face! That's it, I thought, that's all it is! A sop to the nausea of our unknowable origin and our terror of the darkness to come. That's all religions are! That natural anxiety which is so slyly manipulated, for the convenience of the mendacious swine who wield the power in our so cynically and knowingly mis-named 'civilisation', to keep children upon the straight and narrow path. Serfs, sots and pillaged sheep! God, as we had been taught to think of Him, was nothing more than the callous, calculating invention of blackguards!

As we passed through the drab gloom of East Ham my eyes happened to pick out the inapposite quaintness of two road signs, Shakespeare Crescent and Hathaway Crescent...'Wherever there's a Will, there's a Way'...It's not true, of course, females outnumber males quite considerably in our importunate young species. Further north, I knew, in the vast City of London cemetery at Ilford, little Polly's corpse lay cold, unmourned and rotting.

The train turned south at Barking, following the river's course through Rippleside...not Ripperside!...South Dagenham, Rainham and Aveley to Tilbury where, in 1588, Queen Elizabeth I and Sir Francis Drake reviewed the English fleet before they sailed out to victory over the Spaniards and the Catholic Juggernaut of the Armada. Why has the whole of recorded history been the tawdry tale of pointless religious strife? What has it all been about, I ask you?!

I looked over at the mournful matron, with *pince-nez* perched, piously bent upon the incessant click-click of her knitting. No other soul had entered the compartment since our departure. How, I thought, how on earth do such people maintain this unassailable pose of righteousness? How could my father, in that same ponderous grandiloquy of my youthful fainting fit, have mocked the melancholy afflictions of Rousseau with the words, "Such, it would appear, is destined to be the unhappy fate of all who, to gratify a morbid singularity, resolutely oppose their own crude notions to the calm, deliberate and healthy judgement of the rest of the world." The self-satisfied, hypocritical old monster, taking it upon himself, as all such do, to assume what is healthy and what is not in the name of the "rest of the world"!

Delve sometime, if you can muster the stomach for it, into the cataclysmically vacuous ravings of my uncle Octavius in his pamphlet, An Affectionate Tribute to the Christian Memory of Forbes Benignus Winslow, oh yes, my own eminent father, published by none other than Shaw of Paternoster Row. It's thirty-four pages long and even has a quotation from Carlyle on the frontispiece! He harks back "with no little honest pride to the Winslows of Massachusetts, the founders of a new Empire, renowned throughout the world for the vastness of its territory, the culture of its intelligence and the purity of its religion." Rubbish! Exclusion, that's what they really want...'For the mind of the flesh is death, but the mind of the spirit is life and peace'...I ask you, what kind of double-brained nonsense is that?!

Mind and spirit and flesh are inseparable, you ditherer! You cannot have one without the others. They live and die together. Peace is not the opposite of death, it is its twin! You must make the best for yourself in this life. We are born from nowhere and die into nothing, that's all there is, let's please just face it. But no matter the pain and horror of life, it is still a gift and a miracle. Why must we require it to have a purpose? Why can't we simply revel in its majestic, heartless, unknowable mystery. The poetry is in the glorious lostness of it all. That's what it means to be an *Übermensch*, living that way, wild and free, not forever clinging to the umbilical, cradle song of religion!

We went on, through Stanford-le-Hope and South Benfleet, the clickety-clack of the undercarriage on the rails mimicked by the tick-tack of the matron's needles, until we reached Leigh-on-Sea where, after the primmest and most orderly preparation, she rose and, with the tiniest possible, disparaging nod in my direction, slid open the door to the compartment and disappeared. It was quite on purpose that I made no motion at all to help her.

Her place was taken by a tiny gentleman, well above eighty years of age, I should say, dressed neatly in visiting clothes and a bowler hat. I guessed him to be some long since retired City clerk, living frugally, with long lists of figures from his ledger-books still totting happily in his head. He looked at me with milk-blue eyes and raised his hat. A few valiant wisps of hair still graced the dappled whiteness of his pate.

"Good morning," he piped, in a high, glottlesome, reedy squeak. "Rain's giving over."

"Mm."

It was hard for me to find any kind of voice.

He sat gingerly and opened his newspaper. Of course, there was nothing yet on the front page regarding Mary. Only some local news and more on the Parnell Commission, I remember. The Commission had been formed at the request of the great champion of Irish Home Rule to challenge Conservative allegations that he had condoned the Phoenix Park murders. Though perhaps the article had been about Parnell's citation, by one Captain O'Shea, as co-respondent in a messy divorce suit, I'm really not sure.

We rattled on in silence, except for the little man's reflex habit of smacking his lips as he turned a fresh page, clearly his drying carcass was no longer producing sufficient saliva, through Westcliff, Southchurch, and Thorpe Bay to the end of the line at Shoeburyness. We both rose and I opened the door and when we reached the steps I helped him down to the platform. There was no flesh at all on his bones, brittle and starved as a bird. He chirruped, "Ta very much," and then, as though we were long lost friends, or father and son, he put his skeletal hand on my arm and said kindly, "Well, look after yourself now, won't you." I think I only managed a rather vacant nod and he was gone.

The face of the station clock read seven minutes past nine. I looked about the platform in a dream wondering what on earth was I doing there. My eyes fell upon a row of newspapers, the Times, the Globe, the Star, the Telegraph, nothing but Parnell again and expectant articles about the Lord Mayor's Show. We'll see about that, I thought. Then I went down to the wicket and bought a first-class express return to London, choosing the departure at sixteen minutes past two. I wandered out of the station taking the road north and west toward Great Wakering and Foulness Island.

'Well, look after yourself now, won't you ... ?'

The little man's words reverberated in the belfry of my exhausted brain. What had he seen? Perhaps nothing at all, I said to myself, and dismissed it. But, despite its smack of 'morbid singularity', I decided it was very good advice.

My steps finally took me away from the road and along the beach. The tide was in and just beginning to turn and the rain had stopped. At length, I came upon a deserted, pebbled cove under some low cliffs and sat down on an incongruous, crumbling, pudding-stone groyne to look at the sea.

You may think it an incomprehensible, frightening deficit in my character but during all this time I had not once thought of the reality of what I had just done. The fact that I had torn asunder the body of a beautiful young woman and thrown her heart away like a rotten melon was not what was bothering me at all. You may not wish to believe it but it wasn't. It simply wasn't. It was finding some reason to live on, some way back to a joyful existence in a universe that was blind and purposeless and utterly, utterly indifferent to me, that was what obsessed my churning soul.

I decided to take a swim in the frigid, gray waters of the Channel. If I came back, I came back, if I didn't, I didn't. Urim and Thummim, *doctrina et veritas*, *logos*, *mythos*, I didn't care what.

Having stripped to the second layer of winter woolies, and after relieving myself in what I can only term a bullock's sluice at the water's edge, I noticed that there was still some considerable pinkness and blotching of blood on my forearms and elsewhere on my skin and on the inside of that last layer of undergarment. I determined to jettison it far in the ocean currents.

Leaving my clothes high under the cliff I plunged, without preparation, into the icy water, ducking beneath a few low breakers near the shore, and swam with a steady crawl straight out to sea. A pale sun was just brightening the thick November clouds. When I stopped to look back, perhaps it was fifteen minutes later, I was at least half a mile from land. I had forgotten the outgoing tide, my progress had been much the more rapid because of it.

I realised that I would very likely have a devil of a time of it getting back, what with the rip and the cold and the strong possibility of cramp, but I didn't panic, rather I calmly relished the challenge. Once I had struggled out of the cumbrous, clinging wool and sent it to its aqueous grave, both my body and my mood were lightened ... 'rid of the machinery of rite and ceremony, over the hills began to creep a thin and watery light' ... Ha! ... I splashed about for a carefree, childish moment, caressed in my nudity, and then made with renewed spirits for the distant shore.

It took me well over an hour and a half, breasting with all my sinew the cosmic pull of that inexorable tide, many times my flagging muscles were tempted to give in but the life force within me was stronger still and at last, frozen to the bone and gasping, the slow whitecaps at the water's edge gently buffeted me into the shallows and I was able to wade onto the level sand. The tide had retreated a hundred yards or more from the pebbled shingle and I loped merrily across that icy stretch of mud to my clothes like some amphibious ancestor first clambering from the primaeval soup of Creation. I stood on the stones, letting the wind dry my skin before I dressed, clean and white, not a trace of guilt upon me ... 'bolt upright and determined to be well'!

To say that I was braced by this great wakening and felt purified of all foulness as I hastened back, retracing my steps to Shoeburyness, will only, I am sure, convince you that my punning strain of mind is beyond all correction, but, I'm sorry, I can't help it. I bought a rather sorry-looking cheese and pickle sandwich at the station and washed it down with a glass of tepid ginger beer and then slept like a log all the way up to London. The express took the shorter route through Basildon and Hornchurch and I arrived just fifty minutes later in the jolting contrast of the East End. Oh yes, rail service in England was as good as that in those days. It was now a quarter past three.

The depressing maw of Fenchurch Station was eerily quiet and deserted. I went to the newspaper kiosk. A grimy-faced lad of twelve behind the shelves announced in a husky adult voice before I had the chance to scan them, "There's been another 'orrible slaughter, sir. Worse than ever. Stopped the parade it did an' all. It's in all the dailies but they ain't come 'ere yet. Late because of the killin', y'see."

"Yes, I see. Do you know anything more about it?"

"No, sir."

"Well, I do," I said jauntily, giving the puzzled boy a silly, mocking, macabre wink and walked away. I can't think why I succumbed to such a daft impulse but I couldn't resist.

Just below London Street as you leave the station is the narrow thoroughfare of Seething Lane... sorry again, I know you don't find these things any fun!... Samuel Pepys set out from there to view the Great Fire... but, be that as it may, I was forced to use neat's leather because there wasn't a carriage in sight. I walked to Aldgate, shutting out all thoughts of a peek in Mitre Square, turning north towards Spitalfields through the winding back passages of Castle Alley... you'll come to know it soon enough... When I emerged on Wentworth Street I found myself amongst a pandaemonium of angry crowds milling noisily about. I came across people I recognised who would stop and regale me with wild, inaccurate descriptions of what had happened. One claimed that the murderer had made clean away with her head!

I winnowed from the breathless, near to hysterical chatter that Mary's corpse had not been discovered until late in the morning, almost eleven, by Tom Bowyer, a pensioner from the Indian army who worked for her landlord. Abberline had sent for the dogs but they hadn't come. Typical of the police, they said. They'd broken out the window and a photographer had taken pictures of the corpse and of her eyes. Her eyes! They was all staring wide though her face was gone, they said. But they hadn't actually entered the room until an hour or two ago. The landlord, McCarthy, had finally forced the door with an axe and nearly fainted dead away at the sight, they said, and had told them straight it looked 'more like the work of a devil than a man'. They'd cordoned off the whole area and weren't letting anybody near. A coffin had been sent for to take away the remains. They were waiting for it now.

I managed to push through the throng as far as the corner of White's Row and Commercial Street but it was almost impossible to get further. There, ironically, I bumped into Charles Moore and Tom Bulling just at the doors of Toynbee Hall.

"Ah, Lyttleton," Moore called out, "Half a minute. We want to talk to you."

Why not, I thought ... little tin god, little tin god ... as they made their way towards me. I could tell they were quite squiffy and enjoying themselves despite the general upset of the crowd. Outside observers, the 'journalist's eye'. I found them both despicable. But wait, but wait, that was a reflex from my older, starchier self. I had shed that skin. I elected to suffer them with playful benevolence.

"You haven't nabbed him, I see," Moore teased, his red cheeks shining jovially, "What do you make of this latest barbarity?"

Bulling, as usual, hung back, eyeing me with a taciturn, sceptical smirk, rolling a rancid nubbin of extinguished cigar between thin, dry lips.

"Still convinced it's, what did you call it, 'religious monomania'?"

"No doubt of it at all," I replied levelly. "It's the same man and we haven't seen the last of him yet, I'm afraid."

And, of course, my comments were parroted in many a lurid column on Saturday morning.

"Did you know Sir Charles has tendered his resignation?" Bulling broke his silence with an unsympathetic rasp.

"I didn't. When?"

"Yesterday apparently," Moore confirmed.

"I suppose it was only a matter of time."

Sir Charles Warren was, as I've told you, an army man and essentially a political moderate. He had been an appointee of Gladstone's Liberal government but now the Conservatives were in power and he felt that he had been unfairly stymied at every turn by the constant interference of Henry Matthews and the Home Office yet, in truth, he was never suited to the job. As a young man he had seen service in Palestine and had published three books on the archaeology of ancient Jerusalem. In retirement he became much involved in Baden-Powell's Boy Scout movement ... Baden-Powell, by the way, had once been an actor, and was, at this precise moment, a young officer serving with the 13th Hussars in Zululand! ... Warren was also, I knew, an evangelical Christian.

"No loss," said Bulling, "Casualties all round, I'd say."

He gestured laconically with his head at the noisy, frightened crush.

"Looks as though this lot's got its own back for Bloody Sunday."

He followed the acerbic acuity of this observation with an unhealthy, phlegm-sogged cackle and spat.

"I expect Monro'll be replacing him," said Moore, laughing uproariously at the absurd justice of it.

James Monro, as you will recall, had resigned his position as head of the CID at the time of Polly's transport because of the friction between himself and Sir Charles. It brought to my mind how this petty factionalism had always seemed to fall so timely to my benefit. But now, of course, now I had come to the mature realisation that such coincidences meant nothing, nothing at all, they were merely the chaotic workings of blind chance. I smiled with inward amusement that Monro, for all his vaunted capability, was a Millenarian, as was his successor as Assistant Commissioner, Robert Anderson, both babes in expectation of the Second Coming of Christ!

"Very droll," I agreed.

At that moment, a great hullabaloo arose amongst the multitude clustering the police cordon at the end of Dorset Street as a one-horse cart covered by a tarpaulin turned the corner from Commercial Street and made its way, with no little difficulty, the last twenty-five yards to Miller's Court. The constables were unable to restrain the mourners and they broke through the barrier and rushed to watch, some sobbing, some railing obscenities, some with ragged caps doffed, as a much-used coffin was taken inside and, after a tense *fermata* during which the whole situation might well have exploded in riot, Mary's shrouded remains were brought out and loaded on the cart, covered with the filthy cloth and driven away, amongst a cacophony of weeping and wailing and angry shouts, to Shoreditch Mortuary.

Now you must remember that through all this time I had stood with Freddy's carvers tucked beneath my arms and, though I am sure I might have convinced the police that they were for self-protection, I doubt if I could have persuaded any member of that distressed and violent mob. I sensed that I would risk considerable danger if I tarried and decided on the instant to go home.

How poignant, I thought, as I made my way north past the market, turning west at Lamb Street to Spital Square, that this whole tragic slum had once been open fields with a view, from the 13th to the 17th centuries, of the not so benign façade of Bedlam, the hospital of St. Mary of Bethlehem, long since removed to Moorfields and now, with its splendid dome, at St. George's Fields in Hyde Park... Mary meets Hyde... I know, I know, I know, I've got to stop it!

I decided that the only hope for a carriage would likely be at Liverpool Street Station so I walked down Bishopsgate and, after a nervy wait of fifteen or twenty minutes, I was fortunate to secure my passage to Wimpole Street from there.

I entered my blessed sanctuary just after seven o'clock. It was hardly more than twenty-four hours since I had politely clapped my hands at Florence Maybrick's singing. What a total reversal of thought, what a transformation had taken place within my soul! For the first time in my life I was truly free! No more crushing pressure to exist as metaphor, torturing beautiful reality through a double-brained looking-glass of the rest of the mad world's craven opinion! No more the lie of gentle Jesus with his crown of thorns and his patient, hooded, downcast eyes and the silent accusation of his beatific smile! No more pious pangs of insidiously inculcated guilt at the agony of the Crucifixion! No more listening to the stupefyingly banal, sadomasochistic epistles of St. Paul and all the rest of his monomaniacally twisted disciples spanning the sorry, vicious ages since! No more phony doxology! No more God! No more religion of any sort, monotheistic, polytheistic, pantheistic or supra-theistic! I was done with the whole ghastly, indefensible pile! What a relief! I threw myself down on Florence Jessie's loving brocade and laughed and laughed and laughed.

Freddy, thankfully, would not come until the morning. Yet, despite my overwhelming fatigue, I forced myself to rise and go to the kitchen where I scrubbed and dried the knives, even though they were already clean, and replaced them in the drawer. Then I went upstairs to the bathroom and removed my clothes, meticulously checking each garment, one by one, inside and out, for any sign of blood. I found two slight stains above the cuffs of my right trouser leg, two tiny splatters that I suppose had flown across the room at the height of my frenzy, but they were hardly distinguishable from the dark colour of the cloth and thankfully no one in my travels that day had noticed. There was nothing on my shoes, I'm sure the rain had washed them long before I had reached Fenchurch Station. I stood in front of the mirror and examined my skin, front and back, but, other than some grains of sand between my toes, I was quite clean. I even checked my fingernails but, of course, any trace of red had been scoured away during my desperate swim against the out-rushing tide. The key I kept as a symbol of my liberation.

Having put the clothes away and donned a dressing-gown, I went to the bed and pulled out the trunk beneath. If Freddy questioned me about the two missing hand-towels or the sea-drowned woolies I would simply claim ignorance but I knew he wouldn't. He was far too polite. He would simply fret and assume it was his own oversight. I took the jars, one still containing a hemisphere of little Kate's kidney, the other Annie's puckered uterus complete with cervix still attached and the cheeky, floating circle of her navel, and went again downstairs to the scullery. There I carefully tipped away the wine-spirit from both jars into the basin, retrieving the organs and placing them on the draining-board. Using the same paring-knife with which I had desecrated the bloom of Mary's face and sliced through the tired wattles of Long Liz Gustafsdotter's neck, I cut them into small sections, scooped them into a mixing bowl and flushed them away in the downstair's water-closet. It took several pulls on the chain and a good scrub round with the brush to completely dispatch them. Then I cleaned up the bowl and knife, wiped down the draining-board, washed the jars and tops with strong soap, finally rinsing the smell of the wine-spirits away in the basin with a long douse of boiling water ... 'for the women of Moab and Midian shall die and their blood shall mingle with the dust' ... what offensive and distasteful drivel!

I dried the jars and took them back upstairs, replaced them in their padded forms in the trunk and carried the whole again to the attic. Then I ran a hot bath and soaked the itch of the salt water from my skin. On impulse I smoked a cigar while I was doing it! ... 'If there were dreams to sell, what would you buy? Life is a dream, they tell, waking, to die.'

What luxury! What luck!

The Tragedy of Woman

You may be thinking, I suppose, that there cannot be much more of interest to my story, but you would be dead wrong. Surely you realise that I did not introduce the Maybricks for nothing. And, perhaps you forget, there is still one more murder. Alice 'Clay Pipe' McKenzie. I need to tell you about my shamefully Machiavellian motive for sending her packing and the subdolous way in which her death facilitated my crowning achievement. Oh yes, have a little intestinal fortitude.

When Freddy arrived at seven o'clock with the morning papers I had already eaten breakfast, but I was ravenous and, when he had time to prepare it, I ate his as well. We immediately discussed the horror of the murder, of course. I told him I had hurried there in the afternoon and that I had seen her body being removed from Dorset Street. He told me he had been directly outside St. Paul's with the family when, as the Star put it, "the well-stuffed calves of the City footmen were being paraded for the laughter of London" and the first newsboys had appeared yelling, "Murder! Another 'orrible murder in Whitechapel!"

Much to Freddy's dismay some young medical students had apparently taken the opportunity to run amok knocking off people's hats in the crowd. His scandalised description of one of them leaping on a constable's back and biting his thumb was, I must say, quite comical. I thanked him for the papers and took them to my study, not to gloat, but rather to bask in the glorious muddle of it all.

The Morning Post, among others, enlarged freely on my comments to Moore and Bulling, and there were, of course, *ad nauseam*, the gruesome details of the mutilations, but I noted with a smile that, although several papers reported, with imprudent and offensive haste, that the killer had stolen away the victim's uterus, the police, in every instance, were careful to conceal that any part of her body was missing.

Sir Charles Warren's resignation was announced and in his name the offer of... 'Her Majesty's gracious pardon to any accomplice, not being a person who contrived or actually committed the murder, who shall give such information and evidence as shall lead to the discovery and conviction... *etc.*' Still no offer of a reward for simple information, Matthews couldn't bear to give in on that point, but a pardon! What a gnarl of furrowed brows there must have been at the Cabinet meeting that decided on this transparent piece of obfuscation! They knew perfectly well that such intervention, besides being pointless, would be immediately challenged in the Commons, which indeed it was. They really were getting desperate.

I was most fascinated to read several eye-witness accounts of people who claimed to have seen Mary in the street, alive and complaining of the 'horrors of drink' and that she had vomited up her breakfast, as late as half past eight or nine o'clock on Friday morning. I was never, even then, absolutely certain that I didn't believe in ghosts. Are you?

The inquest was to be held at Shoreditch Town Hall beginning on Monday morning and I resolved, come what may, to attend.

After consuming Freddy's delightfully well-presented repast, I had a sudden impulse to telephone Florence Jessie and tell her that I would come down to Brighton that afternoon. Will it offend you when I say that I had a very pleasant visit? Dulcie was blooming, reading Dickens and discarding boyish admirers right and left, it would appear, at least from her giggling description of it. Florence Jessie, too, seemed much more buoyant than on any of my previous trips in the past year, and, though the cloud of Percy's unsettled future still hung over us, Ashton was doing exceptionally well in his last year at Rugby. It had been six months at least since Florence Jessie and I had made any gesture toward lovemaking but that night we did so with a joy and freedom and, dare I say it, abandon that had not been the case since almost before the children were born.

It was, surprisingly, more on her initiation than my own. I must confess when I became aware of her desire I was quite anxious that I would be entirely unable to perform the act with Mary's so recent image hovering in my mind. We lay afterwards in each other's arms and talked sincerely and lovingly about many intimate matters. It was beautiful.

I returned to London on the last train on Sunday evening.

The inquest began the following morning at eleven o'clock before Dr. Roderick McDonald. He was an exacting Scotsman and a Radical. He was known as the 'crofter's M.P.' and sat in the House of Commons as representative for the constituency of Ross. I did not arrive until two o'clock because I knew that the jury would be taken to the mortuary first to view the body and likely visit the crime scene in Miller's Court as well but when I did Abberline told me of the ridiculous dispute over jurisdiction that had taken place at the outset of the proceedings between several jurors and the coroner. It began with one of the jurors objecting to having the inquest 'thrown on our shoulders when the murder did not happen in our district but in Whitechapel.' Another insisted that Wynne Baxter should therefore rightfully preside. After which, McDonald ... 'the merciless' ... 'showed like a rebel's whore' ... sorry! ... had reprimanded them severely, saying:

"Do you think that we do not know what we are doing here? The jury have no business to object. If they persist I shall know how to deal with them. I am not going to discuss the matter. The jurisdiction lies where the body lies, not where it was found. It was taken to my mortuary and that is the end of it."

A bit abrupt, perhaps, both Abberline and I agreed.

I listened to the evidence. Joe Barnett told the jury about Mary's past and that he had last seen her early in the evening with Maria Harvey. I learned, with both delight and chagrin, that the corner of the window by the door had been broken out in an argument sometime before Joe had lost the key and afterwards they had simply thrust through it to open the latch. My leprechaun's gift, my pot of gold, my lighthouse beacon, my Acceptance from on High had not been necessary after all! I could merely have reached in! Ha! And there was much inane discussion about the murderer having to have had a key because the door had been locked when they found her. But it was a spring lock, it fastened automatically!

However, there was one eerie thing. Amidst all the deposition and depiction of the various people with whom Mary had been seen on that last evening of her young life, needless to say there were several 'Jewish-looking' suspects, it was by now almost *de rigueur*, two independent witnesses described having heard a voice crying 'Murder!' at precisely the moment of her death. You know that I had heard it too, though, of course, I alone was aware that she had not made the slightest sound other than in the echoing corridors of my febrile imagination. Clearly, the two women, Sara Lewis and Elizabeth Prater, despite being much less than perfect specimens of the female sex, were a great deal more in tune with the unseen vibrations of this universe than the man who had so blithely extinguished the gas-lamp!

Dr. Phillips, the medical examiner, only got so far as to state that the cause of death had been the severing of the right carotid artery when McDonald cut him off saying that more detailed evidence could be given at a later date. After Abberline's testimony, which, poor chap, perforce involved a rather sheepish admission regarding the dogs, their absence was not at all his fault, McDonald asked the jury if they had enough evidence to conclude the proceedings. Following a few minute's consultation, the foreman stood up and said, yes, they would return a verdict of 'willful murder against some person or persons unknown.' And that, to everyone's astonishment, and my inward hilarity, was that!

I realised that I had taken a considerable chance in going because of the total void in my memory of events during my agonised sleep-walk from Miller's Court to Fenchurch Station. I had checked all the news reports carefully but I couldn't be perfectly sure that someone who might have seen me would not be there and cry me out. In this, however, as in so many other things, I was incredibly, undeservedly lucky.

I wasn't entirely spared. My heart took a leap into my throat the following morning. Moore telephoned me from the Central News office shortly after eight o'clock to tell me that they had an eye-witness who could identify the killer! He had been in customary attendance at one of Melville Macnaghten's Corinthian dinner parties after the inquest when they heard that a man named Hutchinson had just walked into the Commercial Street station and given a statement that the police were taking very seriously. It would be in all the evening papers but, infuriatingly, he said he hadn't time to tell me the whole story and rang off. As you can appreciate, I was more than a little on tenter-hooks until I read them.

As it turned out it was of no danger to me, though the testimony did contain one marvelous, coincidental oddity. Hutchinson claimed that he was a friend of Mary's and that he had seen her with a well-dressed, 'foreign' gentleman at about two o'clock that morning. The man, he said, was carrying a parcel wrapped in 'American cloth'! He had watched them go into Miller's Court and had waited for a time outside Crossingham's rooming-house on the other side of Dorset Street for the man to reappear. When he didn't Hutchinson got fed up with the rain and cold and went away.

Now, assuming his story to be true, it must have been that gentleman's back I had seen turning the corner into Bell Lane. How exquisitely close our paths had come! I imagined some stingy cheap-jack who had in all likelihood waited for Mary to fall asleep after their sordid assignation in order to recover his fee before stealing away because she was deep in the arms of Morpheus when I entered the room. There was certainly no mention of any money having been found amongst her possessions in any of the police reports. It's more likely, however, that there had been no such gentleman at all and it was Hutchinson's back I had seen turning the corner. The veracity of his statements was seriously to be doubted. Perhaps he had been standing outside vacillating in his desire for her and finally, faced with the obvious stumbling-block that he had no money, simply got cold feet.

Whatever the facts, this man led Abberline a merry chase. Moore told me that he was out with Hutchinson for several nights thereafter scouring Whitechapel for another glimpse of his 'gentleman'. I had decided independently, just on the off-chance, that it might be the better part of valour to stay home.

Moore had also discovered that Hutchinson, in his original testimony, described the man as 'Jewish-looking'. In their quite useless dilution of this to 'foreign-looking' and, as evidenced in their qua-vering reticence to speak of Mary's missing cardial pump and the obviously higher-directed truncation of her inquest, the authorities were exhibiting their typical tight-lipped paranoia. What, I ask you, is the actual motive lurking behind all such official censorship? Is it to protect the public as they always claim? Never! It is ever the need, as with unconfident children, to have little secrets, to bolster up their flagging self-delusion of importance and power!

Melville Macnaghten, by the by, was the son of the last chairman of the East India Company, the family had a fortune in tea plantations, and a friend of James Monro's. They had made acquaintance in India. In 1881, Macnaghten had been knocked senseless by land rioters and Monro was then the Inspector-General of the Bengal Police. On his return to England the previous year, Monro had offered him the post of Assistant Chief Constable with the CID at Scotland Yard but the Home Office had finally rejected the appointment because Sir Charles didn't want 'the only man in India who had been beaten by Hindoos'! It was a good part of the reason for Monro's earlier resignation. I ask you, what possible chance did fools of this nature have of catching me? The wonderfully acid lyricist, William Schwenk Gilbert, lampooned all such pompous 'poo-bahs' and 'model major-generals' to perfection in the Savoy operas!

Thousands of people were outside St. Leonard's Church in Shoreditch on the following Monday to watch Mary's coffin carried from the mortuary. None of her relatives had ever made themselves known but the good verger of St. Leonard's, Henry Wilton… You'll be grateful that I refrain from reference to the 'coincidental' appellation of my brother Edward's parish! Such nonsense, I promise you, is all in the past!… paid for her funeral so that she would not have to suffer the indignity of a pauper's grave. I admit I felt a slight twinge of such sentiment, a wish that there might have been some way that I could have contributed without arousing suspicion. It was apparently a proper affair, the hearse drawn by two horses with two mourning coaches behind. The police had a difficult time making a path for the cortège through the wailing crowd with people scrambling forward to touch the coffin and throw flowers and women sobbing and crying out, "God forgive her!" The procession, once launched, carried her shattered remains all the way across the Hackney Marshes to the Roman Catholic cemetery at Leytonstone. It was with genuine sympathy the next day that I read in the newspapers of these simple-hearted outpourings. Of course, for the reasons aforementioned, I kept well away.

Let me try, as succinctly as I can, to clarify for you what had happened to me. I sense that there may be some lingering confusion in your mind. It was not at all that I expected Almighty God to magically leap forth from Mary Kelly's loins and confront me with His august and white-bearded Presence, bestowing instant sainthood upon my humble person in that vile stew of a room. Surely even the devout among you cannot have thought me as infantile as that. No, no, it was rather that I was seeking an ultimately transcendent leap of faith within myself brought about through a perfect intimacy with life's pulse and death's mystery... 'Lord of the candent lightenings'... Like St. Simeon Stylites perched on his pillar, or Christ delirious in the wilderness of Sinai, I was hoping for much, much more than the fleeting glimpses of Paradise that I had experienced in tantalisingly exalted increments with the others. I was convinced that I could attain to a permanent state of uncontrolled bliss in which the heavenly cadence of God's Music never stopped. I was the same as any opium-eater in his den. I had become a slave, addicted to the adoration of an illusion. I tore away her flesh in a misguided attempt to tear away the burden of my own and live as an ecstatic, disembodied spirit. Such futile obsessions have, alas, been all too common through the ages. They have manifested themselves in many forms and many guises, all dangerous and doomed to failure, from the shivering emaciation of the desert hermit to the Roman Legions on their Juggernaut march to world dominion, from the circus fakir on his bed of nails to the narcissistic agony of Christ on the cross. An unassuageable dissatisfaction with the given conditions of our earthly life!... 'man's reach should exceed his grasp or what's a Heaven for!'... This was the very human madness from which my uncontrollable and shocking penile malfunction had finally, mercifully rescued me. At last I could put the itch of Edgar's 'foul fiend' behind me and become, simply and joyously, Lear's 'thing itself'. No more the cobweb veil of religious sophistry but 'unaccommodated man', alone, fearless and free! Truly at home, a perfect beast.

Well, *mutatis mutandis*, I hope that clears it up for you. It's the best I can do and I'm not going to talk about it any more. You're too polite to say it but I'm sure that will be an immense relief! From this juncture, I promise, I shall speak solely of results. No more excess, just success.

There was much of the farcical in the aftermath to Mary's death. Queen Victoria herself got into the act and sent a chiding telegram to

Lord Salisbury... the prime minister was a scion of the Cecil family whose powerful influence in the affairs of the realm stretched back to Lord Burghley, the secretary of state, treasurer and wily confidant of Elizabeth I...

"This new most horrid murder shows the absolute necessity for some very decided action. All these courts must be lit and our detectives improved. They are not what they should be."

Ha! Such touching concern! How did so tender a heart manage to condone her country's imperial ambitions in Africa, the ruthless crushing of the Zulus, the blood-lust for diamonds or Cecil Rhodes' grotesque and maniacal vision of 'British rule from Cape to Cairo'?! Those were some of the questions that occurred to me!

It is a merely anecdotal irony, to which I cannot resist allusion, that one of the main reasons the prime minister refused to dismiss his clearly incompetent Home Secretary, Henry Matthews, was because Matthews was Catholic. Indeed, he was the first Roman Catholic who had been a member of the Cabinet since the Elizabethan era and Salisbury was fearful that his entire government might fall if Matthews either resigned or was removed from his post. So delightfully arbitrary is the tergiversation of history. The only constant is the struggle for power which, once attained, will never be relinquished without a fight.

Practical jokesterism had a brief run in the West End. Some youthful bright sparks took to invading the posh suburbs and generally disturbing their sanctified peace by bellowing at the top of their lungs late into the night about further counterfeit murders and mutilations. One furious resident of Pembroke Square wrote to the Telegraph, "... is it not monstrous that the police do not protect us from such a flagrant and obscene nuisance?!"

'O monstrous, monstrous!'

The police had their hands full protecting innocent citizens in the East End from becoming the unwitting victims of the violent mobs that roamed the streets. One had merely to attract the slightest suspicion to light the fuse of vengeance. Woe betide you if you in any way resembled 'a tall, sandy-whiskered man of rough appearance', 'a short man of German appearance', 'a gentleman with a black bag and a moustache', 'a foreign-looking man with a brown paper parcel under his arm', 'a swell with spats on his boots, a gold watch-chain and an astrakhan collar to his overcoat', 'a blotchy-faced fellow who looked like a labourer', 'an elderly respectable-looking man with the appearance of a clergy-man' or any of the other so-called 'eye-witness' descriptions.

Although, of course, they dutifully investigated every lead and interviewed hundreds of suspects in the weeks and months following the ninth of November the police, as we know, got nowhere. James Monro took up his position on the twenty-seventh and shortly there-after procured extra funds to support an increased force of nearly one hundred and fifty officers in plain clothes. I had known these secret patrols had been in operation since my waltz with Dark Annie but to a lesser degree. They were untrained amateurs, easy to spot, and I had little trouble remaining invisible, even to them.

However, as the new year of 1889 wore on into the spring with absolutely no progress in the case, the general public, and therefore, of course, the press, lost interest, the plain-clothes patrols were dis-banded, even the Toynbee Hall students who had been part of the first Vigilance Committee formed at St. Jude's by Thomas Hancock Nunn gave up the chase due to exhaustion, the excitement gradually died away and I began to feel as though I had lost the best of a golden opportunity. I determined to rectify this but you'll have to wait a bit to see quite how I managed it. It was necessary to create an ever-ex-panding cobweb of untruth, some of which I have already described to you at length.

More than anything else though, as throughout this 'strange, eventful history', it was luck.

On the evening of May the eleventh James Maybrick died and three days later his wife Florence was formally taken into custody by the Liverpool Police on suspicion of his murder.

It was alleged that she had systematically mixed arsenic with his food and also in his drinks. He had suffered from bad health for some time but the acute and baneful symptoms, it was said, had only developed a few weeks before his death. As I read the report of this in the Times I realised on the instant that she was innocent. I had clearly detected the signs of his addiction during our one meeting at his brother's the day before Mary's death. I decided to take an active part in the case and to see what I might do for her. The Grand Jury date was set for the twenty-sixth of July.

For some months prior to this it had been forcing itself upon my consciousness that, in order that I might finally be acknowledged through all England as the man who arrested the murderous hand of 'Jack the Ripper', which had always, as you know, been a large part of my double-brained plan, I would have to commit another sensational atrocity. It made me very nervous frankly, it had no appeal at all, and yet I became more and more convinced of its necessity. After my glorious rebirth as a carnal being in Miller's Court I had let the issue grow cold. I would have to rekindle it. Once the date of Florence Maybrick's trial was announced I knew, don't question how, that July would be the perfect time.

In the early part of the month I was called to examine a man named Currah who had murdered one Letine, the proprietor of a troupe of acrobats. Currah had a daughter, Beatrice, who had been engaged by Letine as one of his troupe but, very shortly afterwards, he had discharged her. As a result of this Currah had brought various actions against Letine for wrongful dismissal and for the ill-treatment of his beloved daughter. In each case the acrobat had emerged victorious and this had apparently affected Currah's mind. To top it all off, the child had died and Currah naturally felt that her premature death had been caused, in no small measure, by Letine. So, one day he had waited at the stage door of the Canterbury Theatre of Varieties and stabbed Letine as he came out. Immediately thereafter he had made a gruesome but unsuccessful attempt on his own life. In consequence of this he was taken to St. Thomas's Hospital where I examined him in conjunction with the house surgeon.

Currah suffered from mental prostration, the result of the tribulation he had passed through, and he had become haunted with auricular and visual hallucinations to the effect that he was pursued by the spirit of his dead daughter who had urged him on to the killing. I was summoned to give evidence at his trial and he was acquitted on my testimony.

This particular case brought me back once again into the public eye and I had an odd premonition that, if I played my hand correctly, Florence Maybrick's plight might soon serve to enhance my reputation even further. It was propitious then, all my instincts told me, that, if I could just summon up the blood for a few final thrusts with Freddy's carvers, I would have a sure foundation on which to bring my already well-laid plot to fruition.

The evening of Tuesday, July the sixteenth, was warm, muggy and overcast. Freddy left to go home, slightly later than usual, at about ten minutes past eight. I had been worrying myself sick all day knowing that this was the night to strike. It was early in the week, you see, and, even though it had been more than eight months since the last murder and the general level of police and public vigilance in Whitechapel had again become quite lax, oh yes, the short memory of our species has always been of immeasurable assistance to the criminal classes, both the poor and the powerful, there was still the habitual assumption that the killer was more likely to perpetrate his horrible crimes on, or near, the weekend. Also, the inquest and the magisterial inquiry into Florence Maybrick's case had been completed and had upheld the charge of murder. I knew that I wanted to be in conspicuous presence outside St. George's Hall in Liverpool on the following Friday and I had promised Florence Jessie more than a perfunctory visit before then.

After two hours pacing my study like a caged animal I went upstairs to dress. I told myself that, even if I could not bring myself to do the deed, some similar murder might well occur that would suffice. Though my familiar woolen suit would certainly be too hot, I had no summer garments of the necessary dark colour. I was also superstitious about any change in tactic. I put it on and the same soft-soled shoes, then descended to the kitchen for the knives. I was even more jittery than before my night with 'Emma' Tabram and had to visit the water-closet to relieve myself though there was not much realistic need. Despite this, as my shaking hands struggled to unbutton my fly, a childish spurt of urine shot down my trouser leg. Damnation, I'll never manage to go through with it, I thought.

Like a juddering automaton, I went back into my study to fetch Mary's key and my two half crown talismans from the locked centre drawer of my desk. For reasons too obscure for my mind to fathom, the touch of these now magical objects brought a welcome degree of calm to my quaking nerves. I placed them, as before, in the pockets of my waistcoat and returned to the vestibule, donned the felt hat and, instead of the overcoat, took a light cape over my arm in case the clouds should decide to open. It was just before eleven o'clock. After several deep breaths to steady myself I ventured out the door.

Whether it was the threatening sky or the yet undiminished panic of the times, the streets were mercifully bereft of summer strollers. I encountered the occasional pedestrian, however, and made sure, as I did so, bidding them a polite 'good evening', that they were not of my acquaintance. In Upper Regent Street a passing constable, who recognised me, enquired sympathetically where I was going and answered his own question, "To attend a patient, I'll warrant." I didn't dissuade him, just smiled and nodded, but, as bad luck would have it, a brougham was clattering by at that moment and the obliging constable whistled it down for me. Of course, he asked me the particulars of my destination so that he might tell the driver. For some reason, I winked and volunteered the lie of Whitehall Place. This, at least, had the effect of silencing further curiosity concerning who my patient might be but, as the carriage got underway, I was overcome with an uncontrollable shiver. Events were unfolding less than perfectly.

By the time I had hailed a second carriage below Charing Cross Station on the Victoria Embankment it was gone half past eleven. Damn the stupid interference! I told the second driver to convey me, with all reasonable haste, to the London Hospital in Whitechapel Road. Yet, I mused, as we trotted along and my irritation subsided, perhaps the little detour had been for the best. Certainly no suspicions would now arise in the mind of the meddlesome constable and he had cleared me of my home turf without incident.

As we entered Whitechapel High Street at twenty minutes past midnight, I noticed two policemen chatting together at the entrance to Castle Alley. I surmised that one, or both, had just traversed it on their beat. Then, not thirty seconds later, I spied a woman, staggering a little, at the corner of Church Lane. At the next, Union Street, I told the driver to stop, that I would walk the rest of the way to the hospital from there. Despite paying him well he grunted humourlessly, wheeled the carriage around and returned the way we had come, barely missing the woman as she stumbled back over to the corner of Brick Lane and continued on down the north side of the High Street. I could see that she had lit a pipe and was puffing on it. I hurried after her.

As I pursued her across Commercial Street, the two constables were lost to view. I caught up to my sad, sacrificial pawn at the precise spot where they had been standing. The sound of my footsteps made her turn. I was glad that I did not recognise her freckled face. We wasted no time.

"What d'you want?" she said, cold, hard and blunt.

I could detect a Cambridgeshire accent and was reminded of my winter sleigh-ride in Croydon with the tutor of Downing College.

"What d'you want?" she repeated.

I was grateful for her insistence. I was so on edge I could not speak. I took out the half crowns from my waistcoat and nodded curtly with my head into the alley.

Unlike Fay, this pug-faced little woman did not take my mute gesturing for innocence. The sight of the half crowns seemed instead to make her angry, a bitter foreknowledge born of crude experience that the amount inevitably would require something perverted and unpleasant that she had no choice but to give. I motioned again for her to follow.

There was a single street-lamp half way along and by its light I could see the alley was deserted. A few paces beyond it I stopped and waited. I held the cold blade of the paring-knife already concealed in my right hand. We were partially hidden from view of the alley entrance by two covered carts. She came slowly up beside me.

"What d'you want?" she whispered with finality.

She, too, was nervous now.

I reached out with my free hand and softly touched her hair. Her eyes were darting, looking for the half crowns, anxious, ready to bolt. Impelled by the necessity of action, as I had always been, and refusing to be swayed by the genuinely guilt-sick feelings of that moment, with a sudden violent wrench, I pulled her head back and, swinging my body round in a single fluid motion, I plunged the knife straight into the left side of her neck. She had no time to squeal. I pulled the blade, flung her roughly to the pavement and fell upon her like a demon. My knees struck her midriff knocking the wind from her with a rib-cracking grunt. Slamming down the heel of my left hand on the breathless gape of her mouth, I thrust Freddy's peeler again to the hilt and carved sideways beneath her chin, this time, I was sure, severing both the carotid artery and windpipe, but, despite the overwhelming savagery of my attack, she still struggled to throw me off. Her teeth bit down hard into the fist-knuckle of my little finger, drawing blood, and with clawing arms and flailing legs and all her fading strength she was desperately trying to escape. Clearly I had not succeeded in separating the rungs of her voice-box for, beneath my ruthless smother, she kept attempting futile calls for help. Alas, she could manage no more than a choked, drowning gargle, since my full body weight was forcing her heart to pump the life away through her wounds into the gutter in ghastly, hissing spouts.

"Die, please," I whispered, "Die."

Her eyes were staring wide in agony. She had no breath to spit at me the contemptuous blood that flooded her larynx and only the barest, eerie, fluted siffle escaped her lips.

"... I .... Know .... You ... !"

Red, salivate bubbles rose slowly through her tar-stained teeth as her heart muscle at last gave way and she succumbed. Of course, there was no music. On the contrary, I remember noticing with a kind of blanched amusement through my nausea that at that very moment it started to rain. I knew that I was about to be sick and staggered to my feet. The horror of what I had just done was swimming everywhere before my eyes yet I had to make it appear a genuine ripping or render it superfluous. I quickly raised her skirts to expose her belly. I had intended to gut her like the others but I was too overcome and could manage only a few feeble incisions before rushing to the far end of the alley to vomit.

I cannot recall as total a voiding of stomach contents at any other time in my life, but then, as I've told you, I had rarely, if ever, been seriously ill. Not daring to turn or look, nor wait for the final, acrid heave, I vanished into the narrow passageway of previous chance acquaintance that brought me happily out to Wentworth Street. I was no sooner there than I heard the shrill summons of a policeman's whistle. I had sensed as much. I dashed across Goulston and Middlesex Streets, passing by the dismal, darkened warehouses of Sandy Row, and entered the relative sanctuary of the City via Harrow Alley. I stopped for a moment in the foul misnomer of Devonshire Square to rinse my hands and the knife at a stand-pipe, then out I sailed, reeking of bile acids, into the calm of Bishopsgate. It was less than five minutes since my wracking evacuation in Castle Alley and I was once again seated in a fortuitous clarence that whisked me toward home from Liverpool Street.

Of course, despite being thus overwrought, trembling from head to toe with shock, momentarily hideous and repugnant even to myself, I was not foolish enough to be conveyed direct to

Wimpole Street. Instead, I asked to be driven to Lowndes Square in Knightsbridge... William Lowndes was a friend of my uncle Edward's... a bookseller's son, he compiled The Bibliographer's Manual of English Literature, the first invaluable reference work of its kind. My father's signed copy had gathered dust for many years on a lower shelf in my study... and from there, after a suitable pause, I walked home across Hyde Park through the meaningless drizzle.

As I passed through the Albert Gate and along Rotten Row to the Dell, there to wash my face and hands and the blade again in the Serpentine, I had to come to grips with a new and terrible awareness, one I had truly never faced before. I was no longer in thrall to religious monomania. All the previous murders might perhaps be excused by the fact that I was seeking a 'higher good', however deluded, but this last could not. I had done it merely to further my own paltry ambition. That I had carried through with it under these circumstances revealed something quite terrifying about me. No doubt the other assassinations had dulled my consciousness to the blood and barbarity of the fell action I had performed almost as routine... yet who was I? Who was I now? No Juggernaut. No *Übermensch*. Just a nasty little man who had killed a perfectly innocent woman for no good reason. Yes. And the ebbing life force sang of no glory. It was nothing but a hopeless, helpless fall into the bottomless hollow of a well. No choirs of angels but a consummation devoutly to be avoided, as the poor little woman had so frantically tried to do.

As I knelt by the softly quacking, sleepy ducks, a flood of hellish images broke teeming through the stubborn breastwork of my conscience. Each murder, one following hard upon the other, viewed from on high and set in stark relief, without any amelioration of heavenly music or Christian sentiment, minutely detailed, brutal, sickening and banal. All their contorted faces, now with blood red eyes and snake-writhed hair and wildly beating wings, accusing, knowing, hating, screeching, none forgiving. None in bliss, none relieved, none 'glad of it really', none 'gone to a better place'. All aggrieved and livid, howling at me in the misty, dripping quiet to restore their stolen lives. No matter the sordid destitution, the misery, the debasement, it was what they had and all they had and I had cheated them of it! For God?! Ha! Ha! Ha! Ha! Ha! Ha! For nothing!

'O let me not be mad! Not mad! I would not be mad!'

The swirling furies tore into my mind, harping relentlessly on my cowardice in Miller's Court, the moment I shrank from self-castration, a fate I well deserved unlike their heavenly progenitor, son of chaos and husband to the treacherous earth, tempting me, daring me again and again to the extreme verge of the precipice, until at last I could bear it no more. I leapt to my feet, shouting at the top of my tormented lungs to the distant, dreaming rooftops.

"I ... do ... not ... care!"

I remember that a flock of pigeons were startled from their slumbrous shelter in a nearby tree and took resentful flight.

I stood skewered, aghast, momentarily exiled beyond time's protection. I could hear no other sound. The infinite mansion of the night seemed to have turned its back in an embarrassed silence.

"I don't care," I repeated quietly.

'Don't care was made to care, don't care was hung ...!'

"You can save your trite yammerings, grandmama. It's true. I don't. I don't care tuppence."

I began to snap out the words, biting them off with growing relief and joy, shaking my arms and hands as though to dispel a haunt of goblins, spinning and dancing like a dervish.

"I don't care that any of you are dead or that you may have died in fear and pain. I don't care that I robbed you of the shrivelled remainder of your worthless existences. I don't even care that it may well have been for nothing! Why in blazes should I? I don't give a fig for the whole absurd, sad, savage history of humanity! I care about one thing and one thing only. Me! What does it matter if my motives are entirely shallow and selfish? Why should I stand aloof and pretend superiority over the rest of my fellow men? Why would you have me stoop to such base posturing? The stale squawk of morality is mere contrivance! Confess it! It's nothing more than the perfidious conformity of the herd! We are all delighted to escape judgement and cruelly indifferent beneath the cobweb veil! Confess! The rest of it is lies!"

I suddenly came to my senses and stopped to look about me, panting for breath, a frightening, otherworldly apparition. I had imagined the greasy black waters of the pond to be on fire but, instead, a saturate gloom hung undispelled in every direction. What a laugh! I was entirely unobserved.

Once my heartbeat had returned to something approximating its normal rhythm, I set off toward Speaker's Corner across what had once been the ancient manor of Hyde ... in the manner of Hyde! ... and later King Henry VIII's deer park.

To say I felt cleansed would be to exaggerate, my body was still in the thrum of a cathartic dream, but I was supremely relaxed and I let my mind wander as I walked to more pleasant remembrances. The jolly time I had with the family during the electric rumblings of last August Bank Holiday, Captain Dale's parabolic exit from the cannon's mouth to cheers and gasps now seemed much to resemble, in essence, my own daring, yet somehow clownish translocation, and, as well, the many sunny, summer walks we had enjoyed. Florence Jessie would sometimes bring a picnic lunch to Kensington Gardens before we were married as I frequently had to attend patients at St. George's Fields in those younger days.

Traversing Tyburn Way, though it had been one hundred and six years since the last public hanging there, I could hear preceding centuries of ghosts laughing with me at my liberty. I would never come to preach at Tyburn cross though I deserved it, though I had a rogue's face and a hanging look to me and was certainly without benefit of clergy! William Burke was hanged in Edinburgh in 1829 amidst general execration but I got off scot-free! Scot and lot, too! A free and accepted 'Bardotto'! With bats in the grotto! This club-eschewing Pacchiarotto! ...*solventur risu tabulae* ... Oops, sorry! I told you my mind was wandering.

I took Great Cumberland Place and Seymour Street to Portman Square. Glancing north on Baker Street ... Conan Doyle was born in Edinburgh and studied medicine there ... a childhood memory overtook me. Burke's grim likeness in the 'chamber of horrors', so dubbed by the editors of Punch, at Madame Tussaud's Wax Museum, now five years since removed to more spacious quarters in the Marylebone Road. I smiled in fancy that it might not be many months, for all I knew it likely already had happened, before 'Saucy Jacky' became crowned the current King of Felons and elevated to his rightful place of honour in this rogue's gallery. But who amongst the model-makers would possibly be able to imagine his true face?!

Madame Tussaud, *née* Marie Grosholtz, had survived imprisonment during the French revolution. Under her uncle's tutelage she learned her craft, sometimes moulding death masks from heads freshly severed by the guillotine. These scarifying impressions and the 'reign of terror' blade itself were a very popular part of her exhibit. My maternal grandfather, 'Raggedy' Holt, ever fond to my memory, treated Edward and I to a clandestine, spine-chilling, never-to-be-forgotten visit in 1850, the same year the grand old lady died at the age of ninety. Mother and father would most certainly not have approved.

I continued on through Manchester Square, crossing Marylebone High Street and Welbeck Street, a few steps then along Queen Anne and I was home. It was twenty-five minutes past four.

Ah, Marylebone … the old village lay within the manors of Tyburn and Lilestone. King James the first had granted it to Edward Forsett in 1611 but a century later it passed to the duke of Newcastle and from thence to the Oxford, Harley and Portland families. Now the haven of mad doctors and scopophobes! … St. Mary at the bourne … brook, boundary or both? … 'from whence no traveller returns' … at any rate, forgive my disjointed musings … 'how far to be beloved' … the name of the parish church where Robert Browning married Elizabeth Barrett when I was two years old. Florence Jessie and I had ourselves forever been joined in holy matrimony at All Soul's in Langham Place. I had walked by it just a few short hours ago! We christened Percy at Holy Trinity. And will you believe that on my way to find the carriage which was hailed down by the inquisitive constable, in retrospect his salacious thoughts may well have assumed me bound for some house of ill repute, there were far too many such along the route from Langham Place to Whitehall, I had traversed the end of Mansfield Street?! But that's neither here nor there!

After removing my shoes and socks in the vestibule and temporarily hanging my hat and cape to dry, I went upstairs to the bathroom to look at myself in the mirror. I had no compelling need to urinate as I had recently done so under an obliging elm in the park. My face was clean, damp and of the same perfect blandness as before. My hands, too, were pink, pristine and uncalloused, except for the gash on my knuckle which I carefully dressed with ointment. However, a quantity of blood had penetrated the fabric on the cuffs of my jacket and shirt. There was soiling also on my waistcoat, the lower front of my jacket and the knees of my trousers. I stripped them off, as well as my undergarments, donned a robe and carried everything back down to the kitchen.

I placed the knives, my talisman half crowns, Mary's key, my bill-fold, keys, watch, fob-chain and a few odd coins on the counter and, with the help of a good, stout pair of scissors, set to snipping all the clothes, with the exception of the cape, into small pieces. Once completed, I kindled a fierce blaze in the hearth in my study and one by one I incinerated every bit. I would most assuredly never need them again and I know you will greet the following with incredulity, I have already alluded to the strange phenomenon in the early stages of this narrative, but, even at this decisive juncture, even as I went about meticulously destroying all evidence of my crimes, down in the deepest part of my soul I could not be completely convinced that I had committed them!

The clothes now reduced to ashes, I put two further timbers on the fire to fully consume all residue lest Freddy find any fragments to concern him whilst emptying the grate, and returned to the kitchen. I cleaned and replaced the knives and scissors, rinsed with ease a few trivial flecks of gore from my waterproof, dried the counter, draining-board and basin with a cloth, taking the other items with me back to the study. There I hung the cape over a chair by the fire to dry, as well as my soaked shoes, thoughtfully protected from shrinkage with a pair of trees. Mary's key and the talismans I locked once again in the middle drawer, leaving my other valuables carelessly on the desk. It was gone half past five before I climbed wearily up the stairs to bathe.

As my body slowly found comfort in the steaming water, I congratulated myself on a job well done. I earnestly vowed to give reason to the little woman's death and make sure it led to success. My mind was released. I was more than happy to be Scylla if the last dregs of my guilt could be swept down the Charybdis of the plug-hole.

I had restored the dry cape to its place in the vestibule, taken my still rather musty shoes down to the cellar where Freddy would find and polish them, was shaved, dressed and discreetly bandaged, as he walked in the front door at fifteen minutes past seven and the telephone rang.

It was Maudsley.

"Whatever do you think you're up to, Lyttleton?!" he growled.

Freddy poked his head into the study to see that I was there. He held the morning papers and was clearly excited. I placed my hand over the mouthpiece.

"It's alright," I said quietly, smiling, "I'll have the usual, thank you."

He tiptoed swiftly across the room and laid the papers out before me on the desk.

"There's been another murder, sir," he whispered.

I looked up at him, raising my eyebrows in what I hoped was a worthy facsimile of shock and surprise.

"Are you there, Lyttleton?"

The sound of Maudsley's muffled, irritated voice pushed Freddy to get on with it.

"It's quite horrible, sir. The same savage monster."

I glanced down at the expected screaming headlines and nodded, frowning.

"Lyttleton?!"

"Right you are, sir. The usual, sir," Freddy acquiesced, in a dramatic *sotto voce*, and beat an unwilling retreat back to the kitchen.

"Lyttleton, what.... ?!"

"Sorry, Henry. Freddy just came in."

"Ah, there you are! Look here, what the devil do you imagine you're going to achieve by this?"

I was already sufficiently startled by his first question.

"Achieve by what?" I queried cautiously.

"This latest hypocrisy with Currah. Getting him off scot-free. The man was a murderer, plain and simple. While it amuses you to wallow like a drunkard in some misguided dream of Christian benevolence the whole structure of civilised society is undermined. You've got to stop it. You'll be arguing next that this Whitechapel butcher was ill-treated by his mama and should so forever remain unculpable. When will you talk some sense into that bleeding heart of yours and admit these people form a separate, dangerous class. They have regressed to a state of isolated barbarity which is beyond all reach of moral suasion."

Now you must understand that, despite my throroughgoing disavowal of all previously held religious beliefs, I kept this transformation entirely to myself. I still attended church each Sunday. I fully realised the value of retaining a pose of perfect normalcy. I had no wish to be ostracised nor, like Shelley, to be 'sent down from Oxford' for the 'necessary' freedom of my newly-espoused atheism. No, no, I was much, much cleverer than that. I was determined to remain 'the secret'st man of Blood' and was very careful to my dying day never to be brought forth upon the subject. Only you have now been given the privilege of these intimate confidences!

"You know as well as I do that we must look at each case individually," I said. "I sincerely believe that Currah was temporarily unhinged by his daughter's death. He was filled with remorse after murdering Letine and immediately attempted to do away with himself. It's a very different situation with our man in Whitechapel."

"Why?" Maudsley snapped, "How do you know he's not filled with remorse? And if he is it proves that he's sane! That's precisely what I mean about Currah! He had no justification whatever for going about murdering people!"

"Of course not," I agreed calmly, "But this man was not a vagrant nor a slum-dweller. He was not an habitué of your vice-ridden, unreachable sub-culture. I'm surprised that you seem to have come round to Savage's Lombrosian viewpoint when I know you loathe him."

George Savage...is his name not delightful!...had written an article in the Fortnightly Review disparaging my use of the term 'homicidal maniac' and at the same time putting forward his own pet theory regarding the similarity between the brains of criminals and monkeys! In the article he had made unforgivably slight reference to Maudsley's seminal work in the field.

Cesare Lombroso was a Jewish-Italian criminologist who also believed that criminals could be identified as a special anthropological type. He became famous for his detailed measurements of the skull, the so-called science of anthropometry, and had recently published The Man of Genius, not yet translated into English, a book that attempted to prove that genius was a by-product of either physical or mental illness! I'm sorry to say it but I really grew very tired of humouring mad people.

"A low blow, Lyttleton," Maudsley rebuked me, quieter now, "That's not what I'm talking about and you know it."

"Well, what's done is done," I said, "I'm sorry that you disagree. By the by, have you any opinion about the alleged murder of James Maybrick?"

I was well aware that Maudsley held the abilities of the female sex in low esteem.

"Come, come, you're trying to trap me again. I'm fed up with you," he said coldly, and was gone.

Before I had time to smile the infernal contraption rang again. I'm sure we were all vastly better off without it. It's bad for the nerves and one's general health in a host of ways. Maudsley lived not five minutes from Wimpole Street in Hanover Square. It would surely have been more salutary for our respective constitutions if, having the rare desire to converse, we had, one or other or both, taken the air for a brisk walk. The world will become a sorry place if this latest gadget ever attains to general usage, I thought. I am cognizant, in retrospect, that it was rather foolish!

Maudsley, you know, quite closely resembled Robert Browning in facial appearance, but, unlike Browning, he became even more prickly and reclusive in his later years and I seldom spoke to him.

"Hello."

"Ah, Lyttleton, I'm glad I caught you at home."

It was Moore. What on earth did he mean by that? It was only half past seven in the morning.

"Of course I'm at home," I said, "I'm just about to have breakfast. And, yes, I'm looking at the papers."

He laughed.

"Good, good. Well, what do you think?"

"It's the same man."

"Why the long wait then?"

"It sometimes happens," I replied, intentionally refraining from too specific a committal, "There could be any number of reasons."

"Yes, yes, but let's have your professional diagnosis."

"He may have had a lucid interval," I said. "Perhaps he simply relishes surprise or he may have thought it cunning to play dead for a bit. I've a reasonably good suspicion about who our man is, you know. I've offered my assistance over and over again. I spoke with Macnaghten just last week but Scotland Yard remain characteristically wooden-headed."

"I don't suppose you'll tell me," he chuckled.

"Sorry."

"But I can quote you about it being the same man?"

"Feel free, Charles," I said, "How could I stop you?"

"Did you know a friend of hers is missing as well? They think it might be another double."

"Really?"

"Yes. Some woman named Cheeks. Gone from her lodgings."

"How dreadful," I said, "Let's hope she turns up."

"Mm. They're wasting no time. Baxter's getting the inquest under-way this afternoon."

"It's understandable."

"Mm. Well, thank you, Lyttleton. I won't keep you. Oh yes, hang on a minute, I wanted to ask you about the Maybrick affair."

"She's innocent."

"What makes you so sure?"

"All things come to those who wait, Charles. I'll see you in Liverpool."

Freddy came in with my breakfast.

"I'm going to eat now," I said pleasantly, and it was my turn to ring off.

James Monro had finally got his wish and appointed Melville Macnaghten as Assistant Chief Constable of the Criminal Investigation Division at Scotland Yard the previous month. The press was initially welcoming, pleased to have a young man of thirty-six in such a position. As a matter of quite unrelated interest, I believe Michael Kidney was treated for syphilis in the Whitechapel Workhouse Infirmary at about the same time. And I learned much later on that Macnaghten was a devotee of the Chamber of Horrors at Madame Tussaud's!

"Thank you, Freddy," I said solemnly, as he placed the tray before me.

He hovered.

"Yes, I know. It's horrid. Just give me a moment to eat and read the papers and we'll have a chat about it."

"Thank you, sir," he said gratefully, and left me to my much-needed repast.

Can you fathom how well everything was going?

The 'woman named Cheeks' was being most co-operative, I must say. My single concern for the inquest was how the medical examiners would interpret the wounds. As you know, I had failed miserably in my intent to disembowel the poor woman. I had been so dry-mouthed with terror that I hadn't even asked her name. I only found out from the papers.

I thought it prudent not to attend that afternoon, in any case the proceedings were quickly adjourned to the Friday to allow time, as I discovered, to satisfy Robert Anderson's desire for a second *post mortem*. When I did arrive at the Working Lad's Institute I was greeted with a decidedly chilly reception. What was my sin really but to point out, as so many others had done, the very obvious flaws in the official approach to the case? Even Abberline, though he was no longer directly involved, seemed to give me the cold shoulder at the start. I did manage a few inconsequential words with him at last, mainly to do, as I recall, with the thankful reappearance of Margaret 'Mog' Cheeks, who had merely been visiting her sister. Oh yes, and the resumption of the plain-clothes patrols. But what did I care now about that?

Alice McKenzie, it turned out, was from Peterborough. I had been right about her accent. She had lived for many years with a man named McCormack. Most recently at a common lodging-house in Gun Street. The two policemen I had seen standing at the entrance to Castle Alley were PC Joseph Allen and PC Walter Andrews...odd, both having interchangeable Christian and family names...It was Constable Andrews who discovered her body and who had come so near to uncloaking me. But what was crucial to my cause was the testimony of Dr. Thomas Bond. He had also examined Mary and I had heard a rumour that he had told Robert Anderson at the time that, in his estimation, the murderer was likely 'a well-dressed, middle-aged man of great coolness and daring.' I can only assume he was clairvoyant! In any case, unlike George Bagster Phillips who felt that, on purely anatomical grounds, the murderer of Alice McKenzie was a different man, Bond testified that, as far as he was able to judge, it was clearly another in the same series. Most important of all, his opinion convinced James Monro.

There was not time to complete the proceedings that day and the inquest was adjourned once again to the middle of August. So much the better for me.

I spent a very lovely summer weekend with Florence Jessie and our beguiling despot. We even took the trouble to travel all the way to Hastings on the Sunday morning to attend dear brother Edward's eleven o'clock service at St. Paul's. Greater love hath no man! I sat serenely and graciously, I felt, through the twittering bathos of his homily, amongst a mainly gray-haired congregation mindlessly immured in the strait-waistcoat of age-encrusted ritual, its meaning and origin long since forgotten. The blind truly leading the blind. Everyone sang Luther's constipated hymn, *'Ein Feste Burg'*. Oh yes, I thought, a mighty fortress from which we cannot escape. Or is it rather that we do not wish to escape it?

Edward treated us all to a pallid, politely monosyllabic lunch at the Rectory and we were back in Brighton in time for tea. After which Florence Jessie and I took a long walk alone along the strand and returned to watch a glorious sunset from the pavilion on the pier. I did wonder briefly whether, as a loving and responsible parent, I should be making some attempt at least to rescue my children from the suffocating clutches of the Church but in the end I decided no, it was wiser to let them fend for themselves. Besides, I would have had to let the cat completely out of the bag, wouldn't I.

I burst out loud laughing on the late Monday morning train up to London. I was looking at a report of Alice's murder in a five-days-old copy of the New York Times. At the end of the article it stated that, some hours before the crime, Scotland Yard had received a letter signed 'Jack the Ripper' telling them he was about to resume his work! How absolutely wondrous if it were true! It set me to thinking about another little wheeze of my own.

Once Freddy had departed on Tuesday evening I sat down in my study and penned this saucy epistle. I didn't take nearly as much trouble as I had before, after all I wasn't enclosing half a kidney, though I did write it with my left hand.

"Dear Boss"

I began, after the original manner of Moore and Bulling.

"You have not caught me yet you see with all your cunning with all your 'Lees' with all your bluebottles. I have made two narrow squeaks this week..."

Why I put 'two' I can't recall. Perhaps some half-brained reference to Mog Cheeks? Or the memory of the sound of my knife's twice passage through the organs of Alice's neck?

"...but still though disturbed I got clear before I could get to work..."

Well, you know the point of that self-serving falsehood.

"...I will give the foreigners a turn now I think for a change. Germans especially if I can..."

It had always given me an idiotic twinge of concern that I appeared to be unfairly singling out women from the British Isles, though I suppose Liz counted as a Swede.

"...I was conversing with two or three of your men last night..."

The over-helpful constable in Langham Place as well as Allen and Andrews.

"...Their eyes of course were shut and thus they did not see my bag..."

A cheap joke. Sorry.

"...Ask any of your men who were on duty last night in Piccadilly (Circus End) if they saw a gentleman put two dragoon guard sergeants into a hansom..."

I actually observed this on the way to Whitehall Place.

"...I was close by and heard him talk about shedding blood in Egypt. I will soon shed more in England..."

I couldn't resist a sly stab at the carnage in North Africa that had continued unabated since 'Chinese Gordon's' death at Khartoum. Perhaps I was reminded of the hypocrisy which surrounded Mary Jeffries' trial the following year. She owned eight fashionable West End brothels and a flagellation house in Hampstead and yet escaped with only a fine. After which she was heard to complain, "Oh, I have been very slack since the Guards went into Egypt." Is it not impenetrably queer that Leopold II, King of the Belgians, was one of her many illustrious clients?!

"...I hope you read mark and learn all that you can if you do so you may and may not catch Jack the Ripper."

The next morning I posted this little gem to Scotland Yard from a pillar-box in Finsbury Square.

Now, before I relate the circumstances of Florence Maybrick's trial and my attempts to effect her rescue from execution, I must tell you about the Callaghans. I speak of them in my collected reminiscences but I do not use their name. If you trouble to wade through the volume you will see also that I artfully fudged some of the facts and the dates on which several events occurred.

The unvarnished truth is this. Edward Callaghan and his wife were the proprietors of a respectable lodging-house at 27, Sun Street, off Finsbury Square. He had come to me in the middle of June as a last resort, having been rebuffed at every turn, he claimed, by the police. As I listened to his story I became very excited because I could see how perfectly it might be made to fadge with my plan.

He told me that, in April 1888, a gentlemanly-looking man had called in answer to his advertisement of a vacancy in the Daily Telegraph. The man engaged a large bed-sitting-room in his house, saying that he was over on business from Canada as an agent of the Toronto Trust Society and might stay a few months or more probably a year. Eventually he established an office in Godliman Street...do you believe in perfection?!...near St. Paul's.

Callaghan and his wife noticed that whenever the man went out of doors he always wore a different suit of clothes from the day before and that, indeed, he would very often change three or four times during a single day. He had eight or nine suits of clothes and the same number of hats. He kept very late hours and whenever he returned home his entry was quite noiseless. In his room were three pairs of rubbers coming high over the ankles, one pair of which he always used when going out at night.

Two days after I had murdered Martha Tabram, Callaghan was sitting up late with his sister waiting for his wife to return from the country. She was expected home at about four o'clock and they sat up until then. A few minutes before she was due to arrive the lodger came in, looking as though he had been having rather a rough time. He told Callaghan that his watch had been stolen in Bishopsgate and that he had made a complaint to the police. Callaghan informed me that he had subsequently investigated this and found it to be false.

The next morning, when the maid went to the man's room, she had run downstairs in a panic and called Callaghan's wife to come and see a large bloodstain on the bed. They found his shirt hanging up in his room with the cuffs recently washed. He had done this himself. A few days afterwards he left, saying that he was returning to Canada but he evidently did not because they were both certain that they saw him getting into a carriage in the Haymarket in mid-September.

While the man had stayed at their lodging-house he came to be regarded by all as a person of unsound mind. He would frequently break out into remarks expressing his disgust at the number of fallen women in the streets. He would talk for hours with Callaghan expounding his views on the subject of immorality. During his leisure time he would often fill up fifty or sixty sheets of foolscap with obscure religious ramblings. These he would read out aloud and Callaghan was vivid in his remembrance of their violent tone and their bitter hatred for dissolute women.

At eight o'clock faithfully every morning, Callaghan said, the man attended service at St. Paul's Cathedral.

Several days after sharing this information, Callaghan brought me some of the man's possessions which had been left behind in his rapid departure from the lodging-house. Foremost among them were a pair of rubber boots covered in dried blood. In addition, there were three pairs of women's shoes and a quantity of bows, feathers and flowers such as are usually worn by women of the lower class. Some of the latter were also stained with blood. These items I had given to Freddy for safe-keeping. I led him to understand what I also had no reason to disbelieve at the time, that Callaghan had, on several occasions, attempted to give this information to the police. Freddy had since maintained them carefully laid out in his workroom in the cellar just like an exhibit from Madame Tussaud's. I assured him that I would make everything known to the authorities at the appropriate moment. You can now appreciate the reason that he was so particularly exercised on the morning after Alice's murder. It took quite a long 'chat' to calm him down and keep him sworn to secrecy.

Can you see that this tale of the Callaghan's had come as a most opportune gift? It was the coincidence that had really spurred me on and steeled me to the necessity of one last killing and there were many more such happy chances to come. I sat steeped in wonder at these myriad blessings as I watched the pleasant English countryside idly passing by outside the window of my first-class carriage, mile after verdant mile, all the way to Liverpool on Thursday afternoon.

St. George's Hall was a typically Victorian, soot-stained, stone edifice which stood, imposing and alone, next to St. John's Garden and directly across the road from Lime Street Station, in the city's centre. I had submitted, and been granted, my request for a seat at the trial some weeks before but, of course, I was not allowed to attend the proceedings of the Grand Jury. The scene outside the courthouse on Friday morning was pure mayhem, with buskers and doggerel-singers and thousands of people pushing and shoving to catch a glimpse of the young defendant, the first American woman ever to be tried for murder in England. It was a shameful circus.

I joined Moore at luncheon in the Poste House and we both agreed that it was a virtual certainty under the circumstances that the jury would return a true bill and the case would go to trial. The judge was Mr. Justice James Fitzjames Stephen. He was at the end of a very colourful and controversial career and we chuckled over our pre-prandial pint at his description in the Liverpool Review.

'A big, burly, brainy man,' they called him. 'His mind is like one of those very wonderful machines that one sees in manufacturing districts which does its work with remarkable, laborious and untiring exactness, but, unless it is carefully watched by the attendant and occasionally set in the right direction, it is liable to go all wrong.'

"You know he smokes opium," Moore said with a wry grin.

I shook my head in dismay.

Indeed, for Florence Maybrick, the appointment of Justice Stephen to the case could not have been worse. The old fool had, in his quite unconscionably prejudicial opening remarks to the Grand Jury, which were, of course, duly reported and elaborated upon in all the newspapers, called James Maybrick, "a man unhappy to have an unfaithful wife."

He compounded this appallingly unprofessional bias by continuing, "If the prisoner is guilty of the crime alleged to her in the charge, it is the most cruel and horrible murder that could possibly be committed." It goes without saying that he made no mention of her husband's frequent and well-known peccadilloes.

There was only one topic of relevance and that was whether James Maybrick's death was caused by arsenic poisoning and, if Florence had in fact administered it to him, did she do so with premeditation and lethal intent. As Moore and I had correctly surmised, it didn't take the Grand Jury long to pronounce the charge and the trial commenced on Wednesday, the thirty-first of July. I trained back up from London on the Tuesday evening and was able to observe this mockery of justice from first to last. As you can see, the case hinged on a primarily scientific issue which only those versed in such investigations could in any way be expected to comprehend. It will be pointful, therefore, to mention the constitution of the learned jury who had been summoned to adjudicate upon this abstruse, toxicological question. One Timothy Wainwright, a plumber, was the foreman. The remaining eleven gentlemen were a wood-turner, a provision dealer, a glazier, two farmers, a grocer, an ironmonger, a milliner, two bakers and another plumber. With regard to their mental equilibrium, a letter I received from a man living at Southport is not insignificant. He wrote, "Until I had read the names of the jury in the Maybrick case I agreed with the verdict but, being acquainted with three of them, I must say they are not fitted to express an opinion on such an important subject, being men of the poorest education. I can vouch that one cannot read his own name." I discovered that another had recently been convicted of thrashing his wife!

The counsel for the defence was none other than Sir Charles Russell, QC, an eloquent Irishman, a former Attorney General and distinguished Member of Parliament, who had been wooed to the case by Florence's mother, the Baroness von Roques, through her solicitors, Arnold and William Cleaver...such names!...The baroness, it turned out, had an unfortunate weakness for titles. She had clung to the honorific of her third husband, a Prussian army officer, despite the fact that he had most dreadfully abused her and squandered all her money. Sir Charles, you see, had a less than successful history with murder cases, O'Donnell had been executed and his prosecution of Adelaide Bartlett, who was most certainly guilty of poisoning her husband with chloroform, resulted in her acquittal, and, alas, he proved not at his flamboyant best throughout this trial either, in part, I'm sure, because of his deep involvement at the time with his taxing duties as chief defence counsel for the Parnell Commission, which seemed never to end...Parnell did eventually marry Mrs. O'Shea, by the by, but died a few months later.

Now, I think that the most efficient way of elucidating Mrs. Maybrick's defence for you will be to quote in detail from the statement she made in court on the sixth of August.

She rose at a sign from Sir Charles and had some difficulty in beginning, struggling to restrain her tears, swaying to and fro for several moments and having to hold on to the dock to steady herself. At last, in a halting voice, she said she wished to make known certain things regarding the charge made against her of the deliberate poisoning of her husband, the father of her dear children. She went on to say that she used the fly-papers, from whence, so alleged the prosecution, led by the always blithe and affable John Addison, QC, the offending arsenic had been decocted, for her complexion. Her mother had known for years past of her custom in this respect. Even Queen Elizabeth I had applied arsenic powder to rid her face of unwanted eruptions!

"My lord," she proceeded, "I now wish to say a word about the bottle of beef essence. On Thursday night, the ninth of May, when Nurse Gore"...they go on and on!..."had given my husband the meat juice, I went and sat down by his side. He complained of feeling very sick and very oppressed and he implored me then again to give him his powder. I declined to give it to him, but I was overwrought, terribly anxious, miserably unhappy, and his distress utterly unnerved me. Only after he had reassured me that the powder would in no way harm him if I put it in his food did I consent. My lord, I had not one single honest friend in the house. I had no one to consult. I was deposed from my position of mistress and from attendance on my husband, notwithstanding, on the evidence of the nurses, he wished to have me with him and missed me whenever I went out of the room. For four days before he died I was not allowed even to give him a piece of ice without it being taken out of my hand.

"I took the white powder into the inner room with the meat juice, and pushing the door I upset the bottle. In order to make up the quantity of fluid spilled I added a considerable quantity of water. When I returned to the room I found my husband asleep and I placed the bottle on a small table and sat again beside him. After a short time, he awoke and had a choking sensation in his throat and vomited. As he did not ask for the powder, and as I was not anxious to give it to him, I removed the bottle from the small table where I had put it onto the washstand behind the basin, where he could not see it. There it remained until his brother, Mr. Michael Maybrick, took possession of it on Tuesday, the fourteenth of May.

"After my husband's death, until a few minutes before the terrible charge against me, no one in the house had informed me that a *post mortem* examination had taken place, or that there was any reason to suppose my husband had died from other than natural causes. It was not until Mrs. Briggs alluded to the presence of arsenic in the beef juice that I was made aware of the nature of the powder that my husband had asked me to give him. I then attempted to explain to Mrs. Briggs, but the policeman interrupted the conversation and stopped it. In conclusion, my lord, I have to say that from the love of our children, and for the sake of their future, a perfect reconciliation had taken place between us, and that on the day before his death I made a free confession to him of the fearful wrong I did him."

By which she meant her affair with Alfred Brierly, a younger rival of her husband's in the cotton trade and the wealthy scion of an established Liverpool family. Their flirtation had, apparently, been developing for some years and culminated in an illicit tryst in London, at Flatman's Hotel in Henrietta Street near Covent Garden Market, at the end of the third week in March. During her stay Florence had contacted her solicitors regarding a separation.

Her trial took place over seven days, the last two of which were almost entirely taken up with Justice Stephen's utterly incoherent summation. Of one thing he left the jury in no doubt, his opinion of her guilt, stating, "For a person to go deliberately administering poison to a poor, helpless sick man upon whom they have already inflicted a dreadful injury, an injury fatal to married life, they must indeed be destitute of the least trace of human feeling." As I've said, it was a mockery. It was clear to me that Maybrick had simply died of kidney failure due to decades of addiction. Not only arsenic, he frequently took strychnine. The baroness had summed it up in a withering aside to Moore, "He made a perfect apothecary's shop of himself."

The jury retired shortly after three o'clock on August the seventh and took precisely forty-five minutes to arrive at a guilty verdict. Justice Stephen donned the black cap and pronounced her sentence. Death by hanging. When asked if she had anything to say why the sentence should not be carried out, Mrs. Maybrick replied, in an astonishingly firm voice, "My lord, evidence has been kept back from the jury which, had it been known, would have altered their verdict. I am not guilty of this offence," and she stepped down, with a slight stumble, from the fatal dock.

Many important witnesses had never been called to testify. Two of Maybrick's brothers, Michael and Edwin, though they well knew of his addiction, had denied it in their testimony and Michael had prevented Maybrick's will, which gave him power over the estate and nothing to Florence, from being entered as evidence. But nearly everyone agreed that had it not been for Stephen's severe comments and lengthy allusion to her wicked immorality the jury would certainly have acquitted her. He was almost lynched getting into his carriage and drove away followed by howls of "Shame!" The next day he had to be protected from the angry mob by a hundred and fifty constables. I suppose, to be fair, I should mention that it was his last trial and he was evidently not in his right mind. He died in a private insane asylum in Ipswich five years later. But he had fixed the time for her execution at Walton Gaol at eight o'clock in the morning on the twenty-seventh of August and I was aware that, in the busy workshop at Madame Tussaud's, they would already be moulding her likeness.

I returned to London on the eighth and on the ninth I began to agitate on her behalf in the press. In a letter of that date I wrote, "Seldom has a case caused so much public excitement as that of Mrs. Maybrick. The judge and jury have acted as moralists while ignoring the testimony of the medical experts. It is the duty of every Englishman to save an innocent woman convicted without one tittle of evidence from the hands of the public hangman."

I also communicated with Callaghan that afternoon and asked him to prepare a detailed written statement of all he had told me about his lodger, which I said I would take personally to the police.

It was felt by many that the only chance Mrs. Maybrick had of reprieve lay in Queen Victoria's deep aversion to the affliction of capital punishment on a woman, yet petitions on her behalf at once began gathering throughout the country. Justice Stephen returned to London to meet with the Home Secretary. They reviewed the evidence and Stephen expressed his entire concurrence in the verdict and his appreciation of the careful way in which the jury had performed their arduous duties. I was given to understand that the clot-poll Henry Matthews... 'who shieldest the rogue?' ... was very much impressed and so remained, for the moment, adamant. But memorial after memorial poured in to his office, one from Liverpool with over twenty thousand signatures, another from Cardiff with five thousand. I do not exaggerate that more petitioners signed for Florence Maybrick's release than had ever previously been known in any other case.

On the thirteenth of August we convened a gigantic public meeting in the great hall of the Cannon Street Hotel. In my opening remarks I made stress that there were few cases in forensic medicine where such grave doubts occurred as in the present one. I told the audience of Maybrick's long history of addiction and asked why no antidotes had been administered by his doctors. I drew attention to the apathy of the jury who, throughout the trial, had not asked a single question. I vouched that among the many medical men I had canvassed for an opinion I had only received one expression of guilt. I also mentioned my letter to the press in which I agreed to take charge of any communications or letters which might be sent to me to be attached to the petition.

Our petition read as follows, "The petitioners pray that a reprieve may be granted in Mrs. Maybrick's case in consequence of insufficient evidence and in the light of scientific knowledge." A sub-committee was appointed of which I was elected chairman. Within a short time we obtained thousands of additional signatures and a memorial was drawn up in the House of Commons by Mr. McDonald, the blind member, and Colonel Nolan.

On the fourteenth of August the inquest into Alice McKenzie's death was concluded at the Working Lad's Institute with a verdict of 'murder against a person or persons unknown'...well, I couldn't have everything my own way...though I felt satisfied that the general public and most members of the investigation team at Scotland Yard were convinced it had probably been the handiwork of 'Jack the Ripper'.

On the fifteenth of August another meeting was held at the Cannon Street Hotel. I informed the audience that I had just yesterday received a letter from the doctor who had originally prescribed James Maybrick arsenic and acting under whose advice he had continued to take the same up to the time of his fatal illness. I read them this excerpt.

"Dear Sir, I should be obliged by your placing my name on your list as one who believes in Mrs. Maybrick's innocence. James Maybrick called upon me several times while I was acting surgeon to the Skin and Cancer Hospital. He was suffering from psoriasis of the feet. I prescribed a solution of arsenic and very distinctly told him that if he did not continue the medicine he might have paralysis."

I was also pleased to tell them of the upwards of five hundred telegrams which had arrived that very morning desirous of placement on the general petition and that I was circulating a special petition of my own amongst the medical fraternity.

The editors of the Lancet devoted five columns to the issue, stating, "We can have no desire that the Royal prerogative veto should not be exercised in this case but, as a duty to the living relatives of the deceased, to a painstaking, fearless and honest jury and to one of the greatest ornaments of the English Bench, we solemnly assert as an unbiased opinion that the verdict was warranted by the evidence."

Arse-lickers and mutton-heads! I made them eat their words.

On the nineteenth of August, when Matthews arrived at the House of Commons, we presented three petitions to him. I believe this is the first instance on record where such an unusual proceeding has taken place. My own medical petition, which I handed to him in person, contained four hundred and ninety-nine signatures, all opposed to the verdict.

A final rally was held at Olympia at which I proved that no fewer than twenty-one irritant poisons had been administered to James Maybrick within six days of his death. Such potent drugs as *nux vomica*, henbane, jaborandi, cocaine, morphia and others. It's hardly surprising that he showed symptoms of gastro-enteritis! There were quite enough grounds for a suit of rank medical malpractice. I also discovered that Fowler's solution of arsenic had been prescribed which would, by itself, have more than accounted for the morbid appearances found. If ever there was a case of wrong and cruel conviction this one stands out prominently in our history, but in England, as in all the sorry dominions of this globe, a government mistake is never quickly admitted and seldom, if ever, rectified.

It was not until the twenty-second of August, late in the evening, that Matthews caved in to our concerted pressure.

This was how they worded the reprieve.

"The Home Secretary, after the fullest consideration, and after taking the best medical and legal advice that could be obtained, has advised Her Majesty to respite the capital sentence of Florence Maybrick and to commute the punishment to penal servitude for life, inasmuch as, although the evidence tends clearly to the conclusion that the prisoner administered and attempted to administer arsenic to her husband, yet it does not wholly exclude a reasonable doubt whether his death was in fact caused by the administration of arsenic."

Well, I ask you, if there was a "reasonable doubt" as to the cause of his death, how on earth could there be justification for keeping her in prison? The convenience of her conviction for murder was simply used by Matthews for the mendacious purpose of punishing her for the even greater sin of adultery.

Our committee met again the following day and we decided that every legitimate means should be taken to get the verdict quashed, in order that she might receive a free and complete pardon. We organised agitation after agitation but no pardon came and I'm very sorry to say that Florence Maybrick lingered on in prison for fifteen years.

I heard, and I'm sure it's true, that no one was offered the post of Home Secretary, during the life of her late Majesty, if he was what was termed a 'Maybrickite'. So convinced was the Queen of Florence Maybrick's guilt that these were the conditions upon which anyone might ascend to that office.

During the length of her incarceration many applications were made for me to visit her. She was, very understandably, physically broken down and mentally depressed and was plagued with continual insomnia and nervous prostration. Sir Charles Russell, who became Lord Chief Justice, once sent her mother to me to urge the energetic continuance of my pleas. In response, I always received the same official acknowledgement which stated coldly that the authorities were satisfied with the opinion and treatment of the prison surgeon.

On her release, just six days before my sixtieth birthday in 1904, she was taken to the Convent of the Epiphany in Truro, Cornwall, for a few months recuperation. It nonetheless came as an unpleasant surprise to me, considering the trouble I had taken and the fact that had it not been for my exertions she would have suffered the full penalty of the law, that in July of that year she left England for Rouen without calling at my house. I immediately wrote to her mother offering my assistance *gratis* in treating her daughter's fragile mental condition, but shortly thereafter I received a terse letter from France in decline.

Florence Maybrick eventually returned to America, I believe, and never once herself penned a word of thanks.

Of course, none of that really mattered very much to me. Of far greater consequence was that, as a direct result of the tragic injustice inflicted on Florence Maybrick and the huge outpouring of public sympathy which followed, I was able to position myself squarely in the spotlight at the precisely opportune moment.

Aids to Psychological Medicine

Two weeks after I had requested it, on the twenty-third of August, 1889, Edward Callaghan brought me his signed affidavit regarding George Wentworth Bell Smith.

Please understand that I had no desire to see an innocent man arrested and possibly convicted for my crimes. No, no, I had recently seen quite enough of such painful misfortune. I was satisfied that there was only the slimmest of chances that Callaghan's lodger was still in London. Besides, I could be certain that Scotland Yard, with whom as you know I was never on the best of terms, would pay scant attention to any new evidence that I might now present to them. The public at large, however, was quite another matter. My sole intent was the continued orchestration of my own celebrity and I hope you will grant my success. I achieved it without ever giving Smith's name to the press, nor did I mention it in my reminiscences and, of course, I knew all along that I could rely on the authorities to remain as tight-lipped on the subject as the Sphinx.

It was just one more in this whole remarkable sequence of adjuvant coincidences, that on the thirtieth of August, at their urging, an acquaintance of the Callaghan's came to me saying that a man had spoken to her in early July in Worship Street and wanted her to go down a court with him. She had refused to do so, but, together with some neighbours whom she told, followed him, walking a little way behind. They saw him go into a house in Finsbury out of which she had seen him coming some days before. The housekeeper then told them that, on the morning after Alice's murder, she had watched the man washing blood off his hands at a stand-pipe in the yard! She particularly remembered the occurrence because of the peculiar look on his face. However, when I enquired at the house the man was gone and the description I received from the other tenants in truth bore only a rather tortured resemblance to the Callaghan's lodger.

Nothing daunted, during the first week of September, I took the affidavit, as promised, as well as the other physical evidences from Freddy's display in the cellar, to Chief Inspector Donald Swanson at Scotland Yard. When it came to part with them, Freddy seemed, in capricious contrast to his earlier impatience, rather soppily reluctant to do so. As it turned out, he needn't have worried.

Swanson was a scholarly Scot. He and Abberline were, in my judgement, by far the brightest members of the investigating team. He was now Monro's desk officer in charge of the case. I had met him years previously as a young detective because he had been instrumental in gathering the information which had led to the arrest of Percy Lefroy Mapleton...a good part of whose mental instability, as is so commonly the case, sprang from the misapprehension of his own importance. He was desperate to become an actor but no one else shared his overblown opinion of his talents...and, alas, he still had a very sharp eye. I had carefully altered the date in Callaghan's statement regarding the late return of his lodger, and the following morning's incriminating discovery of blood-stained sheets, from August ninth to August seventh, 1888, so that it would exactly tally with Martha Tabram's murder. Callaghan's penmanship was crude and I thought my forgery would pass unnoticed but Swanson quickly spotted it. It caused me no little embarrassment at the time. I was finally forced to concur with him, in the privacy of the station, that the testimony being offered was likely worthless, and the upshot was that I took everything back with me to Wimpole Street.

This rebuff, which I had partly expected as you know, was of no consequence whatever to my overall plan. The visit to Swanson was simply to legitimise what was to follow and to satisfy Freddy and Callaghan. My concern for the latter had evaporated during the interview when Swanson determined that there was absolutely no record of his ever having brought any evidence to the police. But the fact that the Callaghan's entire story might be a pack of lies was perfect. I had his written statement and I had the boots and clothing and even if they were spattered with red paint, I didn't care.

Bright and early on Monday morning, September the ninth, I contacted the London office of the New York Herald and said that I knew the identity of 'Jack the Ripper' and that I would share my information with them as an exclusive if they immediately dispatched a senior editor to my house. This they did and this is the gist of the cobweb veil I spun.

First, I reiterated my well-known theory that the murders were all committed by the same man, unaided and unassisted, who suffered from religious monomania and had lucid intervals during which he was in every way unconscious of what had taken place.

Second, I said that I knew the man changed his lodgings after every murder and that I had been able to trace him from these.

Third, that the lodging-house keepers, on the next morning after each murder, had found stains of blood in the house and pieces of ribbon and feathers strewn about the room which had been occupied by their now vanished lodger.

Fourth, that in some of these lodgings he left behind him long written scrawls bearing directly on the subject of his imagined mission, oftentimes boasting that he had just 'performed some wonderful operations.'

Fifth, that I was in regular communication with those persons who possessed these writings. I showed them Callaghan's statement and the blood-stained evidence but I would not let them have his name, nor the document, nor take any pictures.

Sixth, that I had interviewed the woman at whose house he lodged on the night of Alice McKenzie's murder when he was seen to come home at four in the morning and wash blood from his hands at a stand-pipe in the yard.

Seventh, that I was thoroughly conversant with his habits in every way...you can see that I danced upon the very knife-edge of confessing!...that I knew his haunts and how he spent his Sundays, that he attended St. Paul's Cathedral every Sunday at eleven o'clock and that I had informed the police that on a certain Sunday he could be arrested there.

Eighth, that the previous week, having completed my private investigation, and having shared the full particulars of the same with one of the chief judges of New York City, who had described it as one of the most convincing and comprehensive that he had ever heard, I had endeavoured to once more take the police into my confidence and get their co-operation and that they had, as usual, declined.

Lastly, that I had warned the police that unless they assisted me in the capture of 'Jack the Ripper' on that certain Sunday morning, which was now, alas, past and gone, and if they continued to allow the mysterious red-tapeism and jealousy which surrounded Scotland Yard to interfere, I would publish my opinion to the world.

Needless to say, the Herald reporters had many questions for me, most of which I declined to answer. I told them that I was still withholding certain facts for the police and that I was driven to publish this information solely in the hope that it might somehow serve to bring the murders to an end.

I can't remember before or since when I have spent quite such a delicious and perfectly satisfying afternoon!

The very next morning Freddy dashed through the front door, almost apoplectic and speechless with indignation, and thrust a copy of the Pall Mall Gazette into my hands. It was fronted by the most outlandishly shocking headline of all.

"Latest East End Horror! A Woman Murdered and Mutilated! The Victim's Head and Arms Cut Off! The Trunk Found in a Sack!"

The article beneath told, in livid detail, of the discovery of another torso, this time mutilated and already decomposing, under a railway arch in Pinchin Street. This was not more than fifty yards from where I had flown over the tracks by the Goods Depot after the murder of Long Liz Stride! The gruesome description was accompanied by a map of the supposed nine murder sites, as you are aware only one was wrong, and this, of course, carried the splendid implication that all had been the work of one man.

Can you give credit to it?! Such impossibly beautiful timing! And nothing whatever to do with me!

"They'll just have to start listening to you now, sir," Freddy proffered earnestly and, indeed, it wasn't many minutes before the telephone was ringing.

First came Moore, who was, of course, understandably miffed that I had not given my exclusive to him, but I knew that he wouldn't hesitate to pick up the Herald story nonetheless. I had shunned him, I suppose, as some sort of semi-conscious revenge for my unwanted and, still to my mind, undignified *nom de guerre*. Also, because he and Bulling and so many others in the British press had so frequently treated my theories with condescension.

Later in the morning I received an extremely irate call from Chief Inspector Swanson. I had been sitting calmly waiting for it. I lied very politely and said that I had been unfairly manipulated by the Herald reporters and that they had taken everything that I told them out of context and had completely misrepresented the tenour of our conversation.

Ha! No more Juggernauts! No more *Übermenschen*! I had become, quite happily, the perfect fake!

I waged my publicity campaign relentlessly throughout the autumn, even penning the two letters already mentioned, the smudged card and the one from 'PSR Lunigi', in case I needed a knockout punch. I didn't, but I kept them, and they only ever saw the light of day in that carelessly deceitful chapter of my Recollections which I published over twenty years later.

My double-brained *coup d'éclat* was, at last, complete! Oh yes, glory, glory ... 'for dappled things, for skies of couple-colour as a brinded cow! All things counter, original, spare, strange. Whatever is fickle, freckled, who knows how?' ... I fathered forth whose beauty is past change! Praise me!

Both Hopkins and Browning died in 1889, by the way. Though the former's peculiar, Jesuitical verse was not much known or appreciated in his lifetime. He was born in the same year as I, but was untimely carried off by typhoid fever. Friedrich Nietzsche was also my birth-twin. His father and both grandfathers were Lutheran ministers. He suffered from insomnia and severe bouts of migraine and had, alas, succumbed to hopeless insanity the previous January. Ironically, this was just about the time that I was in full recovery from the pressures of my own humourless upbringing! He was fortunate to spend the last eleven years of his life in the care of his mother and sister.

Some months after I was traveling in a train. There were two strangers engaged in conversation in the compartment and the topic of the Whitechapel murders cropped up. One said, not knowing who I was, to his friend, "At all events, if Dr. Forbes-Winslow did not actually catch 'Jack the Ripper', he stopped the murders by publishing his clue." I should like to have said, 'Hear, hear,' but my companions alighted at the next station. I was more than satisfied that what they said was the general opinion in England expressed by everyone except the Scotland Yard authorities, who would have deemed such an expression of gratitude towards me as unworthy of the great dignity of their office. I should like to ask them one question though, if I did not arrest the murderous hand of 'Jack the Ripper', who did, and what part did they play in the transaction? Ha, ha, ha!

The rest of my life was, in a way, a *dénouement*, though I remained continually in the public eye. I published a great deal of singularly high-sounding verbiage, took up fishing and made a very comfortable living as a much-sought-after psychological consultant.

In 1890, with perfect dissembling piety, I founded an outpatient clinic for the poor which honoured the memory of my father, the British Hospital for Mental Disorders, in Camden Town. Of course, it was greeted with the usual sneer of professional jealousy but it did do some good in the world.

In that same year, I was involved in the case of a woman named Pearcey. She had killed another woman named Hogg, mutilated the body, nearly severed the head from the trunk, cut the remainder into pieces and placed it in a child's perambulator which had been found in St. John's Wood. The barbarity shown previous to the murder led many to believe that the act could not have been done by a sane woman and the suggestion was *prima facie* for the investigation as to her mental condition. Her modesty of demeanour and behaviour in court created quite a sensation. It was argued that her conduct was inconsistent with that of a murderess and it was found difficult to imagine that anyone who behaved herself so quietly and with so much propriety could have been guilty of such a heinous offence.

She was epileptic. I agitated on her behalf and managed to induce the Home Office to order a medical examination, unlike in the case of Lefroy in which the wretched man was given no opportunity to have his mental condition tested. Despite my lengthy efforts, I'm sad to say, Mrs. Pearcey was hanged in Newgate Prison. Thankfully, she was only the fifth female to have been hanged there in the preceding fifty years. Of course, after her death her full confession was found and circulated far and wide. Such transparent forgeries are commonplace in justifying the use of capital punishment.

In 1895, I received an invitation from America, from Mr. Clark Bell, the president of the Medico-Legal Congress, to act as chairman of the branch relating to mental diseases at an international conference in New York.

I chose to convey myself to the other side of the 'herring pond' on the St. Louis, twin vessel to the St. Paul, of the American line. As always happens on these occasions, every possible berth had been secured by rich Americans, with many of whom I became on friendly terms before the end of the voyage, and who individually handed me their cards with pressing invitations to stay at their various houses as their guest. I pondered, with amusement, the blank astonishment that would have been occasioned had I actually turned up at their respective estates with all my luggage, my Remington and the large tin box of books which always accompanied me on my travels. Of course, I was never foolish enough to afflict myself with such excruciating tedium.

I passed the typical Custom-house examination, with no opportunity given to the surly officials to pronounce me a smuggler, and set off in a car for the Westminster Hotel. This was quite near Irving Place where Charles Dickens used to stay. Immediately upon my arrival in the lobby, I was accosted by a gentleman of the press and subjected to an hour's interview on 'Jack the Ripper'. A second hailed me and demanded my opinion about ladies riding bicycles, an issue, I was told, about which all New Yorkers were 'crazy'. It was my unwitting introduction to the puzzling fact that Americans are sadly devoid of a sense of humour. I answered the man, tongue-in-cheek, that I should not wish to see my own daughter riding one and that the proper place for a woman was the nursery. Well, as you can imagine, the American press, who suffer from acute xenophilistinism, if you will indulge my quaint coinage, never let me forget it. Three or fours days later a letter was printed in one of the New York papers from 'the lady doctors of Chicago' in which they berated me as 'an old woman who had better go home in the Valkyrie.' I suppose they felt this was the greatest condemnation that could be rendered to an Englishman at the time. The Valkyrie was a yacht belonging to Lord

Dunraven which had been beaten in a race by the American yacht, the Defender. I soon realised I had been called to no 'banquet where the gods rejoice'!

In fact, what made the greatest impression on my mind during the whole of the congress was the extraordinary level of intoxication that was achieved at the dinners and the profuse promises that were made there never to be fulfilled. I was content to partake of their rather sickly ginger ale, being, as you know, more or less a total abstainer.

I had originally intended to stay in New York for only a month but, being quickly retained to testify in several murder cases, of Mrs. Fleming, who offered me six thousand pounds to defend her, and Holmes and Hannigan and Durrant, I had no choice but to remain longer. I filled my time by writing an article every week for the New York World on the 'progress of women', and I again had the opportunity to see Richard Mansfield perform. He was the first to introduce the works of George Bernard Shaw to America and I attended both Arms and the Man and The Devil's Disciple. His acting, though it was as intensely skillful and exciting as I remembered it, had become, I felt, rather self-consciously stiff, a trifle grand and pompous, and I never let him know I was there.

I left, the day after I had concluded my cross-examination in the Hannigan case, aboard the City of New York, the same ship on which Sir Henry Irving and Ellen Terry had often made passage. It will not, I hope, cause offence when I say, with decided understatement, that I was delighted, on the twenty-first of November of that year, to arrive back in the Valhalla of my study at Wimpole Street and put my feet up with a delicious cup of Freddy's freshly brewed tea.

The Reading mystery, in 1896, created much excitement. Mrs. Amelia Dyer managed a baby-farm and was charged with drowning a number of children entrusted to her care. I once more found myself in the unsatisfactory position of being an expert witness in a case of a most unsavoury nature and one which had, in all probability, been prejudged. I visited the woman twice in Holloway Prison. She gave the impression of a kindly nurse and seemed not of the murderess type, but she suffered from hallucinations and heard voices and remarked, "My only wonder is that I did not murder all in the house when I have had all these awful temptations on me," and this I testified to at the Old Bailey.

I was endeavouring to graphically describe what she had told me, that she 'had visions of animals and worms crawling over her, eating her very vitals,' when I overheard one of the jury say *sotto voce* to a neighbour, "She may have dreamt it but it will soon be a reality." It was staggering. Her conviction was a foregone conclusion.

The evening before her execution she wrote a letter to her daughter, the last words of which were this couplet: "My hope is built on nothing less, than Jesus' blood and righteousness." Is that not abysmally sad in every way?

I could describe case after case which followed in the ensuing years, the hereditary insanity of Mary Ansell, the so-called 'twins mystery' of Arthur Devereux, during which Maudsley and I had yet another fundamental clash of opinion, the arson of Dr. Story, the paranoid eccentricity of Mrs. Cathcart or the strange hypnotic power that Robins had over the Marquis of Townshend, but I will refrain. I'm sure you would agree that they contain nothing truly germane which might add to the general argument of this narrative.

My beloved Florence Jessie passed away, just two years following the release of Florence Maybrick, in 1906. Eventually I was gladdened in the company of another dear lady, Margaret Anna Gordon Gilchrist. Though very much my junior she consented to become my second wife. We decided to make a fresh start and moved around the corner to 57, Devonshire Street. Anna didn't take to Freddy for some reason, besides, like myself, he was nearing the age of retirement, and I reluctantly let him go with a very generous severance. We occasionally met for a toddle in Regent's Park and, of course, reminisced about how we chased 'Jack the Ripper' from England. I believe he still kept those boots. I won't bore you with the many and varied accomplishments of my surviving children. What, after all, would be the point?

On my sixty-sixth birthday, in 1910, I sat down to write my Recollections and some months later, in July of that year, I received an impossibly perfect communication which I shall not be able to resist sharing with you in full. I also included the entirety in the final pages of my chapter on the murders. It was in consequence of certain articles of mine which had been appearing in the press with reference to various statements made by Sir Robert Anderson on the matter.

Anderson had been knighted in 1901 and was now publishing his memoirs in serial form in Blackwood's Magazine. He had declared for years that he knew the identity of the murderer and now pointed the finger at a Polish Jew, named Kosminski, I believe, though he didn't say, whom he wrongly assumed to have died in Colney Hatch Asylum. It was a lot of guff and quite offensive, to wit, 'his people were low-class Jews, who knew of his guilt and refused to give him up to justice.'

The letter I received was signed by a lady and sent to the Postmaster-General to be forwarded to me. Sound familiar? But it's true. The names were given in full but I still think it right to suppress the same, though I did hand the matter to the police for further investigation at the time. Why not add confusion to confusion? The letter in every way seemed to corroborate my publicly held view of the case, and might possibly, I told them, finally lead to the arrest of the right man.

'Be my guests, fell sergeants, and be swift!' Ha, ha!

I shall read it to you. It's really quite extraordinary.

"G.P.O. Melbourne, 10/6/1910.

"Your challenge is more than justified regarding 'Jack the Ripper'. You indeed frightened him away, for he sailed away in a ship called the Munambidgee, working his passage to Melbourne, arriving here in the latter part of 1889. He is a native of Melbourne, Victoria, but before his return had been in South Africa for several years. He was educated at the Scotch College here; the late Dr. Blair was a great friend of his family, and it was from him he gained his surgical knowledge, the doctor taking him with him to *post mortems*. When he arrived in Melbourne he married a Miss..., who lived only a little over a year, but she died of natural causes; she was only dead a short time when I met him. He told me he had a hard time in London, and he was always buying sensational newspapers. I said to him, 'Why do you buy those horrid papers? They are only full of police reports of terrible crimes.' He said, 'I want to see how things are in London.' Then he commenced reading me the trial of a man named James Canham Reade, who married and deserted several women, and finally killed one, for which he was hanged. I said, 'What a fearful fellow!' He said, 'Yes.' I then said, 'What about Jack the Ripper?' He said, 'Strange those crimes ceased once I left England.' I was astounded at his remark, and said, 'My God, Jack...'"

Isn't it fantastic?! Even I wouldn't have dared invent it!

"'... I believe you did those crimes,' he having told me about living in that part of London previously. I tried to banish the thought from my mind, as I loved him; but I referred to it many times after, and finally he told me he did do them. I said, 'Why did you do those crimes?' He first said, 'Revenge,' then said, 'Research.' I said, 'But you never made use of the portions you removed from those women; what did you do with them?' He said, 'Oh, there are plenty of hungry dogs in London.' I wrote to Scotland Yard telling them all. Sir Robert Anderson answered my letter; but as I had told him all I had to say, I did not write again till last year, but have heard nothing from them. It is my opinion they all bungled this matter up and do not like owning up to it. I even gave him up in Melbourne in 1894. The police examined him; he told them he was in Melbourne in 1890, so they found this was true, and without asking him where he was in 1889 they let him go. He laughed, and said, 'See what fools they are. I am the real man they are searching for, but they take me in one door and let me out of the other.' I even gave one detective a letter of his, but he only laughed at me. I asked him to have the writing compared with that at home signed 'Jack the Ripper', but he did nothing. Now I have burnt his letters long since, but the monster's name is …, called Jack by relatives and friends. His brother told me he is in Durban, South Africa, employed by the South African Railway Co. He left here for South Africa about six years ago. Your plan is to get a sample of his writing and compare with yours. If you cannot find him there, place an advertisement in the papers purporting to come from his brother … …, who has been lost sight of for many years and has never claimed money left by his father to him. Advertise, and Jack will soon answer this, but to some address in London or South Africa. However, get his writing. He was a very good writer. He often used to attend St. Paul's here, and I would tell him what a hypocrite he was. I only wish I could see you.

"I am certain as I am writing this he is your man. If only to prove how wrong they were to accuse that poor Irish student, I would be pleased if the charge was sheeted home to the right man, when I think of the suffering it has caused his people. As to Sir Robert Anderson saying it was a Jew, he must be a dreamer of the dreamiest sort, for he was the man who answered my letter years ago; but they served me as they served you, with too little consideration, for I am certain we are both right. He always carried an ugly sheath-knife in his belt. When you frightened him away he came straight to Melbourne, and remained here till six years ago. What I regret most is that that poor demented Irish student should suffer for this man's crime. I did not know till this week that anyone was charged with those crimes, or I should have made a great deal more noise than I have done, knowing as I do the real culprit. Since starting this letter I have ascertained his proper address.

"You ought to have no difficulty in getting a sample of his writing. Go very careful about all enquiries, as he always told me he would never be taken alive, but would kill himself on the first inkling of being captured. That is all I can say at present till I hear further from you. I am sending this letter c/o P.M.G. to insure its safe delivery, as I only got your name and opinions from a newspaper cutting; but you are quite right.

"Wishing you success with this, and hoping to hear from you soon ..."

My life was a veritable cornucopia of such gifts!

The day following the publication of the letter I managed to unearth the Irish medical student mentioned. His name was Grant. He was not 'demented', yet had been peached, by the very solicitor who defended him in 1895 on the charge of stabbing a woman in Whitechapel, as 'Jack the Ripper'.

"I swear solemnly that I was wrongly accused," he said.

He had been sentenced to ten year's penal servitude.

"I was set upon by a lot of hooligans and robbed. I took out the knife to protect myself. The hooligans wounded me and fled, having beaten and robbed a woman that was there also. The police then came down the court and the supposition was I had attacked her. I deny it on my soul. A solicitor was asked to defend me at the preliminary proceedings but threw up my case at a later date, leaving me to the tender mercies of an English court of justice, undefended. This solicitor told the police he thought that I was 'Jack the Ripper' but after many investigations they were convinced otherwise. Ever since then he has been publishing letters in the press to the same effect, also claiming that I died while I was in prison. I implore you to take up my cause and help to have me reinstated. I was studying for the same profession as yourself as a medical student."

I believed in the genuineness of his story and took steps in the matter. I made an application to get him righted and to make public what I knew to be a great injustice.

I wrote a letter to the solicitor, asking him to call at my house so that I could bring him face to face with his 'late' client. He replied he could not come, saying, "With great respect, I believe your information and conclusions generally to be very incorrect." This made me quite dottily indignant so I attended at Bow Street the next day and convinced the presiding magistrate to put a stop to his unjustifiable cruelty. The magistrate agreed it was actionable.

In order to confirm his identification, I accompanied Grant to Scotland Yard to examine his photograph and to verify the statement which I had been upholding, that the man defended by this solicitor in 1895 was not dead but very much alive. After a great amount of preamble and secrecy, my application to examine his photograph was taken up to the presence of the Assistant Chief Commissioner of Police. The usual answer was returned, that it was against precedent and custom to show a prisoner's photograph unless for extraordinary reasons, but I might make a request in writing. It mattered little as Grant was well known there. "Hullo, Grant, how are you?" the desk sergeant had asked with a grin as we arrived. That sufficed.

Grant called upon me soon afterwards to tell me that he had just bumped into the solicitor on the street. He rushed over to him saying, "See, I am not dead yet, but very much alive." The man apparently threw up his arms in horror and bolted to the other side.

Can you appreciate the fierce rivalry that was immediately spawned by the murders? Competing theories as to my identity have abounded, with noisy and infinite variety, ever since. But I was the first and original 'Ripperologist'!

In 1912, by the by, I spoke several times with Marie Belloc while she was writing her novel The Lodger and was able to provide her a deal of further insight. Just enough, mind, and no more! During the murders she had been working for Stead at the Pall Mall Gazette. Her husband, Freddy Lowndes, was a good friend and a distinguished editor at the Times.

As for the lady with the flushed, melodramatic imagination from Melbourne ... what is it about my little crimes that seems to hold such an endless fascination for these people? It can't just be the mystery of my identity, can it? Surely from within their cobwebbed cocoons they envy the freedom of my lawlessness! ... needless to say, I did not reply to her missive. Nor did I wish the police in any way to persecute her histrionically obsessed young man in South Africa and I never followed the matter up with them. I was warned off, if nothing else, by her phrase, 'I only wish I could see you.' It seemed rather pressing, between the lines, like a premature proposal of marriage. But were you not as tickled as I by the letter? Her use of the word 'research'? And her delicious reference to the dogs?

In the days following the publication of my Recollections I found myself somewhat at a loose end and began to cast about in my mind for one final, gloriously peccaminous jest.

Many a time during the wee hours in the twenty years since the murders I had lain awake reliving them amidst a teeming flux of emotion. I decided to try and give these feelings some poetic shape, and perhaps by doing so, to expunge the most violent among them. It was an idle experiment, but, as I fiddled away at it in secret late one evening after Anna had retired, a quite devilish idea bubbled up from the depths.

Why not, I thought, give it form as the erratic raving of a madman's diary? And why not, I was chilled at the vengeful brilliance of it, make that madman an addict, as I once was, but that addict not me but James Maybrick?! I hated the man on sight. I had loathed his conceited manner. He was vicious and selfish and indolent and weak and had callously caused deep suffering to a beautiful and guiltless young woman more than two decades his junior. Not only that, but I knew a great deal about him. A dedicated copy of Alexander William MacDougall's six hundred page Treatise on the Maybrick Case lay that moment before me on my desk. MacDougall and I were firm friends before our vigorous attempt to secure Florence Maybrick's reprieve, having worked closely together on the eerily similar circumstances of the so-called 'Penge mystery', the murder by starvation of Harriet Staunton, at the very beginning of my career in 1877. In contrast, on that occasion one of the defendants, Alice Rhodes, instead of walking to the scaffold, had walked into my study herself to thank me for the efforts I had taken to prove her innocence.

Over the ensuing weeks, as I steeped myself once more in MacDougall's eloquent dismantling of the prosecution's case against Florence Maybrick, my spitefully false hemerologium of her husband's sins fell easily into place. I'm sure you must have read it. Quite a chortlesome little pastiche, is it not? The forged diary of 'Jack the

Ripper' by 'Jack the Ripper' himself! I believe that one among your fellows has divined my authorship. To that bright spark, I offer my hearty congratulations.

It took several months before I was completely satisfied with the voices and the psychological tone. In the end I recopied the entirety in the rear half of an old scrapbook which I had recently received from Edward, having carefully excised and burnt nearly fifty initial pages of cuttings relating to my father's life and works.

In 1905, I had been given a small trunk by Arthur Devereux for safe-keeping, filled with a miscellany of his collected possessions which I had never examined, and which he wished me to hand to his surviving son Stanley after his execution. He had killed his wife and twins. His son had, understandably, been quite unwilling to accept this and it had languished for years in the cellar. However, since Anna and I removed to Devonshire Street she had many times enjoined me to get rid of it. This I was only too delighted now to do and I used it as a way of leaving my forged daybook to posterity, like a wave-tossed cry for help in a shipwreck's bottle. I placed it at the very bottom of the trunk and dispatched it to the last address I had for Stanley Devereux in Coventry and what happened to it for all those years afterwards I have not the slightest idea. However, it has finally come to light as I hoped it would. Oh, those naughty maggot-pies and choughs!

You may also be interested in a certain watch. Yes, that, too, was mine. The silly doodlings etched within it on the mechanism cover are of my origin though in my intent they had nothing to do with James Maybrick. In a moment of pure whimsy, I handed it to a beggar in Trafalgar Square one scudding, leaf-blown autumn afternoon in 1912, after having tea with Marie and Freddy as I recall. I'm sure it took no more than ten minutes to find its way to a pawnshop.

"What do you think of yourself now?" I hear you asking. "Why have you come forward after all this time to reveal yourself?"

In answer to the latter question, it began to fester within just six short days after my death on Sunday, June the eighth, 1913 ... I happen to think it fascinating that you were born on precisely the same day thirty-three years later though I know you don't consider it of any consequence ... with those mean-minded, niggardly insults, those slender and neglectful obituaries in the British Medical Journal and the Lancet! Barely a paragraph! How glibly cavalier the dismissal! How serpentine the envy of one's surviving contemporaries! Surely you can understand, after nearly a century of rising gall, that I wish to require my rightful plenitude of fame!

And what do I think of myself? Well, let's see. I feel rather numb. Dispassionate. Like all our species, forever unable to perceive the brave boundlessness of the wood for the momentary distractions of the trees. I told you at the very outset of this macaronic that I was dull. As I've expounded, 'the tragedy of mental obscurity.' The bats fly squeaking on and on, round and round in their sightless, lightless, irrational gyres, forever and ever, amen. I was a man, as others, no better, no worse. Anna always said that I was jolly and kind. If I were you, I wouldn't cast the first stone.

It would be most completely accurate, I suppose, for you to think of me as just another of your own light-hearted friends.

'So out of Life's fresh crown fall like a rose-leaf down. Thus are the ghosts to woo; thus are all dreams made true, ever to last!'

Ha!

Postscript by Clanash Farjeon

Doctor Winslow wanted it known that this 'confession', though he felt many of his colleagues might benefit from the perusal, is primarily offered to the world at large in the hope, as he put it, "that certain helpful and pregnant quiddities may be found engrafted therein."

At the risk of a seeming betrayal it should also be noted that not all of the 'facts' contained in this account are strictly true. Whether the victims of time's diffusion or the gentle shuffling of artifice remains for the reader to judge.

Doctor Winslow left his estate in its entirety to his second wife. Its gross value was less than thirty pounds. He was able to leave nothing to his children.